The Seven

Also by Peter Newman

The Vagrant
The Malice

Short Stories
The Hammer and the Goat
The Vagrant and the City

PETER NEWMAN

The Seven

HARPER
Voyager

HarperCollins*Publishers*
1 London Bridge Street
London SE1 9GF

www.harpercollins.co.uk

Published by Harper*Voyager* 2017
An imprint of HarperCollins*Publishers*
1

A catalogue record for this book
is available from the British Library

HB ISBN: 9780008180171
TPB ISBN: 9780008180188

This novel is entirely a work of fiction.
The names, characters and incidents portrayed in it are
the work of the author's imagination. Any resemblance to
actual persons, living or dead, events or localities is
entirely coincidental.

Typeset in Sabon LT Std by Palimpsest Book Production Limited,
Falkirk, Stirlingshire

Printed and bound in Great Britain by
Clays Ltd, St Ives plc

MIX
Paper from
responsible sources
FSC
www.fsc.org
FSC™ C007454

To my parents,
for your unfailing support.

CHAPTER ONE

Alpha of The Seven stands in an alcove, encased in rock that is eggshell thin. A fragile prison made of grief, of stone tears that flow briefly, hardening, smothering.

For a thousand years, he and his siblings have dwelled in their chamber, wallowing, their gaze turned inward, falling further and further from humanity. It was not always this way.

Once, when the Breach first stirred, they sent their sister, Gamma, to aid their people. It was her time to shine, to do the creator's will and do glorious battle against the infernal.

But there was no glory. Only death.

When Gamma did not return, The Seven wept anew, a river of tears for the life that should have been. Endless.

And when a lowly vagrant returned Gamma's living sword, the relic had changed. They offered it rest at their side and it rejected them. It judged them.

So they retreated from pain and grief, returning to a haven of memories.

Years passed and a new threat arose from the Breach.
The Seven turned their backs.
And Gamma's sword ventured into the world once more.
This time a girl bore the sword back to them, and where
the man had been silent, she had plenty to say.

Alpha remembers her words. They sting and stir, making
grief into anger, inaction into action. Rage shakes him. Cracks
form in the eggshell-thin layer of stone. Individual chunks
fall, like a jigsaw of a man unmaking itself, each piece
revealing a glint of silver, a hint at the form that dwells
beneath. Wings stretch: a cascade of stone as Alpha steps,
shining, from the alcove, a halo of flying dust around him.

As his essence flares into life, so too do his brothers and
sisters. They wake slowly, reluctantly. Compelled but hesitant,
curious but afraid.

Alpha's eyes are the blue of the sky. He looks to each of
the alcoves, to his brothers, Beta and Epsilon, and his sisters,
Delta, Theta and Eta. Silvered wings flex, and stone crumbles
away, revealing bodies that gleam. The fragments shatter in
a cloud. A wing-beat, two, and the cloud is dispelled.

They stare at one another for a long time as dust settles
and thoughts begin to form. Then, one by one, they step out
from their alcoves to join Alpha in the centre of the room.

Six metal figures, perfect, gather together in a circle. Their
voices are music, each weaving with the others, harmonious.
Slowly, they sing of what has happened while they slept, of
all that has gone wrong, and begin to debate what is to be
done and how many will have to die.

Nearby, Vesper fidgets as feathers are woven into her hair.
'Is this really necessary?'

At her question, hands pause, and three sets of eyes flick to the other authority in the room.

Overseeing the team of people dressing the girl is Obeisance, the only human allowed within The Seven's inner sanctum. Wrapped in her feathered cloak, her skin is hairless, her toes and fingers without nails, her life and body dedicated to service. Obeisance's voice can soothe immortals, it has no trouble with Vesper. 'You do not approve?'

'It's not that,' says Vesper. 'I'm sure it looks . . . lovely. But it's not really me. I think they should see me as I am.'

'Do you believe you are defined by your appearance?'

She scratches at a cluster of tiny white scars on her cheek, thinking. 'No.'

'Then appear to them as a leader. You are the chosen of The Seven, Bearer of Gamma's sword. It will be your voice that leads us into a new age. Change is unsettling, and the people of the Shining City must put their faith in you. This,' she gestures to Vesper's outfit, 'will make it easier for them.'

Vesper shrugs, Obeisance gives a nod, and the team get back to work.

Adjustments are made, tiny details agonized over. Her long coat is carefully arranged, the plates on the shoulders given a final polish. Vesper's boots add an inch to her height, her hair another two. She does not feel any taller.

'Are you ready?' asks Obeisance.

She is not. 'Yes,' she replies, lifting the sword and putting it onto her back.

Obeisance gives a rare smile. 'Good. It is time.'

They gather around the steps leading upwards to the sanctum of The Seven. Thousands of them: a ceremony to welcome the Bearer back from her travels. Prominent residents of the Shining City and proud members of the Empire of the Winged Eye. The Seraph Knights in their gleaming armour, the soldiers in their perfect formations, and the citizens, modestly dressed, uniform in appearance and thought. Even the children are here, organized by choir, synchronized and silent.

Like a living sea they swell around the great silver steps. A dazzling monument of seamless metal, fifty feet high, that ends, abrupt, in mid air. Another thirty feet of empty space separate the steps from the great floating cube that is the sanctum itself, turning slowly, featureless, suspended above by powers no longer understood.

A small opening appears at the base of the cube, two figures framed within.

Far below, the assembled crowd lower their heads in reverence and the knights draw their singing swords in salute.

One of the figures, Obeisance, steps out, her feet finding purchase in the air, descending, her weight borne by The Seven's love. This is an act of faith she makes daily. The second, Vesper, draws the sword and holds it out. Silver wings unfurl from the hilt, feeling the currents of essence mixed with the air. An eye is revealed set within the crosspiece. It opens and Vesper looks into it.

The young woman gives a half smile and steps out after Obeisance.

Neither falls.

One walks gracefully, the other with a quiet confidence.

When they arrive on the uppermost stair, Vesper frowns. The eye in the sword has not closed, instead, staring up over her shoulder, it is wide and worried. She risks a glance but sees only the side of the great cube and the two suns above.

Such concerns are soon banished from her mind, for the eyes of the Shining City are upon her. When she speaks, they will listen. And, at her request, every word will be spread throughout the remains of the Empire, via chips whispering into the mind, via runners, traders and all of the networks at the disposal of the Lenses.

Her own chip feeds the words of the speech to her now. She knows what to say but, as Obeisance tells her, only the ear hears the words. It is up to her to win their hearts.

She looks for support, a last boost of confidence before beginning.

She finds it in a pair of amber eyes watching from several steps down. Her father appears strange dressed in armour. Even groomed in the style of the city, he stands out, uncomfortable. Despite all the honours, she knows he'd much rather be at home, tending goats and making wonky additions to the house.

The thought makes her smile. She is both surprised and warmed to see him there.

Her father smiles back.

It is enough.

She takes a breath and begins to speak, holding up the sword. 'Our war with the infernals has been over for ten years. The Breach remains sealed. But the wounds from those times still linger.' For the briefest of moments, she pauses, searching for any kind of reaction. There is none. 'The south has been ravaged by war. When the demons first came our people called to the Shining City for aid and we did nothing. Time and again they repeated that call. Time and again, we did nothing. Now, we have to put that right.

'Some of our colonies, like Sonorous, felt abandoned by

the Empire, and so they left us. And they were right to be angry because we let them down when they needed us the most. We've lost Sonorous now, just as we've lost the southern Empire. But it isn't too late to form bonds with them again and make amends. They don't need our swords anymore but they do need our help.

'You see, the world out there has been forced to change. There are new powers across the sea, human, demon and half-breed, and wonderful mixes of all three. Some of those powers stood with me against the worst the Breach had to offer.'

She falters, her gaze travelling across the hundreds of staring faces. Only her father's head moves as she speaks, nodding, encouraging. The others, in their multitude, are motionless, their expressions frozen. Do they agree with what she is saying? Do they even understand?

'We can no longer see the infernal simply as our enemy. Some are hostile, yes. But not all. And some of them have extended their hands to us in peace.

'In New Horizon, our people were made into slaves and it was not the might of the Empire that freed them. It was an infernal. It was not the Empire that tended their wounds or saw them fed and clothed, it was an infernal.

'I'm going to go south again soon to visit our estranged people. But I won't be marching at the head of an army, I'll be going there as a friend.

'If we want to find our place in the new world, we need to change too. We need to find a new way. To that end, I've arranged a gathering of the greatest leaders of the age. Together we will find a way to live and work alongside each other. Put the past behind us and make a better future for our families and friends, together.'

There is no applause when she finishes, no sign from the crowd that they have heard.

Her father smiles up at her, eyes scrunched with pride.

She wonders whether to go off-script, to say more, find some way to reach past the numberless masks, inscrutable, and get a reaction.

In her hand, the sword begins to hum.

She looks at it.

It is looking past her, looking up.

So is Obeisance, her father, and the crowd.

Twin shadows lengthen, falling across her, making her shiver. Behind her, something moves between her and the suns, red and gold, something vast.

As realization dawns, the assembled drop to their knees, a great wave of dominoes, toppling together.

Vesper does not need to turn round to know what is happening.

She turns anyway.

The sanctum of The Seven, a cube of shining metal – one mile across – is rising. Turning slowly as it goes, the Sanctum blocks out the suns.

Everyone watches the ascension, open mouthed, confounded.

A curve of blood-red light peeks from beneath the cube, glimmering, then a second of gold can be seen. Clouds part long before the cube reaches them, seeming to bend away, reverent.

Still higher the cube floats.

None dare take their eyes from the sight. Unspoken questions hover on the edge of lips. What does this mean? Is it a sign of The Seven's triumphant return, or of worse things to come?

Like a balloon on an invisible string, the colossal cube continues its journey, straight up, until it appears smaller, a silver moon joining the stars.

When it is nothing more than a glinting speck in the sky, attention returns to the top of the steps. Vesper looks across the sea of faces, licks lips suddenly dry. She has no idea what to say. No pre-prepared speech is fed to her via her chip, and she has no insight into The Seven's actions.

Seconds tick by, agonizing, slow.

A bead of sweat appears on Vesper's forehead and runs down to her ear.

Her father gives her a nod, then, after a beat, raises his eyebrows and circles his hand three times.

She opens her mouth, takes a breath . . . and then Obeisance speaks.

'People of the Empire, attend to me. For truly, today is a day of greatness. The Bearer stands before us all and asks us to rise and meet the challenges ahead. And behold! The Seven have risen, an inspiration to Their people. For Their eye is upon us, and They expect only the best. We must not disappoint. Go now, back to your duties, and carry the words of the Bearer with you, and the grace of The Seven in your hearts, and know that They are watching.'

In orderly rows, the crowd disperses. Fervour fizzes within measured steps.

Obeisance turns to Vesper. 'It seems The Seven do not leave you to toil alone any longer.'

'It's true,' she replies, forcing a smile. 'We're very lucky.'

But the sword in her hand suggests otherwise, its eye still staring at the sky, troubled.

* * *

Vesper meets her father on the outskirts of the Shining City. It is the first time she has been alone with him since she left on her great tour five years ago. It takes a moment for her to marry up the man standing before her with the image of her father. The amber eyes are the same but they seem to have been transplanted into a different face, a younger one. Long hair has been trimmed short, stubble banished. Though the collar is loosened, his clothes are crisply cut, a symbol of the Winged Eye woven into the shoulders. The scarring on the side of his head has been treated. There are still stripes running into his hairline but they are less stark than she remembers them. His frame is fuller too.

'Wow,' she says.

When he steps towards her there is no sign of his limp and when he hugs her, she is lifted from the floor, just as she was as a child.

For a few precious moments, the worries of the world disappear, unable to break through her father's arms. She hugs him back, fierce.

The sound of a nearly human shout makes her jump. It comes from the other that has been waiting for her to come out of the city, and Vesper's face shifts instantly to delight. The kid has grown, become a buck. The buck stands tall, struts proudly where once he scampered. Where the kid's bleat was cute, endearing, the buck's is a thing of horror. Sometimes a shout, sometimes closer to a scream, not quite a goat's call but neither a man's. An awkward, ugly, in-between noise. Vesper alone finds it charming.

The buck dashes over to her side, eager, his mouth already watering.

She doesn't disappoint, popping a thick, fibrous shoot into his mouth. 'You're looking magnificent today.'

The buck's eyes sparkle, though whether this is due to the food or the compliment is unclear. Jaws set to work and the shoot squeaks, indignant. Vesper chuckles, ruffling his ears. The buck whimpers and her fingers retrace their path slowly, until they come to rest on the edge of the buck's right ear, finding a jagged edge where things were once smooth. 'And don't worry, I'll be talking to that monster when we get home. She won't bite you again.'

The buck's expression is forlorn.

Vesper sets off, arms waving as she talks to her father, while the buck trots alongside, chewing, enthusiastic. On her back the sword's eye is open, staring hard into the horizon.

'You really think the speech was good, then?'

Her father nods.

'I know I keep asking, it's just . . .'

He reaches out, putting a hand on her arm.

'Thanks. And The Seven coming back now, what do you think it means?'

Her father shrugs.

'Obeisance says it's a sign of Their favour. That's what she's got the Knight Commander to tell everyone anyway. I'm not so sure. When I looked up, I didn't feel hopeful, I felt . . . scared.'

Her father frowns, stays quiet.

Vesper slows as she approaches the hill. She expected to be excited, perhaps a little nervous, but in truth she is reluctant.

It has been ten years since she sealed the Breach. Ten years of rebuilding, renewing, trying to restore some of what was lost during the war with the infernals. During that time, she has grown into herself. Though the Empire of the Winged Eye is dedicated to The Seven, the immortals have been silent for as long as she has been alive. Her orders, given in Their name, are what shape the future now.

For the last five years she has travelled the world with her knights, the Order of the Broken Blades, meeting with demons, half-breeds and humans, a disparate group of leaders forged by misfortune and hardship. Not all of those meetings were pleasant, but through a combination of persuasion, natural enthusiasm and, where necessary, a demonstration of power, she has managed to establish working relationships with most of them.

Progress at home and abroad is slow but she is close now, so close to realizing her vision. And yet coming here that sense of triumph fades. She has been away too long, neglected things at home to work on her great vision. Now she has to face up to that.

She feels a squeeze on her shoulder and glances down to see a small silver wing draped across it. She brushes it with her fingers and smiles.

As she walks, the grass beneath her feet becomes shorter, neater, testament to the work of many goats. They dot the landscape, dull whites and patchy browns against the green, big and small, nearly twenty generations of them. There was a time when Vesper knew every goat by name. That time is long gone.

Two buildings come into view. She stops to marvel at how they've changed. The first, the house she grew up in, has grown. A new extension has been built on the side, lopsided.

Clearly this was not built by the Empire's engineers. Each brick is placed by hand, laboriously. But to Vesper, the imperfections add charm.

She turns to her father. 'You've been busy.'

He looks at his work, then away again, embarrassed, before going into the house. She does not follow. She is not quite ready to face what awaits, not yet.

The second building is smaller, a shelter for their animals and a storehouse. As Vesper walks towards it, the buck slows, lagging further and further behind.

Inside it is dark, ripe with aged and musty smells. Vesper peers into the shadows until she makes out a shape in one corner.

Hands go to hips. 'Wake up, you miserable thing.'

A head raises slowly, unsteady on a scraggly neck. The dark eyes do not see as well they used to but hate just as hard as ever.

'Now, I don't care how old you are, if you don't stop biting everyone I'll have you turned into stew, okay?'

The goat's eyes narrow.

'I'm serious this time.' Vesper points a finger for emphasis, then reaches into her bag. 'But I got you this. I don't know why I bothered though, you ungrateful monster.'

She tosses a leathery strip to the goat and pats her on the head. The goat sniffs at the offering and then starts to eat it, ignoring the affection as best as possible.

Vesper goes back to the house and stops at the door. Her hand lifts as if to knock but hovers there, uncertain. She can just make out sounds from inside. Adult voices talking, and a younger voice rising above them. Yelling? Is it play or some kind of argument?

A knot forms in Vesper's stomach and her hand remains poised.

At her back an eye opens and the wing squeezes her shoulder again. Vesper does not need to turn round to see the sword's silent encouragement.

'Alright,' she murmurs. 'I'm going in.'

She knocks once, so soft as to be inaudible. The sword frowns at her back and the wing squeezes more firmly. Vesper knocks a second time, louder.

The sounds on the other side stop.

She takes a deep breath, lets it out slowly, then opens the door and goes inside.

Vesper passes through the hall quickly. Each glance is bittersweet, conjuring childhood memories and showing their inaccuracies. Cupboards are the wrong colour, the walls show signs of age, and everything is smaller than she remembers it.

Except the kitchen. One of the walls has been knocked through to make space for a new table. Around it, four faces gawp at her.

She waves and smiles, awkward. 'Hi.'

As one, they rise to greet her.

It is hard to know who to attend to first. Before she can decide, Jem is on his feet, moving in close. He leans in, kissing her, arms circling her shoulders only to stiffen as they knock against the sword.

She has barely had time to register the kiss or enjoy it before he is pulling away.

They study each other, noticing the little changes. She has grown as tall as him but seems taller, standing straight where he slumps. His eyes are as sharp as ever but there are smudges underneath, hinting at sleepless nights. A good diet has softened his features, save for his smile which remains feral.

Looking at his face, she cannot tell if that smile is aggressive or not.

Before either of them can speak, another voice interjects. 'Vesper, is that you?'

Her Uncle Harm is reaching out for her, tentative. She takes his questing hand in both of hers and squeezes. 'It's me.'

They embrace, and Harm's fingertips move up to her face, skimming over cheeks, the bridge of her nose and her forehead. He nods, content. 'No new scars. That's a good sign.'

'I could say the same to you.'

He chuckles. 'It's good to have you home.'

Of all of them, Harm has changed the least. A few extra laughter lines, a couple of grey hairs. Taking comfort from that, Vesper turns to her father and the little girl standing next to him.

She looks down.

A small face is staring back up at her.

Dark curly hair frames sullen eyes and downturned lips. The girl's skin is darker than hers but lighter than Jem's. The swirling lines that cover her body have become more pronounced in the intervening years, not less as Vesper had hoped. This is why her daughter has been kept away from the Shining City. The people of the Empire of the Winged Eye are not ready to deal with such obvious signs of the taint, however slight. Inwardly, she swears that will change in her lifetime.

The girl glances up to Vesper's father, nervous.

'Hello, Reela,' says Vesper. 'It's me, your mother. I'm back.'

There is a pause. Her father gives a reassuring nod to the little girl before gently nudging her towards Vesper.

Vesper goes down on one knee and opens her arms. 'It's okay, I won't bite.'

The girl comes forward and accepts her mother's hug. Vesper wonders if perhaps things will not be as bad as she feared.

They all flinch when Reela screams. Ducking under Vesper's arms, she runs past, the scream bouncing up the stairs until it is silenced by the slam of an upstairs door.

For several minutes, Vesper talks, banishing the rejection of her child with talk of bigger things. Increasingly, her arms wave with enthusiasm. Three men sit round the table, listening: her father, her uncle and her lover.

Reela remains upstairs. From time to time she can be heard jumping around her room and squealing. The sound of boards creaking and high-pitched laughter grow steadily louder.

Vesper tries to ignore it but her right eyelid twitches in time with each new interruption.

'And,' Vesper concludes, 'it means we'll have a place to meet and solve problems, but more than that, we'll be creating another way to live, where we talk first instead of fighting.' Another bang from above makes Vesper wince. 'Where children like Reela can grow up without knowing fear.' She pauses but nobody speaks. 'Well, what do you think?'

She looks at each of their faces. Harm's is a delicate balance, support laced with concern. Her father looks down at the table, frowning. Jem just looks angry.

Several thuds and a shriek from the heavens do little to break the tension.

Harm leans forward, his voice soft. 'I think it's very brave what you're trying to do.'

'But?'

'But I'm not sure the Empire is ready. Have you thought about how it might hurt Reela?'

Vesper shakes her head. 'I'm doing it for Reela and all the others like her. She shouldn't have to hide in the shadows because the Empire is too small-minded to deal with change!'

'I agree but you risk making her into a target.'

'But when you came to the Shining City, Uncle, you didn't hide.'

Harm smiles sadly. 'That's true but I came of my own free will and I knew the risks. And I wasn't accepted until I'd been purged of taint, and even that is conditional on me living out here.'

'It shouldn't be that way. I'm going to put it right.'

'The people of the Empire have followed you this far because you've moved slowly but if you start to directly contradict The Seven's law . . . Well, it could end badly for all of us.'

An awkward silence descends. Vesper's father continues to frown at the tabletop.

'We saw the cube rising,' Jem says. 'Did The Seven do anything?'

'No. They just flew off, into space maybe? I don't know, and to be honest, I don't care. We've waited for Them long enough already.'

'What are you going to do now?'

She looks at him, puzzled. 'Exactly what I was going to

16

do before. If The Seven decide to make things better, maybe I'll come back and live here. Until then, the Empire needs us.'

Jem swallows. 'But . . . aren't you afraid?'

She closes the gap between them and takes one of his hands in hers. 'Of course I'm afraid. But it isn't going to stop me.'

'Us,' adds Harm. 'It isn't going to stop us. We're in this together. A family.'

'I'm glad to hear it. Actually, it's a relief. I don't think my plan's going to work without you.'

Harm smiles. 'This sounds ominous.'

She smiles back. 'I want you to guide the people here, the way you guided me.'

'I'm no instructor.'

'No, and I don't want one. I want someone that can tell them about life across the sea. And, I want you to help them get the idea that not all infernals are the same. That's what I tried to tell them in my speech but I don't think they understand. It's too big.'

Harm nods slowly. 'It won't be easy but I have a few ideas. Perhaps I'll tell them some of my old stories.'

'Yes, tell them about the city of Verdigris and about Tough Call.'

'Alright.'

'Oh, and you have to tell them about the Usurperkin there and how they're part of the city.'

'I will.'

'And I think –'

Harm laughs and Vesper swiftly joins him. And then the two of them are recalling old times, trading names back and forth, swept up in the excitement. Vesper doesn't notice Jem slipping to the back of the kitchen to make himself a strong drink. Her father does with narrowing eyes.

'And don't worry about Reela,' adds Harm. 'She's not usually this bad.'

'I'm not sure if that makes me feel better or worse.'

'She'll come round.'

'Was I . . . like her? You can be honest.'

Harm shakes his head. 'No, you were easier. But don't worry, she'll get through it. I think she just misses you.'

'She's got a funny way of showing it.'

'Love can make people behave in very odd ways.' He coughs, polite. 'I can't imagine where Reela gets it from.'

Jem clears his throat, the glass in his hand already half empty. 'When are you leaving us?'

'Soon.'

'And how long will you be gone this time?'

'I don't know.'

'A month? Six months?' His lower lip curls down as he speaks, 'A year? Another five years?'

'I told you, I don't know.'

'Harm's right, you're going to put us in danger. The Shining City hates us.'

'That's ridiculous.'

'Is that why the Lenses spy on us? They're probably listening in right now.'

'The Lenses have a whole world to monitor. They barely know you exist!'

Jem drains his glass, gets up. 'Sounds familiar.'

'Where are you going?'

'Nowhere. If you change your mind, you're welcome to join me.'

Vesper blinks back tears. 'I have to do this, don't you understand?'

'Yes,' replies Jem, bitter. 'I do.' He walks out of the kitchen. Shortly afterwards the front door slams.

The rhythmic bouncing from upstairs is interrupted by a loud thud, a brief pause, and then crying, shrill and persistent.

Vesper's father glances towards the sound, then looks at Vesper.

She buries her face in her hands. 'Not now . . . I can't.'

With a sigh, her father rises. He touches Harm's arm briefly, walks around the table to rest a hand on Vesper's shoulder, then leaves.

They hear footsteps on creaky stairs, a door opening and closing. The crying becomes muffled, begins to move slowly from left to right above them. Gradually, it subsides.

Harm speaks into the quiet. 'Why don't you go up and see her? She misses you.'

'Alright. Then I need to talk to Jem while there are no other distractions. There are things I need to say, in private.'

'Good luck.'

She starts to head upstairs, giving Harm a grim nod. 'Thanks.'

Somehow dealing with her daughter is more exhausting than managing an empire. Handing Reela back to her father and leaving the house is a relief.

She finds Jem standing by the base of the hill, looking out towards the Shining City, reminding her of when she used to do the same.

'Here goes,' she murmurs to the sword, strolling down until she stands alongside him. 'Hi. Mind if I join you?'

He shrugs, sullen.

'Look,' she says, taking the sword from off her shoulder and laying it down. 'I'm sorry I haven't been around.'

A guilty look crosses his face and he seems to deflate. 'Ah Vesp, I'm sorry for what I said in there. Ever since we got word you'd returned to the Shining City I've been waiting for you to come back, and at the end of each day I couldn't understand why you hadn't. I'd tell myself that you'd be coming tomorrow, or the day after, and look forward to us being close again. Believe it or not I've been excited. I even had plans for some nice things that we could do together.

'And then when you did show, you started talking about leaving barely five minutes after you arrived. Another long trip overseas . . . I just couldn't believe it. That's when I lost my temper.' He gives her a lopsided smile. 'But I suppose you've worked out that last bit already.'

She matches his expression. 'I had a bit of an inkling.'

'You know, the last thing I wanted was to push you away again.'

'I do. That's why I'm here.' He nods, the last of the tension ebbing from his stance. 'Would you like to start again?' she asks. 'Pretend I've just got back?'

'Please.'

They talk, fingers occasionally touching, tentative, negotiating the bad feelings to find their way to the good. By the time the suns are setting, the conversation flows more easily. Inevitably, it becomes nostalgic, returning to their early days together. There is laughter, genuine, and when it passes, an earnestness in Jem's eyes.

20

'I've missed you.'

'I've missed you too.'

'I hate to sour things,' says Jem, 'but I need to talk to you about Reela.'

'Okay. She was tough today. Was she always this noisy?'

'Yes. But it's not her fault, it's your father's.'

'How is it his fault?'

'For one thing, he treats her too much, and for another, he lets her get away with murder. If she breaks something, or is naughty and I'm telling her off, he just picks her up and gives her a cuddle. It completely undermines me. And he gives me one of those looks, you know the ones?'

She sighs. 'I know the ones.'

'As if I'm the one that's done something wrong.'

'Have you tried talking to Uncle Harm?'

'Yes, but he's just as bad as your father. Most of the time he finds Reela's behaviour funny. They're getting her into bad habits and stopping me from sorting it out.'

'I'll talk to them before I go, okay?'

'Okay. Thank you. Look, it's getting dark. We should probably get back inside.'

'Let's just stay out here a bit longer.'

'It's getting cold.'

She takes his hands in hers. 'But I'm warm, remember?'

A different kind of glint appears in Jem's eye. 'I think so, but it's been a while. I'm going to need some serious reminding.'

Vesper steps in close, sliding her hands around his waist, kissing him. His nose is like a lump of ice against her cheek, his hands startling on her hips.

She kisses him again, pulling him more firmly to her.

It turns out that Jem does not need much reminding at all. In fact, his memory is very good on the subject. Despite this or perhaps because of it, they stay out long after the suns have set.

CHAPTER TWO

Vesper leaves the next day. Her father watches her march towards the coast with the buck and her personal guard of Seraph Knights, the Order of the Broken Blades. Each member is devoted to Vesper, owing her a personal debt. Their armour glints in the sunslight, pride adding crispness to their movements.

When they are nothing more than a spot on the horizon, he remains, and when that spot has vanished entirely, he remains.

Finally, when even that memory of it has undeniably gone, he sighs and turns back towards home.

Business resumes in the Shining City, each denizen returning to their appointed tasks. But something has changed, excitement infusing even the simplest of actions. The twin statues of Duet that stand either side of the southern road are cleaned. The gardens that curl, unkempt, around the great platinum pillars are cut back. Buttons are polished an extra time, bodies held slightly straighter, a mix of worry and excitement fuelling the drive towards perfection.

Without anyone explicitly arranging anything, the choirs of children meet for additional devotion sessions. When squires train, they lament their mistakes far more, and the knight instructors punish them all the harder.

In quiet industry and whispered speculation, a few days pass.

Like most of the citizens of the Shining City, the Knight Commander spends his spare moments looking up at the sky. Sometimes, at night, he thinks he sees the Sanctum of The Seven, a new star glimmering in the heavens. With the Bearer of Gamma's sword abroad, and Obeisance in silent meditation, out of his reach, it is up to him to prepare the Empire for whatever is coming next.

And there is an undeniable sense that a change is coming. He likes to think that the return of The Seven is a reward for their good work, that finally he and his people are worthy to receive the blessings of their immortal guardians again. He does his best to ensure that worthiness, exhorting his people to work harder, to be better, than they ever have before. Each day, the Shining City behaves as if it were on parade, its citizens outfitted in their best, moving purposefully through corridors that gleam. Every corner is scoured, every piece of equipment cleaned, and any inhabitant that does not come up to the Knight Commander's high standards is given tasks that keep them out of sight.

When the call finally comes, he is prepared, his armour finely polished, and a score of officers are on standby to be given the word, whatever word that will be.

The Seven

The familiar form of Obeisance is projected in front of him, lines of light describing her shape. Despite the magnitude of the occasion, she does not seem any different, but then he does not expect her to. Obeisance communes with The Seven daily, her life a string of abnormal events threaded together by brief periods of sleep. Their wonder is her mundanity.

'Knight Commander.'

He salutes. 'Obeisance.'

'Do not look so solemn, old friend. Rejoice. For we live in glorious times. The Seven have spoken, Their light shines upon us again, and we have been chosen as the instruments of deliverance.'

'How can I serve?'

'You are to gather the fleet for Their pleasure and prepare Alpha's sky palace for travel. Have them assemble on the southern coast, at Greyspot Three.'

'If I may, Obeisance, Greyspot Three is a civilian port with a troubled history. Skylanding would much more suitable for such a historic occasion.'

She does not reply immediately and he wonders if she is considering his words or if there is interference.

'You misunderstand, Knight Commander. You are being given an order, not a recommendation. In any case the sanctum has begun its descent, and Alpha has already taken wing. He is on His way to you as we speak. I trust everything will be ready when He arrives.'

'He's coming here? Now? I don't see how –'

But her image has already winked out. Cursing, the Knight Commander blinks the flickering afterglow from his eyes and starts barking orders.

*   *   *

25

Minutes later the Knight Commander is standing at the base of the silver steps. Somewhere high above is the Sanctum of The Seven, and in the space between them, diving through the ether, is Alpha.

He has had to run to get here, and beneath his armour the Knight Commander is sweating. Behind him a row of Seraph Knights have formed up, hastily, several rows of soldiers rushing into position at their backs. He hears the last stamp of boots, the snap of people standing to attention. Then silence.

They all stand in perfect formation, watching the sky for the first sign of Alpha's arrival.

Though his body is still, the Knight Commander's mouth continues to move, organizing, giving orders via comms link, coordinating the fleet. To meet Alpha's needs he has taken from all over the Empire, stripping the coast and the nearby colonies of protection.

He checks in to see if Vesper's father, the Champion, remains in the Shining City but he has already left, on foot. The Knight Commander shakes his head at the bizarre custom. The Champion has not gone far, is only just reaching the gates but he does not call him back. This is to be a historic moment, and he has no wish to share it.

With magnification from his visor, he makes out a speck directly above, growing quickly, and his heart starts to pump faster. Despite the fact he is standing still, he continues to sweat.

In the scant time that remains the Knight Commander considers what kind of greeting would be appropriate, and how best he can appear both humble and strong at the same time.

Meanwhile, Alpha continues to dive.

Thoughts flicker, disjointed, through the Knight Commander's mind.

Perhaps I should have summoned Alpha's sky palace here instead of sending it to Greyspot Three.

Would it be better to sing in honour of Alpha's arrival or remain silent?

Is it odd that I have not called the citizens here to greet Him? Surely it is better to have a small, perfectly formed greeting, than a great, ugly one. There were too many to organize in the time. This is better. I'm sure this is better.

A song would be more appropriate, I think. Yes, a song would be best, and I should lead it. The image of him singing, his knights a supporting chorus, is pleasing. It seems right. *But which song?* He wonders.

Alpha is close now, wings drawn tight to his sides. The Knight Commander takes a breath, still unsure which note to begin with.

He's coming in awfully fast. A nagging sensation begins to build in the Knight Commander's stomach, a sense that something is wrong. *He's not going to stop. He's going to crash into us. Is this some kind of test? A test of our resolve?*

He can almost hear Obeisance admonishing him for trying to predict the actions of The Seven. If Alpha were a sky-ship or even a bird, then perhaps there would be a danger of him not slowing down in time. He is far beyond either of those things, far beyond anything the Knight Commander can imagine. Shaking the doubt from his mind, letting the awe grow within him, the Knight Commander begins to sing.

Flawlessly, as if rehearsed, the knights join in.

Alpha continues to dive, to accelerate.

He's not going to stop! He's not going to stop!

Ignoring the growing terror, the Knight Commander continues to sing, clinging to his faith.

And at the last, Alpha's silver wings unfurl, and he moves from dive to glide, cutting over their heads, cutting through their song, silencing, and carrying on, leaving the Knight Commander and his followers behind.

On instinct, they have all turned to watch the immortal's progress, a line of confused faces.

'Sir?' asks one of the knights, an irritating quake in her voice. 'What does this mean, sir?'

A good question, he thinks. *What does it mean?* 'Get me airborne!' he shouts. 'Where He goes, we follow.'

The journey to the landing pillar takes too long. The capsules that spirit them up to the pillar's top take too long. The Knight Commander can feel Alpha moving further and further away. He berates himself for not having predicted this. What a fool he was to imagine that The Seven would care for welcomes or parades. They are above such things. Alpha must have come ahead of his brothers and sisters for a reason, to do something glorious for the good of the Empire. And while the Knight Commander cannot guess what that is, he is determined to be a part of it.

Only a handful of Seraph Knights fit into the hold of the sky-ship with him, the rest forced into land vehicles.

They race south, over neatly ordered hillsides and lines of trees, tall and straight, that look like points on a grid when viewed from above.

Reports of Alpha's progress come in fits and starts. Brief sightings reported in terms of wonder directly into the Knight

Commander's ear. The immortal is flying in a straight line, but when his course is plotted on a map, the Knight Commander is surprised to find it is not taking them directly to Greyspot Three.

A call comes through from one of his soldiers. 'Report.'

'He's here, sir. I can see Him!'

The Knight Commander confirms the soldier's location. A small village known as Diligence to its inhabitants. There is little to recommend it. In fact the place is not connected to any major settlements, forcing traders to walk hard paths to get there. A backwater, mostly forgotten.

Could Alpha remember it as something more? Is this a site of significance that we have unwittingly neglected?

He turns his attention back to the soldier. 'What is Alpha doing now?'

'Circling, sir.'

'Just circling?'

'Yes, sir.'

'Then hold your position. We'll be there shortly. Keep me informed if there are any changes.'

'He's seen something, sir. He's . . . diving.'

The soldier sets a flare off from his position, and the sky-ship zooms in on it. Diligence is a grim and rocky place. The power stations and main gathering areas are built under the earth, along with half of the housing, but it has grown over the years, simple extensions jutting directly from the walls. None of these extensions appear to be to standard and the number of them indicates a much higher population than is currently registered.

Even without the flare to guide them in, it is easy to see where Alpha has landed. A circle of charred grass surrounds a new hole in the ground, a new entrance to Diligence's underground network of tunnels.

They set down, leaping from the hatch the moment the sky-ship has settled, and rush toward the hole. The footing is unsteady near the edge, and more than one knight wobbles, graceless, as they try to stay upright.

Around them the air feels charged and angry, making it hard to breathe.

Suddenly nervous of what he will see, the Knight Commander peers over the edge. Below he sees Alpha of The Seven, his sword drawn, shimmering as the echoes of song slowly fade.

At the immortal's silver feet is a smear of ash, making the loose shape of a body.

Alpha holds up his other hand. In it is a visor, black, featureless. The Knight Commander has seen pictures of it before. It is the kind of armour preferred by the First, largest and most powerful of the remaining infernals.

He finds his eyes drawn to Alpha's. Their blue is like a second sky, a better horizon. When Alpha speaks, each word strikes deep, a hammer to his chest.

'Diligence is tainted.'

'We will evacuate the town at once, destroy it, cleanse the ground, and send the inhabitants to the purging centres.'

The visor crumples in Alpha's fist. 'Destroy, yes. Cleanse, yes. But send none away.'

The Knight Commander swallows at the thought. He has just looked at the population figures for Diligence. They number in the hundreds and are likely conservative. *Surely the majority are in ignorance? Surely it is only a few that have been colluding with the First?*

Even as he thinks this, he is drawing his sword. His knights have already done so. Anything else would be an act of defiance.

There is no further reflection. The Seraph Knights begin to sing, their swords flaring to life, and Diligence begins to burn.

Vesper's father nods to the soldiers as he makes the long walk out of the city. An endless cycle of salutes and responses, nods and smiles, polite. They have become especially sharp of late, exhausting in their exactitude.

His lips move as he walks, silently counting steps until he is well beyond the outer boundary. Then he stops, pulling eagerly at his collar, loosening the straps on his armour.

A deep breath and a long sigh follow as his body settles, changing posture, relaxing.

The next part of the walk is taken at a more leisurely pace, thoughts of the day playing across his face in a series of frowns, raised eyebrows and the occasional smile.

Many times, the Knight Commander has offered him a room at the city or transportation home, and he has refused them. The Knight Commander doesn't understand why but tolerates the decision out of respect for past deeds and honours.

Vesper's father slows, stops. He glances over his shoulder but nothing is there. Then, gradually, as if lifted by an invisible hand, his head tilts towards the sky.

He lifts a hand to shield his eyes, squinting against the light of the evening suns. A shape is just discernible, descending, distant, yet getting closer. A cube.

The sanctum of The Seven returns.

There is something different about the way it comes down compared to its ascent. Not faster but more purposeful.

He stares at it, face darkening despite the glare.

Because of this, it takes him far longer to notice the movement at ground level. From the Shining City comes another shape. A snake of metal, mechanized, a machine of war to carry Seraph Knights and soldiers. Caterpillar tracks pull it swiftly across the countryside, towards him. Towards his home.

He stops staring, turns, and runs.

A few miles away Jem stands on a hill holding a battered scope to his eye. Through it he sees high platinum pillars capped in green, gardens decorating their sides in leafy spirals. These pillars visibly mark the Shining City's border. Another border, invisible, runs along their perimeter, a fizzing screen of energy to keep the infernal at bay. Jem cares little for the screen or the pillars, his interests lie deeper. But his attempt to find the sanctum of The Seven is doomed to failure. Even at full magnification it is nothing more than a vague shimmering.

He begins to wander down the hill, leaving Harm and Reela at the house. Twice he stumbles on uneven ground, his attention kept on the air.

Finally, the cube comes into focus, and something else. At first he thinks it is a bird, but it is too close to the Sanctum for that to be true. And it is the wrong shape, far larger than any of the wildlife at this end of the world.

One of The Seven has left the Sanctum.

It is flying towards him.

Directly beneath it, keeping pace, is a metal snake. At this distance it seems to slide over the hills like a boat riding waves.

Jem nearly drops the scope. Fear grips him, an old friend embracing hard. He has but seconds to act. If they have not seen him already, it is only a matter of time. He looks back to the house, thinks of Harm, of Reela. The fear grips tighter. There is nothing he can do. If they see him, they will judge and find him wanting. If they see Reela – he shakes his head, cutting off the thought.

Fear leaves no time for deliberation. Keeping low, moving between the hills, he makes for a destination. Not towards the Shining City and the approaching forces, not towards home, but away, to a hiding place where the trees grow wild.

From there he watches, shivering among the leaves.

His daughter is in danger. She needs him! An impulse to go to her is checked by an older, more cynical one. He cannot get to her in time and any act of heroism on his part would be suicide. What could one man hope to do against an immortal and the armed might of the Empire?

Nothing.

He has stood up before, for his mother, and paid for it in years. The memories are knife sharp, cutting still. Jem has learned from past mistakes, been shaped by them.

But Reela needs him!

He shakes his head, knowing that he cannot go to her, hating himself for it. Better to wait, to choose the right time. And if that time does not come, better to live. He repeats the words a second time, silent, bitter, and forces himself to swallow them.

*　　*　　*

On silvered wings, Delta of The Seven soars. It has been a long time since she has flown, too long.

Behind her, mirror-like, is her brother, Alpha. He flies away from her towards the coast, in search of other prey.

Orders have been given, the worthy have been mobilized. Soon, the purge will begin. The thought of it weighs heavy in Delta's mind. For it is their failure as much as their people's.

She does not disagree with Alpha's plans. He is the first of them, the strongest, and she admires his purpose. And yet . . . she wishes there was some other way to restore the creator's perfect vision.

Though she is awake and active once more, the weariness remains, and a sadness, deep, that she carried even in the earliest days.

A dwelling comes into view. Two houses, ugly, messy shapes. The sight displeases her. Why would the remnant of her sister choose to be here rather than at their side?

She comes down to land, feet making gentle contact with the earth, wings folding behind her like a cloak.

Unmoved by what she sees, yet curious to find its hidden appeal, she looks around while her knights catch up, the hissing of the snake that bears them half a mile distant.

The smaller house has no door. She approaches to find it is a home for animals, nothing more. Despite the space, only one ancient goat seems to dwell here.

Irritated by the disturbance, the goat looks at Delta.

With eyes like bleak winter clouds, Delta looks at the goat. She sees fading strength and many flaws, but all are natural. No taint clings to the creature. It is not the source of wrongness that she senses hidden close by.

She moves away, towards the main house.

Behind her, the goat snorts, derisive.

She ignores it, drawn by lingering echoes of her sister's essence. Metal fingers brush an uneven wall. Once, Gamma's sword rested here. She feels a faint sense of contentment, of peace.

Greedily, she lets the experience wash over her. All too soon it is over. And it is not enough.

She moves to the door and opens it.

Running footsteps approach and a voice, loud, high pitched. 'I'm bitey goat! Baaa! Baaa! Bite! Bite!'

A girl comes into view. Unruly, messy, tainted.

Delta's hand moves to the living sword at her side, grasping the hilt.

The girl sees her in the doorway, skids to a stop, her babbling voice cutting off in shock.

Delta finds her sword, herself, reluctant. She cannot imagine Gamma permitting this tainted thing to exist. It makes no sense to her.

The girl finds her voice and starts to scream.

A man walks slowly over to her, his voice soft, soothing. 'It's alright, Reela, it's alright. I'm here now.' He keeps one hand lightly on the wall, letting it guide him to the weeping girl.

Through Delta's eyes his essence is scarred. Hints of taint remain at the edges, a sign of something far worse that has been burned away, something centred where his eyes once were.

He pauses, head tilting in her direction. 'Hello? Hello? Is someone there?'

Delta does not answer, her hand makes a fist around the hilt of her sword. *Gamma spurned our love, for this?*

'I know you're there. What do you want?'

Shaking her head, Delta turns away.

The metal snake comes to a sliding stop nearby, disgorging

knights from its open mouth. They kneel before her, waiting for her to pass before carrying out their orders. She has seen nothing to make her interfere with them.

As the knights advance on the house, she sinks to her knees, dragged down by misery.

Raised voices soon reach her.

'I will not stand aside! And I will not leave my home! I took your trials years ago and I passed them. I earned my right to be here.'

The knight's reply is amplified by his helmet. 'This house is tainted. It will be purged. If you do not leave, you will be purged with it.'

'Contact the Bearer, she will not stand for this!'

'The Bearer serves The Seven in all things. Our orders come direct from Them. Strip off your clothes, step away from the house and report for re-purging immediately.'

'Just contact her, please.'

'You have sixty seconds to get out of our way.'

'Don't do something you'll regret.'

Delta listens despite herself.

'You have fifty seconds, failure to obey will be seen as rebellion.'

'I will not leave. If you're going to hurt an innocent girl you'll have to go through me.'

'Thirty seconds.'

'Wait!'

'Twenty seconds.'

The knights charge their lances.

'Ten seconds.'

A tear of liquid stone rolls down Delta's cheek.

*　　*　　*

Flames dance, reflected in amber eyes that widen, horrified. He slows on the hillside, taking it in. When he sees Harm's charred body in the doorway, he stops completely. Tears well, falling fat and fast down creased cheeks. One hand claws at his chest, stricken. No sound comes from his mouth but it twists open, grief shaped.

His home has become a pyre. Those he loves, ashes. Himself, a vagrant again.

But above the crackle of fire, almost buried, there is a sound, a voice, familiar, wailing.

Teeth bare, fists clench, and he is running again, past the kneeling winged figure, past the circle of knights with lances, spewing fire. They call out a warning, too late, too surprised to intercept him.

He veers from the front of the house where the heat is strongest, diving in through a side window. Shoddy joinery is, for once, an asset, his body punching the whole plasglass sheet from its frame.

With a heavy thump, he lands. Smoke already clouds the room, making the space strange. The Vagrant keeps low, covers his mouth and moves forward.

Heat buffets from all sides, pressing on exposed flesh, making breath painful.

The Vagrant pauses, enduring discomfort to listen.

Like a siren, the voice comes from the kitchen. He follows until he crouches by the dining table. Ducking under, he comes face to face with Reela.

She stares at him, howling, incoherent, snot bubbling from nostrils to mix with tears and soot.

The Vagrant lifts a finger, puts it to his lips.

Still sniffling, she copies the gesture.

The Vagrant nods, then looks round, squinting against the smoke until he finds what he is looking for. Leaving Reela where she is, he pulls his old coat from its hook and moves to a tank of water. Coughing now, he kicks the tank, then kicks again, and again, until it splits open. As the water gushes out he holds his coat underneath, turning it, soaking it, before rushing back to Reela's cowering form.

It is harder to see her, the smoke encroaching ever lower. She has not moved, her finger still pressed, firm but shaking, to her lips.

He reaches under, grabs her arm and drags her to his side. Desperate, she flails, trying to cling to him, but before she can get a grip, he sweeps the sodden coat over her head, bundling her up.

Reela gasps but does not cry out.

Lifting the bundle in his arms, the Vagrant runs for the nearest window. He can no longer see it, the smoke forcing him to navigate by memory alone.

His recollection is off by an inch, and he jars painfully against the wall before diving out, through fire, through cracked plasglass that shatters, rolling smoking into the last of the evening light.

For a moment he crouches on the grass, breathing heavy. His armour is blackened but not broken, steaming but not alight.

Parting the coat, he checks that Reela still breathes. She does, in ragged gulps. Picking her up again, the Vagrant starts to run.

The Seraph Knights surrounding the house see him. Commands are relayed from chip to chip, the ones furthest away running over, the others closing ranks to cut off escape.

The nearest knight steps into his path. 'We have no quarrel with you, Champion! Drop the – uhnn!'

The Vagrant's elbow connects with the knight's helm and, as the woman staggers back, the Vagrant takes stock. There is nowhere to run, no allies to turn to.

He runs anyway.

The knights raise their lances and a gout of fire shoots out to his right, turning him left, then another comes from his left, trying to pin him.

Ducking his head, raising an arm, he goes under it, mostly. Ignoring the way his backplate sizzles, the Vagrant presses on until he reaches the kneeling figure of Delta.

This close to one of The Seven, the knights do not dare to fire. They put their lances away, and draw their singing swords.

The air trembles with sudden song and Reela flinches in the Vagrant's arms, stung by the sound.

As the knights move into a circular formation, the Vagrant looks down at Delta on her knees. She seems oblivious, a line of stone drying on her face.

He swings Reela under his arm and reaches down, carefully.

'Step away!' orders one of the knights. 'It is a sin to touch Her!'

When it is clear the Vagrant is ignoring them, one of the knights closes in, sword raised.

He grits his teeth, takes the hilt of Delta's sword.

Nothing. No pain, no reaction.

He pulls Delta's sword free, swinging it up and out, opening his mouth to direct its power.

The knights pause, the nearest one stepping back in shock.

Unlike their swords however, Delta's doesn't sing. Silver wings wrap tight around its eye and the weapon feels heavy in his hand, dull.

Quickly, the knight recovers himself and moves to attack.

The Vagrant frowns, glares at the sword, then shakes it hard. In answer, the wings tighten even more.

There is no more time, he parries the first attack, then the second, each blow jarring his arm. Only the proximity of Delta holds the other knights at bay. They are painfully careful, terrified of bringing harm to their beloved immortal.

One of the knights keeps the Vagrant occupied while the others move in behind, advancing together.

He glances over his shoulder at them, barely making the next parry. Forced down to one knee by the impact, Reela slips from his grasp, rolling away.

The knight he has been fighting steps back, raising his sword over Reela's body. The others are now behind him, ready.

'Surrender, Champion. This is your last chance.'

The Vagrant grips the sword in both hands and points the tip at Delta's neck.

There is a pause. Such blasphemy has never even been considered before. A whispered conference is had within the knights' helmets. Would he dare? Could he do Delta actual harm? There is no precedent, no protocol to follow.

The Vagrant makes eye contact with Reela, beckoning her with a twitch of his head.

Without a sound, the girl stands up.

Dumbstruck, the knights watch her as she walks past them, dragging the old coat like a blanket behind her.

When she reaches the Vagrant, Reela wraps herself around his leg.

There is a pause. The knights dare not attack, dare not report what is happening. Too afraid to act, they become spectators to a tale of horror, unfurling slowly in directions they cannot fathom.

The Vagrant touches the point of the sword to Delta's throat.

There is an audible clink, then he lifts the sword under her chin, levering her to her feet.

Two of the knights cover their eyes, five others begin to recite the litany of the Winged Eye.

Silvered wings spring open on the sword's crosspiece, alarmed, and an eye opens wide in surprise.

At the same moment, Delta's eyes open, locking with the Vagrant's, forcing him to look up.

Softly, Delta begins to hum. Her sword takes up the tune. The Vagrant finds his hands starting to shake. Muscles lock all over his body, trembling in time with Delta's melody. Stiffly, against his will, he rises on tiptoe.

Delta raises her hand and the Vagrant's mouth opens. She reaches inside, fingers finding the old scars there. As if reading music, her song changes as she traces the lines, learning their history and that of the man marked by them. Her voice and her sword's fall to disharmony, becoming a thing of grief and pain. The air around them darkens, tints blue. Briefly, it threatens to spark, then dies down, the hand leaving, and Delta covers her eyes, her song little more than a moan.

Released, the Vagrant slumps down, clutching at his throat.

After a few moments, his vision comes into focus again. He sees Reela looking up at him, afraid and hopeful. She clings to his leg, a dark-haired barnacle.

He blinks at her, then nods, reassuring.

Switching to a one-handed grip, he takes Delta by the arm and starts to walk. Delta does not resist, allowing herself to be dragged alongside him.

The Vagrant moves with an exaggerated limp, Reela still firmly attached to his leg. In other places, the image would be comical but the knights see nothing funny in it. They give ground to him, and when he points for them to step aside with Delta's sword, they comply.

Delta is manoeuvred into the metal snake. The driver is pulled out. Reela is unpeeled and belted into one of the chairs in the snake's head. The Vagrant sits in the other. He looks at the controls, frowns.

A button is pressed, a stick twisted. Nothing happens. More options are exhausted, manipulations becoming increasingly forceful until, at last, the hissing of the engines grows in volume and the snake turns away from the burning house and the staring knights, making towards the coast.

One Thousand and Fifty-Two Years Ago

The Empire of the Winged Eye holds power, undisputed. A great engine made of millions of people, machines and essence-fuelled weapons. Its purpose is simple: protect the world from infernal threat.

The Empire stands ready to do its duty. Spheres of metal orbit the globe watching for trouble, and the Lenses, the Empire's watchers, have agents on land and sea, ever vigilant. Legions of knights train daily, keeping senses and swords sharp. Harmonized humans, their souls linked to better withstand infernal possession, train with them as living shields. Armies of soldiers march with essence guns and launchers, keeping constant patrols on the Breach.

There is but one problem.

The Breach has not yet opened.

Massassi, who alone was able to perceive the threat, created the Empire of the Winged Eye in answer to the coming invasion. But she was born too early, has readied humanity too soon.

While her loyal servants keep watch, other voices whisper dissent in the shadows. They question the reality of the threat and if the huge resources required to maintain the military could be better spent in other ways.

She knows that none will dare oppose her now, but after she is gone is another matter. And Massassi already feels her years of struggle, feels each weary pump of her scarred heart.

Despite her godlike power, she is getting old. She will be dead, the skin rotted from her bones, long before the infernals find their way into her reality.

But she is as much a mechanic as a deity. The Empire is simply a complex solution to a complex problem. She has already modified it many times as new data came to her. This is no different. As the problem evolves, so too must her creation. Only politicians and idiots ever think that things are finished or perfect. Massassi is neither.

Leaving the world in the hands of her commanders she returns to her workshop, one last project in mind.

CHAPTER THREE

A metal snake moves effortlessly over hills, matching their undulations. Inside the head, the Vagrant works the controls. Anger manifests in his gestures, making course corrections sharp.

He looks over his shoulder often but Delta of The Seven remains folded in the space behind them, a placid statue. Her sword is on the floor by the Vagrant's side. It too, has gone quiet again, its eye closed tight.

Reela sniffles quietly in the seat next to his. As he works, she tries to get closer to him but straps hold her tight, thwarting the effort. A hint of a storm crosses her features and she begins to wail.

The Vagrant glances over, touching a finger to his lips.

Reela copies him.

Her stormy expression abates and he goes back to managing the vehicle. Calmer now, she attends to the Vagrant. She positions her left hand like his, her fingers hovering over imaginary buttons. With her right, she mimes holding the control stick. She straightens her back, raises her chin, and after another glance at his face, adds a frown.

When the Vagrant looks through the viewing screen, staring intently, she leans forward to do the same. When, briefly, he presses his fist to his forehead, the frustration is mirrored in miniature.

The Vagrant does not notice.

Gradually, the hills flatten out and the snake winds its way over flatlands and between trees planted in orderly rows, wide spaced, with branches that only start high up, shade-making and unobtrusive.

There is a scratching sound from behind the head of the snake.

Instantly, the Vagrant tenses. He releases the straps that hold him then turns, one hand still on the controls, the other reaching down for Delta's sword.

Reela's eyes light up with new knowledge. She presses the central buckle where the straps cross over her chest but nothing happens. She presses it again, using two fingers, then again with her fist. With a soft click, the straps spring apart.

The scratching sounds again. It is close, coming from the other side of the metal that separates the head section from the body of the snake.

The Vagrant raises Delta's sword, his eyes flicking between where Delta sits and the intruder's location.

There is a click, then a soft exhalation of machinery, and the panel slides back to reveal Jem. He has mud on his face and in his hair but appears untouched by sword or flame.

'It's me! It's just me! I was out tending the goats when the knights came. By the time I got here it was . . . too late.

I managed to climb in the back while they were all distracted with you.'

The Vagrant stares at him for a moment, then places Delta's sword back on the floor.

Jem's face splits in a relieved smile. 'Reela! You're alive. Thank—' he notices Delta, springs back against the wall. His voice is much softer when he speaks again. 'Is that . . .?'

The Vagrant nods.

A moment later, Reela nods.

'But you can't just take Her! What are you thinking?'

The Vagrant shrugs.

Reela shrugs.

'What are we going to do?'

The Vagrant holds up a hand. Jem's face sours as Reela does the same. Before he can comment however, something over the Vagrant's shoulder, on the other side of the viewing screen, grabs his attention. 'Look out!'

The Vagrant whirls back to the controls to see they are heading directly towards one of the great pillars. Proximity alerts rapidly ramp up in volume, streams of numbers representing distance and time to impact appear on the view screen, flashing to show their urgency. He jerks the controls, throwing the snake to the right and everyone inside the cockpit to the left.

Only Delta does not move, her serenity untouched. Jem is thrown into the opposite wall, Reela and the Vagrant hurled from their seats.

A musical array of flesh smacking against hard surfaces follows.

While the humans recover, the metal snake continues to veer to the right, until it catches sight of its own tail, making circles of muddy brown in the grass beneath its tracks.

The Vagrant hauls himself back onto his chair, one hand pressing against the new bump on his skull, the other taking the control stick, pointing the snake forward once more.

Jem also gets up, going to where Reela curls on the floor. 'It's alright,' he says, gathering her into his arms. 'It's alright. Ohh, you poor thing.'

She begins to cry and Jem holds her tighter. 'Are you hurt? Does it hurt anywhere?'

Reela blinks, looks over to where the Vagrant is, then takes a deep breath. She squeezes her face, squishing the tear on her cheek and forcing down the other ones.

'Reela?' Jem asks. 'Are you okay?'

She nods.

'Does it hurt anywhere?'

She shakes her head and Jem moves her over to the empty chair. As he fixes Reela into place, he glances at the Vagrant, mutters, 'She should have been strapped in.'

The Vagrant's mouth opens in protest but he says nothing.

The snake travels on, its eyes lighting the dark ahead. On the viewing screen, green lines fill in details for frail human eyes. The gradations in the landscape, the outline of trees and, on the horizon, the line where the sea begins.

Unlike the vast majority of the citizens of the Empire of the Winged Eye, no one in the cockpit is in possession of a working chip. The Vagrant has never had one, neither has Reela. Jem does have one but it is poorly made, a cheap replica of those in the Shining City. It malfunctioned years ago. Now it is a purposeless lump, a little bit of junk in his brain. Because of this, none of them hears the broadcast.

Delta does. She does not need a chip to translate the

sounds for her. She hears all, understands all. Her head tilts to one side, her mouth opens, 'Obeisance.' Even speaking, there is resonance to her voice. It fills the cramped space, charging the air.

The humans are rendered motionless by its beauty.

Fluidly, Delta rises to her feet. 'I am here,' she says. 'Exactly here.'

As if in answer, new lights flash on the viewing screen, and something ripples in the sky above, a ship dropping out of cloak.

It matches the metal snake for speed, flying directly overhead.

The Vagrant points at Jem, then towards the gun turret on top of the snake.

'I'm not going up there! It's suicide.'

The Vagrant points again, Reela joins him.

'I can't. I don't know how.'

The Vagrant sighs, pushes the snake to go faster.

The sky-ship has no trouble adjusting its pace.

A warning flickers on the screen: there is an incoming object. Before the Vagrant can react there is a thunk of something attaching itself to the snake's roof.

A patch as wide as an adult's palm distorts above their heads, turning red, then white, so bright that all but Delta are forced to turn away.

When the light fades, a hole is left behind, just the right size for the sphere to drop through. It rolls a few inches until it is perfectly positioned in the centre of the space, then lasers project from every point in its surface, making grids of green fall like nets over every object in the room, mapping and highlighting all at once.

The Vagrant abandons the snake's controls and picks up Delta's sword. The grid over his face fades from green to red. The ones over Jem and Reela do the same, though Delta's remains green, vibrant, safe.

The Vagrant raises Delta's sword as squares on the grid fill with colour, specific, marking in the locations of major organs.

He tries to sing as he brings down the blade but no sound comes from his mouth and the sword does not wake. The blade makes a dull thud as it hits the sphere.

The laser grids stutter, fizz, and return to life.

At the control panel, new proximity warnings sound. Everyone ignores them.

The Vagrant hits the sphere again.

Delta's sword wakes with a start. It tries to close its eye again but the Vagrant has other ideas. He hits the sphere, singing, and this time the sword reacts, the sound passing down the blade, shimmering as it parts the sphere neatly in two.

Instantly, the grids die out.

The Vagrant stabs a finger in Jem's direction, then stabs it towards the controls.

'But I . . .' Jem begins, but stops as soon as he meets the Vagrant's eyes. He moves instead to hover by the controls, ineffectual, as the Vagrant runs deeper into the snake's belly.

The Vagrant reaches a ladder and climbs up into the turret. The plasglass dome that normally covers it is nothing more than jagged shards around the base, the guns reduced to slaggy tubes. As the Vagrant looks up and down the length of the snake, he sees plumes of smoke where the other weapons are. They have taken away the snake's teeth.

Above him, the sky-ship descends, getting so close that the figures leaning out of hatches are easy to see as they prepare to jump.

Taking a breath to sing, the Vagrant checks on Delta's sword. As soon as it realizes what is about to happen, the sword squeezes its eye shut. He bangs it against the side of the turret until the eye opens again, then admonishes it with a finger.

The eye in the crosspiece trembles but doesn't close.

Again, the Vagrant takes breath, thrusting the sword straight up as he sings. Delta's sword sings with him, and the air burns blue around it, the force of the song travelling beyond the reach of the metal, surging up until it meets one of the light drives in the sky-ship's wing.

There is a muffled explosion, followed by a whine as the engine gives out and the sky-ship falls sharply to the left, scattering its cargo of soldiers onto the ground below. The Vagrant watches their brief fall and the individual bounces and tumbles as they land. The sky-ship only bounces once before grinding to a halt.

Satisfied, he climbs back down.

Jem is happy to relinquish the controls, moving to stand behind Reela's chair.

The Vagrant drops Delta's sword on the floor with a clatter, frowning at all of the new warning lights on the screen. The display on the screen is no longer augmented, forcing him to squint against the plasglass to try and penetrate the dark. With a shrug, he takes the control stick and pushes it as far forward as it can go.

Delta continues to stare at the hole in the ceiling. She speaks so softly, as to be barely audible. 'Obeisance, where have you gone?'

The eye in her sword gives her a guilty glance before closing.

Delta's lips move one more time, soundlessly. 'Obeisance?'

The Knight Commander stands on the edge of the cliff, soldiers and knights forming up behind, ready. Greyspot Three spreads out below him, a ramshackle sprawl. He sees the metal walkway that leads down into the shelter of the rocks. He sees the buildings, noting again how many have been built without authorization and without reference to any guidelines. They will find more undesirables here, those that operate outside of imperial law, tainted souls, criminals, the enemy.

His head shakes, disgusted, involuntary. He had not realized how bad things had become, though he is sure the Lenses know, which means Obeisance knows. If the First dares to walk their lands, what other monstrosities might they find here? How has this been tolerated for so long? And, foremost in his mind: *why didn't she tell me?*

On the edge of Greyspot Three he sees the docks, and beyond them, the Empire of the Winged Eye's armada, gathering. Their presence forms a floating wall, cutting off escape by sea, just as he and his forces block the cliff paths, sealing the port.

Shadows fall across him and he looks up. Alpha's sky palace has arrived. It drifts over his head, a vast battle platform defying physics, defying explanation. He does not hear the huge light engine, its thrumming at a pitch beyond mortal ears, but he feels it, the short hairs prickling on his neck and arms. He exults at its majesty, another miracle, the likes of which has not been seen since Gamma's great exodus.

Somewhere inside are Beta, Epsilon, Theta and Eta of The Seven. With them is Obeisance. Delta is conspicuous by her absence. He has heard that she is attending to some other business inland but Obeisance has been typically obscure on the matter.

Alpha is already down on street level. As the Knight Commander and his troops march down the walkway, boots clanking in synchrony, he sees the immortal moving from house to house. Seraph Knights struggle to keep up, forced to scurry to match Alpha's giant strides.

By the time the Knight Commander has reached the base of the cliffs, he sees a number of people have been pulled from their homes, rounded up and pushed to their knees.

He raises a hand and all of his troops come to a fluid stop, their discipline impeccable. The Knight Commander feels a tiny morsel of relief. No mistake is permissible when The Seven are watching.

A single Seraph Knight hurries over and salutes.

'Report.'

The knight points to the kneeling citizens. 'Alpha says these ones are to be spared.'

The Knight Commander does a quick head count, his chip confirming the details as he tries to ignore their calls for help, for reassurance, for any kind of recognition. There are one hundred and thirty people here, less than one percent of Greyspot Three's population.

'I see.'

'What should we do, sir?'

His voice quivers. The knight is young, barely more than a squire. He has never seen battle before, but then, neither has the Knight Commander.

'What we always do when we receive orders: we follow them.' He turns his head slightly, speaking to officers further away via comms. 'Captains, have your troops form a perimeter around the port. Nothing and no one gets through, understood?'

Within his helmet, a chorus of affirmation echoes.

The knights form up with him, their lances charged, ready, their eyes on him, waiting for the order.

Doubt flickers within the Knight Commander's chest. He wonders if they are really about to destroy an entire port. *Is this some kind of test? Surely we must be able to save more than these few? Even the tainted can be purged.*

Doubt turns to fear as Alpha's gaze falls upon him. If he does not act now, and immediately, he will be judged and found wanting. Perhaps he already has been.

The Knight Commander swallows in a dry throat.

He gives the order.

The knights level their lances.

By now, the people of Greyspot Three have realized what is coming. Those with weapons ready them. Those without take cover. Despite the lack of time or cohesion, a resistance forms quickly. Houses become bunkers, windows gunnery ports. Those without conventional firearms resort to throwing whatever comes to hand.

It is a swift and spirited response.

The knights' lances spew fire, a wave of destruction, setting buildings and people ablaze. The rebels return fire, less spirited than before.

Back and forth it goes, three times, with the resistance fading more and more. And then, Alpha sings. It is a long note, sharp, that seems to go on forever.

The Seven

A migraine starts behind the Knight Commander's eyes, the sudden pain throwing off his aim. The other knights struggle too, their sword-points lowering, wilting. While, further back, the soldiers stop firing altogether.

In one of the houses, a half-breed begins to scream. She is not tainted badly, not on the surface. But, behind her skin, the blood vibrates, burning up. Similar cries join her from scattered locations, and through it all, Alpha sustains the note.

The Knight Commander is not sure how much more he can take and he is not the target of Alpha's song. The rebels have stopped firing now, hands too busy, covering ears or staunching blood that flows from nostrils, to handle weapons.

Three streets away, on a roof, a lone woman stands. Her clothes are well-worn, faded, but something in her posture speaks of command. Though the sound buffets her just as much as the others, she finds the strength to stand. In her hand is a Slingpistol. She points it at Alpha, putting his silver face in her sights, and fires.

A single shot, flung at a giant. For a moment all attention goes to it, soldiers and citizens alike forgetting their pain as they gape at the unlikely attack.

The Knight Commander cannot believe what he is seeing. He has time to realize that the woman's aim is true, time to pose the question of what he would do if Alpha fell, but not time to answer it.

Set into the winged crosspiece of Alpha's sword is an eye. It tracks the incoming projectile. The Knight Commander is not sure whether it is sword that moves arm, or arm that moves sword, but one moment, Alpha's blade is at his side, the next it is arcing up, swatting the shot from the sky.

Alpha stops singing, and three eyes turn to the woman on the roof. As the immortal's sword swings in her direction, the Knight Commander sees her turn, jump down, trying to put the house between them.

Alpha sings a second note, and for a moment it is too bright to see anything, the Knight Commander is forced to shield his face from a world turned searing blue. When he looks again there is no house, no woman, no resistance. Just a pile of ashes smouldering in the breeze.

Then Alpha is moving towards the next house, and the Knight Commander is shouting orders, mobilizing his forces. This time, when the soldiers and knights fire, the rebels have no answer.

Hours pass as the metal snake continues to work its way towards the coast. Despite its size, the vehicle moves swiftly. Smoke trails at sharp angles from shattered turrets, and the caterpillar tracks make short work of the uneven terrain.

Delta of The Seven blinks, returning from thoughts of the past. She has been staring at a tiny hole in the ceiling, waiting for Obeisance to come. But Obeisance has not come. Her brothers and sisters are expecting her return. Alpha will be displeased at the delay. The thought concerns Delta, for she has always tried to be in harmony with the others, prided herself on it.

She realizes that no immediate aid is coming and that she should take action herself. But what action? More information is needed.

In turn, she regards each of the people sharing the cockpit with her.

The child, Reela, sleeps badly. Straps meant for an adult

ride up under her chin, digging in. Her dreams are reflected in Delta's eyes. She is trapped in a house that burns, and visored faces stare at her through windows, blocking escape.

Studying her essence, Delta sees little to cherish, and the proximity of the taint, however slight, is unpleasant.

The smaller man, Jem, is looking at her. He is afraid. He is right to be. She sees his mind making its petty calculations, the network of small lies that permeate his being and, beneath them, a heavy sense of bitterness and regret she cannot help but feel empathy for. But more than all of this, she sees that he is tainted, spoiled by years of infernal contact.

The other man, the one that once bore Gamma's sword, and has now dared to use hers, is not tainted. Though he is easy to read, a simple example of the species, she does not understand where he fits. Like a spare part left in the box after construction is completed. There is a temptation to keep him around, just in case, but really, there is no need for him. She lingers briefly on the freshness of the man's grief, how it threatens to overwhelm him, the tidal surge of it held back by adrenaline, fear and the demands of the moment.

Delta knows what is expected of her. She closes her eyes, imagines Alpha giving the order. So easy is it for her to picture her brother, it is as if he were there, demanding their destruction.

Her hand opens as she turns to where her sword lies. It is next to the Vagrant's chair, feigning sleep. It does not respond to her summons. She considers picking it up. Certainly, none of the humans present could stop her. And yet, she does not pick it up.

Even as the outrage runs through her that it has not

responded, she realizes she does not want it to. Delta has always carried weariness within her and she has little spirit for fighting. She did not leave the sanctum to bloody her hands. She left it to investigate her sister, to understand why the last fragment of Gamma acts the way it does.

She tells herself that these humans are not worthy of her wrath. Tells herself that it is only a matter of time before the Empire comes to collect her, and so it is not worth the effort of leaving. She tells herself that she is choosing to wait because it suits her.

And then, because it is habit and because it is easier, she sits down and closes her eyes.

Both suns are in the sky, casting lights, sparkling, across the sea. Water dominates the view now, from the unbroken line of the horizon to the waves smacking against the shore.

Throughout the dawn and early morning, the metal snake continues its journey, tireless. Thinning smoke leaks from ravaged turrets but, despite the battering, it moves as fast as ever.

Jem comes over to stand next to the Vagrant's chair. He glances at Reela, asleep in the straps, and lowers his voice. 'We're making good time.'

The Vagrant doesn't register the words at first, his attention elsewhere, in the past, on things lost. Amber eyes focus again. He blinks away tears, nods.

'Do you think we can get to Vesper before they do?'

The Vagrant shrugs and Jem looks past him, towards their destination.

Up ahead is a port, but not the great northern sea base that Jem expects to see. 'I thought you'd be taking us to

Skylanding.' He leans forward, squinting, trying to recognize a landmark. 'It's not Northwing either. Where are we?'

The Vagrant points at the navcom, shrugs.

'You don't know?' asks Jem, incredulous. The display is damaged but he is able to make out enough detail to guess. 'It's taking us to Greyspot Three, isn't it? But Vesper will be going to Crucible. We should be heading to Skylanding, that's the most direct route.'

The Vagrant gestures back to where Delta sits and shakes his head.

He imagines the kind of welcome they'd get from the Empire's forces at Skylanding or Northwing and reconsiders. 'Alright, you have a point, but we can't take Reela to Greyspot Three. It's not safe. It's full of refugees and rejects from the Shining City. For suns' sake, I've even heard rumours that the First's nomads use it as a trading spot!'

Reela stretches, yawning, and whatever Jem is about to say is bitten back.

The Vagrant pulls gently back on the control stick and the metal snake eases to a stop. He rubs at his eyes, blood-shot, before resting his hands on the dashboard. There is a pause, long enough to take a breath, to sigh, and then he is pushing himself out of the chair.

Jem goes to unstrap Reela but finds she has already stood up, a big frown on her little face. 'What's wrong?'

Reela looks up at him, solemn, but says nothing.

The Vagrant collects Delta's sword from the floor and opens the hatch. There is a hiss, and fresh air wafts into the stuffy room, enlivening.

Jem moves to his side, pulling Reela behind him. He leans in close. 'What about Her?'

Both men look at Delta for a moment. If she is aware of their scrutiny, she gives no sign.

'Maybe we should just leave Her here?'

The Vagrant thinks for a moment, nods, and takes a step towards Delta.

'What are you –? Actually, I don't want to know.' Jem retreats towards the exit hatch. 'Before you do anything, I'm going outside.' He looks down, adds hastily, 'To keep Reela safe.'

The Vagrant nods.

Jem ushers Reela out, turning briefly before following her. 'Whatever you're going to do, be careful.'

The Vagrant raises an eyebrow.

Alone, save for Delta, the Vagrant seems to sag, the weight of recent events folding over his shoulders like a cloak. He pinches the bridge of his nose, knuckles tired eyes and walks to where Delta sits.

Carefully, quietly, he kneels down opposite her. The top of his head barely lines up with her shoulder.

She does not stir.

With reverence, he returns her sword, leaving it at her feet. He glances up, but her eyes remain closed. Neither sword nor immortal show any sign of having noticed each other. He stands slowly, leaves quickly, and doesn't look back.

Outside, Jem and Reela are waiting. The three of them walk towards the cliff's edge. Up here, they are exposed, the wind knocking at them, playful, tugging hair and making speech difficult. The smoke that rises from the other side is whisked away as soon as it peeks above ground level.

The Vagrant sees the smoke and his frown burrows deeper.

'I don't like this,' murmurs Jem.

They move nearer to the edge, battling the wind for balance. Jem holds one of Reela's hands, the Vagrant holds the other.

Slowly, by inches, Greyspot Three comes into view. Houses smoulder below, glowing red, a scattered cluster of dying stars. Jem pulls out his old, battered scope. He sees details he could have done without, a high heap of bodies, stacked, blackened limbs rigid. Shattered buildings and bomb-scarred streets.

The Vagrant takes the scope, his jaw clenching as he takes in the details.

Reela's scope is imaginary, but the grim set to her face is convincing nonetheless.

'Oh no,' says Jem, tapping the Vagrant's shoulder.

He looks over and Jem points, back to the metal snake. 'Look!'

Delta of The Seven stands between them and the vehicle. She is watching them, her expression unreadable. One of her silvered hands rests on the hilt of her sword.

'What do we do now?' asks Jem.

The Vagrant looks over the edge of the cliff. The walkway that leads down the rock face is mostly intact. He runs for the nearest platform, pulling Reela behind him, pulling Jem behind her.

'But,' Jem protests, 'we can't go down there!'

The Vagrant ignores him, and when Jem gives a second look over his shoulder, he sees that Delta has started to follow them, and his protests die.

Rusted walkways clank with every step. The top layer has disguised the damage further down. The side of the cliff has chunks blown out of it and there is blood caked in the lattice of metal either side of them. There are no bodies here, however. Each has already been taken, fuel for the pyres in the port below. As they pass the worst of the damage the walkway leans out, alarming. Four of the main supports have broken free of their housing, leaving power cables to hold up the structure.

The Vagrant stops.

Reela stops.

'Go on,' urges Jem.

The Vagrant looks down, very quickly looks up again, leaning back against the rock.

'You know what they say, you should never look dow— Wait! Don't you look, Reela! I said don't look!'

The girl begins to overbalance, sliding towards the side. Tugging on an arm each, the two men pull her back. There is a long creaking sound as the cables adjust to the shifting weight.

They all freeze until it settles, clinging to the wall, to each other.

Jem is the first to move, pushing the others into action.

They work their way down, zigzagging back and forth along the rock face. About three quarters of the way, a cable twangs loose.

There is a lurch, brief and fast, then the remaining cables catch.

As the three of them ease their way along, the lean of the walkway becomes more pronounced, slowly succumbing to gravity. Like a drunkard falling over, it takes its time.

'Run!' shouts Jem.

And they do.

The Vagrant scoops Reela into his arms, head low as he accelerates, Jem at his heels.

Their feet hammer fast, raindrops on a rooftop, echoing loud all around them. Only two levels up now, the Vagrant's feet start to slip, unable to cope with the acute angle of the floor; he leans back, trying to keep from falling over. Jem, unable to stop, unable to get past the slower man, shouts, 'Come on—'

Rock groans, final cables come loose. The entire walkway falls away from the cliff, bellyflopping into dirty sand and stone.

The three inside it slam together against the mesh wall, then bounce, to fall again, a tangled heap of arms and legs.

For a while, all is still.

Reela sits up, her younger body managing the impact better than the adults. She holds up a hand and inspects it. The crisscross imprint of the walkway runs up her palm and the outside of her little finger. There is blood where a nail has been torn. At the sight of it she starts to shake. A bottom lip falls from formation, trembles.

Jem springs up, suddenly alert. He presses his face against the mesh trying to see through it, then turns back to the others. 'Is everyone alright?'

With a sigh, the Vagrant levers himself up onto one elbow.

Reela shows them her hand with a look of infinite woe.

'Ouch,' says Jem. 'That looks painful.' He goes back to the mesh. 'I think we're safe. I can't see anyone else nearby.'

The Vagrant looks at her hand and, with a flourish, produces his own. Amid the calluses are new bruises, a bleeding knuckle and a thumb twice as big as its counterpart.

Reela nods, impressed. She takes a deep breath and her lip settles again.

Climbing out of the wreckage of the walkway, they see Greyspot Three from ground level. Aerial bombardment has destroyed any sense of landscaping the place might have had. Craters have given buildings new shapes, added ugly valleys. Lumps of churned earth make new hills, some of them still burn, slowly melting into puddles of slag.

It is a dead place but not everyone here is dead. Survivors sit and stand, united in shock, blending with the debris. They barely notice the newcomers, barely even notice their surroundings.

Jem does. He picks up on glints in the rubble, moving from one to the other, searching for treasures amidst the chaos. He finds a few coins, one of them platinum, precious, and a bonding gun with half a cartridge still intact.

While he does this, the Vagrant looks back up to the top of the cliff. Sunslight glints off a silver figure as she steps off the edge. Wings open, dazzling, turning a fall into a dive, then a glide as she swoops low over the ground, heading straight towards them.

The sight of her returns the survivors to life. As one they scream, scattering in all directions.

Jem, Reela and the Vagrant run too, but do not get far before her shadows rush overhead. The three come to a stop as Delta lands in front of them. She looks from left to right, her eyes bleak as she surveys the wreckage, before coming to rest on a nearby corpse pile.

Jem starts to edge away but the Vagrant takes his arm, gripping tight. He drops slowly to one knee, pulling the other two with him.

Delta pulls out a body from the pile. The arms are asymmetrical, one thicker and longer than the other. She pulls out a skull, ordinary, small, and raises it in the palm of her hand. 'How has it come to this?'

The question is rhetorical but the Vagrant stands, drawing her gaze. He points out to sea, and when she looks, she sees a set of receding specks riding distant waves. A fleet bearing the symbol of the Winged Eye. Above them, ponderous, floats Alpha's sky palace.

Delta closes her eyes.

One Thousand and Fifty-One
Years Ago

Massassi makes the final adjustments to the metal by hand. Somehow, this feels appropriate, as this is to be the most personal of her creations.

The work is a slow race. It does not matter if she finishes today or tomorrow, in a year or three years. The Breach is quiet and her empire is stable. The threat here is internal rather than external: Massassi is racing her own degeneration.

For some, this would lead to depression or collapse but for Massassi it is a spur. There is a clearly defined challenge and a theory on how to meet it. She'll be damned if something irrelevant like her physical body is going to get in the way.

The main shell that she works on has already been shaped by powerful machines. The form of a man cast in metal. She knows people respond instinctively to height and so she has made him taller than any normal human, imposing, authoritative. The kind of shape that demands obedience.

Broad shoulders are added, and the suggestion of curves,

muscular. Such things are unnecessary and bear no relation to her creation's actual ability, but she is making a symbol as much as a tool, one that should inspire confidence.

She works long hours, finding hidden reserves of energy now that she has removed herself from the demands of politics and rulership.

As she hammers and smooths, a face begins to take shape beneath her tools. A strong face, proud, regal. It is only when she is finished that she sees the amalgam of her past in there. Features of her supervisor blend with Insa's, which in turn blend with the Neuromaster she met decades ago, and with the first man sent to kill her when she was still a child. A disparate group to draw upon but all were confident in their abilities, many of them opposing her, and all were bent to her will.

Standing back to look at the shell, she cannot escape the sense that something is missing. It is not enough that the chosen form be large, impressive. She needs it to be bigger than humanity, something to stand above, to provoke wonder.

Then it comes to her: Wings. She will give her creation wings. She intends to instil many qualities and gifts, practical, important, why not add something for fun? A rare smile finds its way to her face as she begins the modifications.

One change soon leads to another, a whole set of new challenges presenting themselves: the need for aerodynamics and the practicalities of functional wings on a humanoid shape.

Good, she thinks. Her life has been one long series of challenges. Why change things now?

Time passes in a blur of thinking, designing, working and sweating, cursing and smiling.

As the shell nears completion, Massassi starts work on its weapon. She has made swords before for her Seraph Knights. Each carries a tiny fraction of her essence, activated through song. She has kept them simple, limited in scope by the skill of the users. No such limits apply here. She intends to make something with its own consciousness. Part ally, part extension, a connected but separate entity.

Metal is folded in on itself, again and again, the edge honed to cut, the blade tuned to focus and discharge essence.

She gives the sword an eye, setting it into the winged crosspiece. Her idea is that the connection will run both ways, allowing the sword to inform its wielder of new developments on the battlefield and, if necessary, guide their arm in combat.

The empty sword is placed in an empty hand, lifeless fingers curled around the hilt.

When all is ready, she climbs onto the scaffolding and raises her metal arm. The iris in her palm opens, and she places her hand over her creation's eyes.

Drawing deep, Massassi directs her will. Her aim is perfection, a being that will have no equal, that will have the power to do whatever is necessary. Essence surges from her, infusing the shell with light, with life. Some of this plays through its arm, flowing into the sword and back again. Like a child in the womb, the shell draws sustenance from Massassi, taking on aspects of her nature. She tries to hold back the regrets and the doubts, projecting only the strongest parts of herself.

The essence within the shell takes shape, harnessed through lenses and cables, flowing like water through internal channels. It finds its own rhythm, becomes self-sustaining.

Massassi releases her hold, falls hard against the scaffolding. All of the late nights, the long hours catch up with her in a rush. Bones suddenly feel their age and it is all she can do to wheeze, more human sack than godlike empress.

As she exhales, the figure in front of her inhales and the air crackles with energy. Three eyes open together and Alpha is born.

A silver hand reaches down, offering its support to Massassi. She has never accepted anyone's help before but without hesitation she takes it, is lifted gently to her feet.

For the first time, she is not alone.

Looking up, she sees eyes of clearest blue, like the sky on a perfect flying day. They gaze at her in wonder, full of love.

She checks Alpha for cracks, faults and essence leaks, finds none. 'You'll do,' she says.

Alpha's chest swells, picking up on buried praise. He speaks and his words reverberate through the workshop, making metal chime and blood sing. 'I am ready, creator. Shall we begin?'

'Oh yes,' she replies, 'you'll do nicely.'

CHAPTER FOUR

The Commander's Rest skims across the sea, trailing a tail of light. Vesper's special unit of knights, the Order of Broken Blades, pack the space above and below deck. They have seen much over the years, endured much, and now they are bonded by experience and respect. Though old prejudice runs deep, their time with Vesper has stretched their minds somewhat, enabling a grudging acceptance of the ship's pilot.

Samael is at the wheel. Like the other knights he wears armour but his is a battered collection scavenged from an old battlefield. A mish-mash of pieces, a mess, functional. Entirely appropriate. For Samael is a half-breed, unique, changed late in life, his human essence mixed with that of the Knights of Jade and Ash's commander. Once a great man, the commander was corrupted, his soul near burned away by a fragment of infernal essence, making him a slave. And like many who have suffered, he passed this suffering on, binding Samael to his will.

And Samael served, mindless, until the commander was destroyed. Since then he has wandered, sometimes serving others, sometimes himself. Now he serves Vesper, and for the moment this pleases him.

A descendant of the Usurper itself, Samael has little love for infernals, save for the one joined to him by an essence thread. Invisible to most, this thread connects him to a Dogspawn, red-furred and mangy, one ear torn off in its prime. The Dogspawn goes by the name of Scout and one of Samael's eyes is in its skull, just as one of its eyes is in Samael's. The exchange of eyes is a bond, permanent, allowing them to share vision and sensation.

At this moment Samael is aware of his hands at the controls of *The Commander's Rest*, but he is also aware of Vesper's hand scratching a spot on the back of his neck, and a tummy that needs feeding.

Vesper stands at the prow, the wind making streamers of her hair. Scout sits next to her on one side, the buck on the other. All three seem to take equal pleasure from the feel of the breeze on their faces.

She raises an eyebrow as Samael joins them. 'Not like you to step away from the controls.'

'No,' he replies, his voice dry, cracked, like a man in need of water. 'But we are here.'

Vesper looks over her shoulder, sees the light drive powering down, feels *The Commander's Rest* slowing to a gentle drift. Frowning, she turns on the spot, searching the horizon until she has gone full circle. 'Are you sure? It's kind of quiet.'

'These are the coordinates. Do you think the First is going to come?'

'Why bother to go to all this trouble and then not show up?'

Samael makes a dry rasping sound. 'Lots of reasons. To draw you away from the Empire so that it might strike elsewhere. Or to attack you in a place where you cannot bring the Malice to bear.'

'Well, when you put it that way . . .'

Scout whines softly and Vesper looks down. 'What is it?'

'He was enjoying your attention,' replies Samael, 'and that itch still isn't quite satisfied.'

'Sorry, Scout,' she says, resuming her grooming duties. 'The thing is, I know the First has every reason to want me dead. My knights aren't exactly pleased about the situation, and if the people back home knew I was out here,' she shakes her head, 'I'd never hear the end of it.'

'They don't know?'

'Well, they know the broad strokes. I've told them I want to make a lasting peace and that we need to think differently about infernals.'

'But you haven't mentioned the First by name?'

'No. I don't think Obeisance, or the people of the Shining City,' she grimaces, 'or my father are ready for it.'

Samael nods, slowly. 'I agree.'

'At the moment, they can't even imagine the changes I want to make. I'm hoping that if I can pull this off, they won't need to. It'll be there for everyone to see.' She looks directly into Samael's mismatched eyes. 'I'm going to do this, whatever it takes.'

'And the Malice is happy with your plans?'

Vesper touches the sword's hilt and it hums beneath her

fingertips. 'I don't know if the sword can ever be happy. But we've talked about it and we're of a mind.'

They fall to a companionable silence. Time passes, the knights talking quietly amongst themselves, Vesper playing with Scout while the buck and Samael watch the waves.

Then, around them, the water begins to darken.

Samael looks up but there are few clouds in the sky, and none of them block the sunslight. He and Vesper move to the rail and lean over.

The shadow is beneath them, growing rapidly as it ascends. Though the taint has made denizens of the deep big enough to match what comes, it is too solid and too static for a life form. This is a ship, made in the Empire's glory days: a Wavemaker. True to its name, it sets the water around it to motion, rocking *The Commander's Rest*. Under their feet, the deck shakes, then a dull boom sounds, and Vesper's boots lift briefly into the air. She grips the rail tight while the knights wait, stoic, strapped into their positions.

Magnetic locks activate within the Wavemaker, attaching it to the smaller vessel. Untroubled by the extra weight, it continues to rise, until the blunt nose breaks the surface, pushing itself and the smaller ship into the air.

Foam sprays in all directions, and the rocking falls into a steady rhythm, decreasing as the two ships and the water around them settle.

A hatch opens in the Wavemaker's side and a black-clad figure emerges, its loose robe flowing easily over fitted armour. With a single leap it sails up, twenty feet, to land on the rail, a boot either side of Vesper's hands.

Knights detach themselves, rushing forward to support

her. Samael draws his battered sword, and, at Vesper's shoulder, an eye springs open, angry.

'Wait!' she shouts, holding up her hands. 'All of you, wait! Stand down.'

Immediately, they stop, though all remain prepared. Samael's sword returns to its sheath.

The First looks down at them. 'I see that your natures remain . . . violent and I am unsurprised.'

Vesper takes a step back from the rail. 'You haven't changed either.'

'This is true. I remain . . . reasonable.'

'Is that why you ambushed us?'

The First raises a gauntleted hand to point at Vesper. 'You are displaying your power. I am simply displaying mine. It interests me that you have told your followers not to attack and yet you have drawn the Malice.'

Vesper blinks, surprised to find that this is true. The sword is in her hand, humming, ready to act. She thinks quickly. 'Not drawn in anger. The Malice is part of this discussion too.'

She closes her eyes, letting the sword show her a different vision of the First. Through its eye, she sees the infernal dwelling within the human body. Swirling essence that moves in alien ways, discomfiting. Within the strangeness lurk more recognizable emotions. Rapid fluctuations that betray anxiety, a lightening of colour one moment, perhaps curiosity, in the next a change of shade that suggests bitterness. There is no sign of aggression, at least not yet.

Opening her eyes again, Vesper beckons the First forward, inviting it on deck.

Lightly, it steps down. 'Are you ready to begin?'

'I am.' She lowers the sword but does not sheath it.

'You do not wish to discuss our . . . business in private? If you wish, we could return to my ship.'

'No. We can talk freely here. My knights understand what we're trying to do.'

The First reaches up, unclasps its featureless helmet, and removes it. A face is revealed, hard, female, the features rendered slightly odd through a lifetime of minor alterations in service to the Empire of the Winged Eye.

Vesper gasps. She knows that face. Once it belonged to two people, both called Duet. The face stirs many memories, of her betrayal of one of them, of being betrayed by the other. Ultimately, Duet was taken by the infernals, though only one of her went willingly.

At the sight, Scout throws back his head and howls.

The First studies Vesper. 'You may be wondering why it is I chose this particular body for our meeting. There are many reasons. I wanted to remind you that people of your Empire have desired alliance with me in the past. I wanted to acknowledge the . . . history that exists between us.'

'Is she still,' Vesper waves a hand, 'in there?'

'No. Her body was fresh enough for me to occupy, but by the time I arrived, her essence had already dissipated.'

Vesper looks down. 'Good.'

'Is it? For whom is it good? Had you not interfered, the woman would have realized her dreams through me. Now she is nothing more than a memory. Look at this face and remember the past. If you do not accept my offer, only death will follow.'

The threat makes the knights tighten their grip on their weapons. Unlike the other orders of the Seraph however,

these knights no longer carry singing swords, having sacrificed them long ago. As such, they pose little threat to the
First.

Scout glares up at the infernal and begins to growl.

'Stop that!' snaps Vesper, shaking her head at Samael.
The half-breed does not reply but the Dogspawn lowers
its head, abashed. 'You were saying something about an
offer?'

'Yes. I have no quarrel with your kind. Many of them
live . . . happily in my cities. For years now, we have proven
an ability to coexist. It is only your Empire that resists me.
Disband it, destroy the weapons made to cause my kind
suffering, and I will make peace.'

Vesper bites her lip and looks out to sea. In her hand, the
sword begins to shake. 'That's it? That's your offer?'

'Yes.'

'Well, I agree on one thing; if we can't negotiate, there
will be war.'

'Then let us negotiate.'

'Alright. I don't have any quarrel with your kind either.'
She gestures to Samael. 'I can, how did you put it? Coexist.
I'm on good terms with New Horizon, West Rift, Red Rails,
Verdigris and Slake. That's only a first step. I intend to
negotiate with all of them, not as individuals, but as a collective. I want you to be part of that collective. Come south
with me. Take part.'

'I have heard of this gathering of yours.'

'It's no secret.'

'These things are not mutually exclusive. If you agree to
my offer, then I would come with you.'

An eye narrows and Vesper's voice rises. 'How can you

be so blind?' She holds up the sword and the First flinches away. 'The Malice is alive, just as much as you are! It deserves to live just as much as you do. The Seraph Knights' swords that you try so hard to break also live. They're not as complex or as clever but they are alive. If you want me to look at you and see more than just an enemy, you have to do the same for me.

'You're offering me the chance to submit to you or be destroyed. That's no choice at all. I'm offering you the chance to be part of something bigger.'

The First's face does not react, its expression disconnected from its feelings. 'This is . . . surprising.'

Vesper allows herself a small smile. 'The Usurper is gone and I speak for the Empire now. There's no need for us to fight anymore.'

'So you say. I remain unconvinced but, I am intrigued.'

Vesper shifts the sword to her left hand and holds out her right. 'A truce then? You'll come with me and take part?'

'I will travel with you, I will observe. Perhaps I will engage. I promise no more than that.'

'That's all I'm asking.'

The First takes her hand, mimicking the human gesture perfectly. 'I accept.'

A few days pass as the Wavemaker and *The Commander's Rest* speed along the sea together. From under the water, a new vessel moves to join them, then another. Both part of the First's fleet.

Vesper and the sword exchange a concerned look.

It does not stop there. A fourth ship comes, a fifth, and so on, until a war fleet of nine follows them, just under the surface. When a half dozen sky-ships drop from the clouds to fall into position above, Vesper demands another audience with the First.

It comes in multiple bodies. Some arriving from the sky-ships, others swimming up from the depths. Vesper watches them through the sword's eye, and begins to appreciate how big the First truly is. A single being, divided into bite-sized human chunks. Though the First has a diverse collection of shells, they dress the same, move the same, making the differences in height and weight hard to remember. Vesper guesses that perhaps a quarter of its strength is here, the rest of the infernal spread out across the world.

They line up along the rail, like a line of ravens watching, waiting for an animal to die.

Vesper gestures to the ships all around them. 'What is this?'

One of figures breaks from the others, jumps down. It removes its helmet, revealing Duet's face. 'You wished for me to come south with you.'

She frowns. 'For talks. We don't need an invasion fleet.'

'I am not here to invade. We have made a truce.'

'I just don't understand why we need all of these ships.'

'You seem displeased. I do not understand. Surely your gathering is important enough to warrant my full attention.'

'Wait. You're calling all of, um . . . you, here?'

'Yes.'

The sword looks at Vesper, its hum felt more than heard, whisper-like. She nods. 'There's something you're not telling me.'

'You once promised to stand between me and the Malice, do you remember?'

'Yes.'

'And while we are at peace, do you promise to stand between me and rest of The Seven?'

'Yes.'

The First leans closer, bracing itself against the invisible force of the Malice's anger. 'You truly don't know, do you?'

'What are you taking about?'

'The Seven. They have awoken and the fires of their rage burn in the north.'

'But there's no hostile force in the north.'

'They see it differently.' Vesper's face falls and the First continues to speak. 'The Seven are gathering Their strength. They call out to Their agents, who in turn call out to others. Factions within the colonies that came over to me have already begun to rebel.

'They are coming south. I believe They are coming for me.'

Vesper's hand goes to her mouth. She thinks of her family, despairs. Have they become another sacrifice? And what will The Seven do to her? What kind of example will they make? Such thoughts are dispelled with a shake of the head. 'You knew this all along. That's why you came to speak with me. You're afraid!'

'Yes. I am afraid. We are united in fear.'

She looks up, defiance colouring cheeks. 'No, we are united in more than fear.'

But when the advance scouts of The Seven's armada appear on the horizon, she goes straight to Samael, and he pushes *The Commander's Rest* harder until it seems to fly across the wavetops.

The First returns to its fleet and they too accelerate, doing their best to keep pace with the sleeker vessel.

The scout ships fade from view but they are not forgotten.

Delta forces herself to look. In one hand she has a skull, in the other, part of a skeleton. The skull is ordinary, that of a human male, the skeleton belonging to a different man, one that has experienced the touch of the taint, turning the bones asymmetrical.

Even without attending to the essence echoes around them, she can tell their end was abrupt, anguished, and at the hands of her brother, Alpha.

A compulsion makes her walk around the ruins of Greyspot Three. Where normal eyes see only the present, pyres, ashes and charred buildings, Delta's see shimmering where the power of her kin was used. Her ears attend to the fading hum of energy, her body sensitive to the soft-vibrations in the air. Together, these sensations allow her to follow in her brother's footsteps. She stops at each place he sang, identifying the corpses he has made, choking on her brother's righteous anger that still lingers, remorseless.

There are so many dead. So many of her people, dead, that it overwhelms her. Finally, on the edge of Greyspot Three, she stops, and thinks.

Her role is to love her siblings, to make a better world with them, and yet she cannot feel love for what has happened. Cannot help but judge.

She has asked how it came to this, and they have pointed to her brother. But this is unsatisfactory. She knows that Alpha did this, knew it the moment they arrived. What she does not understand is why he did it, nor why it was done in such a manner.

The need for answers bubbles in her, converting despair to action.

Jem pulls on the Vagrant's sleeve, lowers his voice. 'How long do you think She's going to be gone for?'

The Vagrant looks in the direction Delta went, shrugs.

'Then let's go before She comes back.'

The Vagrant nods and strides off towards the docks.

Reela strides after him, little legs working double time to keep up. With a last glance at Delta, Jem follows her.

The air here is smoke-heavy, smelling of burnt rubber and cooked meat. The Vagrant covers his mouth and, for different reasons, the two behind do the same.

The ragtag array of ships usually found in port are gone, their wrecks thickening the water. Most are sunk, some still sinking, the odd stray mast protruding from the surface in final salute.

The Vagrant looks out to sea. Alpha's sky palace has already lumbered from view, leaving an empty, peaceful vista.

After a moment's contemplation, he frowns and walks along the corrugated jetty, amber eyes searching.

'What are you doing?' asks Jem. 'We need to get out of here. If we follow the coastline far enough we'll hit another port. Maybe we could get passage on a ship there. Or we could go inland, find somewhere remote, where nobody else goes. Somewhere with lots of goats!'

The Vagrant pauses to direct a hard stare over his shoulder.

'What? You love goats!'

The Vagrant turns back to his task, dismissive.

'Look, it doesn't matter what we farm or even if we farm. We have to get out of here, now. The Empire will be coming for Delta and we don't want to be here when they arrive.'

Jem checks again to see if he can see Delta, only to find she is a hundred metres away, and that he is staring directly into her eyes. She seems purposeful, angry, and he looks away quickly, shame dousing him like a sudden blast of icy water. 'We have to go,' he says, then again, louder. 'We have to go!'

He hears a splash, turns back. The Vagrant is reaching down, pulling objects from the water like a magician from a hat. Each one is tossed onto the jetty. Jem examines the objects, seeing nothing more than broken junk.

The Vagrant plunges his arm under, pulls hard. The water nearby bubbles and a small sea-shuttle bobs up from the depths, cheerful. No longer bound to its stricken mother vessel, the sea-shuttle floats easily, only a few dents marring its flanks. Built for speed and short-distance travel, the sea-shuttle resembles a triangular dart, a shallow deck cut into the topside.

Reela looks wary of the boat but allows herself to be lifted onboard. Jem needs no encouragement, jumping on as soon as there is space to do so.

'How do you turn this on?' asks Jem.

The Vagrant frowns at the blank display.

They try a few experimental prods at the screen and search around the sides of the steering column. Neither of them are familiar with the design.

Nearby, Reela carries out her own experiments, touching places at random.

The Vagrant smacks the steering column.

Nothing happens.

'Don't break it!' says Jem.

Reela smacks the side wall.

'Reela, stop that!'

With a sudden hum the steering column activates. Lights sparkle on its surface, diagnostic checks begin, and on the underside, steering flaps open, close, open and close again.

The Vagrant, Jem and Reela all share a smile, each taking credit for their good fortune.

There is a ping, and the lights of the steering column display blue and green in all the right places. The sea-shuttle is ready to sail.

As the hum of the startup sequence fades, they begin to hear a second hum, identical in pitch, coming from behind them.

The collective smile fades away. Reluctant, the three turn round as Delta steps onboard.

The Vagrant kneels, Jem presses himself against the far side of the sea-shuttle. Reela just stares up, mouth open, her eyes as wide as they will go.

Delta stares back. 'Go,' she says, and the word jars through them all. Jem wonders if she wants him to leave but does not dare to move. In any case, she is blocking the exit. Perhaps, he wonders, bitter, she expects him to jump over the side.

The sea-shuttle's engine starts up, eager.

The Vagrant stands. He turns to the steering column and places his hands into the moulded surfaces on either side. Mutigel adapts to the contours of his fingers, pressing snug against his skin. He adjusts his footing, squares his shoulders and tilts his hands forward.

The sea-shuttle begins to move, parting the debris around it with ease. The Vagrant tilts his hands further, the sea-shuttle accelerating as it clears the worst of the wreckage.

With the Vagrant steering and Reela busy pretending, Jem is left alone to worry about Delta. He tries not to look at her but cannot help himself. He sees she still carries the bones from the pyre, poised between her index finger and thumb. The slightest use of her strength would reduce both to powder. Jem wonders at her restraint, applies a pattern to the behaviour, knowing it is foolish. So long as she does not break those bones, he decides, they will be safe.

Vesper feels her hand move to the hilt of the sword. She doesn't fight the compulsion, allowing herself to be guided. Drawing the weapon, she sees that the eye is already open, staring straight up. She follows its gaze, sees nothing but cloud-smeared sky.

She looks down at Scout. 'Does anything seem wrong to you or Samael?'

Scout sniffs the air, while behind him, at the wheel of *The Commander's Rest*, Samael looks around. Neither have anything to report.

But the sword is insistent, concerned even. Vesper sighs. The sword has been concerned ever since the Shining City. Reading her thoughts, the sword vibrates in her hand. *No, it seems to say, this is different.*

Silvered wings point, underlining the sense of there being something above them.

Vesper closes her eyes, letting the sword see for her.

The physical world remains as she saw it, there are no

sky-ships, no winged figures, no threats of any kind but the currents of essence, usually invisible, are disturbed.

There is a communication, a song, that travels from her pursuers up into space. She cannot fathom its meaning but has the sense of an order being given, recognizes that it comes from Alpha of The Seven.

Though the immortal is far away, separated by miles of ocean, she can feel him reaching out, almost as if he could touch them.

And then, as she watches, something does become visible: a tiny glint in the sky, like the first star of the evening arriving early.

Without knowing why, Vesper's heart beats faster. Eyes still closed, she calls back to Samael: 'We've got trouble incoming!'

She barely hears his reply over the ocean. He is asking for clarification. Does she want him to change course? To slow down? To speed up?

'I don't know!' she shouts. 'Just be ready!'

Scout barks an affirmation.

The buck's dark eyes twitch from left to right. He senses the change in mood but cannot see the cause.

Around her, knights prepare their weapons, their lips moving to prayer, automatic: 'Winged Eye, watch over us, protect us, deliver us.'

They do not appreciate the irony, for an eye is watching them, a sphere of silver-steel high in orbit. But its attention does not herald salvation.

An answering song is given, emotionless, flat, directed back to Alpha.

Vesper opens her eyes again, runs to Samael. 'The Seven! They know where we are!'

'Yes,' replies the half-breed, unsurprised. 'You hold the Malice.'

She remembers what the sword was trying to tell her. 'This is different. They know exactly where we are. Signal the First.'

Samael does so, then adds, 'We're already at top speed and there is no sign that they can match it. Could this be a way to make sure we don't lose them?'

'No. Well, it could be but that doesn't feel right. The sword knows The Seven are in that direction.' She points without thinking. 'They must sense where we are. Why bother with anything else?'

'To know our strengths.'

'That makes sense but . . .' She trails off, looks at the sword. It is looking back the way they came, across open ocean, expectant.

Then she sees them.

A cloud of missiles, each one spinning, air playing across fluted surfaces to create a collective buzz. Their approach is so fast that by the time Vesper's brain has made sense of what she is seeing, the missiles begin arcing down, splitting into clusters, each one targeting a specific vessel.

The First's fleet springs into action. None of the sky-ships are targeted, leaving them free to fire on the missile clouds, thinning them. Warships submerge, leaving countermeasures in their wake.

Meanwhile, Samael turns *The Commander's Rest* as tightly as he dares, the whole ship tilting, threatening to flip over. Knights are thrown against their harnesses, forced to watch and hope.

Vesper runs to the back of the ship, staggering as the lean

of the deck sharpens. Slamming into the back railing, she gasps down a breath and holds up the sword, singing. Air flashes blue around her and the nearest missiles tremble, their spinning suddenly erratic.

An eye flashes, angry, and missiles veer away, crashing into the sea.

In spite of this, in spite of everything, many missiles find their targets, puncturing hulls, ripping holes, and fire flares underwater. With each detonation comes a smaller pulse of essence. None trouble Vesper, but within its many shells, the First pauses, momentarily stunned. Samael flinches, pressing a hand to his head, and Scout howls wildly.

The First's fleet remains intact but four of the vessels have been forced to return, smoking, to the surface, and one of them has stopped entirely, its engines ruined.

Vesper grips the railing, catching her breath as *The Commander's Rest* slows to a crawl. She doesn't relax, the sword won't let her, and when the second wave of missiles comes, she is already straightening, drawing breath to sing again.

As they travel, the Vagrant pushes the sea-shuttle faster, until his hands meet resistance on the column, feedback from the mutigel informing him that he has reached the craft's safety limits.

The water is choppy here, the sea-shuttle launching from one wave-top to another, haphazard. Jem hunkers down in a corner, holding Reela to him. Hard surfaces smack against his back and legs with each new impact. Delta unfurls her wings, for balance.

The Vagrant squints at the empty horizon, scowls, and

presses his hands forward again, until his fingers are curling against the back edge of the steering column.

A humming engine becomes a whining one, though the sound is barely heard over the wind. Emergency flaps open at the front of the sea-shuttle, bravely trying to prevent the high speed from flipping the ship over.

Onward they go, the sea-shuttle so fast now it threatens to defy gravity. Water soaks them all, whipped cold, numbing hands and stinging eyes.

The Vagrant grits his teeth.

Jem tries to talk to him, but the words are torn away. Terrified, but more scared of moving than staying, Jem reverts to watching Delta's hands and the bones within them.

At last, Alpha's sky palace comes into view. Such is its size that it confounds the mind, like a half-rendered image where the mountain that surely supports the structure has not yet resolved itself. But there is no mountain, no ground beneath it.

Ahead of them, on the water, they see rows and rows of Alpha's ships, an armada, too many to count. War cruisers, frigates, scouts, all moving in perfect formation. Such a fleet has not been assembled since the Battle of the Red Wave.

And then, from the battlements of the palace, a glimmering cloud issues, a swarm of missiles streaking away, soon lost to sight.

Jem shouts, his voice an insect's whine against elements and engine. 'Now what?'

The Vagrant ignores him.

'You're not just going to sail through that? You can't!'

The Vagrant ignores him.

'I won't let you do this to Reela!'

A shadow looms over them, making both men turn.

Delta has stepped forward, she steps again, so close that the hilt of her sword nearly pokes Jem's chest. Knees bend and she leaps skyward, the sea-shuttle lurching dangerously in the opposite direction.

Seawater briefly rises above ankles, diving over boot-tops to chill toes.

Delta's wings beat, the downdraught plastering the Vagrant against the steering column, and Jem and Reela against the floor.

Spluttering, Jem sits up, looks up.

Delta's wings beat again, long and fluid, propelling her, catching currents that draw her swiftly away, a silvered arrow pointing unerringly at Alpha's palace.

CHAPTER FIVE

Delta looks at the ships beneath her. They carry the same troops that razed Greyspot Three, the ones that turned the people living there to the bones in her hands.

She looks at Alpha's palace in the wake of its just-launched volley of missiles. Distantly, she feels their tiny impacts. Deep inside her, the misery grows until it becomes too much to contain.

Her mouth opens in song.

The air shakes with it. Nearby clouds weep, and below, waves pause, collapsing in on themselves.

Without being ordered by their commanders, the pilots of each of the ships cut their engines.

Everything stops.

But Delta is not done.

She turns her gaze to the sky, singing out as her brother has done, connecting with a distant orbiting body. But her order is different. The satellite glimmers one final time, and is gone.

Silver wings carry her over the top of the battlements, soldiers gasping at the sight despite themselves, awestruck. She ignores them, diving into the courtyard where Alpha is emerging, followed quickly by Beta, Epsilon, Theta and Eta.

He glances past her as she lands, sky-blue eyes darkening with rage. As that stare turns on her, she feels his displeasure, like fists pushing at her chest. Bracing herself, Delta raises her hands, opens them so that they can all see the charred, misshapen bones in one and the small skull in the other.

'How did it come to this?'

Three volleys have come, each a rain of singing missiles. Vesper waits to see if there will be a fourth. Around her, the crews of the First's ships swarm over their decks, putting out fires, plugging holes, pumping out unwanted water.

The interlude of peace continues, extending well beyond the rhythm of the previous attacks. An eye closes, and she puts the sword away.

Two of the nine ships escorting *The Commander's Rest* have been sunk, another five damaged and unable to submerge. The Wavemaker has sustained hits to one of its engines, slowing it substantially.

Unlike conflict on land, there are no other scars of battle visible. If anything, the water is calmer than before.

Vesper takes a drink to soothe her throat. Use of the Malice has left it raw, and it complains each time she speaks. She watches in silence as her knights, of the Order of the Broken Blades, tip one of their number into the sea. There is time to see the shrapnel wound, to appreciate the misfortune, before the sea claims the body.

A gloom falls across her people. They are used to death

and struggle but they are not used to this. One of them raises a hand.

'Yes?'

'That attack, it came from the Empire.'

It isn't phrased as a question but Vesper answers it anyway. 'Yes . . . and it was directed by Alpha of The Seven.'

Dismay does not sit well on the usually stoic faces. Eventually one of the older knights says, 'If The Seven wish us dead, should we not oblige Them?'

'No,' replies Vesper. 'It's not that simple. Alpha started the attack but the sword, Gamma's sword, protected us and another of The Seven stopped it.'

'But . . . The Seven speak as one! What does this mean?'

'It means They don't speak as one. Perhaps They never have.'

Another knight speaks, full of despair, though his courage has never failed before. 'What will we do?'

An eye flicks open at Vesper's shoulder and her own widen with anger. 'What will we do? What will we do! We've lived our whole lives without The Seven, up till now. Gamma helped us before and she's still helping us now. We survived the Usurper and the Yearning without Them. We've just started making sense of everything and I'm not going to stop now.' She looks at the crippled ships around her and her scowl only deepens. 'Damn Alpha! How dare He attack the people who faced it all alone while He wept in the dark!'

The knights don't answer, shocked by Vesper's defiance. They are utterly loyal to her but they are also loyal to The Seven. Up till now they believed these loyalties to be one and the same.

There is a whisper that reaches Vesper's ears. 'We're not worthy, we have failed Them. We have broken our oaths.'

'No!' replies Vesper, her voice cracking. 'No. Don't you see? They have failed us, but we need to keep going. If we don't, then thousands of people are going to die. Can you do that? Will you stand with me?'

She looks at them. One by one they meet her eyes, nod. She nods back, relieved, proud.

As she returns to Samael, she notices how unsteady he is on his feet, one hand pressed against the side of his battered helmet. 'Are you alright?'

'Yes,' he replies.

Vesper suspects that there is a longer and more complex answer but doesn't press for one. Scout whines nearby, lying flat on his belly, paws over his head. 'And him?'

'He'll recover.'

'Glad to hear it. Have you seen my goat anywhere?'

Samael points down. Tucked between his legs and the wheel of the boat is the buck. Only an act of desperate contortion has enabled his large frame to fit within such a small space. The buck's head sticks through a gap in the bottom of the wheel, the angle awkward.

'There you are. Now just stay still a moment and . . .' she trails off, her attention taken by the First. It moves towards her in leaps, launching from the deck of one ship to land on the next, an armoured flea.

'Don't worry,' she says to the buck. 'I'll come back.'

By the time she has stood up, the First is landing in front of her. 'There is conflict among The Seven. Do you perceive it?'

'I do,' she replies.

'We should leave before it resolves.'

'Agreed.' She checks in with Samael for confirmation. 'We're ready, are you?'

'Our mobility has suffered. If they pursue again, they will catch us easily.'

'Then we've got no time to lose.'

The First returns to its ships, Samael goes to the wheel and Vesper goes back to trying to liberate the buck. Moments later, engines stir in the still water, and eight ships continue their journey.

Though not as impressive as Alpha's sky palace, the armada sailing beneath it is comprised of the Empire's finest ships. Greatest of these is their flagship, *Resolution*.

Functioning as a launch station, command ship and artillery platform, *Resolution* would appear massive if not sailing in the shadow of something greater. The bridge is raised above the main deck on an articulated mast of steel, S-shaped, like a dragon's head drawing back to breathe fire.

Standing within is the Knight Commander, highest military authority in the Empire of the Winged Eye. Around him are officers, crew, all poised at their stations, all waiting for him to say something.

But for once, he has nothing to say.

'Knight Commander,' says one of his officers, 'the Bearer and the First's ships are moving away from us.' They consult their screens before adding, 'They are two down.'

He turns toward the officer. 'Only two?'

'Confirmed, sir. Two down.'

Unlike his predecessor, the Knight Commander has seen nothing of the battlefield during his tenure. He is, therefore, unduly troubled by the way simple things are rarely as plain as they appear. The missiles, for example, should have wiped out the enemy entirely.

But the failure of missiles to live up to expectations is the least of his worries.

'Knight Commander, they are still moving.'

'Understood,' he replies, irritated at the needless update and the nerves that prompted it. 'Inform me if this changes.'

He clasps his hands behind his back and checks the impulse to pace. He of all people must appear calm.

Alpha's orders are clear. Their purpose is to purge the world with fire and song. They are to become legend, immortalized in canon for future generations. Or so he thought. Delta's order was equally clear: stop. In the absence of specifics they are forced to err on the side of caution. They have stopped their pursuit, powered down their engines. Now there is nothing to do but wait.

The Knight Commander looks up. Beyond the metal above his head, somewhere in the floating sky palace, The Seven are together and, as far as he can tell, they are arguing.

The thought is ludicrous, going against everything he was taught, from his earliest days in his choir, through to his squire training, even the many lectures received from Obeisance. For the first time in his life, the Knight Commander feels the bedrock of his certainty crack and begin to crumble.

In the courtyard of Alpha's sky palace, two essences rage back and forth, a pair of storm fronts colliding, colliding again.

Delta's and Alpha's argument is elemental, made up of words, will and song.

For the humans unfortunate enough to witness the display, it is too much. Blood runs from ears overwhelmed with furious song, pupils gape wide, blown forever. They are not dead but there is little of life left in them.

Others distributed throughout the palace are merely driven to their knees in terror. Some weep, some cover their faces, others pray, enacting the rite of mercy. All responses are equally irrelevant.

Beta of The Seven watches, aghast, while Epsilon, Theta and Eta simply wait as they have always waited.

The bones that Delta brought with her from Greyspot Three have been destroyed. Too fragile to be exposed to such energies, they have been reduced to ashes that swirl briefly about the two immortals to be scattered, forgotten. She came with a question and it has been answered. This leads to more questions, each a stab in the eye, and more answers, like slaps across the face, coming faster and faster, rising in volume and anger until even Beta looks away.

Abruptly it ends, with Alpha's hand on Delta's throat. At the contact something in her seems to break and her eyes half-close, body flopping, going slack. Alpha does not let her fall, not yet. His anger is not done.

He walks up winding stairs to the battlements, dragging Delta after him, her heels ringing against each step.

Beta follows and, after a pause, Epsilon, Theta and Eta do the same.

Past bowed heads and trembling bodies, Alpha goes, ignoring all. Displeasure radiates from him in waves, driving people from his path like iron filings from a magnet, flipped the wrong way.

Raising Delta over the edge, he draws his sword. Its eye

is open, glaring balefully at Delta as she dangles, a puppet, stringless.

When Alpha draws back the weapon the light around it sparks so brightly that the blade turns black within it.

And then, Beta is at his side, one hand on his wrist.

Alpha looks down.

Their eyes meet.

One Thousand and Forty-Nine
Years Ago

Massassi lets the slab take the weight of her body, groaning with pleasure as it lowers her into the vat. Nutri-fluid oozes between toes and into armpits, thickening at the base of her neck and the points along her spine, supporting, warming.

Damage sustained long ago has led to a regimen of treatments. Injections, tablets and organ stimulation are all daily routines. Some to manage the pain, others to keep her alert. Such things have taken their toll, however. Her hair is gone and her nails have fallen out. The metal studs she used to plug old wounds were not her best work, a rushed solution, plaguing her with regular inflammation and infection.

For years she has endured such things, a small price to pay for the safety of the world. No longer. At last she is able to rest. Alpha is here now, and he is more than able to run the Empire, giving her a well-earned break.

She tries to remember the last time she felt this relaxed and finds she cannot. The Nutri-fluid has eased her physical aches and Alpha has taken away the awful responsibility. It may have cost her the best years of her life but she has done it.

Hours pass, happy dozing punctuated with periods of self-satisfied reflection. Normally, her quick mind would be getting bored but she feels no need to move. Perhaps this is part of getting old, taking pleasure in the smaller things. Perhaps it is just that she is tired. For once, Massassi feels no desire to dig deeper. Understanding is not necessary. She could lie here until the end of time.

Her slumber is disturbed by knocking, insistent, on the side of the vat. Massassi wakes unwillingly.

It is Peace-Fifteen. One of the best of the new generation. Massassi only has to glance at the girl's essence to know that something serious is going on. A bad tempered command sets the slab into motion, raising her from the vat into colder, more miserable air. 'What is it?'

Peace-Fifteen bows, making the sign of the Eye. 'It's Alpha.'

She forces herself upright, ignoring her protesting back. 'Well don't just stand there! Help me up!'

Massassi is quickly wrapped in a self-sealing robe and ushered out of the chamber. She sees the fear in the girl, and some of it begins to leach into her. 'What's happened to Alpha?' A flurry of possibilities already runs through her mind. Has her beautiful creation broken after a fall, a miscalculation on her part allowing the essence to slowly leak from him? Or perhaps she has failed to calibrate his wings properly. They worked well at low altitude but what if he has gone higher, trusting to her designs? What if she has made another mistake as she did with the Breach?

Peace-Fifteen shakes her head. 'Nothing's happened to him,

Your Imperial Majesty. I have come to ask you to stop him.'

The relaxed feelings have evaporated and Massassi feels a familiar dread return. 'Show me.'

Along corridors and through transport chutes they go, rushed along by automated platforms and assisted walkways, until they reach a set of doors that lead to a comms tower.

At Massassi's approach the doors open, revealing the full extent of her failure. Four bodies litter the room, utterly broken. A fifth person makes muffled noises, his skull stuck between the wall and Alpha's hand.

Unprepared for the sight, Massassi stops to stare for a moment. In that moment, Alpha squeezes and blood streaks stark red against silver skin.

Too late, her lips move. 'What is this?'

Alpha turns, his eyes lightening with love. 'Creator!' He strides over the bodies towards her, opening his arms.

Massassi raises her hands, warding him off. 'I said, what is this?'

He stops, arms still open while Massassi looks into his essence. It is easier to read than most, brighter, purer, and he makes no effort to hide from her.

The first man died because the calculations he presented Alpha with were imperfect, a reduction of zero point three required to balance it again. The second died because he dared to judge Alpha's action monstrous, which, in Alpha's mind was a suggestion he had made a mistake. This was of course a criticism of his creator as much as himself, and he could not allow such words to stand. The third and fourth died for much the same reasons as the second, and the fifth had been unable to cope with what he saw. His essence was showing signs of fracture and Alpha had decided it best to terminate him immediately to avoid the danger of the man cracking in an unsupervised space.

Replacements are already being summoned. Within the hour, the mess will be cleaned away and perfection restored.

Massassi finds no concern for any other ramifications of these actions and no regret over the deaths. For Alpha lacks the capacity for regret, having been created without any. He is perfect and he expects perfection in all things. He can neither understand nor tolerate anything that fails to meet those expectations.

She sees a new future for the Empire when she is gone. One where Alpha slowly destroys it from the inside. She feels a slight sympathy. Many a time have the incompetencies of her fellows driven her to break things. But no, this will not do. Alpha's role is to lead the Empire, to watch over it. It appears that he will need some help.

Massassi turns from the room, and Alpha follows without the need to ask.

They go back to her workshop and Massassi starts on a new project. She is grateful that Alpha is there to assist, making matters easier. Even so, she struggles.

Where before, with Alpha's creation, she aimed for an ideal, this time she is more restrained. The body they craft is grand, more than human, but it is not quite so large. She still gives it wings however.

The new creation is designed to be a balance for Alpha. Where he is single-minded, ruthless and exacting, she will make someone more cautious, who thinks about the bigger picture, who considers the details.

If Alpha charges headlong into battle with what's coming, then he will not be alone. There will be another there to watch his back and keep him safe. She crafts a second great sword and it is lighter than Alpha's, quicker.

When the time comes to infuse the body and the sword with essence, she tries to capture the spirit of being an engineer, remembering that it is this training that has saved her in the darkest times. She tries to make him careful, thoughtful, analytical, logical. Like her on her calm days.

Essence flows from the iris in her palm and into the body and the sword, creating life, diminishing hers.

She sways but before she can fall, Alpha catches her, taking her weight. She feels his love around her like a physical thing.

In front of them, Beta is born. Where Alpha's eyes are the blue of a clear sky, Beta's are the blue-black of night.

Massassi is the first thing that Beta sees, and she feels his love for her just as she feels Alpha's. Gentler, but no less powerful.

She pats one of the silver hands supporting her. 'Alpha, this is your brother.'

Alpha tilts his head down.

Beta tilts his up.

Their eyes meet.

CHAPTER SIX

The sea is so unnaturally calm it resembles a vast lake, the echoes of Delta's power calming currents, smoothing waves. The armada sailing across it is equally still, collectively holding its breath until The Seven resolve their dispute.

Half a mile above them sits Alpha's sky palace, also motionless.

Intruding into the serenity is a small sea-shuttle, a mosquito in an otherwise quiet room. It is the only thing moving, and operators on every ship watch its progress on scopes or through plasglass viewing ports.

Though the occupants of the sea-shuttle cannot see the watchers, they feel their scrutiny.

'This was a bad idea,' says Jem.

The Vagrant doesn't respond, forcing the other man to address his back. As they approach the gap between two larger Empire craft, the Vagrant eases back on the steering column, slowing down to adjust their positioning.

'I just don't see why we can't go round them.'

The Vagrant presses his lips together, continuing on his course.

Jem is left to seethe. Powerless, he raises the scope to his eye, moving it from ship to ship, checking to see if guns are tracking them. They are not. Safe for the moment, he trains the scope on Alpha's sky palace.

'I can see movement on the battlements . . . I can see The Seven!' he shouts, making the Vagrant flinch and Reela jump. Then, in a whisper, repeats. 'I can see The Seven. I think that's Alpha. He's . . . He's holding Delta . . . She looks bad. Is She dead? He's throwing Her!'

The Vagrant looks up. Even without the aid of the scope, he sees her, sunslight glittering red and gold over her as she arcs in the air, corkscrewing, falling.

His hands twist on the steering column, push forward. As he does so the sea-shuttle pivots in the water, then accelerates. The engine starts to whine, an unhappy noise.

'I don't know about this,' says Jem but there is little force to his words. He is already resigned to the fact that the Vagrant isn't listening.

The sea-shuttle slips easily between the back rows of the armada, cutting through the calm, racing towards the front where Delta falls.

Jem watches through the scope. 'We'll never make it in time.'

He is right.

Ahead of them, Delta turns awkwardly in the air one final time before impact. Water sprays up. When it comes down again, there is no sign of the immortal.

Something in the air changes and waves once more ripple across the surface of the water.

104

The Seven

Jem looks around, nervous. 'I really think we should leave now.'

The Vagrant pulls back on the steering column, reversing the engines to cut their speed. The sea-shuttle drifts to a near stop over the spot where Delta fell.

'What are you doing?' asks Jem. 'She's going to sink like a stone!'

The Vagrant shrugs out of his long coat and pulls off his boots.

'Even if you do find Her, you won't be strong enough to pull Her up.'

The Vagrant presses a smooth section of the sea-shuttle's wall and it splits open, revealing a compartment. From this, he produces a breathing mask.

'I don't understand what you're hoping for! She doesn't care about us!' He gestures to all of the ships behind them. 'But they do! They all want us dead, remember?' He reaches for the Vagrant's arm. 'You can't save Delta but you can save us.'

Shrugging him off, the Vagrant dives into the water.

Exasperated, Jem looks down. Partway through cursing his situation, he notices a small pair of boots have been placed next to the Vagrant's, arranged at the same angle as the larger ones.

His eyes widen as the thought hits. 'Oh no, Reela!'

He looks up just in time to see the splash.

'Reela!' he shouts again, and dives in after her.

On the bridge of *Resolution*, the Knight Commander watches the sea resume its normal behaviour and hopes it is an omen of things to come.

'Have you identified that sea-shuttle yet?'

'Yes, sir. It's one of ours. It was lost in action over twenty years ago. I'll put it on the screen.'

The Knight Commander looks at images of the sea-shuttle taken minutes ago, magnifies them. 'What do we know about the crew?'

'The Lenses report the Champion is on board. There are two more, both off-record. One of them is confirmed tainted, the other, suspected. Do you wish us to bring it in?'

'Not yet.'

'Forgive me, sir, but –'

'But what?'

'Nothing, sir.'

The Knight Commander does not punish the near insubordination. He understands it. Whatever they decide to do, they are damned. To take action contravenes a direct command of The Seven. To do nothing contradicts their edicts. To fail The Seven is punishable by death. *I wonder*, he muses bleakly, *if we will be damned for doing too much or too little.*

The officer monitoring their other prey speaks up. 'Forgive me, sir. I know you did not wish to be disturbed but they are reaching the edge of scanning range.'

'Impossible. They can't have got so far away already.'

'It's not them, sir. Since The Seven . . . Since Delta . . . Well, a portion of the network has gone down over where they are. The eyes are blind, sir. If we don't send a scout or a sky-ship to monitor them, we'll lose them.'

'Understood.'

One set of targets is slipping away while the other sits in their grasp and he can do nothing about either of them.

Delta has told them to stop. Until she or another of The Seven says otherwise, he dare not act.

The Knight Commander starts to pace, catches himself, curses himself and stands still again. He remembers to have faith in The Seven. When they are ready, they will lead the way. Until then, he must be patient.

But the image on the screen taunts him. A pathetic little ship, a glorified lifeboat, mocking the might of the Empire! He focuses on the anger, tries hard not to think about what fell from the palace, or what that means. It is not his place to question, it is his place to serve.

'If we don't launch in the next five minutes, sir, we'll lose them completely.'

The Knight Commander draws himself up, puffs out his chest. 'Let them run if they want. It doesn't matter. Their time will come when The Seven are ready.'

The officers nod, satisfied, while the Knight Commander considers history and quietly panics. It took The Seven a year to decide what to do about the Breach, and after the Battle of the Red Wave they fell silent for over two decades. He worries about how long it will take The Seven to recover this time and what he will do when the rations start to run out.

The Vagrant plunges into the water, letting momentum take him as far as it can before starting to swim. Strong strokes pull him deeper but Delta has a head start.

Amber eyes search the depths, see a glimmer of silver and a shape, tantalizing, far below. He makes towards it, lungs working hard, muscle memory stretched, recalling actions from youth long gone.

Fish keep their distance, peeling away from the intruders.

Other things don't, drawn to investigate by the promise of food. The nearest appears as an inverted shell with tentacles extending from it. A closer look would reveal that the shell is the remains of a submersible, curled around another form of life, and that each tentacle is in fact a human body stripped of limbs and stretched. Each body plays host to a minor infernal, servants to the thing within the shell. The heads remain, bobbing on rubbery necks, with white sightless eyes and mouths full of broken teeth. In place of hair, each scalp is covered in long translucent antennae that twitch as they read the disturbances in the water.

News of fresh prey is absorbed, along with a sense of size and current speed, by one of the minor infernals. This information then moves through its essence, down the body to where there were once feet, to be whispered through membranes into their master's ear. The creature shudders as it digests the news, before floating up, beginning the hunt.

The Vagrant is getting close to Delta now, occasionally breaking rhythm to grab for her. But under the sea, appearances are deceptive, and his fingers curl around empty water.

He continues to chase, the light from the suns lagging further behind, allowing the cold to creep in. Fingertips brush wingtip to slip away. Another reach, a stretch and they slide over smooth feathers, foiled. A frown, a mouthed curse and another try . . . success!

The Vagrant pulls himself alongside Delta, turning her so that they are face to face. The light is poor here but he sees no obvious wounds. It would be easy to imagine that the immortal is merely sleeping.

He tries tapping her face but there is no response.

There is a brief pause and a brief sigh, allowing tired legs a taste of respite before being called to action again.

Establishing a grip under her arms he begins to kick for the surface. Being made for flight, Delta is light for her size, but she is still heavy for the Vagrant. Their ascent is slow, hard work. Perspiration clouds the inside of the Vagrant's breathing mask.

He keeps going, establishing a steady rhythm, sticking to it, dogged.

From the depths, several knots of antennae rise. One of them touches a foot, tenses.

The Vagrant frowns at the contact.

At the next kick, the antennae rush forward, feeling their way up the Vagrant's extended leg. The head that they're attached to snakes after them, winding around the Vagrant's ankle until a once-human jaw is rubbing against his shin.

The Vagrant gasps, making fresh bubbles stream from his mask. Then he looks down. Amber eyes widen. He tries to kick free but the boneless neck tightens around his leg, and the body-made-tentacle that it is attached to draws him deeper.

He shifts his grip, moving his right hand from Delta to the hilt of her sword, his left holding the immortal tight, bracing against her so that he can pull the sword free quickly.

But the sword doesn't move, staying in its sheath, stubborn.

He lets go of Delta entirely, using his free hand to prise open the eye.

It looks up at him, afraid, guilty. It must have sensed the infernal, yet it did nothing, took no action, gave no warning.

He glares at it.

It looks away, quivers, then closes again.

His eyes widen, astonished.

Teeth sink into his calf, making him buck with pain. Instantly, a set of antennae are on his other leg, while a third begin to explore his back.

The Vagrant makes a fist, raising his middle finger slightly, making a spike of his knuckle, before driving it into the sword's eye.

It springs open in shock and he yanks it free, taking a breath to sing, and reaching for his breathing mask with his free hand.

A head rises up alongside, clamping its jaws around his left forearm.

Keeping his own mouth shut, holding that precious breath, the Vagrant pulls against it, inching his fingers towards the lower edge of the breathing mask.

Something slides across his back, following the line of his ribs until a second head nuzzles against his stomach.

The mask comes free.

The Vagrant sings, a weaker note than normal but Delta's sword picks it up, amplifying. Around them water vibrates, clouds of antennae retract, curling tight into themselves. Jaws go slack as the minor infernals retreat deeper into their shells, and their master quivers in surprise.

Meanwhile, untethered, Delta begins to drift away.

Pressing the breathing mask to his face again, the Vagrant takes another breath, then removes it to sing a second time, stronger now, swinging the sword downward. Water crackles, bubbling in the sudden heat and, with a sudden convulsion of blank-faced tentacles, the infernal is gone, swallowed by the depths.

The Seven

The Vagrant blinks away the nightmarish after-image and goes after Delta. His wounded leg no longer kicks so well, making progress halting but he manages to get hold of her.

He sees the eye in the sword trying to close and shakes it angrily. Now with its full attention, the Vagrant holds the sword out, uncurling his fingers one by one.

It glances from the depths to his face several times, its look becoming increasingly pleading.

The Vagrant narrows his eyes, flicks them up.

At the crosspiece, silvered wings come to life, starting to beat. The Vagrant joins in with his good leg, pulling Delta close, keeping a firm grip on her.

In uneven bursts, they move, a strange lopsided swimming mess.

Gradually the shadow of the sea-shuttle gets closer, until, at last, they bump against the hull.

Jem and Reela are waiting for him. 'There!' shouts Jem, and two pairs of hands, one big, one small, grab hold and begin hauling him up. As soon as he is able, the Vagrant throws the sword, hard, onto deck. It lands with an anguished clunk, the eye already closed.

Delta is harder to get onboard. Between the three of them, they manage it, grunting, wheezing, and in the Vagrant's case, wincing, as the effort squeezes more blood from his wounds.

It is only afterwards that he notices how wet Reela and Jem are. Lips purse to frame a question, then he shakes his head, dragging himself up the steering column.

Moments later the sea-shuttle leaps into life, powering away from the armada and Alpha's sky palace.

Not a single ship moves to stop them.

*   *   *

111

The Vagrant pushes the sea-shuttle's engines as hard as they will go until The Seven's armada is banished from sight. Only stopping when they are far away and the red sun dips below the horizon.

This time, when he picks up Delta's sword, it wakes at his touch, obedient. He hums low, sending soft vibrations along the blade, and places it against his calf. There is a hiss, of steel on skin, of breath through gritted teeth, and then he moves Delta's sword to the bite on his arm.

The Vagrant nods to himself, then sways, his gaze unfocused.

'Watch out!' calls Jem, rushing over as the Vagrant stumbles sideways. Catching him before he falls, Jem eases the bigger man down until he sits on the deck. 'Are you alright?'

The Vagrant nods blearily.

'Those wounds look nasty, we should bind them.'

The Vagrant shakes his head but Jem is already getting an emergency box of supplies from the sea-shuttle's cabinet. 'The stuff in here is old but it's better than nothing.'

The Vagrant holds up his hands, tries to wave Jem away.

'Don't worry, I know what I'm doing. Back when we liberated New Horizon from the Demagogue, I learned how to patch people up. Nothing clever, but I can clean and stitch if I have to.'

The Vagrant's cheeks pale and he rests his head against the wall.

When Jem takes his arm, the Vagrant flinches, making Jem smirk.

Afterwards, Jem looks for rations, finds little. Most edibles are already perished or plundered but a couple of sustenance bars have been overlooked. Each is broken into three pieces, shared out, and chewed slowly.

Jem waves the end of his at Reela as he talks. 'No wonder these were left behind, they're unflavoured. I used to hate them when I was your age.' He watches her and the Vagrant chewing together. 'What do you think?'

Reela shrugs.

'That's it? Are you saying you actually like it?'

Reela shrugs again.

'If you could have anything to eat, right now, what would you have?' He smiles to himself. 'I'd have some fried lizard wings. The ones that are so crispy you can snap off bits with your fingers and eat them. The trader my mother, your grandmother, used to go to had this special sauce. I dread to think what was in it but the stuff was delicious. It was spicy and salty and made my mouth tingle. I'd be desperate for a drink after but I made myself wait because the tingling feeling was so good.' He looks back at her. 'Okay, your turn.'

Reela's brow scrunches in thought and she licks her lips but she says nothing.

Jem's smile melts away and he shoots the Vagrant an unhappy look. 'It's alright. Take your time.'

It is nighttime. Clouds blanket the stars, a lightless sky reflecting emptiness on the ocean. A sea-shuttle drifts in the dark, a lone speck in the void, its engines quiet, three of its four passengers asleep.

Jem wishes he could join them but cannot. Thoughts play in his mind, restless, repetitive. He checks on Delta regularly, half expecting her to be awake, half expecting her to be dead. Both possibilities fill him with dread.

The sneeze is unexpected, taking Jem by surprise. The usual sense of its approach is fused with the sneeze itself, making a sound that jars with the rhythm of waves against hull.

Wiping his nose, Jem looks to see if any of the others have woken. Delta remains utterly still, Reela twitches and rolls over, sighing noisily in her sleep, and the Vagrant sits bolt upright, as if someone has applied a small electrical charge to his toes.

In the darkness, Jem smiles.

A bit of time passes, both men listening to the sighs and fidgets of the sleeping girl.

'Are you awake?'

The Vagrant nods.

'Did you just move? I can't see you in the dark.'

The Vagrant gives him a gentle kick.

Jem sighs, dramatic. 'You know, it would be a lot easier if you just talked.' He pauses, allowing time for a response. 'No? Well, that's okay, I've got some things to say. To be honest, I don't care if you speak or not. That's up to you. But I do care about Reela. I don't know what you've done to her but she's stopped talking and it's all your fault. You know when you went after Delta she followed you into the water?'

Jem has the sense of the Vagrant leaning closer. 'That's right. And you know how bad a swimmer she is. You need to talk to her before she really hurts herself.' The next words come out without his meaning to say them, moving under their own power. The kind of words only said at night. 'Everyone else thinks you're something special but I know the truth about you, remember that.

'The thing I don't understand is why you'd risk all of our lives to save Delta when you wouldn't lift a finger for my mother? She died in New Horizon, did you know that? She's dead because of you. And because of you I was a . . .' he searches for the words, 'a slave and a toy and a . . . fucking curio for the Demagogue, for over ten years. Because of you.'

As the first light of the suns brings colour to the sky, little has changed on the sea-shuttle. Delta remains where she was put, a silver statue stuck somewhere on the spectrum of sleep, coma and death. Reela also sleeps while Jem and the Vagrant wait awkwardly, neither communicating, both busying themselves with trivialities.

The horizon remains clear ahead and behind. The gold sun greets the day fully as the red starts to climb behind it. Final checks are made and the sea-shuttle's engines are warmed. They whine into action, making the sea-shuttle judder, ominous.

With a shrug, the Vagrant pushes forward on the steering column and the little ship cuts a smooth path through the water.

Jem and Reela take turns to sneeze and shiver, huddling together for warmth.

After a few hours, Reela drifts off again and Jem joins the Vagrant, not looking at him directly but standing close enough to talk. 'There's no more food. Can you fish?'

The Vagrant raises a hand, horizontal, and tilts it left to right several times.

'That's not very encouraging. I'll see if I can find anything to fish with. We need to find a port. I've been looking at the charts. They're years out of date but they do show a couple of places. There's an old drilling station called Ferrous we could try, or there's an island. It's not got a name, just a designation.'

The Vagrant raises an eyebrow.

'Well, I don't see you suggesting anything. If Ferrous is still active it's our best bet but if it isn't, I doubt there's much left there now. The island is an unknown. I think . . . I think we should go for Ferrous. It's a gamble but it's our best bet if we want to catch up with Vesper before The Seven do.'

The Vagrant pauses, nods and Jem puts the details into the sea-shuttle's navcom.

Time passes, the ocean being gentle with the ship. Little is said though Reela's belly often gurgles and grumbles. Jem and the Vagrant smile at the sound, but not at each other.

Reela prods at herself, experimenting, hoping to make the others laugh. Before her efforts can bear fruit however, there is a different kind of grumbling beneath her feet.

The deck gives a violent shudder and the sea-shuttle lurches forward one more time, a desperate leap to nowhere as, with a final whine, the engines die.

CHAPTER SEVEN

'We're the problem,' Vesper mutters to herself, then looks to the First for confirmation, knowing it will have heard her.

'Though I suspect The Seven would echo your . . . sentiment, I do not understand.'

She looks to Samael but the half-breed appears equally baffled. 'When you discovered that The Seven were back, you came to me for protection, yes?' The First nods. 'And when we realized they were chasing us, we ran, and we're still running now.'

'Yes.'

'Yes! But that's not good enough. You said you thought The Seven were coming after you. I believe that but they're also coming after me, and everything that came from the Breach, and everything that has been touched by the taint.

'We can't just run and hide from this, we have to start taking action.'

'I hear rhetoric but little more.'

Vesper takes a deep breath. 'Okay then, I'll get to the

point. Your ships are too slow to evade pursuit. They need time to repair. We can give them that time by drawing The Seven away. You and me. If we are both together, I'm sure The Seven will prioritize us.'

'How is this different from running away?'

'Because we won't be running away. We'll be running forward. You have sky-ships. We're wasting them here with the main fleet. We can use them to get messages to our allies, warn them of what's coming and coordinate a response. That means: New Horizon, Verdigris, Slake, Red Rails, West Rift and Reachers Cove. Oh, and any of the big Usurperkin tribes and infernals that you know about as well, just so long as you save one sky-ship for us.'

'One? It will be too small. I am far more than a single body.'

'We'll just have to pack as many of you in as we can and hope it's enough to hold The Seven's attention.'

Samael clears his throat. 'You're leaving *The Commander's Rest*?'

'Yes,' she replies. 'And so are you. I'm sorry, but I need you with us. The First's people will have to take care of it.'

'And where,' asks the First, 'will we be running to?'

'To Wonderland, and an old friend.'

Sitting heavy in the air, the sky-ship skims over tainted tree-tops. The First occupies the pilot's chair and the co-pilot's chair. It also packs out most of the hold, with several standing in open doorways and out on the wings. Samael has been wedged into a seat, his armour making tatters of the fabric. Vesper sits between him and one of the First. Tucked beneath their feet are Scout and the buck, who have so far remained mercifully quiet.

None of them is happy. The First is torn between the reassurance of having so much of itself together again and the sense of vulnerability that comes from such close proximity with the Malice. Samael worries about *The Commander's Rest* and the fact that Scout is transmitting queasy impulses through their link. Vesper worries about the knights she left behind, about her family, about the future, about so many things that she begins to worry about her ability to remember them all. Meanwhile, the buck is getting hungry, and the Malice continues to radiate misery.

'Do you know what I hate?' Vesper says into the silence.

'No,' replies Samael.

'Not being able to see where we're going.'

The half-breed nods, sympathetic. 'I hate that too but the thing I hate the most is not being in control.'

The sky-ship has a number of systems in place to keep the flight smooth and stable; as a result, Vesper has little sense of movement. Such systems do not fool the more sensitive Dogspawn however. Scout's head jerks forward in a dry heave and the buck bleats nervously, edging as far away as he can in the cramped conditions.

'You truly . . . hate these things?' asks the First.

Vesper jumps in her seat but the straps do not allow her to get far. She gives a half smile, sheepish. 'Sorry. I know this sounds ridiculous but you hadn't moved for so long I forgot you were there.' An eye glances up at her, unimpressed. 'Sorry,' she says to the sword, then, to the First she adds, 'When I say "hate" I mean I find it very frustrating.'

'Words are such imprecise tools. When my kind converse, understanding is total.'

'What's it like when you talk to each other?'

'When my kind meet, our essences touch and there is a merging. It is as if I become you and you become me. I do not just hear you, I am you. I know the concept you wish to share and I know it as you do. We do not divide emotion and understanding, they are one.'

'It sounds a bit like when the sword talks to me. We don't use words but I know what it's trying to say. It's hard to explain, like we're communicating on a deeper level.'

'Are you aware that the Malice is changing you?'

Vesper looks down at her hands. They rest across the sword on her lap. 'Yes.'

'That is why my kind are solitary. To deal with another is to risk losing yourself.'

'But demons travel in groups all the time.'

'Yes but only one of them is itself. When the Usurper walked your world, only a few of us remained free. The rest were slaves to the Usurper's desires. For all their flaws, words allow us to remain distinct.'

'Oh I don't know about that,' replies Vesper. 'Words control people too.'

'And bind us,' adds Samael in a hoarse whisper.

'I have another question,' says the First. 'You have a child.'

'A daughter, yes.'

'How is she?'

Vesper looks up, surprised. 'Difficult. Noisy. Funny. I don't know, to be honest. I haven't spent much time with her and now maybe I never will. I fear for her. And my father and my uncle. I'm hoping that The Seven are so intent on coming for me that They haven't even noticed my family.'

'But you do not believe this.'

She crumples in her seat. 'No. My daughter, Reela, bears the taint. And I know They don't like my father.'

'I thought he was Their Champion?'

'He is. But he disagreed with Them, and I have the feeling They won't have forgotten about it.'

Scout coughs a few times and then begins to retch. The buck sounds an alarm.

'He's not going to . . . ?' asks Vesper.

'A hairball,' Samael replies. 'But that may change. Flying doesn't suit him.'

Vesper leans down to stroke the buck, calming him. She is surprised to find the First has also leant down, its visored face only inches from hers. 'Er, hello?'

'I do not understand you.'

She pauses, then murmurs. 'Okay.'

'With others of your kind, it is simple. I see into them, I know them. Not as well as if I touched my essence to theirs, but enough. The Malice makes that difficult. It keeps a wall of hate between us.'

'If you're asking me to put the sword down so that you can study me, I'm going to have to say no.'

'Before, you said you hated not being able to see.'

'Yes.'

'Then why not move to the cockpit? There is a viewing window there.'

'Well,' she remembers Genner's lecture from when she was a girl, a lifetime ago, 'because of protocol and safety regulations and . . . and none of that matters here does it? Can I go into the cockpit?'

'Yes.'

Vesper punches the air. 'Yesss!'

121

Buckles are released, straps retracting into their housings and Vesper is on her feet. It is awkward squeezing past the various shells of the First, but enthusiasm and determination win through.

She is nearly through the hold when Samael's armour creaks behind her. 'Can I come too?'

'This is much better,' declares Vesper.

The cockpit is built for two, the First occupying both of the designated spaces. Vesper kneels on the lap of one, and looks over the shoulder of the other. Samael stands at the entranceway, bent forward so that his back can follow the curve of the roof. He has removed his helm to better position his head, revealing white skin, bloodless and inflexible. It also allows his long black hair to fall freely, giving Vesper a second fringe and tickling her ear.

Despite her view being limited to the square formed by the crush of bodies, Vesper's grin is bright. She marvels at the landscape blurring by beneath her.

Through his canine eye, Samael transmits the sight to Scout, who remains crouched in the hold; making sense of the sky-ship's movement and settling his stomach.

As the sky-ship slows down, details come into focus. A forest of stalks, yellow-gold, thick as birch trees and easily as tall. Hidden inside are all manner of tainted creatures: giant spiders spinning webs like cable, swarms of wasps grown too fat to fly, and thorny plants that take root in the soft flesh of the living.

Wonderland sits in the middle of this mess, an island of grey and blue. A great city taken to new heights by the Uncivil, its turrets continue to stand proud, great walkways arcing between them. The lights and life of the city have long been extinguished however, leaving a pale ghost of what was.

'We should come across a courtyard soon that we can land in,' says Vesper. 'Right about . . . yes! There it is.'

They come to a stop above five towers, each joined by a wall obviously built much later to create an enclosed area. Where the towers are seamless metal structures, the wall is a thing of mud and bones and junk, glued together with filth.

The First brings the sky-ship down, light drives rotating to vertical, allowing a straight descent. Old bits of refuse dot the space, broken bits of stone and glass. Otherwise, it is empty, the remains rotted or squirrelled away for darker purposes.

When the hatch opens, the buck is the first to bound out, bleating, triumphant. Scout quickly follows, racing around in a happy circle.

Samael comes next, his helmet back in place, then Vesper, who stretches out her arms and neck. Vertebrae click and blood finds its way back into extremities.

'That's odd,' she says aloud. 'There used to be a giant fake monster here.'

The First begins to exit behind her, marching in single file. 'This place appears abandoned. I was given to understand that it was . . . cursed.'

'No, it isn't cursed. It's . . . it's a long story. We need to go to the Don't Go. If my friend is still here, that's where she'll be.'

Vesper leads the way around the side of one of the buildings to a small corrugated shed. She pulls open the door to reveal a rusty chute. 'It's down there.'

'I remember,' says Samael, ushering Scout into the chute

and climbing in after. He pushes off, metal squealing against metal, and he is gone.

One of the First steps forward, the other black-armoured bodies spreading about the courtyard. It ducks low, infernal eyes untroubled by the lack of light, and runs headlong down the chute.

'Show-off,' mutters Vesper.

Nearby, one of the First's bodies turns its visored head towards her but says nothing.

Vesper sits down on the top of the chute, beckoning the buck to join her.

The buck stops its bounding and regards her.

'Come on, come over here.'

Dark eyes blink but the buck does not move.

'Come on! Don't be scared. You've done it before and you were tiny!'

The buck makes a derisive noise.

'Fine, you can stay here with the First.' She waves. 'See you soon!'

The buck stares at the empty space where Vesper was moments ago. He bleats at it, stares, bleats again. When Vesper does not reappear, his mouth opens wide, an approximation of horror. Taking a deep breath the buck lowers his head and charges, screaming all the way. Nearby animals pause to sniff the air and swarms of insects change direction.

The buck does not stop when it reaches the chute, and soon hooves skid on sloping metal. Legs work hard to find purchase, to stop, to go back. They fail. Screaming changes pitch, panicked, and the buck's charge becomes a fall.

*   *   *

Vesper comes off the slide at speed, landing off balance, her feet skipping on dusty stone, skidding, wobbling, before coming to a stop by the opposite wall. She grins to herself. 'Not too bad.'

Scout barks approval. 'Better than last time,' agrees Samael.

A living wallpaper of beetles covers the room, little clicks of them scurrying up and down and over each other forming a constant background noise.

Samael walks forward, eager, and they part for him, recognizing his essence. A honeycombed surface is revealed beneath, and a doorway. As he passes through, Scout at his heels, Vesper hears the buck's catastrophic descent. The clatter of hooves on metal, the thud of body smacking chute, the wail of torment.

She covers her ears.

There is a final thud as the buck slides off the end of the chute.

Vesper soothes quickly, the sight of her and the liberal application of sympathy appeasing the buck.

The First studies them. 'Where is the . . . symbiosis in this relationship?'

'The what?'

'You take this animal with you. You tend to it and endure its company. Why?'

'Oh. I love him.'

The First is quiet for a moment while it considers the buck, then it repeats, 'Why?'

'Lots of reasons. He saved my life once, but it isn't that. We grew up together, we've gone through a lot.' She strokes the buck's head. 'You've never come across people having pets before?'

'I have. Normally these pets are either functional or are . . . pleasing to the eye.'

'He is pleasing to the eye! He's lovely!'

The First says nothing.

The buck looks smug.

Vesper gets up. 'I think you'd better stay here.'

'Because I do not find merit in your choice of pet?'

'No! Because my friend hasn't met you before. I'll talk with her first and come back for you.'

The First consents and Vesper chases after Samael. The beetles have covered the door once more but when the sword hums at her shoulder they scurry from the sound, drawing back like a curtain. Vesper steps through. Beyond is a simple passageway, old and worn. She sees changes from the last time she came this way. Parts of the floor have been taken up, revealing the impression of pipes that once ran underneath.

Holding up a navpack, she puts it to torch setting, the light catching on little shadow patches where pieces of the structure have been removed. She and the buck make quick work navigating the holes but, despite their haste, Samael is nowhere to be seen.

A feeling of uneasiness begins to grow in Vesper's stomach. She isn't sure if it comes from the sword or from her own instincts, the two so intertwined, but it is there.

She passes several chambers, glancing in and shining her torch. The layout remains familiar to her but the rooms themselves are just blank spaces, stripped of furniture, of personality. They don't match with her memories of the place.

'It looks abandoned,' she murmurs to the buck.

They continue onwards until she hears Scout's bark, distant, excited. Hurrying, they turn two more corners before seeing the Dogspawn and Samael talking to a tall, robed figure, green eyes glowing softly within a deep hood.

'Neer!' she calls, waving.

The woman in the robe turns towards her. She does not wave back. 'I was beginning to wonder if the pair of you were ever coming back.'

Scout barks.

Vesper and goat come close. 'It's so good to see you again!'

Scout barks, several times. Samael mumbles something, and Neer's face creaks as she turns back to him. 'Yes, yes. I gave my word, didn't I? They're waiting for you, you know where.'

Samael and Scout leave, an unusual eagerness in the half-breed's step.

'Neer, I have news. You know what I've been working towards?'

'Your little utopia? Yes, I remember.'

'Well, it's really happening.'

Eyes flash green in Neer's dead face. 'And?'

'And I want you to reconsider getting involved. Come with me, you could make such a difference.'

The eyes flash again. 'And? There's something you're not telling me, girl. Out with it.'

Vesper sighs. 'Well, you might not have much of a choice about leaving Wonderland – The Seven are coming, coming here, and they won't like what they find.'

'And you won't be putting in a good word for old Neer because?'

'They want to kill me and do suns know what with the

sword. They've gone crazy. According to the First, they've started burning parts of the Empire. I dread to think what they'd do to you.'

'Oh, you're on speaking terms with the First now?'

'Yes. As I said, this is happening and the First is on board. It's here now, actually.'

'You brought the First to my doorstep! Do you know how careful I've been over the years to hide my presence? To keep my work a secret?'

'Yes, of course I do. But the time to hide is over. Things are so desperate now, we can't work alone anymore.'

Neer shakes her head. 'Don't try the innocent face with me. You know what you're doing. You're forcing my hand.'

'I came here to warn you.'

'And to get my help.' Vesper nods and Neer tuts. 'Well, the essence is out of the shell now, you might as well introduce us.'

The First is soon called and stands before them.

'This,' says Vesper, 'is my friend, Ferrencia, otherwise known as Neer. She was the surgeon general to the Uncivil when it was alive. And this is the First.'

The two size each other up.

'Interesting,' says the First. 'The state of your shell's decay is advanced and yet it does not impede you.'

Neer's reply is heavy with sarcasm. 'And you've got quite the silver tongue for an infernal, eh?'

'Your essence is only partly connected to your shell. Unlike the rest of your kind, you are not completely bound. You inhabit it at a slight remove. In this regard, you are not unlike . . . me.'

'Are you done?'

128

'No, I am just beginning. I wish for you to understand that there is little point in hiding secrets from me. I already know what it is that you want, and I am willing to negotiate.'

'And what is it that I want so badly?'

Vesper's head turns back and forth as each speaks, the buck's does the same. In contrast, the sword keeps its gaze fixed on the First.

'You want what all of your kind want. What all of my kind want. To live. The connections between the altered parts of you and your essence are thinning. Parts of your shell are wearing out. I can see the repair work. Artful, but only delaying the inevitable.'

'And you can offer me something better?'

'Yes.'

Neer chuckles. 'I believe you but I'm far too old to believe in kindness. What do you want in return?'

'I've already told you.'

'You look alive from where I'm standing.'

'This,' replies the First, gesturing at itself, 'is existing. It is not living. Do you understand?'

Neer's eyes glint, intense. 'I think I do.'

'If you want to trade with the First,' says Vesper, 'you'll need to help me. It's under my protection.'

'Fine,' mutters Neer. 'I'll consider it, though it isn't much of an offer.'

Vesper says nothing, doesn't need to. She and the sword know the half-alive is already hooked.

'Come with me,' Neer snaps, trying to hide her excitement beneath a veneer of irritability. She looks at Vesper and raises a finger. 'But not you.'

*   *   *

Scout's ears prick up. Through them, Samael hears Vesper's approach, picking up on her angry tone as she talks to the buck. He pulls the cloth back over the stone slab and its contents, moving to the doorway before she arrives.

Vesper comes into view, words still flowing, her hands making cutting gestures in the air.

The buck shouts at them and Vesper pats his head. 'There you are. I've been trying to find you for ages but Neer gave her directions so fast I forgot the last part. I'm sure she does it on purpose, to try and belittle me, as if I'm still the same little girl I was when we first met. I tell myself it's just a way of hiding affection but sometimes that's hard to believe.' She shakes her head. 'And I don't know what she and the First are up to, and that bothers me.'

Samael checks to see if she's finished. 'Can I talk to you?'

She looks up at him, suddenly focused. 'Go on.'

He takes a step towards the slab. 'This is not easy for me to explain. Do you remember when we first travelled together and in the swamps around the Fallen Palace I had to make our case to the Backwards Child in order to pass?'

'Of course. But that was years ago, what has it got to do with now?'

'When my essence touched that of the Backwards Child, it changed me. It . . . made things clearer.'

'What do you mean?'

The half-breed thinks for a while. 'When I was made into this –' he nearly adds the word mockery '– by the commander of the Knights of Jade and Ash, the man that I was became mixed with his infernal essence, and that essence was also a mix. It was made up of the commander, of his infernal life and the human life before it. It also contained traces of other infernals that had touched his essence, like the Uncivil.

'For the longest time my head was a mess of images and feelings. I didn't know which were mine and which were theirs. Sometimes a piece of knowledge would appear out of nowhere when I needed it or I'd remember someone I'd never met, but I had no way to access that knowledge. It was the same with emotions. I had them but they often came from my creator or from the Uncivil, and I had no way to know which was which. The Backwards Child changed that.'

Vesper reaches into her bag and pulls out a flask, sipping soup slowly as Samael continues.

'Because of the Backwards Child's intervention, I can see where they start and I begin. Inside I feel more ordered, and I can call upon their knowledge when I need to.'

She takes another sip. 'That sounds great.'

'Then I'm not telling it right.' He pulls off his helm, sliding his long hair free. 'I used to want to fight all infernals. I hated them.'

Vesper smiles sympathetically. 'They took your life away.'

'Yes. They did. But which life? I thought my desire to destroy the infernals was my human side winning out. But it was more complicated. The infernals often fight each other. What I considered my hatred had its roots as much in the Uncivil and the commander as it did in the human from whom I take my name.

'What I am trying to say is that when we first met I was clinging to the idea that inside here,' he bangs his fist against his chest, 'was the soul of a man. But that isn't true. I'm not a man and I'm not an infernal. I'm something else, a sum of the different parts of my heritage.' He looks up at her. 'I have to honour them all.

'For the fisherman that I was, I have my life on the sea, my own ship and the freedom that it brings. There's Scout too of course.'

The Dogspawn barks cheerily.

'For the parts of me that once loved the Empire, I have my service to you. It's always seemed fitting that I became part of your Order of Broken Blades. But to be a real knight I wanted to have a sword.'

Vesper gestures towards the slab. 'Which is why we're here.'

He pauses, aware that he is stalling, aware that she knows it. 'I know that I will never wield a Seraph Knight's weapon but some vanity in me needs a sword. A special sword. Something that suits me. I believe that your knights also suffer the lack of a proper weapon. They broke something of themselves when they broke their blades.'

Vesper looks down. Samael's half-breed eyes see the change in her emotion: she knows he is right.

'Yes,' she agrees, 'and I need them whole again if we're going to stand against the Empire. So. What about the new weapons? Did your experiment work?'

He beckons her to follow and moves over to the covered slab. Vesper does so as Samael takes the edge of the cloth and pulls it back to reveal a set of swords, cloudy grey blades with red hilts and brassy pommels. A similar shape to the swords of the Seraph Knights but a shade lighter and an inch longer. 'What do you think?'

An eye opens at Vesper's shoulder, and a soft hum fills the air. 'There's essence inside them.'

'Yes. Essence that I harvested during the fight for New Horizon. It's inert. The swords won't react to lies or infernals but they can be directed by the song of a knight or by my will. It is a form of Necrotech, but Neer has used it to animate essence rather than flesh.' He looks at her for a moment, then adds in a quieter voice. 'You haven't told me what you think.'

'What do I think? I think it's incredible. I'm not sure what my knights will make of it though. It's exactly what they need but I know they'll struggle to accept the Necrotech.' She smiles at him. 'Don't worry, I'll speak to them. I want this to work. These aren't just weapons, they represent a new way. They're a symbol. Just like you are.'

Samael gives a slight bow. 'Thank you, Vesper. This means a lot to me.'

'I have a question though. When you were working with Neer, did you get a sense of what she's trying to achieve here?'

'Yes. Neer is dying. She is looking for ways to transfer her essence into another shell. To that end she has been restoring parts of Wonderland.'

'I don't understand.'

'This city was once one great shell for the Uncivil to inhabit. The Malice destroyed her before she had a chance to finish it. Neer intends to complete that work.'

'Neer wants to become a city?'

'Not exactly. The Uncivil was big enough to fill Wonderland and they had to keep expanding the city to accommodate her growth. If Neer had been successful she would have been more like a ghost inside it.'

Vesper claps her hands together. 'That's why she wanted to study Duet! She was looking for ways to join her essence to other things.'

Samael nods. 'Yes. She has the skills to make a new shell, be that a human body or a necrotic structure, like this one. But she cannot transfer her own essence. Without help, she is trapped in her body.'

'Could you do it?'

'I don't know. I might be able to assist.'

'Could the First?'

'Possibly.'

'That's what I'm thinking. Pack up the swords, it's time for us to go.'

CHAPTER EIGHT

The engine casing is open, allowing smells of burnt rubber and scorched metal to waft freely. A hot, fused lump is all that remains of the light drive.

The Vagrant stares at it for some time.

'Can you fix it?' asks Jem.

The Vagrant gives the engine an experimental prod. Then he hits it. Then he shakes his head.

'I knew it! I told you, didn't I? I told you that if you kept pushing the engines over their safety limits they'd fail. I told you several times and you didn't listen! And now were fin—' He notices Reela is watching him and catches himself, forcing a brighter tone. 'Now we're finding another way to get to Ferrous. Any ideas?'

After a long sigh, the Vagrant digs into a slot and brings out a short plastic stick. With a flick of his wrist, it telescopes out, one end unfolding to form a paddle. He hands it to Jem.

'You're kidding me! We'll never—' the Vagrant gives Jem a pointed look '– get there until we start.'

The Vagrant nods, smiles at Reela and then snaps out a second paddle.

As the two men get to work, one either side of the sea-shuttle, Reela investigates. To her delight, she finds another stick in the slot. She gives it an experimental shake.

Nothing happens.

She tries again, more vigorous this time.

Abruptly, the stick opens up, its paddle end smacking her in the face.

Reela gapes at it, shocked. She blinks rapidly, taking in a shuddering breath, putting a finger to her lips. No tears come. Nodding to herself, Reela moves to the side and joins in the paddling.

Hours pass, all three fixed on their work. Every so often, Jem glances over at where Delta lies on the deck. For a moment he thinks her eyes are open, staring blankly at the sky, but when he checks again, he finds them closed. Occasionally, when his muscles are aching, or when the reality of the situation strikes, he pauses to glare at the Vagrant.

'Let's take a break,' he finally announces, flopping back.

The Vagrant raises an eyebrow but stops paddling.

While tired arms get a brief respite, the Vagrant checks the navpack. The display suggests they are veering off-course. He shows it to Jem, stabbing a finger, accusing.

'What? It's not my fault. You're paddling too fast!'

The Vagrant rolls his eyes.

'If we're going to keep straight, you need to match my rhythm.'

They try again, the strokes more synchronized. When Jem pauses to look at Delta, he falls out of time. The Vagrant taps his paddle on the side of the sea-shuttle.

'Sorry,' mutters Jem and gets back to work.

Reela forgets about the paddling, focusing her attention on Jem. Every time he slows, an imperious tapping sounds, Reela prompting him to redouble his efforts – and to mouth something dark. Each time, the smile on her face grows and the urge to giggle gets harder to resist.

For once, the Vagrant's face mirrors hers.

Time passes.

'It's no good,' says Jem. 'I have to stop.' He points at the Vagrant. 'Don't say anything. And don't give me that look either. I'm doing my best, I'm just not very good at this. If you hadn't ruined the engines then it wouldn't be a problem, would it?'

He notices the Vagrant has stopped paddling, and is resting his head on his palm.

'Are you alright? You look . . . awful.'

The Vagrant glances up at Jem, revealing a face lined in sweat.

'You're burning up!'

By way of confirmation, the Vagrant slides from his position at the rail, flopping onto the deck. He holds up a finger, then passes out.

Jem and Reela rush to his side. A quick investigation confirms a fever. Jem digs out some of the old meds from the sea-shuttle and shoots them into the Vagrant's arm with a medgun. He then gathers some cold water and soaks a cloth, applying it to the Vagrant's forehead.

Reela watches his every move, chewing nervously on her fingertips.

'Don't worry,' says Jem. 'He'll be fine. It's just exhaustion . . . I think.'

Uncertainties go over her head and she nods, content, snuggling in next to the Vagrant.

Jem goes to the sea-shuttle's navcom. It suggests that they are close to Ferrous now. He takes out the scope, checking for any breaks in the ocean and, to his surprise, finds one. A slender tower is just visible. Thick plastic cables hang from a crown at its top, synthetic dreadlocks, uneven. Lights wink like flawed jewels along its surface. Several are missing.

He takes up his paddle again, but alone he makes no headway against the waves. He tries signalling to the tower, lighting up the scope and waving it repeatedly.

All the while, the sea-shuttle drifts in the wrong direction.

Getting desperate, Jem goes back to the medgun, loads it with a cocktail of stims and uppers and presses it against the Vagrant's thigh. He pulls the trigger.

Amber eyes spring open.

Soundlessly, the Vagrant's mouth springs open.

The Vagrant is sitting up.

The Vagrant is standing up.

The Vagrant is looking around, left, right, up, down, left and right, and . . .

'Over there!' says Jem, pointing to the tower.

Together, they paddle the sea-shuttle towards it. The Vagrant works like a man possessed, sometimes running to Jem's side of the sea-shuttle to straighten them out.

As they draw close, the cables skirting the tower begin to twitch, magnets bringing them to life. Of their own accord, they slide across the water to clonk into place on the sea-shuttle's hull, gathering the small vessel in a machine's embrace.

Stiffening, the cables raise it out of the water until it's

level with a hatch in the tower's side. Next to the hatch is a circular plate of darkened plasglass. Tiny green LEDs play across it, sparkling.

The Vagrant moves up to the hatch and looks into the panel. Light maps his face, highlighting scars. There is a pause, then a buzz of rejection.

Jumping back onto deck the Vagrant picks up Delta's sword. It just has time to open its eye in surprise before the Vagrant leaps over to the hatch again, pressing the crosspiece against the panel.

There's a muted hum of alarm from the blade, followed by a resonant ping of acceptance.

The hatch swings open.

With a grin, wild, the Vagrant turns back to the others. He holds up a hand to them and then steps into the hatch.

'Hold on,' says Jem. 'I think we should stay together.' He moves to the Vagrant's side and adds in a lower voice, 'I don't feel safe with Delta here.'

They both look at Delta and nod.

As they're about to leave, Reela holds up a hand.

Bemused, they watch her cover Delta with the Vagrant's old coat, tucking it in around silver shoulders.

The Vagrant nods four times in approval, excess energy shifting him from foot to foot.

'Ah, how are you doing?' asks Jem.

The Vagrant gives him a thumbs up and plunges through the open hatch.

A moment later, a smaller thumb is also raised as Reela runs after him.

Jem pauses to mutter something under his breath before following.

As they enter, lights come on inside the tower, blink off, stutter a few times, then stabilize, casting the space in harsh white light. The room is circular, empty, with featureless walls and a studded metal floor.

Behind them, the hatch swings shut, its seal sucking into place. They all jump.

'Now what?' asks Jem.

Reela and the Vagrant shrug.

They don't hear any movement but they feel it in their bellies. A sudden lessening of gravity as the room begins to fall.

Reela holds out her arms, Jem steadies himself against the wall and the Vagrant crouches down, fingers resting lightly on the floor for balance.

There is an ugly screeching sound and the room shakes, slows, then resumes its progress.

Down it goes, into the depths. Like an iceberg, only the tip of Ferrous is visible above the surface, most of its bulk spread across and under the sea bed.

Stomachs return to their normal positions and, on the opposite side of the room from where they came in, a new hatch opens.

Any lights that once worked in this part of the station failed long ago. Jem switches the scope to torch mode and shines it nervously into the corridor. The beam of light shakes as it describes the way ahead. A ridged tube stretches before them, the opaque surface mottled with shadows. A few of them move, suggesting life of a sort on the outside.

Fixing his gaze firmly at his feet, the Vagrant sets off, holding Reela's hand in one of his, Delta's sword in the other.

Jem keeps close, twitching every time something moves beyond the curved walls.

At the other end is another hatch. This too opens for them. In the darkness revealed on the other side, something screams.

At the sight of it, Jem screams too.

Delta of The Seven remains where she was placed on the deck of the sea-shuttle. The sound of Alpha's song, far away, carries on essence currents.

Eyes of storm-cloud grey open.

Motionless, she stares up, listening, understanding, reflecting.

And tears of stone slide down the sides of her face.

The Knight Commander straightens at the incoming call and, on the bridge of *Resolution*, officers pause in their work, sensing the incoming change.

Obeisance's smooth features project in the air before him and her voice is fed like a balm into his ear. 'Knight Commander, I trust you are well.'

'I am, and ready to serve.'

'As are we all. I have resumed my place at The Seven's side and They have spoken. Prepare yourself, old friend, there is much work to do and The Seven are keen to hunt down the traitors.'

The Knight Commander braces himself. 'I am sorry to report that the quarry has eluded us. We believe the First and the Bearer have separated from the other ships but we're unclear as to where either is going.'

'You are mistaken. Our Lenses in the south have already

told us their destination. You are to make your way there with all haste, stopping en route only to purge the locations I am sending to you.'

Her face is replaced with maps, full of blinking lights. The Knight Commander responds, 'It would be most efficient if I split the fleet, dividing the targets between them.'

'Proceed as you see fit. We trust you to make the right decision.'

'You honour me.'

Her face reappears. Even across a link, he finds her scrutiny wearing. 'There is one other thing. Assemble a squad of your most experienced troops and dispatch them to Ferrous at once. Consider them at my disposal. It is unlikely they will return.'

'Understood.'

'Pick only those whose faith is unshakable.'

'Understood.' But he does not truly understand. Surely all of them have unshakable faith? Why say that unless there was reason to doubt? Or perhaps she has reason to doubt his people. Or doubt him. Unpleasant thoughts about Obeisance swim to the surface of his mind. Unworthy but insistent, they plant a seed of doubt that forms quick roots. None of it shows on his face.

'Good. We will rendezvous with you on the coast. May the Winged Eye watch over you.'

'And also over you,' he intones.

Cutting the link, he addresses his officers. Minutes later the armada splits into four fleets and a sky-ship peels off, its passengers loaded with secret purpose.

Trembling torchlight sketches features. A half-breed, nearly as wide as it is tall. Skin so pale the veins look like wounds.

Even internal organs are visible as watery impressions. Rolls of rubbery fat strip the figure of sex, tufts of hair sprouting in all the wrong places and none of the right ones. A thin membrane covers the spaces between lips and ears, the nostrils reduced to two shades in the skin.

Thick arms end in fat fingers, webs of flesh hanging between them. They are pressed in horror against its face as it screams.

Jem screams back, prompting it to scream again, prompting Jem to scream again, a game, passing back and forth until the Vagrant holds up a hand, firm.

Jem stops. A scream later, the other stops too.

The Vagrant looks at Jem, gestures towards the half-breed.

He takes the hint, clearing his throat. 'Er, hello? We're not here to fight. My name is Jem. Do you understand me?'

There is a pause, then a grunt. 'Ehrn?'

'I said, do you understand?'

Another pause. 'Ehrn?'

Jem looks for support but the Vagrant repeats his previous gesture.

'Hello,' he says slowly. 'I'm Jem.' He points to himself for emphasis, then repeats: 'Jem. We are hungry.' He rubs his tummy a few times. 'Hungry. Understand?'

Cautiously, the half-breed approaches Jem. The Vagrant steps out of the way. Reela does the same.

Jem flinches as the fat webby fingers reach out, moist where they touch him, like being rubbed with wet jelly. 'What are you . . .?'

It stretches the membrane of its mouth wide, then snatches the torch out of Jem's hands.

'Hey!'

Prize in fist, it turns away to lope off down the corridor.

'I . . .' Jem says to the Vagrant, spreading his hands. 'That wasn't my fault.'

The Vagrant sets off in pursuit, pulling Reela with him.

'It wasn't,' he mutters, hurrying after, before the light leaves him behind.

Torchlight shows slivers of rooms, suggestions of the overall state of Ferrous. Something of the sea has found its way inside. Spores nestle in corners, glowing softly in the damp air. Crates lie scattered on their sides, contents spilling out and abandoned. The sound of a pump can be heard, working, rhythmic, getting louder.

Boots begin to splash as they step, seawater sneaking in through a tiny crack that is never fixed, then pumped out only to sneak back again, a stalemate.

The half-breed leads them deep within the station, until they reach a heavy looking door, hexagonal, lined in pulsing neon. With a hiss, the door opens, revealing a small room. The walls and floor are blank. No exits, nothing of note. The half-breed jumps straight in.

'Do you think it's another lift?' asks Jem.

The Vagrant doesn't answer, stepping inside with Reela. When Jem has joined them, the door closes.

Seconds pass and the walls lose their density, going from dark grey to light, to transparent. Revealed on the other side are rows of cylindrical tanks. There are fifteen in all. Four are broken and dark. The remaining eleven are filled with a pale yellow liquid and three of them contain bodies. These last three glide forward on hidden means of locomotion until they press against the glass, the faces within magnified and

144

distorted. A man and woman with old wrinkly skin and another man, younger, almost as wrinkled.

From a speaker somewhere a simple tune plays and the half-breed flops down. The tune repeats and the half-breed's head lolls forward. A third repetition and it is asleep.

Jem bends down and picks up the torch.

The speaker crackles and then a voice can be heard, matching the movements of the older man's mouth. 'Apologies for the lack of a proper welcome but as you can see, we have some difficulties here. I hope Giblet didn't cause you any troubles. He's well-meaning but he gets over-excited sometimes.'

Jem points to the sleeping half-breed. 'That's Giblet?'

'Yes. When they're born, they look like giblets. He can't talk much yet but he understands a lot. Not bad for a twelve-month-old.'

The Vagrant and Jem exchange a look and the speaker distorts with laughter. 'Oh I know! Imagine what we said when we first found out. I'm sure you're full of questions. Actually, we have a few of our own. I hope you don't mind but we will expect you to answer them all.'

'Before that,' Jem replies, 'is there any chance of something to eat? We've come a long way and . . .'

The speaker snaps off but it is clear that the man is still talking. The other two tanked figures interject occasionally, the fluid wisping around them, making expressions and lips hard to read.

A minute passes while the Vagrant twitches with unused energy.

Reela yawns.

Giblet begins to snore, the air catching some loose flap of skin inside his throat, making wet vibrations.

The three figures turn towards them again and, with a slight pop, the man's voice returns. 'Yes. This will suit us all. Giblet will bring you food and you can eat and rest while we discuss our position on your arrival amongst ourselves.'

'Your position?' asks Jem. 'Is there a problem?'

'Problem? No. Not a problem. Not even close to a problem. Nothing to worry about, just some little kinks to straighten before we decide what to do with you.'

As the walls darken, removing him from sight, the man in the cylinder puts a hand to his mouth, his expression that of a naughty child caught with a hand in the sweet jar.

A simple tune plays and Giblet jerks awake.

'Feed our guests,' comes the man's voice. 'Use only the special stock. Feed them, Giblet, only from the special stock. Feed them well.'

Giblet is gone for some time. When he returns, he is carrying a bulging plastic sack under one arm and a tube with a nozzle under the other. When the sack is put down, there is an audible squelch.

With practised ease, Giblet fastens the other end of the tube to a valve on the top of the sack and then offers the nozzle.

'After you,' Jem murmurs.

The Vagrant takes the nozzle and lifts it up to the eye in Delta's sword. It opens, obliging, and stares into the nozzle. It looks up at the Vagrant, indifferent, then closes again.

Satisfied, the Vagrant puts the nozzle to his mouth and Giblet gives the bag a squeeze.

A thick gel eases from the end, the yellow hue remarkably similar to the liquid inside the tanks. Giblet waits for a curly pile to collect on the Vagrant's tongue before releasing the sack.

The Vagrant closes his mouth. He looks up at the ceiling as if searching for something, then swallows.

'Well?' asks Jem, holding Reela back as she reaches for the nozzle.

The Vagrant raises a thumb.

'Really?'

The Vagrant nods and Jem lets Reela past.

Giblet squeezes the bag for her and then Jem has a turn. 'It . . . It's really good!'

Reela is already reaching for nozzle again.

They take turns, uneven, stuffing as much of the nameless substance into their mouths on each rotation, until the sack is empty and three bellies stretch happily to capacity.

When they are done, Giblet takes the sack away, the large door opening just long enough for him to leave.

Soon, they are all sat against the wall. Jem looks at the Vagrant. 'I hope we don't come to regret eating that.'

The Vagrant yawns.

Reela yawns.

'I suppose we didn't have much of a choice.'

Reela starts to flop over but the Vagrant catches her and leans her against his side.

Jem clutches at his stomach in panic. 'Do you think it was drugged?'

The Vagrant frowns, then shakes his head.

'But how can you be sure?' He fights the sudden urge to yawn. 'I don't like it here. At least one of us should stay awake.'

The Vagrant nods slowly.

'I think it should be you.'

A smile twitches at the corner of the Vagrant's mouth, then amber eyes close.

'I hate you,' whispers Jem. He holds the scope close, taking comfort from its light. He cannot be sure but it seems as if the walls are losing their colour. Not completely transparent but different somehow. Another yawn threatens, is stifled. He thinks about the stims he injected into the Vagrant, wonders if they have lost effectiveness due to age or whether they have been neutralized by other, stronger medication.

The next yawn gets past his guard. The one after that overcomes him completely.

One Thousand and Forty-Six Years Ago

Massassi wakes with a start. She is sitting in her control chair, a comfortable enough design but hardly built for sleep. How long has she been dozing? She looks at the globe of screens all around her, each one monitoring a different corner of her vast empire. Even so there are not enough to show every relevant feed and so the images flicker, moving to whatever seems most important, the globe revolving to bring the newest developments to eye level.

It has been a long time since she sat here. Too long. Her senses are no longer attuned to the screens in the way they were and ocular fitness has gone.

Massassi tuts at herself. She is losing her edge. And that should be fine! Alpha should have more than enough edge to carry them all, and Beta should be enough to stop it cutting too deep.

She is confident in her new creations but not confident enough to rest. After a time of recovery, she has come to check on their progress, to make sure that they are getting things right.

So far the numbers are not quite what she was hoping for.

Certainly there have been fewer deaths since Beta joined his brother. Indeed, the Empire is functional, stable. It is not getting worse but neither is it getting better.

There seems to be something missing. Massassi cannot put her finger on why, but her creations lack spark and innovation. It also bothers her that they are both cast in male forms. Should she not leave something closer to her own image behind as well?

An uncommon sensation runs through her at the thought, that of doubt. She is aware that it has taken longer to recover from Beta's making than it did for Alpha's. She is getting weaker. With each new creation, there is less of her own essence to draw upon.

Nonetheless, once she has had the idea of making some-thing new, it will not leave her. It nags her as she endures her daily treatments, bothers her as she attends to the latest overview reports from Peace-Fifteen, and forbids her from getting any meaningful sleep. The next day, less than twenty-four hours later, she is standing in her workshop, weary limbs supported by a slender exoskeleton, Beta to her left and Alpha to her right.

She senses their excitement and curiosity. It mirrors her own. They do not ask what she is doing and she does not explain. They love her without question. It is far more than mortal love, for Alpha and Beta have powers like hers and their emotions are tangible things that change the world around them. Their loving attention is a force so powerful that Massassi feels her aches lighten.

Without preamble, she commences her next great work. With Alpha she sought perfection, with Beta she tried to capture wisdom and practicality. Now she tries for something less defined, the desire to strive for more, a replica of her will.

A female form takes shape under her hammer. Broad shouldered and winged like her brothers but curving differently at the chest and hips. The face is modelled after her own though even Massassi admits that this is an artist's rendition, flattering, based on a nostalgic memory of younger features.

She gives the body a sword to match Alpha's and then stops.

There is a nagging feeling of something not being quite right and she is too tired to identify it. It can wait till tomorrow.

Alpha and Beta walk beside her, patient, as she shuffles back to her bed.

The next day finds Massassi just as tired, her body sluggish, her mood black. Fresh eyes find nothing wrong with the previous day's work, in fact she is pleased. She asks Alpha and Beta for their opinion and both agree it is flawless. Of course, to them everything Massassi does is flawless. They are incapable of seeing otherwise.

Satisfied that all is ready, and resigned to the fact that she is not going to feel any better no matter how long she waits, Massassi raises her metal arm. Alpha and Beta lift the platform that she stands on, bringing her within easy reach of the statue's silver head. The iris in Massassi's palm opens and she presses it to the inert face.

The plan is to imbue the creation with drive and ambition,

a lack of satisfaction that will not allow rest or slothfulness. But as the essence begins to flow, she finds other feelings taking over. Unbidden, thoughts of her life float to the surface, of the way she was used as a child, worked hard without care for her safety or sanity. This world she works to save is a bitter one, an ungrateful one. And she is angry, so, so angry!

That rage courses through her new creation, flooding through the sword to the body and back, like a river bursting the walls of a dam. Massassi cannot stop it, her essence seeming to move with a will of its own, filling the shell to the brim until it radiates such heat that the air shimmers and bends.

Three eyes open, sudden, and Massassi is repulsed by what she sees, stumbling back into Alpha's ready arms. It is like looking at a younger perfect version of herself and it is too painful.

Gamma's eyes are sky-blue like Alpha's but hers are colder, a mirror of Massassi's disapproval.

Where Alpha and Beta's love is bolstering, Gamma's stare is like a stab in the face, a voice shouting that she should have done better.

She turns her head away, letting it rest on Alpha's chest, and instantly regrets it, knowing the gesture to be weak and knowing that Gamma will see it. The trouble is she feels weak, weak and empty. Rage has driven her through years of adversity and now it has gone into Gamma, leaving only a faint shadow behind.

That is what she is becoming, she realizes, a shadow. A watermark where once there was an ocean.

'This,' she croaks, 'is your sister, Gamma.'

The Seven

At the sound of her name, Gamma steps forward, bending down so that her lips can move close to Massassi's ear.

'Get up, creator,' she says, her voice as hard as the blade she carries. 'There is more to do.'

CHAPTER NINE

Vesper walks back and forth as she talks. The buck follows her, contrite.

Samael and Scout watch them, listening. They are packed and ready to go, only waiting on Neer's return before they make their move. They have been waiting for some time now.

'This was a mistake,' she says. 'I've made myself reliant on the First. Maybe we should have stayed on *The Commander's Rest.*'

'We could leave.'

'No, we won't get to the meeting place in time. There's still a lot to organize and even Genner can't do everything without me.'

'Do you want me to find out how long they'll be?'

Vesper grimaces. 'No, it will make us look weak, and Neer will only get cranky. You know how difficult she can be.'

'Yes. But she's fond of me.'

She stops walking, looks at Samael. 'She does a good job of hiding it!'

'Not to my eyes. The Malice would show you the same, I'm sure.'

'Yes but she's my friend. It feels wrong to use it on her.'

'She has no such compunctions. The Malice is as much a part of you as Neer's implanted eyes are of her. I don't see the difference.'

'The difference is me. I'm not Neer. I have to do what feels right. Besides, if the sword thinks there's a problem, it will tell me. And if it doesn't, I've got you.'

Samael nods and Scout's tail wags happily.

'On second thoughts, go and tell them to be ready to leave, we've waited long enough.'

Samael is not gone long. When he returns, Neer is with him.

'Well,' she says, 'the First needs to work on his small talk but I have to admit, he makes a good case.' At Vesper's worried expression, she tuts. 'Do I need to spell it out to you? I've been convinced to help.'

'You're coming with us?'

'Eventually. The First will take you where you need to go while the rest of it comes here to help with my travel arrangements. This body doesn't travel easily anymore and there's a lot to move, and if we're going to get it right there's a lot to do . . . but I think we'll be in time for your gathering.'

'That's good. Wonderland has its place at these talks as much as any of the other settlements.' She pauses. 'Neer, what kind of deal did you make with the First?'

Green eyes narrow. 'A private one.'

'You haven't given away too much, have you? It drives a hard bargain.'

Neer's body goes rigid and she grabs at the nearest wall,

155

shaking. It takes Vesper a few moments to realize she's laughing.

'Oh! Oh that's priceless!'

'What is?'

'You, trying to give me advice about being naive!' The laughter stops and Neer's eyes narrow again. 'You don't need to teach me about the world, girl. I've been on it a damn sight longer than you. As for me and the First, I'll just say that we have an agreement and it'll see us both happy.'

'I hope so.'

'Hope is for the weak and stupid. I don't need hope and nor should you. Now, you better get going. The First is waiting for you at the sky-ship.'

Vesper gives Neer a careful hug, making the older woman grunt in surprise. 'Just be careful, okay?'

'Don't worry about me. Worry about uniting the south and getting them ready for war. I haven't spent all these years preserving the Necroneer's art and keeping the survivors of this city alive, only to have some damn fool immortals come and tear it all down.'

With only two of the First's bodies making this leg of the journey, the sky-ship seems spacious. Neither Vesper nor Samael appreciate the difference as they are both stuffed into the cockpit, leaving the entirety of the hold for Scout and the buck to enjoy.

'We're nearly there,' explains Vesper, pointing into the distance. 'Crucible. I can't wait to see how it's changed since my last visit.'

'You are excited?' asks the First.

'Yes. This is where we're going to start really changing things.'

Muddy fields rush along beneath them, rich soil so tainted that plants explode from it overnight, full grown, only to die again by day's end.

Birds with brown bodies and orange wings flock down to steal seeds, unaware that they are taking on the indigestible: passengers that wait for a few hours before burrowing up into avian brains.

Beyond the fields is a valley, and in the valley is a huge dome, sitting like an eye in a socket. The top curves up above the valley, allowing those inside a view of the surrounding countryside. Silver struts form the skeleton of the dome, transparent plasglass revealing circular rings inside, each one a platform for visitors to stand on, each joined by walkways to a large stage deep within.

Figures crawl over the structure both inside and out, locking panels into place, connecting fittings, attaching doors.

The sky-ship makes a single pass over the dome and then comes down to land next to the valley.

Engines power down and a hatch opens, allowing Vesper to climb out. She sees someone is already running over. A slim man in black, a silver eye at his collar, his hair a sprouting bush of greying red. Her lifelong friend, her rock. At the sight of him, a little of her stress eases.

'Genner!' she shouts, waving.

The man stops and salutes. 'Vesper?'

'Yes! Who else were you expecting?'

The gun that had been quietly drawn is palmed and slipped away. 'The sky-ship, it isn't one of ours. I'd expected to see an infernal face, not yours.' He smiles. 'A nice surprise for once!'

She jumps down to join him. 'I've got more for you but you're not going to like it.'

'Understood.'

'But first, tell me how it's going here.'

Genner gestures back towards the dome. 'Construction of the main structure is nearly complete. We're watertight, airtight, and all of the section seals are active. There's a lot of work to do inside. Not on our sections, we could have the gel installed and shaped in half a day, but some of the other delegations have . . . requirements.'

'It's important that they feel comfortable here.'

'Comfort I understand, but carcasses? The leader of the Boneweavers wants dead animals in their section. Isn't that a bit much?'

Vesper shakes her head. 'No. This way we're saying that everyone is equally valued. If we furnish it like an imperial base, then it'll look like the Empire is running things. I want people to feel on equal footing.'

Genner's expression cools as Samael climbs from the sky-ship. It cools still further when Scout follows. 'I take it he isn't the surprise?'

'No.'

The smooth black helmet of the First rises from the hatch.

Genner nods. 'You did it then. You said you were going to but I never quite believed it.'

The First jumps to land lightly beside them. It looks at Genner. 'I know you.'

Genner looks back at the featurless visor only for a moment before turning away. 'I'm sorry, Vesper. I can't do this, not yet.'

Vesper watches him walk back towards the dome and bites her lip. 'That was bad timing,' she says to the First.

'He does not like me. He finds my presence troubling.'

158

'Of course he does! You held him prisoner and interrogated him!'

'That is one . . . possibility.'

She sighs. 'For now, just keep your distance, okay? I'll talk to him.'

'For now, I will comply with your wishes.'

'Good.'

Behind her, the buck hops out and begins sniffing at the local flora.

'What about me?' asks Samael.

She bites her lip again. 'Best that you stay here as well, until I've broken the news.'

He nods. 'Good luck.'

She walks away, steps slowing as she considers her approach. Genner has not gone far. He stands at the top of the valley, looking down at the dome and the crews suspended by cables at various points on its curve.

'As soon as I saw the sky-ship I suspected it was here,' he says, gaze still fixed below. 'You'd told me what you had in mind. It's not like it was unexpected.' He pauses. 'But when I saw the First again, actually saw it with my own eyes I . . . I found I wasn't ready. I submit myself to your judgement.'

Vesper shakes her head. 'Don't talk like that. I'm not angry with you. In fact, I wanted to apologize to you.'

'To me?'

'Yes, for putting you in an impossible position, and I don't mean with the First.'

He listens as she explains the situation with The Seven, that they are coming for her, to destroy her dream of a new world before it can begin, and that, if he stands with her, he will be branded a traitor to the Empire he loves. As she talks an eye opens slightly at her shoulder, regarding the man through a slit.

'It's okay,' he says before she can finish. 'I already know about The Seven.'

She gawps at him. 'You do?'

'I'd be a poor Lens if I didn't.' He stops a moment, choosing his words with care. 'I wish things could be different, I really do, but my place is here and I'll do my duty, no matter the cost.'

'Thank you,' she says, warm. 'I don't know if I could do this without you.'

Cheeks pale and he nods. 'You don't need me, Vesper, not any more. You've come a long way from the little girl I met on the hill all those years ago.'

Neither speak for a moment, a tension rising between them. Vesper is aware of how close he is, that it would be so easy to reach out and touch him. Meanwhile, an eye continues to stare, suspicious.

Eventually, Vesper clears her throat. 'I want you to know that I'm going to try and talk to The Seven when they get here. If there's any way to avoid bloodshed, I'll take it. That said, we need to be prepared for a fight. And for that I need a strategist. I need you.'

'It's hard to plan when we don't know what kind of army we'll have.'

'Do we know what kind of army we'll face?'

Genner nods. 'There's no sea access here so we can assume they'll offload vehicles and troops at the coast and travel overland the rest of the way. Alpha's palace will be with them so they'll have a base to launch artillery and maintain their sky-ships.

'If we create a good defensive position, I can see us holding against their army, and I know we have some sky-ships of our own to field against the Empire's. But if Alpha commits His palace to the fight, I don't see how we can hope to counter that. To be honest, your best chance is to scatter. They'd have to spend years hunting you down and might never find you at all.'

Vesper frowns. 'That isn't good enough. If we break here, they'll pick us off one by one. Our only hope is to stand together.'

'Do you think that's possible? I've seen the files, and most of these people are used to being in charge. Peace talks are one thing but when the time comes to fight, and it will, what makes you think they'll listen to you?'

'I'll worry about that. You worry about the sky palace.' He nods. 'I want options, Genner.'

He nods again, not meeting her eyes.

Vesper stands at the bottom of the valley, the dome at her back. Samael is at her right shoulder, the First at her left. The buck has taken up a dramatic pose halfway up the valley wall.

Entering the valley are a group of Usurperkin, half-breeds made massive by the Usurper's tainted touch. A mix of male and female, they run with abandon, like dogs let off the leash. Each one is nearly twice Vesper's size, each of their biceps a match for her head.

She leans closer to the First, keeping her voice low as the green-skinned giants approach. 'I thought the Usurperkin were getting smaller with each generation.'

'This is true. The Thousand Nails are the . . . exception. That is why I asked them to come.'

Many of the Usurperkin are armoured. Plating taken from vehicles, beaten into submission and fastened to their skin. Most carry mêlée weapons though a few have steel bows and one carries a harpoon gun ripped from the deck of a ship.

Their leader is not the largest of them but she is by no means small. A plate of black iron has been riveted to her forehead, sloping back from her blunt nose, as if her face were a ramp. Scars peek out from round the edges, hinting at ancient injuries.

She stabs twelve foot of pipe into the ground. Attached to the top is a flag, a simple sketch of a skull, green, with nails for teeth. 'We here,' she announces, gruff.

'Yes,' agrees Vesper. 'Welcome to Crucible. I'm Vesper and this—'

'You small,' interrupts the Usurperkin. 'I am Flat Head. Thought you'd be bigger.' She points at the First. 'We know that one. Respect.' She points at Samael. 'We know Handlers. Respect less but respect. Don't know you.'

Vesper puts on a big smile. 'That's the reason we're here, to talk and get to know each other. At Crucible we're all equal.'

Flat Head laughs and the others laugh with her, the sound echoing inside the valley. 'We not equal. And talking is slow. I want to know your arm.'

Vesper's smile falters. 'My arm?'

'Words easy. I want to feel the truth of your arm.' She flexes her fingers, making knuckles crack. 'Come. Let our arms meet.'

Vesper exchanges a look with the eye at her shoulder. It is not impressed. 'Can't we just talk?'

Flat Head's heavy brow furrows, making the plate cast a shadow over her eyes. 'Arms!'

'Right, yes . . . arms.' Vesper flexes her own fingers. They seem awfully delicate in comparison. She wonders whether it is better to face humiliation or to back out. A hopeful part of her wonders if this is just a request for a handshake but the sword twitches in its scabbard, suggesting otherwise.

Vesper takes a hesitant step forward and Flat Head lifts a hand towards her, waiting.

She takes another step, committed now, accepting that it will probably hurt a lot but that even bones will heal in time.

An eye twitches to her left in warning, and then the First is moving. A blur of shiny black, the infernal overtakes Vesper, and grabs Flat Head's outstretched hand. It pauses, giving the half-breed time to brace herself before slowly, casually, driving the giant to her knees.

'You know me. I am the First and I have an . . . accord with Vesper. Know that I am her arm and I am but one of them.'

Flat Head tries to push upwards, the great muscles in her thighs trembling with effort. Finally, she smiles. 'Good. Now you have our arms too. They're bigger.'

The First releases her and backs away behind Vesper who offers her hand to the Usurperkin.

Flat Head takes it and stands. 'We will follow you.'

'Thank you, but really I see us as equals, finding a way forward together.'

Flat Head squeezes her hand, surprisingly gently, then throws Vesper onto her shoulders, as easily as a cloak. Vesper's gasp is masked by the delighted roar of the Usurperkin.

'The Thousand Nails follow Vesper!'

Together they march towards the dome, Vesper's flush of embarrassment gradually evolving into a grin, delighted.

Vesper looks at the room she's been given, a small but functional space, currently devoid of furniture. She tries to decide what to put inside it, what would make it feel like hers. At the moment, a set of mutigel cubes have been squished together to make a bed, and her things are in a pile next to it. Hardly homely.

And yet, when she tries to think of home, none of the images in her mind quite fit. She remembers the house she grew up in, with its myriad flaws, characterful. She remembers her quarters in the Shining City, featureless. Both are lost to her now.

In any case, Vesper's mind tends towards the horizon, her fondest memories of the Shining City are when it was viewed from a distance, a glorious mystery. By contrast her fondest memories of her house were conjured when she was in peril on the other side of the world. As soon as she gets to either, the longing to travel starts again.

She moves to the outer wall and presses a hand to it. At her touch the plasglass clears, allowing a view of the top of the valley and a peek at the countryside beyond. It also allows a view of the buck, who is wandering along the top on business unknown.

Her hand stays flat on the plasglass as she leans into it, watching the buck's meanderings, thinking of other times and deeds.

A soft ping from the door interrupts her.

'Come in.'

The door slides open to admit Genner, who steps inside and salutes. 'Forgive the intrusion but there are things to discuss.'

She nods, suddenly envious of the buck's freedom. 'Go ahead.'

'Are you sure the Thousand Nails are under control?'

'Why? Have they done something?'

'Not yet but we have more delegations arriving any day and none of them are expecting the Thousand Nails to be here. We're totally reliant on your relationship with them until the Order of the Broken Blades arrives. If anything happens before then, we won't have the manpower to contain it.'

'They'll be fine. I'll handle them.' She tries not to think too hard about the casual way Flat Head has of throwing her about. 'Anything else?'

'We have another, bigger problem. Word has got out that The Seven are coming. While a few are preparing to fight, many people are fleeing. I've got reports of overloaded ships sailing south and hordes of people just packing up and going from settlements between here and the coast.'

'That's good isn't it? Didn't you say that the best way to survive was to scatter?'

Genner remains by the door, awkward. 'I said that was your best chance of survival. I'd be lying if I said it was theirs. It remains the best way of avoiding The Seven but there are lots of other ways to die outside of the protection of the cities.'

Vesper frowns. 'Why are you telling me this?'

'Some of them, a lot of them, are coming here. They're hoping you're going to give them sanctuary.'

'And they're right to hope,' she replies, immediate, 'make the arrangements.'

'At once. That is, if you're sure?'

She turns from the plasglass wall, pulling her hand away and letting the surface mist over. 'What is it, Genner? Something isn't right. You don't seem yourself.'

'I was worried you'd want to protect them all. But do you appreciate the scale of it? This place is big but it's not a city. You have multiple armed groups coming here that aren't used to working together, much less living together. It's already a volatile situation. If we add thousands of desperate and hungry people to the mix, we'll lose control. The war will be lost before it even starts.'

'We can't just turn them away . . .'

Genner's face is sympathetic. 'The world doesn't deserve you, Vesper.' Both of them blush and he pushes on swiftly, sadly. 'Sometimes in order to win, and for the greater good, we have to make tough decisions. Even if it means sacrificing those we love.'

Vesper's expression hardens with thoughts of the past. 'I understand that better than you will ever know. If it comes to it, if there is no other choice, I'll do what it takes to win. I'll be a monster if that's what it takes. Until then, we do what's right. Send out word that we'll provide sanctuary to those that need it. Coordinate with the First. Let's use those sky-ships for something other than fighting, and get them bringing in extra supplies. I'll talk to the Thousand Nails, have them escort travellers here and help transport heavy goods.'

'The Thousand Nails? They're little better than animals! They're as likely to slaughter people as help them.'

'No. They're proud. If they agree to do something, they'll do it well.' Her voice softens a little and she sighs. 'If this is going to work, all of the people here need to trust each other, and quickly. The only way I know to do that is by example.'

'Forgive me, but even with extra supplies and the resources we've stockpiled, you'll be cutting the amount of time we can hold out from months to weeks. And when supplies run low, our forces will turn on each other. You're handing victory to The Seven.'

'If it comes to that. I'm still hoping we won't have to fight.' She pauses, nearly says more, then shakes her head. 'You have your orders, Genner.'

He salutes again, smartly. 'Understood.'

For a few minutes she watches the space where he stood, churning words over in her head. A bad feeling nestles in her stomach, nearly pulling her over. She does not let it.

Doubts are tucked away to be dealt with later. She picks up the sword, straightens her shoulders and walks to the door.

CHAPTER TEN

The Vagrant shifts a little. His mouth works sloppily a couple of times before being consumed by a yawn. Amber eyes open without focusing. He blinks slowly, then a few times more, rapid.

He tries to stretch, but his wrists are held above his head, bound by straps, ankles fastened tight to the table that he lies on.

By straining he manages a little movement of the head. The room appears to be the same one as he went to sleep in. A second table, thin and metallic, with wheels on the end of each leg, is to his left, Jem strapped securely to it. The man is sound asleep.

He looks to the right, finds Reela has been left against the wall, unbound. He whistles at her, hopeful, but her features do not flicker.

Bonds are tested again, found more than up to the task. The table judders as he fights them, rocking from side to side, alarming.

At the sound of the door opening, he stops, the table rocking left, right, then left once more before settling.

Giblet lurches into the room and slaps Jem's face playfully. When there is no response, the half-breed leans over the Vagrant and brings back a webbed hand.

Amber eyes glare and the hand pauses.

Giblet begins to jump up and down making happy grunting noises until the walls fade to transparent and the tubes filled with orange liquid and old wrinkled bodies glide into view once more.

'Well done, Giblet,' says the man's voice from the speaker. 'Well done. Now settle down.'

A tune plays, simple, and Giblet's enthusiasm leaches away, the large body flopping immediately onto the floor. Two more repetitions and he is sound asleep.

'Congratulations,' says the speaker. 'You're the first to wake up and this means you're the first to be interrogated. I don't know if you recall but I mentioned earlier that we would have questions and that you would be answering them.' There is a brief crackle. 'This is what's going to happen now. If we're happy with your answers then there's nothing to worry about. Nothing to worry about at all. Are you ready?' He doesn't wait to see if the Vagrant will answer, his voice cheery. 'Good! Then let's begin.'

The Vagrant glances around again. He sees the bonding gun that Jem had scavenged in the corner, along with Delta's sword. By stretching the tie on his wrist to its limit, he is able to get his fingers to the wall.

'Something easy to start with: what is your name?'

The Vagrant pushes. Wheels turn easily on the polished floor and the table drifts towards the opposite corner where the weapons are. There is a moment of hope before momentum trails off, stranding the table in the middle of the room.

'You know, my colleagues didn't want to bother talking to you at all. You're clearly not a rescue party from the Empire, they said. Best to use you as breeding tissue, they said. But I said no. Because that would hardly be civilized. Surely you'd rather answer a few simple questions than be turned into gestation tubes for Giblet's descendants?'

The Vagrant stretches out his foot, trying to reach Jem's table but the toe of his boot is held in the empty air, the ties too tight for his plans.

'I'm not sure what you're hoping to achieve but it won't work. Now tell me: Who are you? Why are you really here?'

The Vagrant sighs, closes his eyes.

'Perhaps you'll change your mind, perhaps you won't. It doesn't matter. Your colleague seemed a lot more forthcoming. He can answer my questions instead. We don't need you. Well, Giblet does.' The speaker stutters with a suppressed giggle. 'But perhaps I'm mistaken. Yes! I see it now. You've become fond of him and you wish to develop your relationship. To become, what's the word? Intimate. So be it.'

A tune plays and the half-breed becomes alert.

Locking his arms and legs, the Vagrant begins rocking the table again, desperate.

'Giblet,' says the old man, his voice sing-song. 'Wake up Giblet! It's time for you to become a daddy.'

A sky-ship drops from the clouds, phasing out of cloak as it does so. Reflective shielding fades, revealing a sleek metallic body, its wings adorned with the badge of the Empire of the

170

Winged Eye. Already, they are rotating, engines moving from horizontal to vertical, allowing the craft to descend directly onto Ferrous.

Coming to a stop twenty feet above the tower, the sky-ship opens a hatch, allowing armoured figures to jump out. Each one is linked to the ship by a cable that unravels behind them, measured, controlling their fall.

Two lieutenants lead the group. The first to land secures the tower's entrance, the second makes her way onto the sea-shuttle that is docked alongside. As more soldiers arrive, the first lieutenant enters the tower and they begin streaming in behind him. Only two soldiers peel off to join the one on the boat.

While their colleagues make their way deeper into Ferrous, the remaining lieutenant and her two soldiers check the sea-shuttle for stowaways, carefully avoiding the prone form of Delta on the deck.

The sea-shuttle is small and the search quickly completed. 'There's no one else on board, ma'am,' reports one of the soldiers. 'What are your orders regarding . . .?' He stops, unsure of the proper form of address in the circumstances. The point of his rifle begins to drift in Delta's direction, to signal his meaning but he snaps it back into place.

'Report that She is here, and that I'm investigating Her situation. Update in five.'

'Yes, ma'am.'

'And watch my back, I don't like it here.'

'Yes, ma'am.'

The lieutenant sees that someone has tried to hide Delta under a dirty old coat. The attempt is laughable as it fails to cover legs, head or the tops of Delta's shoulders. Then it occurs to her that the attempt might not be to hide the body

171

completely but to cover up an injury or other blasphemy. She moves closer, wary of any reaction, but none comes. Though Delta's eyes are open, they do not respond to any outside stimuli, staring straight up.

She finds those eyes mesmerizing, like looking into the sky of another world.

When one of her soldiers speaks, the lieutenant jumps.

'Ma'am? Command wants to know if Her sword is here.'

'Negative. I repeat: Delta's sword is not here.'

She admonishes herself for allowing herself to become distracted and pulls the coat away, tossing it into a corner.

Delta blinks, her eyes focusing on the movement. Both the lieutenant and the immortal find themselves watching the coat as it lands in a crumpled heap. Then, slowly, magnetically, they turn back to face each other.

It is one thing to watch a storm at a remove, through the protection of a screen, another to stand naked before it.

For a moment, the lieutenant experiences an instant of total openness, as if all of her thoughts were laid out, cards on a table, carefully labelled.

After that, all she feels is Delta's displeasure.

After that, nothing.

The table falls over with a clang, the impact jarring through the Vagrant's body. He is now agonizingly close to Delta's sword but arms remain tied, unable to cross the short distance to the hilt.

However the noise has woken the blade, wings parting to allow a wary eye to peek out.

The Vagrant catches its eye with his own, a silent plea for help.

Guiltily, it looks away, closing again.

Lips curl, disbelieving, exasperated, before parting in surprise as a rounded shadow falls over them.

Wet palms slap against the sides of the table, a soft grunt sounding as the half-breed lifts it off the floor.

Delta's sword vanishes from sight, replaced by a wall, a ceiling, then the other wall and, briefly, Reela's face. The girl is awake! Then he is moving the other way, the table set right and the horizon is suddenly full of Giblet.

The half-breed is excited, something akin to sweat oozing milkily from his pores. Thick fingers struggle to find the fastenings on the Vagrant's chest plate and, when they do, they struggle to work them.

The Vagrant struggles too but his efforts do little to weaken the bonds.

'Well,' says the man through the speaker. 'If you'll excuse me, we have more unexpected guests that need attending to. I'll come back when this is over. It's Giblet's first time so he won't be gentle. If it's any consolation, you're going to serve as such a potent example to your companions, I'm sure they'll answer my questions without hesitation.'

As the speaker cuts off, Giblet gives a grunt of delight, lifting the chest plate away from the Vagrant's shoulders. Another tug and he is able to toss it over his shoulder, nonchalant.

Amber eyes widen as they notice the unusual bulge in Giblet's stomach. Folds of flab peel apart, revealing a translucent tentacle.

The Vagrant struggles harder, threatening to topple the table until Giblet puts his weight on it, straddling the smaller man. As the Vagrant catches his breath, Giblet rips the fabric away from his chest, exposing skin.

The tentacle swells at the sight, its tip hardening into a ridged point. Tiny blobs swirl inside it, like shoals of fish, barely visible to the naked eye.

The Vagrant turns his head away.

Giblet pulls himself further up the table, positioning his tentacle directly over the Vagrant's sternum. The pitch of his excitement changes, his whole body tensing.

The Vagrant takes a breath, closes his eyes, and begins to hum. It is a simple tune, and the sound of it freezes Giblet in place.

Taking another breath, the Vagrant hums the tune again, and again, until the tentacle retracts back into Giblet's belly and his head droops forward. The weight of it brings the body after, until Giblet flops onto the Vagrant, silencing, squeezing the air from his lungs.

Precious seconds pass as his mouth opens and closes, futile. Veins bulge at temples and then, just as vision begins to blur, Reela's face appears.

The Vagrant tries to mouth something but the girl stops him, putting a finger to her lips.

She releases his right arm from the straps, then his left, and together, they attempt to roll Giblet onto the floor. Both man and girl strain until the cords stand out on their necks, tilting the blubbery form until gravity takes over. The half-breed lands with a soft squelch but doesn't wake up.

Reela goes to the other end of the table and begins to untie ankles while the Vagrant wheezes, working air into his body and blood into his extremities.

They quickly release Jem, who remains asleep, blissful, and gather their things. The Vagrant ties the tattered remains of his top together and gets Reela to help him reattach his chest plate.

Abruptly, the speaker switches back on, bringing a sentence half started to their ears. '. . . Of course, as loyal servants of the Winged Eye we knew there was something wrong with them and kept them here until such time as we could report to the proper authorities . . .'

'Show us,' demands a second voice.

The man's reply betrays a little too much dread. 'Show you? Well, this may not be the best time to . . . I mean, perhaps they should be cleaned up first?' Then it switches to resignation. 'Of course, of course, at once. Don't say I didn't warn you.'

The wall's colour fades, revealing the row of cylinders, including the three occupied ones. Soldiers in Empire uniform also stand in the room. A lieutenant nods as he takes in the contents on the Vagrant's side of the wall. 'Sighting confirmed, command. I repeat, sighting confirmed.'

'Just as I promised,' says the man in the cylinder, relieved.

'Wait,' demands the lieutenant. 'By the Eye, what is that?' He points and all eyes go to the slumbering half-breed.

'Oh, him? That's just Giblet. He's a distant relative. A great, great, great, grand cousin or some such.'

The lieutenant doesn't answer, just turns to the cylinders and slowly raises his rifle. Without needing to be commanded, the soldiers copy the gesture.

'Don't shoot!' begs the floating figure. 'We are loyal to the Empire!' When his words fall flat he reaches for a button on the inside of the cylinder, pressing it as the soldiers squeeze the triggers of their guns.

Bullets spray in a wide arc, punching holes through plas-glass and the bodies within. They writhe artfully, dancing their way to death. Orange gel spurts rudely from holes, forming lumpy puddles on the floor.

A new tune begins to play, different from before and Giblet wakes with a snarl.

Leaping to his feet, the half-breed runs through the rapidly opening door, making a strange keening sound. Distantly that sound is echoed, once, and again, from an assortment of nooks within Ferrous' web of walkways.

The Vagrant blinks, looking from the fresh corpses beyond the wall, to the soldiers, to the space where Giblet was. He grabs Delta's sword from the floor and begins to push Jem's table towards the exit. On instinct, Reela hops onto one end, sandwiched between the Vagrant and the table, her feet braced on the table's legs.

'Fire. Fire at will,' commands the lieutenant.

Rifles flash, peppering the wall. At each impact a small circle of the wall mists, as if the soldiers were decorators, obscuring themselves with a thousand tiny pellets of paint.

The Vagrant doesn't wait to see if the wall will hold.

Through corridors he goes, running blind in the poor light. Uneven floors make the table bounce in his hands, Jem's head bounce on the table, and Reela's teeth clatter.

Ahead, he sees light and another half-breed run from left to right past the end of the corridor. Not Giblet but not unlike him. The keening is louder now, the various makers of the noise growing in number, gathering together.

Pausing, the Vagrant looks at unfamiliar surroundings, squinting, hopeless.

Reela leans over the table and rummages in Jem's pocket,

producing the old battered scope. She switches it on so that light shines from under her chin, ghoulish.

The Vagrant nods, approving.

She nods back, then shines it about, the light bouncing from place to place, before settling on a ridged tunnel.

The Vagrant frowns at it while Reela nods repeatedly.

A change in the keening prompts the Vagrant into action. It is moving now, a mass of sound accompanied by the thudding of many webbed feet.

The Vagrant moves in the opposite direction.

Reela's use of the torch is imperious, picking their route without need to consult others. There is no time to argue, the Vagrant struggling to keep the table from tipping over as he runs.

Somewhere behind them the half-breeds make contact with the soldiers and there comes the sound of gunfire, sporadic, and hasty orders, screams, and through it all, that strange gurgling wail.

The Vagrant runs that little bit faster.

It is hard to tell if they are going the right way or not. The route has only been done once, in the opposite direction, mostly in the dark. The Vagrant glances worriedly down every passage they don't take but always follows the light from the scope.

Incredibly, they pass through a doorway into a lit area of the base. It is familiar. The Vagrant pauses to catch his breath and shakes his head, amazed.

Reela gives him a self-satisfied smile and he ruffles her hair.

Briefly encouraged, they round the final corner, arriving at the base of the tower and the way back to the surface.

Two soldiers await them.

For a beat, both soldiers and Vagrant freeze.

Whatever the soldiers have been expecting to come, it is not the Vagrant pushing a table.

As the two look at each other, the Vagrant launches the table forward, scooping Reela from the back one-handed and running after it.

The soldiers ready their guns.

The Vagrant raises Delta's sword, head-butting the cross-piece, so that the eye snaps open. He takes breath.

The soldiers fire.

The Vagrant sings.

And Delta's sword channels the note, shaking the air ahead of them. The bullets are knocked off course by the sound, parting from the Vagrant to drive harmlessly into the sides of the corridor.

One soldier takes aim again while the other reaches for a knife. So intent are they on their target that neither attend to the table as it slams into them.

The Vagrant slams into them moments after, a pommel kissing two skulls in quick succession, and then he is moving past, the bodies left to groan in his wake.

Reela is swung into the lift, Jem hauled off the table and dumped next to her.

A single glare is all it takes for the sword to sing, setting the lift into action.

As the doors close, there is a faraway sound of a lone gun firing and firing, until it becomes the click-click-click of an empty cartridge, and then it too is gone.

Swiftly it is smothered by a score of voices, keening.

The lift begins its ascent.

*   *   *

Jem coughs as he wakes up. He is quickly alert, taking in the scant details of the empty room. The Vagrant nods to him, Reela does the same. Though things appear still, he feels the sensation of movement in his belly, and knows they are going up.

With no immediate threat presenting itself, the aches and pains of his body come forward, shy at first but growing in confidence. 'I feel terrible,' he announces, carefully probing the new lump on the back of his head. 'What happened?'

Two faces look at him. One raises an eyebrow, the other contorts with effort before raising both.

'Well, at least they let us go. There was something really wrong with those people . . . and that Giblet,' he shakes his head. 'Urgh.'

The sensation of movement fades and the doors slide open. The sea-shuttle remains connected to the tower and waves still sweep from horizon to horizon.

Hovering above is a sky-ship, cables dangling from its underside like a sparse skirt.

The Vagrant gives it a wary glance and moves to the door.

'You're not going out there!' exclaims Jem. 'You're not though, are you?'

As the Vagrant edges out, Delta's sword raised and ready, Jem pauses to consider his options. Reela doesn't. She is already moving to the doorway, following in the Vagrant's footsteps.

He races after her, grabbing her hand and forcing her to take cover by the sea-shuttle's edge.

Ahead of him, the Vagrant drops down onto deck. Jem watches, tense, waiting for a reaction from the sky-ship. None comes.

The Vagrant crouches down, examining something.

Jem feels his hand being tugged, and after a last worried glance upwards, allows himself to be led onto the sea-shuttle.

Delta remains where she was left, the Vagrant's coat covering her like a blanket. Around her are three soldiers of the Empire of the Winged Eye spaced out on the deck, each curled up tight in a ball. The Vagrant is crouched by one of them, watching a foot twitch, spasmodic.

As Jem gets closer, the Vagrant looks up, puts a finger to his lips, then moves to the next one. Each is alive, their bodies clenched tight and unhappy.

'Are they . . . dreaming?' he whispers.

The sight is so strange that he does not notice Reela leaning down or her little hand prodding at one of the soldiers until it is too late.

Instantly, the soldier jerks upwards, grabbing the girl by her shoulders, nearly pulling her over. 'I'm sorry!' he shouts, the voice distorted through his helmet. 'We didn't know!' Fingers press tightly into Reela's skin, and she hisses in pain.

'Stop it,' Jem urges, 'you're hurting her!'

Unaware of the Vagrant suddenly standing behind him, the soldier turns his head to Jem. 'You have to for—'

The Vagrant's arm loops around the soldier's neck and pulls tight, making hands open in surprise, releasing Reela. The Vagrant walks backwards, dragging the soldier clear before twisting sharply, sending the other man to the floor.

There is no resistance, no use of combat skills. The soldier simply curls up where he has fallen, defeated.

'What's going on?' asks Jem.

The soldier doesn't answer.

180

The Vagrant shrugs, looks at Delta's sword. Its eye is fixed on Delta, suspicious.

One of the others, a lieutenant, has moved to a kneeling position. 'Please,' she whispers. 'I can't take this any longer. In the name of the Winged Eye: task us, use us, forgive us.'

Jem and the Vagrant exchange a look.

'Wait,' begins Jem. 'You're offering to help us?'

'Yes. I'll do anything, anything! Please.'

'But why?'

The lieutenant's gaze starts to slide towards Delta but with an effort of will she fixes it to the floor. 'Because She is displeased with us and we need to make it better. Just tell us what to do and we'll do it.'

'Can you pilot that sky-ship?'

'Yes.'

He leans in to the Vagrant, lowers his voice. 'Do we trust her?'

The Vagrant holds out Delta's sword, letting the blade pass over the kneeling lieutenant, once, twice. He frowns, then nods. Reaching down he pulls her to her feet with his free hand.

'What are your orders?'

He points up.

She goes to the edge of the sea-shuttle and one of the cables is suddenly alert, swinging towards her, enthusiastic. The end of the cable curves about her middle, locking into place on the back of her belt and several points along the spine of her back plate.

The Vagrant goes with her to the rail and tries to catch one of the other cables. They sway on the edge of his reach, taunting.

'I can take you,' says the lieutenant.

With reluctance the Vagrant goes to her. She puts her arms round him. 'Hold on.'

The Vagrant complies.

'What are we supposed to do?' asks Jem.

The Vagrant gives a slight shrug as the cable goes tight, whisking him and the lieutenant upwards at speed.

Reela watches them, her head tilting up and up, her jaw slack. As the sky-ship swallows them, her hands begin to wave about her head, venting excitement in all directions.

Jem reaches for the bonding gun, finds it isn't there. Desperate, he picks up one of the paddles, flicking it to full extension and then places himself between the two remaining soldiers, the paddle raised above his head. His eyes are constantly moving, from one twitching body to another, to Reela, who continues to stare at the sky-ship, her face a stretched mask of delight.

The cable pulls them directly into the open hatch, swinging the Vagrant and the lieutenant into the hold.

Most of the soldiers have gone down into Ferrous or onto the sea-shuttle but not all. Four remain, a captain, two pilots and a comms officer. Of these, only one still lives.

The eye in Delta's sword closes, unwilling to see any more. The Vagrant has no such luxury. Stepping away from the lieutenant, he moves to each body in turn. There is no sign of any struggle, and with two of the bodies, no sign of any wounds. One of the pilots has died in her chair, the captain seems to have expired where he stood. By contrast, the comms officer was killed by a shot to the head. The Vagrant looks at the pistol in the comms officer's hand, his frown deepening.

Though the co-pilot survives, he shakes in his seat, only held in place by straps, trapped in some nightmare that can only be guessed at.

Together, the lieutenant and the Vagrant drag the bodies to the hatch, letting first the sky, then the sea take them. Each time, they wait for the solemn splash before launching the next one.

The rest of the sky-ship is checked. It appears undamaged, save for the communications array, which has been shot several times with a pistol.

Gentle attempts to wake the co-pilot fail, so the Vagrant removes the man's helmet. Beneath it is a sweaty face, eyes screwed shut but still moving beneath the lids. The Vagrant taps his cheek, shakes his shoulder, even flicks a little water at him but the man does not stir.

After some silent consideration, the Vagrant replaces the helmet.

He walks back to the hatch, points down to the sea-shuttle. In moments he and the lieutenant are being lowered by the cable at considerable speed.

Reela applauds their arrival.

'At last!' exclaims Jem.

Amber eyes linger on one of the soldiers who is more still than the other, a paddle-shaped dent in his helmet.

'It's okay,' says Jem. 'There was some trouble but I handled it.' He glances up at the sky-ship. 'Can it fly?'

The Vagrant nods.

'And she can fly it?'

'Yes,' replies the lieutenant.

'But?'

'But we have no comms and no co-pilot.'

183

'Do we need one?'

'No.'

'But?'

'No,' repeats the lieutenant. 'We don't need one.'

'Then let's go.'

The Vagrant points to the motionless form of Delta.

'Maybe,' Jem says, lowering his voice, 'we should leave her here.'

The Vagrant shakes his head.

'Do you think, with enough cables, we could lift her up there?'

The Vagrant stares at them for a while.

'I don't know how we'd attach them,' says Jem. 'I mean, how you would attach them but I think it's possible.'

The Vagrant holds up a hand. When he turns to face Jem, he seems purposeful, a slight smile threatening on one side of his face.

'What is it? Have you had an idea?'

The Vagrant doesn't answer, putting down Delta's sword and relieving Jem of his paddle. He moves to the rail, leaning out as far as he can, and uses the end of the paddle to hook one of the cables, drawing it to his side. After passing the cable to Jem he leans out again, fishing for another.

Gradually, more and more cables find their way into Jem's hands. When he can hold no more, the lieutenant is waved forward. She comes without question, though both she and Jem are obviously curious.

Reela waits patiently alongside them, arms open and is rewarded with a single cable end. Delighted, she wiggles it, making small ripples, like a snake, dancing.

The Seven

When all of the cables save the one attached to the lieutenant have been gathered, the Vagrant nods to himself, takes one from Jem, and sets to work.

CHAPTER ELEVEN

To the north of the valley, Vesper's people labour. Trenches are dug, and holes punched into the soft earth. From above it would resemble writing gone wrong, wavy lines divorced from their punctuation.

She knows that such measures will not stop The Seven's army but hopes it will slow them down, give her a chance to take action. She also knows the importance of giving people things to do.

Though it raises many eyebrows, the Thousand Nails have joined in the digging. They did not ask if they were needed nor even if their presence was desired. No one can question their enthusiasm however and, so far, the two groups remain civil to each other, both seeking to prove themselves the more effective. For the moment, competition motivates, channelling the mutual sense of superiority into more productive endeavours.

Vesper leaves them to it, going down into the valley itself. Samael and the First go with her.

The delegation from Slake travel slowly, pushing carts, beasts and backs laden with possessions, parts, tools and trinkets.

At the front and sides of the procession are soldiers in junkyard armour. They stand several feet above the others, mounted on stilts powered by spring and steam. In their hands they carry shrapnel guns tipped with long knives.

A man and a woman lead them. The woman has short hair, gaudy red to match her painted lips. Her jacket, top and trousers fit perfectly, a contrast to the ragged bunch behind her. Though old, she does not need the cane she carries. It is a copper plated vanity, a badge of power.

The man wears clothes designed to show off his ageing body. His skirt and top are full of slits, revealing glimpses of thigh and armpit, and machinery where his abdomen should be. There is no hair to dye on his head but lips shine equally red. His cane is iron plated rather than copper, he does not need it either.

Both bow, the motion slight, bordering on respectful.

'Gorad,' says the man, pointing to his companion.

Gorad reciprocates, gesturing to the man, 'Gut-pumper.'

'Hello,' says Vesper, 'and welcome to Crucible.'

The two place their canes on the ground and lean on them, studying Vesper. 'Gut-pumper has a question,' says Gorad.

'More of a thought really,' adds Gut-pumper.

'Yes, more of a thought. You see, he was wondering about the way things are going. You've been wanting us to come here for a long time.'

Gut-pumper nods. 'Years.'

'Yes, years. And now, all of a sudden, we have to come to here, you know, for these talks.'

'More than that though.'

'Quite,' Gorad agrees. 'Now we have to commit even before the negotiations start. No choice is there? Not with The Seven on the move.'

Vesper spreads her hands. 'I'm sorry.'

'Thing is . . .' continues Gorad.

'Yes,' says Gut-pumper, 'my thought is . . .'

'His thought is,' cuts in Gorad, 'that it's very interesting timing. No activity and then all of a sudden, they turn on you and us all at once. Very interesting.'

'Convenient,' Gut-pumper adds.

An eye opens at Vesper's shoulder, irritated. 'Are you seriously suggesting that I'm trying to trick you into negotiations?'

'Gut-pumper isn't suggesting anything. He's just thinking how odd it is that you, the great Bearer of Gamma's sword, the hero of the Empire, is being attacked by The Seven, especially when you've got one of them on your back.'

Vesper thinks for a moment. 'I understand. That's why Crucible exists actually. It's a place where we can get to know each other properly and shed these misconceptions. I'm sure that now we're here, face to face, we'll be able to see the truth in each other.'

'I'm sure we will,' agrees Gorad.

'My people will show you to your quarters and the areas marked for your followers to camp. But before you go, I have a thought of my own.'

Gorad and Gut-pumper both pause. 'Oh?'

'I've not been to Slake, but I've heard it's a big place with a population in the tens of thousands. So I can't help but think that your group seems small.'

'Ah,' says Gorad. 'Well, that's the thing with large numbers, they're hard to manage.'

'Complex,' adds Gut-pumper.

'We can't force people to come with us. And we can't force them to stay either. Not everyone is convinced about this threat of The Seven coming. Even we have our doubts as you know.'

An eye narrows at Vesper's shoulder. 'Yes. Well, I'm sure you'll want to get settled in.'

Scout grumbles to himself as the delegation passes, Samael shakes his head.

'I know,' says Vesper, 'I don't trust them either.'

The First watches the rows and rows of people passing. 'I see little loyalty here. You could remove them and put more . . . agreeable individuals in charge.'

'No we can't,' says Vesper, firm. 'If I do that, I undermine this process before it starts. Half the delegations would turn round and go home and the other half would be waiting in fear.'

'It is your choice, but I would suggest a little disruption now will make things much easier in the long term.'

Vesper folds her arms. 'I'm not here to make this easy. I'm here to do this right, to build something that will last. If we start this with bloodshed, it will end that way.'

'Very well, though I remain curious as to the value you place on this morality. How many will have to die before you change your mind?'

'Let's hope we never find out the answer to that question.'

The buck pays little attention to the bedraggled humans and half-breeds trudging along the bottom of the valley. He is much higher than them, safe at the top of his sloping kingdom.

Grass is abundant here, along with all manner of things nestling in the sloping earth and rock. The buck is content to spend his days exploring, finding delicacies at all manner of strange angles.

But something is not quite right.

The buck pauses in his chewing, listens. There is no sound but the feeling persists until the buck straightens and looks up.

The valley remains unchanged but his gaze is drawn by instinct until he is looking up at the top of the dome. As the source of the distraction is revealed, his tongue flops out in surprise.

Another goat is there, a doe, brown and white, with mismatched horns, one straight, the other crooked. Her beard is crooked too but the buck finds his dark eyes drawn to it. However, the doe turns from his stare, coy.

The buck watches for a moment, then resumes eating, assuming a nonchalant air, until the feeling of being watched returns.

Eagerly, he looks up but the doe has already turned away. They repeat this ritual several times, the buck's chewing becoming increasingly drawn out.

While her attention is elsewhere, the buck dips his head between his legs, dousing his beard in his own urine. Prepared, musky, he waits for her.

And waits.

And then, at last, the doe is not looking away. She is staring right at him.

Joy turns quickly to panic. Now the buck looks away,

looks for any kind of inspiration. Spotting some particularly long grass, the buck rips off the biggest clump he can manage, so successful that his lips cannot touch around it. Slowly, certain that she can see, the buck lifts his head in a triumphant display.

But the doe is no longer there. She has vanished without trace, like a dream upon the dawn.

Grass falls from his mouth, forgotten, and for some time after the valley is filled with anguished bleating.

As the days pass, more delegations come. Next are the people of Red Rails, more than three quarters of which are ratbred. They are led by their self-proclaimed prince, Savmir, who has a list of requirements, dietary, decorative, and diplomatic.

After that are the warriors of West Rift. Survivors of a nameless plague, they are so badly scarred, and so carefully wrapped in cloth and steel, that it is impossible to tell which are tainted and which are not.

Vesper greets them all equally, keeping her smile in place and the sword in its sheath despite what sometimes seems to be the best efforts of those she seeks to help.

However, when the news comes that a group from Verdigris have arrived, all frustrations are replaced with excited nerves.

Vesper appears early to meet them, forcing her people to wait with her. Rain pours from a dark sky, making rivers in Vesper's hair and miniature lakes at her feet.

At Vesper's request, the First is not present but Samael and Genner are there, enduring the elements alongside her. Genner's training forbids complaint and Samael has little connection to his body, leaving Scout to grumble for all of them.

As soon as Tough Call comes into view – one-armed,

tattoed, face set against the wind – Vesper breaks into a run, throwing her arms around the older woman.

Verdigris' leader seems bemused by the display of affection. She returns the embrace firmly, if a little more restrained.

'You came!' says Vesper, delighted.

'Said I would.'

'You did but that was when it was just for talks.'

'Well, difference between talks and fights isn't much in my experience. Besides,' she adds dryly, 'we'd have brought the guns anyway.'

Vesper looks at the weapons they carry. Lances and launchers of elegant silver, made in the Empire of the Winged Eye's earliest days. At her shoulder, the sword laments. Vesper brings a comforting hand to its hilt. 'These were meant to protect people, not kill them.'

'I reckon we count as people too.'

'Oh yes, of course, I didn't mean . . .'

Tough Call shrugs off any offence, waving her fellows forward. Vesper is re-introduced to some of Veridgris' senior figures. She tries to hide her surprise at how much Marshall Max and Marshall Maxi have aged. Time has worked quickly on the Usurperkin twins, cycling them from birth to their prime, towards their death beds in a third of an untainted human's span. Hair spikes are almost completely yellow now, straw-brittle, and green skin is mottling, going white in places. However age brings its advantages too, curbing legendary tempers and, for now at least, their muscles remain firm, their strength barely diminished.

Doctor Grains approaches next, his white jacket adorned with a simple symbol of the Winged Eye. He kneels before Vesper and she smiles at him, awkward.

He does not see, his head down, reverent. 'May the Winged Eye watch over us, measure us, judge us.'

'I'm hoping we'll be able to watch over each other.'

Doctor Grains nods. 'Yes. I'm sure that together, we'll be able to do what's right.'

'And for the right price, yes?' adds a new voice. It belongs to a large man, dripping in wealth and self-satisfaction, sat atop a waggon that is just pulling up.

Doctor Grains glares at the newcomer. 'Not everything is about coin, Ezze.'

'Ah, but there are many kinds of coin, my friend. We are all to be trading here, selling one thing or another. Do not look down on Ezze because he has a fondness for the physical.'

'Alright,' cuts in Tough Call, 'I'm sure Vesper's got better things to do than listen to you two bicker.'

'Ezze could not agree more, great leader,' replies the merchant, his smile generous. 'We should embrace the spirit of friendship and the mutual winning, hold it to our bosom, yes? And this is why I wish to speak to our great and young and kind Vesper, to make her an important, time sensitive offer.' He turns his smile on Vesper, pats the seat next to him. 'Perhaps you would wish to be hopping up here? Or would you prefer a more private setting, away from the wagging of tongues?'

Vesper holds up her hands. 'I'd love to talk to you Ezze, to all of you.' She makes sure to acknowledge Doctor Grains as she speaks. 'But first I'd like the chance to speak to Tough Call, alone. The rest of you should make yourselves welcome here. We'll speak soon I promise.'

Max and Maxi wait for Tough Call's subtle signal, then grunt appreciation, leading the rest of the group into Crucible.

Doctor Grains pauses as he passes Vesper. 'Forgive my boldness, but if I could speak to you at your earliest convenience, it would be appreciated.'

'Of course.'

Ezze's waggon rolls by shortly after. 'And don't forget to come to Ezze. To win, first you must be in!'

Vesper waits for Tough Call at the top of the valley, watching as the rest of Verdigris' delegation trudges into Crucible. Her attention is briefly taken from greater worries by a goat she hasn't seen before. 'Oh, hello there,' she says.

The doe watches her from a distance, cautious.

Without thought, Vesper reaches into her bag and pulls out a pink-skinned piece of fruit. 'You want some?' she asks.

The doe takes a few steps forward, then stops, uncertain.

'It's okay, I'm not going to hurt you. My name is Vesper and this is my place but you're very welcome to stay.' Kneeling down, she peels a strip off the fruit's outer skin and puts it on the ground, backing away. With each step, the doe advances, maintaining proximity.

On the other side of the valley, the buck stretches his neck, straining for a better view.

A few more paces and the doe works up the courage to take the peel, watching Vesper carefully as she picks it up.

'There you go! It's good isn't it?' She takes a bite of the fruit herself and for a while the two chew in companionable silence.

With an excited shriek, the buck plunges down the far side of the valley.

Not long after, Tough Call arrives. 'This is quite an operation you've got here.'

'Thank you,' says Vesper.

'Care to talk me through it?'

They walk along the valley, Vesper pointing out the newly dug trenches and sinkholes, then moving on to the bunkers being built by Slake's engineers. She talks about the army already massing, her own people, the Thousand Nails, the units from Slake and Red Rails and West Rift. She adds that the First has nomads making their way from the coast, that they have their own sky-ships, and that her knights are travelling with them. When she is done, she glances at Tough Call, inviting comment, desiring approval.

'Like I said, quite the operation. We've got Usurperkin of our own. Most of them are third generation. Not as big as your Thousand Nails but not as wild either. And we're bringing the big guns to the table.'

'I know,' replies Vesper, 'and I'm grateful. But what I really want is your expertise.'

'Go on.'

'Can I speak to you honestly? I know that you're here as Verdigris' leader first but you've always been a good friend to me. I feel like I need you now more than ever.'

Tough Call smiles. 'Reckon I can be here for you as both.'

'Good. Because you've been leading a city of mixed groups for a long time, successfully too. How do you do that?'

'There's not much to it. I keep a few simple rules. Real few and real simple. If I can give folk what they want, I do it every time, but I make sure they know I'm giving it and

195

what I expect back. I don't play favourites. Things like our talk will always be noticed so if you haven't been having private chats with the others, it's time to start.'

Vesper blushes and nods.

'Don't promise anything unless you have to and always deliver on your promises unless it kills you. And don't take shit from anyone, especially people like me.'

For a moment Vesper blinks, surprised, then she bursts out laughing.

'You know, we nearly didn't come here. Grains and his believers feel a lot like The Seven do when it comes to anyone with the taint, and Ezze suggested we wait until after the battle before pitching up.'

'But you came anyway, why?'

'Because times have been hard, they've made me hard too. Sure, I'm holding Verdigris together and that's no small thing, but you? You're trying to make something new, something better. Seems like times have made you shine and if we're going to have any kind of future, I reckon you're our best shot.'

'Thank you. Most of the time it just feels impossible.'

'Yep. Don't expect that to change anytime soon. And don't expect anyone to thank you either. And you better know, whatever seeds you plant are only going to be seeds in your lifetime. We're doing this for our grandchildren's children. They're the ones that are going to benefit, not us.'

Vesper sags. 'My daughter was in the Shining City. I have no idea if she's still alive.'

'That's tough to bear but you can't let it own you.' Tough Call sweeps her one arm over the various groups working. 'These are all your children now. And it's on you to keep them safe, and teach them not to be shits to one another.'

The two women talk until duty drags them back to Crucible. As they are descending, the buck leaps onto the top of the valley. He scampers around, looking left, then right, but the doe is long gone. Dark eyes shimmer with dismay, eventually alighting on Tough Call and Vesper's backs, narrowing, blaming.

Doctor Grains smooths the Skyn along the side of Vesper's palm, glancing up at her as she winces. 'Don't worry, the pain meds will take effect any moment now.'

'Thank you,' replies Vesper. 'I feel a bit silly asking you to do this.'

'It's really nothing. You saved my life, this is the least I can do. Besides, I'm always keen to expand my knowledge and I've never treated a goat bite before.'

She shakes her head. 'I don't know what's got into him, lately. He's usually so gentle. Anyway, you said you wanted to talk to me. This seems like a good time.'

'Yes. Since you came to Verdigris, things have continued to change. Many of our citizens have returned to the ways of the Empire. I've heard that it's your intent to negotiate on our behalf when The Seven come, to save us from Their wrath.'

'That's right. I'll only fight if I have to.'

The quote comes easily to Grain's lips. 'And so it was that Gamma always knew when to hold back and when to strike.' He looks at her, his expression intense. 'I want to offer my aid when you go to them, to prove that some of us have not fallen from the path.'

'That's kind of you. I'll give it some thought.'

'Whatever you think is best, of course. I wish only to serve.'

After he is gone, Vesper paces, shaking her hand until the Skyn settles and the stinging subsides. Over by the wall, the sword stirs, an eye looking towards the door.

Vesper goes and opens it. 'Come in, Samael.'

The half-breed knight does so. 'The First's nomads have arrived. The Order of the Broken Blades is with them.'

'Great.'

'I was wondering if this might be a good time to give them the swords I made.'

'Yes, of course. I'll be right there.' She thinks about how small her order of knights are in the grand scheme of things as she picks up the sword. They make up a tiny fraction of the forces assembling at Crucible, their needs almost insignificant in the face of what comes. In fact, despite the grand nature of her endeavour, most of her days are filled dealing with petty requests. But for Vesper they are not petty, just those of individuals rather than empires. *And what*, she thinks, *is the point of having an empire if the people in it are overlooked?*

Samael remains in the doorway. 'Do you think the order will accept them?'

'The swords? Yes. But maybe not at first. You need to understand that my knights might take a while to adjust.'

'Yes.'

He remains stranded in the doorway and for a moment, she sees him. Not the monstrous knight or the half-breed with mismatched eyes and a patchwork soul. She sees a person, alone, anxious, struggling to find his place in world. He needs the knights to accept the swords, she realizes, because she needs them to accept him. 'Come on, my friend,' she says, taking his arm, 'I'm with you.'

He does not really feel the contact, but when it registers, she sees his head tilt in surprise, and his hand moves carefully over hers. 'Yes.'

The Order of the Broken Blades make a semicircle, neat, around Samael, Vesper and the new swords.

Samael speaks at length about their usage. Though enthusiastic, his voice is hard to hear, forcing Vesper's knights to lean forward.

'. . . And that is all. Who wishes to try them first?'

The knights lean back. Covert glances are exchanged. One of the knights in the front row wrinkles his nose.

Vesper's tut is audible. 'What are you waiting for?'

'Forgive us,' says one of the older knights. 'But aren't these swords tainted?'

'No,' says Samael. 'The essence is inert. I have stripped the infernal from it.'

'Then why is it called a Necro-blade?'

'Because it was made from the essence of the dead and the skills involved are those refined by the Necroneers of Wonderland.'

The knights lean back a little further.

'Oh for goodness sake!' snaps Vesper. 'This is a great gift. I've looked at them myself and there is nothing to fear.'

Shamed, the older knight steps forward and picks one up. He tests the weight, and after getting a nod from Samael, gives a few practice swings.

'Now, try singing,' the half-breed urges, pointing to a wooden target.

The knight sings, and the essence within the blade is charged by it, setting the weapon to humming. When he attacks, the enhanced edge cuts through the wood, clean.

'It has no song of its own,' Samael explains, 'but it can empower yours.'

The old knight takes it in, thinks, then: 'I have one question.'

'Yes?'

'Can I have another go?'

One Thousand and Thirty-One Years Ago

Sometimes, Massassi wishes she could not read essences. It would make the concern of others easier to ignore. She is sitting in her room, turning a bolt over in her hands. She is sure the idea for a new project is lurking just round the corner, and that if she is quiet for a while, it will come.

Peace-Fifteen stands nearby, wringing her hands.

'What do you want?' Massassi snaps. It is a cruel question as Massassi knows what the girl wants, why she wants it, why it's important, just as she knows that she is doing what's right. Massassi is cruel anyway. More and more, she takes pleasure in little acts of spite.

'It is time for your medication.'

'Is it? Haven't I had enough for one lifetime? Maybe I just want to be left alone.'

Peace-Fifteen makes a show of checking the time. 'Yes, it is definitely time. May I connect you?'

'What if I said I didn't want it?'

201

'Then I would do nothing.' There is a pause but Massassi can see she has not won yet. 'Of course, I would remind you that a delay in treatment can cause discomfort, increased risk of clotting, put a strain on your heart, negatively impact on digestion, impair sleep—'

'No more,' cuts in Massassi, letting the girl experience a moment of heightened panic before adding, 'No more of your arguments. I'll take the thrice-damned medication and all the side effects it brings.'

Peace-Fifteen knows better than to say anything, getting straight to work. The valve in Massassi's side is connected to a thin med-tube. Dosages are measured within the wall, fed through machinery directly into her body. Peace-Fifteen presides over every stage of the procedure, an extra measure of security, unnecessary. Massassi cannot help but be moved by her care, cannot help but hate herself for having turned into such a strange and bitter thing.

Overwhelmed by a rare touch of remorse, she keeps her complaints to a minimum, only a slight groan slipping out as Peace-Fifteen disconnects the med-tube.

Good intentions soon fade, however. 'Why are you still here?' she grumbles.

'I thought it would be good for us to go for a walk,' ventures Peace-Fifteen.

'Why?'

'To get some air.'

'No, I don't want to.'

'You haven't been outside for three days now.'

'No.'

'But you hate sitting around.'

'No.'

Peace-Fifteen thinks for a moment. 'We could go and see how Alpha, Beta and Gamma are doing. They love it when you visit.'

'Gamma doesn't.'

'Of course She does. Only yesterday, She was asking where you were.'

Massassi looks at the bolt in her palm. It has come from another machine and is weathered from use. A piece of junk, as likely to ruin something it was put into as to fix it. Scrap. She tries to ignore the fact that Peace-Fifteen is still there, looking at her. Massassi hates that look! She is used to fear and reverence, but she finds reverence coupled with worry unbearable.

'Go away.' Massassi is aiming for a brusque command but, to her horror, achieves something more akin to a plea.

Peace-Fifteen bows, unable to hide the hurt from Massassi's eyes, and walks away.

Alone, she takes in her surroundings. A tank for her daily immersions, a slab for sleeping badly on and very little else. She hates this room. It is empty and cold and is not made to sit around in. Stimulation is needed, something to engage her mind and distract her from the vague feeling of guilt that is becoming far too common in her life.

A fit of coughing takes her, requiring all of her attention. Fragile bones are shaken until her chest aches and the breath turns thin in her throat.

The bolt slips from her fingers, landing with a clang and rolling out of reach.

Massassi watches it, wheezing curses and making angry

hand gestures, until warning lights begin to display on her monitors and Peace-Fifteen hurries back in.

The girl bows quickly. 'Is everything alright?'

'I've . . . decided,' gasps Massassi, 'that I want . . . to go . . . for a walk.'

CHAPTER TWELVE

A sky-ship flies low across the ocean, twin plumes of light streaming from the wings. Cables run from its underside at a forty-five degree angle, taut, linking it to a small sea-shuttle, towing it over wave-tops.

The Vagrant stands at the prow, a smile on his face. Jem and Reela stand with him, while Delta remains flat on the deck, still covered by the Vagrant's old coat.

Every so often, the Vagrant glances at Jem, until the other man exclaims: 'Alright! I admit it. This was a good idea.'

The Vagrant raises his chin slightly, catching Jem's eye before bringing it down, a grand nod.

Because they only have one able pilot, they are forced to stop at night, the sky-ship putting down on open water. There has been a natural segregation during the day, Reela, Jem and the Vagrant staying on the sea-shuttle while the lieutenant and the other soldiers keep to the sky-ship.

At night, Jem crosses that line, going and sitting with the

lieutenant as she tends to the one conscious soldier and the two unconscious ones.

'How are they doing?'

'They're alive,' replies the lieutenant, matter of factly. 'For now.'

'How about him,' he points to the conscious soldier, the one with the dent in his helmet.

'Not so good. He's barely talking and not accepting any food.'

To his surprise, the soldier they're discussing has already fallen into a light, unhappy sleep.

'How about you?'

'I'm able. Tired from the flying and . . .' she trails off for a moment. 'I'll be ready to pick up again in the morning.'

'Good. My name is Jem by the way, what's yours?'

'Why do you want to know?'

Jem starts to smile, then puts a hand to his mouth, self-conscious. 'Because a very wise person once told me that it's harder to be angry with someone when you know who they are.'

She doesn't look convinced by his argument but replies anyway. 'Lieutenant Mazar. No, just Mazar. They've probably already stripped me of rank and condemned me for this.'

'Do they know what's happened?'

'They know enough,' she says. 'It's obvious that we failed. Details don't matter.'

Jem bravely tries to save the conversation. 'Good to meet you anyway. Hungry?'

'We have rations.'

'Oh.'

There is moment, awkward, then Mazar says, 'I have to rest.'

Defeated, Jem returns to the sea-shuttle.

Mazar waits to be sure that Jem has gone before slumping with relief. She was sure he suspected. Why else would he come with questions?

She doesn't know what to make of the man, hasn't known what to make of anything since Delta destroyed her world. Only two things are clear. She cannot live with Delta's displeasure and she cannot die until she has found some way to atone.

Whenever she closes her eyes, Delta's stare back, twin windows to another world of storm and shade. There will be no rest tonight, sleep more of a threat to her now than a comfort.

Her soldiers have broken under the pressure. Unable to reconcile their duty with Delta's judgement, unable to live with themselves, unable to act, they retreat to a place of twilight, paralysed.

Nobody should have to suffer this way, she thinks. *Nobody.*

She gets up, checks that Jem really has gone and isn't hiding nearby. No one lurks on the other side of the hatch and no one clings to the wing outside. A light plays on the sea-shuttle opposite, highlighting chattering faces. To Mazar, their happiness is alien, a thing to be studied at a remove, no longer understood.

The hatch is re-sealed and she returns to her seat. For a while the display on the inside of the cockpit entertains. Repeated warnings flash that comms and navigation have failed, jarring next to the serene state of the primary systems.

Soundproofing keeps the noise of the waves at bay, and she turns off audio output. In the quiet, it is easy to hear the sounds of her companions breathing. Steady, slow, save for the occasional gasp as some new dream-terror presents itself.

Mazar nearly breaks into a litany to ask forgiveness but catches herself. She does not expect to be forgiven for this, would not take it even if offered.

They are calming now, the three soldiers settling into a deeper, more natural sleep. Their breath seems to find a rhythm, not quite in time but complementary, three waves whispering on neighbouring shores.

Mazar takes off her helmet. Her attempt to stow it in the nearby shelf fails. Preoccupied fingers fumble and it falls, hitting the floor, sounding sharp, angry, bouncing twice, rolling before coming to a scraping stop.

Her hands move quickly, covering her crumpling face. Tears come and shoulders shake, wretched, while one set of breathing slows nearby, hushing, hushing, to a final sigh.

She catches herself, wipes at tears and strains to listen. Only two sets of breathing remain, softer now, a pair of divers leading each other to the unexplored deep. Slowly, they fade, taken by the poison she administered. In the dark it is as if they are moving further away, wandering together, leaving Mazar alone.

In the morning the sky-ship resumes its journey. There are no communications active, the link to the network completely severed. This has several effects: the sky-ship cannot communicate or update navigation data, and it cannot be interfered with remotely, blissfully ignorant of any shut-down orders coming from the Knight Commander.

On the sea-shuttle, Reela plonks herself down next to Delta. She fusses, tucking a corner of the coat back under the immortal's shoulder. Such is Delta's size that the coat cannot cover her completely. Reela has given up worrying about feet or lower legs. However, one of Delta's arms sticks out, elbow, wrist and hand exposed. Reela looks at it for a while, trying to decide what to do.

Neither Jem nor the Vagrant have noticed, one talking, worried, the other, equally worried, listening.

Reela works her fingers under Delta's wrist, first one hand, then the other. It isn't easy and by the time she has managed it, small cheeks are flushed with effort. Setting her shoulders, Reela tries to lift Delta's arm onto her lap. With a grunt she gets it off the floor but can't raise it over her knee. The arm flops down again, Reela dragged with it, hair leaping forward to ambush her face.

Hands trapped under a metal arm, Reela can only blow irritably at her hair. Eventually, it flops aside, releasing the left side of her face.

Reela begins to rock back and forth on her bottom, gaining speed. Twice, three times she goes, pulling lightly on Delta's arm. On the fourth attempt, she throws herself back, adding momentum and body weight to childish strength.

Her labours bear fruit. When she is settled again in a sitting position, Delta's hand is in her lap.

She puts her hand against the immortal's, comparing them. Her fingertips barely cross the silver expanse of palm. This observation leads to a more in-depth exploration. A lack of lines is noted, the skin smooth, flawless, unlike the craggy surface of her own. Perhaps it is the smoothness, perhaps it is the surprising warmth, but Delta's hand feels almost soft.

Reela leans down, planting a kiss in the centre of the palm, then turns her head, nuzzling, making a bed for her cheek.

Hunched over, the girl should be anything but comfortable. Childish biology triumphs however, and sleep comes soon after.

The Vagrant patrols the front rail of the sea-shuttle, checking each cable is secure. Eyebrows raise as his gaze falls on the horizon, where sunlight breaks the sea's illusion of infinity, picking out cliffs and making cove shaped shadows.

Above them, the sky-ship alters its course, pulling them towards one of the many darknesses that eventually reveals itself to be a beach.

The sea-shuttle is eased onto the stones, and the Vagrant begins detaching cables even as the sky-ship comes down to land.

Jem comes over. 'I think we have a problem.'

The Vagrant pauses, looks up at him.

'It's Reela.'

Whirling round, the Vagrant finds Reela sleeping at Delta's side, both of them covered by his coat. He moves closer, frowning at the way the girl is so well tucked in.

'I just found them like that.' At the Vagrant's shake of the head, he adds, hastily: 'I'd only turned away for a second and she knew not to go near Delta. I'd told her lots of times. It isn't my fault!'

Amber eyes glare and Jem takes a step back, involuntary.

The Vagrant bends down over the prostrate pair. Though Delta's eyes are open, they stare straight up, unfocused. He reaches out very slowly, very carefully, pausing at the slightest twitch or sound, until he has a good grip on the coat's collar.

Behind them the sky-ship settles onto the beach, hatch springing open, allowing Mazar to jump down and begin jogging towards them. She is armoured for battle, a rifle slung over her shoulder. As soon as she sees what the Vagrant is doing, she accelerates. 'Don't do it!' she cries.

The Vagrant flinches in surprise and Jem ducks.

Mazar clears the last of the distance between them, hauling herself onto the sea-shuttle. 'Don't,' she pleads, 'don't disturb Her.'

The Vagrant points at Reela and raises his hands, exasperated.

'You can't help the girl now.'

The Vagrant shakes his head, continues with his work. Further attempts to persuade him are ignored and both Mazar and Jem back away.

He eases the corner of his coat from under Reela and slowly peels it back until she is uncovered. Eyes flutter open, meeting his.

The Vagrant puts a finger to his lips and Reela does the same. Nodding, the Vagrant supports her weight as Reela slips her arm from Delta's.

Silver fingers curl, eclipsing Reela's hand, holding it tight.

Feeling the resistance, the Vagrant freezes.

Mazar swings off the side of the sea-shuttle and Jem ducks, both moving out of sight.

Reela's arms have become a slope that run from Delta up to the Vagrant. While the Vagrant holds very still, Reela tugs harder.

Delta blinks.

Reela tugs again and Delta's head turns to look at her.

There is a moment where nobody moves.

Then Reela smiles and nods towards the sky-ship. The Vagrant also nods, beckoning her with a finger, offering her a hand.

Delta's surprise strikes them both like a strong breeze. She takes the Vagrant's hand, though she needs neither man nor girl to help her up, and stands in a single fluid movement.

The coat falls in the space between them, making a worn puddle of fabric at their feet.

Delta looks down at it and the Vagrant finds he has been released. He crouches down and picks up the coat, offering it up to Delta, who accepts without comment.

At another tug from Reela, Delta allows herself to be guided towards the sky-ship.

The Vagrant goes to follow but a plaintive hum from the deck stops him. The source is Delta's sword, lying abandoned, staring at the space where recently there was a winged back, forlorn.

He gets up, walks over to it, and the eye swivels towards him, plaintive.

Sighing, he picks it up, hurrying to join the others.

Soon, they have all climbed into the sky-ship. No longer tied down, it rises easily into the air, leaving the sea-shuttle to the mercy of the waves.

Mazar keeps the sky-ship low, making regular adjustments to accommodate uneven scenery. Cliffs are left behind, replaced with sodden marshland and deep lakes. Tower tops and antennae, rusted, break the surface in places, giving hints of buried civilization.

These too give way to watery fields, long grasses sprouting in clumps, wild patches on the head of a balding man.

The Vagrant leans forward, pointing at the transparent panels by their feet.

Mazar slows the sky-ship and looks down. She sees a long caravan, strung out, meat runners transporting their trade. A variety of animals are with them; even from a distance they are sad and scrawny specimens. The caravan's passage is clear, its progress ploughed through soft earth. However something is wrong, one of the heavy waggons leans, its wheel sunk too low. Beasts are brought forward, the humans working quickly to try and pull the wheel free. It is quite a show.

It is not what the Vagrant is pointing at.

Things are pulling themselves from the ground nearby. They move like worms but are too big to be worms, each about the size of a large dog. Mazar guesses there are at least a dozen of them.

'Doesn't look good for those meat runners. Have you fought that kind of infernal before?'

The Vagrant doesn't answer, just points down again more firmly.

'You want me to go down there?' Mazar asks.

The Vagrant nods.

Jem steps into the cockpit, drawn by the noise. 'Something wrong?' His quick eyes take in the scene below. 'Why are we getting closer to that?' Realizing the Vagrant is behind this, he grabs the other man's outstretched arm. 'This is a mistake. We need to get Reela to safety. We need to get us to safety! And,' he drops his voice, 'what about Delta? Who knows what She'll do. It's too risky.'

As the sky-ship descends, Jem's voice takes on a pleading quality. 'Just for once, please, can we do things my way?' Nobody answers and the pleading stops, replaced by bitterness. 'We'll regret this.'

'I have no assisted targeting,' Mazar says. 'Do you want me to fire anyway?'

The Vagrant shakes his head, continuing to point down.

'I'm wary of landing in that soup. We could get snarled. If it were up to me I'd bring us in low enough for you to jump out but keep us airborne. That work for you?'

The Vagrant nods.

'Okay. Move to the hatch, we'll be green in sixty. I'll get you as close as I can.' As the Vagrant leaves, she adds, 'There's a lot of them, you sure you can handle it alone?'

This time, the Vagrant does not nod, his gesture non-committal.

Jem's voice rises to a shout. 'You don't know? You're going down there and you're not even sure you'll survive? You're an idiot!'

The Vagrant pushes past Jem, going through the hold to the hatch, and sure enough, a minute later it is opening. The ground is getting closer, near enough to jump, far enough for second thoughts.

The Vagrant grips the sides of the hatch, takes a breath, and heaves himself out, jumping, flailing, falling.

Luckily, he does not fall for long.

Boots connect with earth already churned by the sky-ship's vertical engines, plunging deep, twin knives into soft butter.

The Vagrant blinks, takes in his situation.

Already, the meat runners have tethered several beasts to the stricken waggon, coordinating the first attempt to tug it out. Meanwhile the wormlike things have nearly managed to struggle free.

The Vagrant can empathize, his own legs buried up to the knee. Finding a nearby clump of weeds, he begins to pull himself out, constantly sprayed by mud and filth as the sky-ship hovers overhead.

Cries are going up now, the meat runners seeing the infernal threat approaching. A few draw slender blades of curving glass, moving to defend their fellows while the rest redouble their efforts.

Now free of the ground, the wormlike things shiver, connecting other joints, waking sleeping tendons. Each one has a set of eight legs, feline, furless, that are tucked away whilst underground. These legs stretch, claws flexing, the movement of muscle easy to trace. One by one, the infernals stand up. Slung back on the top of their worm mouths is what appears at first glance to be a ridge of skin but is in fact a second head. Like hoods, the infernals pull them down and there is a succession of wet clicks as each sphinx-head locks into place. Pointed ears flick into life. Eyes, some blue, some green, all glowing, adjust to the light, pupils narrowing to razor slits.

The living quickly draw their attention. Though the infernals have arrived together, they do not act as one, picking targets seemingly at random, some advancing towards the meat runner guards, others prowling round, seeking softer targets.

Beasts and humans wail together, their panic blending, indistinguishable.

At last, the Vagrant is able to stand up. He claws the mud from his face and draws Delta's sword, rushing forward, taking breath as he closes on the nearest infernal.

215

Something catches in his throat however and singing makes way for coughing.

Glass blades flash out, and claws flash back, faster. Both find their targets but the infernals feel no pain, the damage to their shells cosmetic. By contrast, the meat runners stagger back, precious blood staining their robes.

Delta's sword watches one of the infernals crouch, preparing to spring. Its eye looks to the Vagrant as he spits out a lump of brown, then back to the infernal as it sails towards them.

The Vagrant jumps sideways, twisting, inhaling, drawing back Delta's sword as the infernal lands alongside. Its jaws snap at him as he brings down the weapon.

Blue light surrounds the blade as it cracks the sphinx head, making contact with the second layer of flesh beneath. Keen metal touches the taut, thin skin, and it splits like overripe fruit, the whole body popping, spilling innards twice burnt, by sword and sunlight.

The remaining infernals all turn to the new threat, snarling.

But Delta's sword meets their gaze, unflinching. Its wings give a proud flap, urging the Vagrant forward.

He steps towards them, singing a second time, Delta's sword joining him. Their song drowns out the growling, each infernal slapped by the sound, flinching away, scraggy ears plastering themselves flat on every head.

The Vagrant advances and they all retreat. Silver wings stretch in newfound confidence and the Vagrant takes breath to sing again.

And then, as if from the earth, something else answers, a shuddering moan that seems to be felt through the feet as much as heard.

A row of ears bounce back up again and sharp teeth are bared, the catlike faces easily conveying a sense of sudden smugness.

While the meat runners redouble their efforts to free the waggon, there is a second rumble. The eye in Delta's sword jerks down, not directly, not beneath the Vagrant, but at an angle. The Vagrant follows the line of its gaze, finds he is looking at a spot directly underneath the sky-ship.

He raises the sword, waving it, giving a signal to Mazar. Too late.

Like an eruption of lava, a pillar of flesh and fangs bursts from the earth. It reaches up, a ten foot wide 'V' of teeth that snaps shut either side of the sky-ship. Wings buckle, light drives snuff out, and the body of the vehicle shrinks in on itself under the pressure with a shriek, sickening.

The Vagrant runs towards it, his sword arm dragging behind him. Silver wings droop and an eye stares in horror.

There is a pop and the top of the cockpit detaches. A second pop and two seats launch into the air, clear of danger.

For a moment the Vagrant is distracted by them. At this height only the undersides are visible, the occupants impossible to see.

The infernals sense that moment, leaping for him. Claws scrape down his backplate, scratching but not penetrating. He staggers forward, feet struggling to free themselves from the mud, and nearly falls.

By the time he has caught his balance they are on him, circling quicker than he can, lashing out at his back. He makes wide swings with the sword, catching one, bursting it. And always his eyes flick up to the floating seats, each time an invitation for the enemy.

The first seat comes into view. A small emergency light drive fires in controlled bursts, fighting gravity and the burdens placed beyond its design. Mazar sits in the chair, sighting up with her rifle. She struggles to do this, in part because she is moving and in part because Jem is on her lap, his arms wrapped around her neck.

The second seat glides in a more stately fashion. It is empty. Reela is still inside.

Amber eyes and single eye go wide, turning back to the monstrous thing eating the sky-ship.

The Vagrant puts his back to the infernals, raising the sword and humming a long note. The air about the blade quivers, distorting in colour.

One of the infernals moves to take advantage, is shot in the eye by a buzzing bullet. Steam hisses from the wound as essence burns. The next to try is shot in the temple, the one after that in the teeth. Locations matter little for the infernals have no vital organs. However, breaks in their shell can be fatal this far north and these bullets sting enough to make them think twice.

Lowering Delta's sword to point directly at the pillar of flesh, the Vagrant opens his mouth, letting the hum expand into song. The air between sword tip and target sparks and shimmers, and a patch of ridged skin bursts into blue-tinged flame.

In surprise, the infernal roars, writhing, shaking the sky-ship, a dog with a rag doll.

The Vagrant continues to sing and Mazar continues to fire; wormlike bodies stagger, stunned, flames lick across the giant infernal, and still they keep going, till lungs burn and trigger pulls make clicks rather than bullets.

With a final inhuman howl, the pillar drops the sky-ship and draws back into the safety of the earth. Immediately, the minor infernals do the same, retracting their feline limbs, casting off cat-faced hoods and burrowing down.

As Mazar comes into land, the Vagrant struggles towards the remains of the sky-ship, forcing tired legs onward. It is a sorry looking thing now, a crushed insect. He does not bother with the buckled hatch, cutting a new entrance in the battered hull.

There is little room to search inside, the hull reduced to an eighth of its former size. Curled on one knee is Delta, a silver ball wrapped in wings, statue still.

He squeezes in, clambering over, and two sets of little fingers hook around the top of the wings. A moment later, Reela's head peeks out.

Amber eyes linger on a new bruise on her temple and one on her cheek, then come to rest on her smile.

One set of little fingers wave.

The Vagrant stops, raises a weary hand and waves back.

She reaches out to him and he closes the last of the gap, sliding her out of the winged cocoon and into his arms.

For a long time, they simply hold each other. Safe.

'We've come into visual range of Seraph's Rock, sir.'

The Knight Commander nods, tired. Seraph's Rock is their last stop before the rendezvous. Behind them, his fleet has left a trail of fire and carnage, no doubt matched by the other half of the fleet travelling with Obeisance. By now, word of their coming must have spread. He wonders if they're going to meet resistance. In a way, he would welcome a real fight. Something to test their mettle. Something more glorious than shooting people as they fled or bombing them out of existence.

'Have they launched any of their ships, captain?'

There is a pause as the captain confers with their scouts and his instruments. 'No, sir.'

His reply sounds more like a sigh than he would like. 'Have they mounted any kind of defence at all?'

'There are people on the walls, and the docks are packed, sir.'

Easy targets, he thinks. 'Can you tell what they're doing?'

'It appears they're welcoming us, sir. They're . . . singing.'

'Singing?'

'Yes, sir. They're singing the rite of mercy. Would you like me to feed the audio to you direct?'

'That won't be necessary, captain.'

The Knight Commander gets up and walks over to the porthole. They are a long way south now, and encounters with the taint are frequent. The chances are that Seraph's Rock is corrupted, and he has his orders direct from Alpha of The Seven. They are very clear. But these people are asking for his help. They are invoking the rite of mercy. Perhaps they could be purged. Perhaps they could be saved. Surely that would be a better solution?

He imagines going amongst them, basking in their song, purging, making them pure again.

Then he imagines explaining his disobedience to Obeisance. Or rather, he cannot imagine it. He cannot think of any words that would breach her disapproval. The Knight Commander shakes his head, defeated. He has his orders. It is not his place to question or second guess The Seven.

The Seven

He gives the word.
The fleet opens fire.
And on the walls and docks of Seraph's Rock, songs are swapped for screams, then silence.

CHAPTER THIRTEEN

Vesper and the buck take a tour of Crucible, struggling to keep track of all the new structures and the steady stream of arrivals. The first refugees have begun to appear. They bring word that The Seven's armada has reached the coast.

Stories of mass purging come with them, of whole colonies left burning. There are counter rumours, of loyal servants of the Empire being spared, even elevated, but these are rare. And most people she speaks to are either too corrupt, too tainted or too cynical to place any hope in them.

Construction continues apace, many of the refugees quickly assimilated into digging teams or building crews. Even the very young are found jobs, passing tools and messages. Vesper cannot help but notice that the old or infirm have remained in their places of origin.

Several of the bunkers have been finished, low walls now being strung between them. Due to the lack of material, the majority of these walls are made of mud. Mercenaries from West Rift spray them with a fine resin.

Curious, she approaches one of them, a man encased from head to toe in bronze-edged armour. The gaps in the armour are covered by a flexible membrane that glistens in the sunslight and a heavy breather tube runs from his belly up to a mask on the front of his face.

'Hello,' she says. 'What are you doing?'

There is a wheeze and a click, then he replies. 'Coating the walls.'

'I can see that. How does it help?'

'It stops snipers being able to see what's on the other side. This mud isn't going to stop the enemy shooting us but it will stop them seeing us.'

'They're not the enemy.'

The man gives a short grunt, unconvinced, and as Vesper walks away, she finds it hard to see the diplomatic centre tucked behind layers and layers of soldiers and military structures. She has a sudden sense of Crucible having its own momentum, that she is tethered to it, rather than the other way around.

The buck seems to share her bewilderment. Though he trots along after Vesper, his head swings from left to right, drawn by random movements. Often, he darts off to investigate only to return to her side shortly after, downcast.

Vesper scratches the base of his horns. 'Do you think I've made a mistake?'

The buck stares into the distance.

'I don't know. It seems like every time we start to get anywhere, there's a new obstacle in the road. I've had to move round so many now I'm not sure if I'm still going in the right direction, you know?'

The buck's head turns at some faraway sight, and he runs

off, a last flick of hooves visible as he ducks round the side of a large cart.

'Thanks for the support,' she mutters.

'Trouble with your beast, yes?' says a voice from behind her.

'Hello Ezze,' she replies, not needing to turn round to identify the speaker. 'I'm sorry I haven't spoken to you yet. It's been . . . hectic.'

'No sorry is needed. You are here and Ezze is here and that is all that matters.'

Vesper rubs at tired eyes. 'Okay. You said something about an offer?'

'Ah, you do remember! Let us be walking and talking. These things are not for the ears of the West Rifters. If we excite them too much, their bits will be falling off!'

Vesper frowns but allows Ezze, still talking, to lead her away.

'Too much? I thought it was a crime to be telling the lies in your presence? Your people of West Rift are not long for these markets.' His voice becomes a theatrical whisper. 'They buy too much of the stitching and the happiness drinks and not enough of anything else. There are messages in people's trading habits and Ezze is the most avid reader of them all.'

'Are you saying they're too ill to fight?'

'No, no. They are sick enough to be great warriors. No fear of death and lots of envy for us healthy ones.' He pats the curve of his stomach and winks. 'They will fight hard and fast. But this is not the deal of which we should be talking.' He waves a hand vaguely. 'Over there are your broken knights practising with their swords.' He waves again, in a different direction. 'And there you have your wild

Usurperkin, the ones with the nails in their brains. Good for the lifting but not the thinking.' Another wave. 'Then there are the good people of Verdigris.' And another. 'The ratbred of Red Rails.' And still another. 'The smelters, workers and winners from Slake, and then all the misfits who fit in not at all. Quite the mess, yes?'

'Where's this going?'

'Ah, truly you are a great lady, with her father's single-mindedness and charm! You see them all, all in their little pockets, with Ezze and his friend Vesper in the middle.' He puts an arm round her, being careful not to touch the sword. 'We should be building bridges together, joining up all of the dots to make something beautiful. You have many dots here. Many, many dots of different sizes but you have no picture.'

'Actually I do,' Vesper protests.

'Ah, but you are talking of the big picture, yes? Ezze is talking of the small ones. What people will be eating tonight. How they will be fixing their broken bed or easing the pain of the swollen foot.

'If they are not coming to you, great lady, then who? Who are the great traders they will seek and befriend?'

Vesper folds her arms. 'You, I suppose.'

His grin broadens and he squeezes her shoulders. 'You are bathing Ezze in your words of honey! It is true that Ezze always seeks new friends and finds ways to make them happy but there is little of the trust here and much of the fear. It is hard to help those too scared to ask, no?

'But you are trusted, great lady. If you were to support Ezze then people would know him as a friend and they would come. Ezze would fulfil their dreams but they would not remember humble Ezze, no.' He squeezes her shoulder a second time. 'They would remember you!'

The sword begins to growl softly and an eye opens, regarding Ezze until he removes his hand. 'That's what all this is about? You want to use me to get the best deals.'

Ezze regards the sword warily. 'Yes, it is true, but these deals are best for your people also. And perhaps, if there is little trust in your heart for Ezze, ask yourself this question: is there more for the First? Or does the great lady prefer the twin rulers of Slake, Gorad and Gut-pumper? For if we do not build the bridges together, they will be building them and Ezze does not think you are wanting that.'

Vesper looks at the sword, her face troubled. It does not tremble at the statement for it is true. She thinks hard, letting the sword share in it, worrying about the future and the different paths stretching ahead. Despite the passage of time, Ezze keeps his face fixed, an exaggerated image of humility.

'Alright,' she says at last. 'I'm listening.'

Ezze claps his hands together, and begins his pitch in earnest.

A group of infernals and half-breeds approach Crucible from the south. They travel without conversation but not quietly, a strange cacophony – buzzing, squelching, wheezing, wailing – accompanying the movement of twisted limbs.

Humans so badly tainted that they will not live to see their seventh birthdays walk in bodies swollen or stunted, their brains flailing, struggling to keep pace with developments.

Minor infernals swarm in a variety of shells, human, animal

and insect: stretching, morphing, searching for the right shapes to please their masters.

Then there are those that stand above but not on top, dangerous and ambitious, they chafe against their chains, unable to break free, unable to bear them.

Near the top of the pile is the Backwards Child. It appears as a little girl sat atop a giant Usurperkin. The girl's head is twisted many times and left facing the wrong way, a small face, solemn, on a bed of coiled skin. Long hair falls down her back, a curtain that drapes the Usurperkin's face. In truth the two bodies are fused together to make room for the infernal itself.

But all here bow to one: the Man-shape. It walks at the front of the group, shockingly ordinary in appearance. It wears clothes that are neat, without holes, that are worn correctly. Essence is folded carefully, arranged intricately within so as not to distort. Like a finely made sword, the Man-shape's essence weaves back and forth over itself, dense, sharp edged. Only the flies give it away, surrounding the Man-shape in a dark aura, gathering at its shoulders as a living cloak.

Vesper waits for them, the sword humming softly on her back, itching to be drawn. Samael and Scout are with her. The rest of Crucible keep their distance, muttering to each other, sharing stories of the cruelty of demons and the hopelessness of the future.

Though detailed communication between infernals requires direct essence contact, simple things, like strong emotions and desires, being blunt, are easily read.

The Man-shape gives no order but its wishes are clear to those that have the capacity to look.

The Backwards Child and the other powerful infernals stop and wait, their bodies motionless, like stuffed animals with glassy, empty eyes. The lesser infernals continue a pace or two before being pulled up short on leashes of the soul, invisible.

The Man-shape keeps on walking until it has left its kindred behind. Fifty feet from Vesper, it stops.

She holds up a hand, signalling Samael to wait, and walks towards the swirling globe of flies that surrounds the infernal.

Insects buzz angrily, bouncing into each other in an effort to get clear, a living door opening for her.

Vesper goes through until she stands opposite the Man-shape, just ten feet away.

With great ceremony, the Man-shape puts one hand behind its back, raises the other, then bows. Vesper inclines her head in response.

She is left to wait as the infernal turns on the spot, putting its back to her. There is a succession of pops and clicks as bones shift from their normal position to one capable of speech. Though she cannot see it from behind, there is a suggestion that its jaw hangs too low, as if dislocated and pulled out from the skull. When it speaks however, the voice is surprisingly mundane.

'Before we begin I would like to engage in some pleasantries. Hello Vesper. It is good to see you again.'

'And you.'

'You appear healthy and I see you and the Malice are closer than ever. I am appreciative that you keep it sheathed.'

'Thank you. I like your jacket.'

'Good, that is pleasing to know. I had it fitted to this body especially. I think I will do this with all of my clothes in future.'

'How are you?'

228

'Strong.' There is a pause and then the Man-shape adds, 'The weather is mild today.'

'I suppose it is.'

'Now that we have exchanged pleasantries we should discuss the future.'

Vesper nods. 'I've assigned an area for your followers to live. Where are the others?'

'Others?'

'New Horizon is a big place. I was expecting a lot more.'

'The majority of humans that live in my city remain there. It is for their own protection, a journey like this would have been hard for them. We do not need to eat as you do and the healthiest of your kind are a hard temptation for my lessers to ignore. I find the trick to maintaining control is to put it to the test as rarely as possible.'

'That's probably for the best.'

'I am ready to negotiate.'

'About that. All of the major groups are here but a lot of them are going to struggle with working together.'

'I understand, Vesper. You and I are alike in our vision but the others see little that is not right in front of them. We are the future and we scare them.'

'Exactly, they're scared and I want to find a way to get past that so people can really start to know each other and work together.'

'It is up to us to lead them.'

'Yes. You've said before that to settle things between other infernals you have a display. We need to give both of our peoples a display.'

'Our displays are made across essences.'

'I know. This one will have to be physical so everyone

229

can see it. Like a symbol. We need to put ourselves at each other's mercy.'

'But then what is to stop me severing you from the Malice or the Malice severing me entirely?'

'Trust.'

The Man-shape stands, silently thinking.

'They are watching us,' Vesper adds. 'What we do here is going to set the tone for everything that follows. We're so close now. Can you come the last few steps with me?'

There is sharp click as the Man-shape's mouth closes, the jaw working back into place. With a subtle shift in essence, the infernal scatters the surrounding swarm, the living globe of flies seeming to disintegrate, exposing them.

It turns round to face Vesper.

She reaches up to the sword, giving one of the wings a reassuring squeeze, then steps forward.

The Man-shape mirrors the movement.

She takes a last step, bringing them together. It is strange, standing so close to an infernal. Next to it, she senses the strangeness more keenly, for while the Man-shape does an excellent impression of humanity it is only skin deep. She takes a breath to brace herself.

The Malice and the Man-shape first met on the battlefield, one made to destroy the other, one destroying the other's master and being destroyed by it. Both have the urge to be elsewhere, to attack, but both also have Vesper, and the young woman realizes that she is the bridge, able to understand each side, to see the beauty amid the scars.

Aware that she is trembling, Vesper raises her arms, going on tip-toe to bring her level with the Man-shape as she embraces it.

An eye widens at her shoulder and the Man-shape looks into it. For the infernal it is like looking into the face of death. But control is ever the Man-shape's strength and it steels itself, inching its own arms up to circle Vesper and the sword.

Vesper rests her head on the infernal's chest, 'Ssh,' she says, soothing. 'Ssh.'

The sword contains its rage.

The Man-shape contains its fear.

Humans and half-breeds and infernals watch, unsure what they are a witness to. Afterwards there is much discussion as to the meaning behind the act. Some say it is submission of one side or another, others a meeting of friends, still others that it is an abomination. All agree it is an omen, though for good or ill, they cannot say. And all feel themselves in the presence of history, and a sense of being made both larger and smaller by it.

Vesper eats as Genner talks. His report is fixed on details, statistics. Food requirements per head, projected population growth versus projected lifetime of supplies, estimates on the arrival of the Empire's army, overviews of grievances with several unresolved cases for Vesper's attention.

When the sword wakes up and stares at the door, Vesper's eyes sliding in the same direction, he stops speaking and opens it.

The First is on the other side.

Genner quickly steps aside, his expression neutral.

'I am leaving,' states the First.

Vesper puts down her lunch. Guilty thoughts fly through

her mind. Is this her fault? Does it know she harbours doubts? 'I don't understand.'

'My people will remain here, as will my sky-ships. They are at your disposal should your desire for . . . peace be at odds with The Seven's.'

'Where will you be?'

'Wonderland. I have a debt to pay and a price to claim.'

'Oh. I'd assumed that you . . . er, this part of you at least, was going to stay here.'

'No.'

'Will you be coming back?'

'It is my . . . intention to do so.'

Vesper stands up. 'I need Neer. I need you too. Promise me you'll come back.'

'Either you trust my intention or you do not. A promise will make no difference.'

'Then I look forward to seeing you again soon.'

After the First has left, Vesper looks at Genner. 'What do you think?'

'It's an infernal, we can't trust it.'

She sighs. 'I know it's hiding something but I can't see what.'

'Where is the rest of it? Spread out like usual?'

'No. The First is gathered together in Wonderland.' Genner's usual composure breaks in a flash of surprise as she continues. 'There might be a few bits of it elsewhere but I doubt it. It's terrified of The Seven. That's what confuses me. I thought it was using me as a shield to hide behind but I can't protect it if it leaves.'

Genner's face is stern. 'I think I see it.'

'Tell me.'

The Seven

'We know the path The Seven are taking to get here and you can be sure the First does too. It's worked out they're bypassing Wonderland to come here directly. It doesn't need you as a shield any more. Do you see? It's using you as bait.'

One Thousand and Twenty-Seven Years Ago

Massassi stands in her workshop once more. An exo-skeleton supports her on the outside, a constant supply of medication via a tube connecting her to the wall, supporting her within.

Peace-Fifteen has warned her that the levels are dangerous, a threat to her health. Massassi has warned Peace-Fifteen to shut up.

Alpha and Beta are delighted to see her in action again, neither able to conceive of her frailty, much less notice it. Gamma is merely annoyed that their creator has not acted sooner.

Massassi empathizes, has wanted to act for a long time. More than ever she is aware of the failings of her Empire. Her Seraph Knights move ever further away from the rest of her citizens. Under Alpha's tutelage they have become stronger, rarified, their dedication setting them apart.

Beta has implemented a series of codes to help mitigate future problems, programming the knights to help their fellow man, should the right requests be made.

And Gamma fluctuates between wanting to improve things and wanting to tear them down. Already she has come into conflict with her brothers and Massassi fears that without intervention, things will get worse.

For all of these reasons, she raises her tools again, and for one other: Massassi is bored, empty without a project. Physical complaints can be endured but not the feeling of uselessness that comes with inaction.

Gamma was too much like her, she realizes, flawed. She still desires to craft something in a female form but this time, it must be more focused, she must be more focused.

The body soon takes shape, very close to Gamma's in appearance but perhaps a little softer, a little smoother. Massassi dismisses the thought of it being weaker, preferring the idea that she is making something more nuanced, a sister that will be better equipped to deal with humanity fairly.

The sword she makes is similar to Beta's, a slightly quicker weapon, as suited to defence as it is to attack.

For days she fusses over details, wanting the work to be perfect, wanting to put off the time when she must give up more of herself to bring the silver body to life.

Deep down she knows there is not much left to give.

Soon, Gamma is making her impatience felt. Unlike her brothers she sees Massassi's fears all too well, sniffing them out with what feels like cold enthusiasm. Gamma's presence is like a fly in the soup of her brothers' love. Not equal but enough to sour the whole thing.

In the end it is as much pride as courage that makes Massassi act. Her silver arm is the only part of her that doesn't tremble, the iris in her palm opening as smoothly as ever. She takes a moment to appreciate the quality of her work, then silently swears to match it again today.

Essence flows, bright, moving from heart to hand, to a silver head then on, through every part of the body, to the inert sword and back again.

Though she never admits it, Massassi has lost the capacity to shape this part of the process. Such is the effort required to push her essence out, she is a slave to the way it flows. This time it is not anger that takes her but regret. A succession of faces wash past her vision. At first the familiar ones, her supervisor, the doctor that tried to muffle her mind with drugs, the men that came to kill her in the early days, the mix of people she tried to elevate to her level and failed. Then others, countless thousands she consigned to death without meeting, too many to name, too many to hold in the mind, a blurring line of ghosts.

Though her exo-skeleton holds her upright, Massassi's body sags as Delta's eyes open.

Like Gamma, the newborn immortal sees her flaws. Unlike her, she forgives them. Instinctively, she embraces her creator.

Alpha comes closer, his approval filling the room with song, Beta joining him, a gentler harmony, complimentary. Gamma remains where she is.

Buoyed by their love, Massassi allows herself to float. She is neither happy nor sad, pleased nor displeased. A great weight has lifted with Delta's creation, leaving her peaceful, calm, almost completely empty.

CHAPTER FOURTEEN

The Seven's armada, reunited after their split, clusters along the coastline, disgorging troops in trucks and knights in metal snakes. Both halves of the fleet have seen their fair share of action.

Island after island has been purged, the tainted and their homes made ash. There has been no resistance to speak of, those with the means to flee having done so, and those without hiding, or running within the confines of their islands, easy pickings for the fire teams.

They had hoped to find pockets of the faithful on their travels, gathering the worthy to their side and growing the army as Gamma did on her fateful journey to the Breach. But the people of the Empire have fallen far in that time, and Alpha's standards are exacting.

Those who have waited on bended knee, with smiles or whispered litanies, have been met with fire.

The Knight Commander knows they are doing good work but cannot help but feel that something is missing. So far it seems as if they do little more than weed a garden, one that will not recover in his lifetime.

Where is the glory? Where is the enemy deserving of their wrath?

As Alpha's palace drifts slowly overhead, the Knight Commander reluctantly leaves *Resolution* behind, the waterways too small and treacherous to support the mighty vessel. At his command, the curving head of the ship comes to life, detaching itself to grind across the launch deck and onto the beach, like a tongue leaving its mouth behind. His command centre appears like the metal snakes favoured by the knights, but is four times bigger, the front raised off the ground, a wingless dragon among the worms.

Separation is successful, smoothly handled, one of the only things to go as smoothly as the drills. The Knight Commander nods, satisfied, and his officers allow themselves a brief moment of inner celebration.

He glances up at the sky palace's shadow, wondering what discussions take place above him, and if an answer to his question will come soon.

He considers opening a channel to Obeisance. Pressuring her or The Seven never ends well but his military training chafes at the delay. His hand moves to initiate contact, stops, moves again, stops. It is all too easy to imagine how she will react. He grimaces. Obeisance has a way of making arguments evaporate and stripping the one making them of dignity.

His fist bangs on the bulkhead, startling those around him.

Things of importance are suddenly found on displays, officers leaning into their screens with utter focus.

238

The Knight Commander curses himself silently, then straightens in surprise as Obeisance's image begins to resolve in front of him.

It is as if she knows! It strikes him then that perhaps she does. He has always thought of the Lenses as a force out there, watching the Empire and its peoples for dissent, has never considered that they may watch him just as closely.

All of a sudden his back feels exposed, his officers no longer harmless. *Could one of them be reporting to her?*

If she harbours any doubts about him, none show in her projected face. 'Knight Commander.'

'Obeisance.'

'I trust the transition is going well.'

'Flawlessly.'

'Good. We cannot help but notice we are overtaking our own vanguard.'

'Apologies, I did not wish to deploy our ground forces until I had an answer.'

There is a pause and the Knight Commander feels a familiar dread. He has said the wrong thing.

'What answer is this? Have your orders not been clear?'

'My orders are clear but now that we know the First is in Wonderland I wanted to know if we were to seize on this opportunity or if we were to proceed after the traitors.'

'If They wished us to change course, do you not think I would have told you?'

'Forgive me, it is just that we have never had the First all in one place before, and never so close to us.'

'The Seven are aware of the situation. We must, as always, trust Their wisdom.'

He bows his head. 'Of course.'

'That said, diligence is all. We will send the Lenses there to observe the infernal, should The Seven wish to know more.' A slight distortion of her eyebrowless face is the only indication of her frown. 'I had believed Wonderland to be a ruin.'

'Perhaps the First hopes to hide there?'

'Perhaps, but I am not in the habit of idle speculation. We will watch and wait, and continue with our great enterprise.'

The Knight Commander isn't sure if there is a rebuke in there or not. He knows he should cut his losses but cannot help adding: 'The sky-ship you sent to Ferrous went dark. Will you require another?'

'No.'

He suspects there are many hidden depths behind the word but knows better than to ask. 'I'm scattering our scouts wide. It will slow our advance, but drive more of the tainted towards our destination. As we suspected, they are clumping together.'

'Lining their heads on the block for us. Good, I am sure this steady, certain approach will please The Seven. Impatience is rarely the way to perfection, as you know, Knight Commander.'

This time, the rebuke strikes him square. 'I will strive to please Them in all things.'

'As do we all,' she intones, her image fading from sight.

He whirls on his officers, catching a few of them staring at him before snapping back to their positions of diligence. *I am watching you now,* he thinks. *I am watching all of you.*

He circles the command platform, moving slowly, lingering briefly behind a few chairs, long enough to make them sweat. 'Are our scouts in position?'

'Yes, sir,' come the replies, one after the other, each squadron present and accounted for.

'Good. Tell them to fire at will. Any settlement not flying our flag, any travellers, anything that moves. I repeat: fire at will. It's time to start closing the trap.'

The meat runners are grateful, full of praise for the Vagrant's efforts, and keen to return the favour somehow. 'You can come with us, if you like? Some extra protection is always welcome and we can give you food and shelter.'

'Where are you going?' asks Jem.

'Same place everyone is going: Crucible. Word is they're going to need our services there.'

'Sounds good to me,' he glances at the Vagrant who is nodding, 'it's a deal. One more thing, we'd be grateful if we could have a spare travelling robe, the bigger the better.' One is brought out and Jem nods his thanks. 'We'll get ourselves together and catch you up.'

The meat runners agree, making their measured way south. This time, two of the younger members of the group have gone ahead, testing the ground with sticks.

Jem and the Vagrant watch them go, Jem's expression darkening as they move out of earshot. 'I know you think you're some sort of hero, but you're not.'

The Vagrant blinks.

'I told you we'd regret coming down. The sky-ship is trashed and we nearly died because of you. You gambled with our lives.'

The Vagrant looks away, his expression pained.

Jem only gets angrier. 'Clearly you don't care about us at all. Is it because Reela's tainted?'

The Vagrant's head snaps up, mouth open, shocked.

'I'll bet if she was perfect, like Vesper, then things would be different. You wouldn't risk Vesper's life to save some stranger, but me and Reela? That's another story.'

The Vagrant just stares.

'Nothing to say?' He prods at the Vagrant's chest, his lip curling. 'You can't even bring yourself to say sorry. Oh yes, I know you can speak when it suits you. Why not say something now? Am I not worthy of your breath?'

The Vagrant starts to shake his head. Lips move but no words come. He looks away again.

'Thought so.' Jem walks over to the remains of the sky-ship, full of angry thoughts.

Reela has managed to coax Delta from the wreckage. Jem beckons her over, being careful not to make eye contact with the immortal. 'Are you okay?'

Reela nods.

'Can you tell me how your head feels?'

Reela thinks for a minute, shrugs.

Jem tries to contain his frustration. 'It would help if you spoke to me. Does it hurt?'

She nods, holds up a hand, the index finger and thumb held slightly apart.

'Just a little? Well, that's good. If it gets any worse or if you feel sick, you have to come and tell me straight away, do you understand?'

She nods.

'Reela, if we're going to take Delta with us, I'm going to need your help.'

She looks up, instantly attentive.

'You know how sometimes you like to play dressing

up at home?' A grin spreads across her face. 'Well, we need Delta to play dressup as a meat runner.' He holds out the robe. 'Can you get her to put this on? I doubt it will cover her feet but if you can get it over her wings, that would be brilliant. And try to get her to pull up the hood. Do you think you can do that for me? It's very important.'

Reela nods.

'Good girl.'

As Reela struts off, a hero on her mission, Jem goes to find Mazar, who is stripping the wreckage.

'Find anything useful?'

'Not much. Bits and pieces.'

He checks Reela is nowhere nearby. 'Are you looking for your soldiers?'

Mazar pauses a moment. 'I . . . Yes.'

'Do you want me to help?'

'No!'

Jem takes a step back. 'Easy. It was just an offer.'

'No. I mean, you can't help them. They didn't make it.'

'Oh, I'm sorry.'

She looks at him for slightly too long. 'I'm not.'

'Well . . . we have to go soon, so if you have anything you need to do, now's the time.'

He leaves her to it, suddenly at a loss. He sees the Vagrant hasn't moved since their talk, he sees Reela, but she is standing on a hill of churned earth, battling to get the meat runner's robe over Delta's head.

With nothing else to do, he waits, feeling useless, his mind drifting, unhappy.

*   *   *

243

The suns circle each other, slow, as they make their way across the sky. Clouds are few while flies are everywhere, gathering around dirty puddles and the people trudging through them.

Gauze veils are pulled over faces, the meat runners well protected with fabric and repellent scents. Their beasts are similarly doused, with thick skins and swift tails to keep the bloodsuckers at bay.

Mazar's armour keeps her safe, as does the Vagrant's, and no fly dares to approach Delta. Reela is close enough to the immortal to be untroubled.

Jem is not so lucky.

By afternoon, a litany of red marks stand proud on his forearms, cheeks and the soft skin of his neck.

The Vagrant watches for signs of pursuit, sees none. The ground, though sodden, is mercifully stable beneath his feet. There is little conversation on the journey, the meat runners saving their energy during the day, only Mazar and Jem's voices breaking the sound of squelching boots and hooves. Without immediate threats or distractions, there is plenty of space for reflection. Several times, the Vagrant's eyes lose focus, watching the horizon but not really seeing it. Lines of sadness appear in his face, old grooves grown deep over the years. He reaches up, touching his cheek, exploring it slowly, mimicking the gesture of another, gone.

Eyes mist and his hand moves, covering his face, but he keeps walking.

By late afternoon, they break free of the marshes, joining a crumbling road. The mag-rails that once ran through it and the guide wires above stripped away long ago. Now only holes are left, like empty gums, useless.

But any road is better than none and many make use of it. A slow moving train of people shuffle on weary legs, laden with possessions, all going one way, all going south. The wealthy have more to carry and more to lose. Food-heavy transports are eyed jealously by starving neighbours only a few feet away.

The meat runners slot easily into the river of people, an unobtrusive addition. Mazar and the Vagrant receive some odd looks but the rifle on her shoulder and the sword on his stave off any trouble.

In the evening the group comes to a gradual stop and sets up camp. Portable heaters are cranked up, battered elements bashed into life. Small fires are lit and judiciously fed. People huddle together, a mix of refugees from multiple settlements, all driven south by the wrath of The Seven. Grudgingly, they share their space with one another, mutual distrust outweighed by the desire for warmth and comfort.

A little food is shared, a little drink. Those with drugs take them, synthetic smiles indistinguishable from natural ones and far more common. In the dark, it is easier to talk. Strangers become less so, swopping names and stories, old jokes and new fears.

The Vagrant stays quiet, listening.

'And I heard,' says a voice, it could be anyone's, identities interchangeable in the dark, 'that she's built a new city for us all to live in. It's like Wonderland used to be, only bigger.'

'Well,' says another, 'I don't trust that Bearer, what's her name? Viper? Veeper? Don't trust no one giving away something for nothing. There'll be a catch, you wait and see. She'll wait till our bits are well truly in her hands and then . . . boom!'

'You watch your mouth,' retorts the first speaker. 'She closed the Breach, so she did. They say she can fly.'

'Bollocks.'

'It's true! And she can talk to the animals.'

'I can talk to animals, don't mean they understand me.'

'But she isn't like you and me. She's Gamma, reborn.'

'If she's Gamma reborn,' asks a third person, 'then how come The Seven are coming after her?'

'They're not. They're coming after us. It's punishment for our crimes.' There are an assortment of grunts and disagreements but everyone feels the guilt hanging in the air. 'I used a little Necrotech in the early days. Everyone did. Most of my friends are dead now because of it. And how many of us gave in to the taint? If we'd been loyal, our bodies would have stayed normal. Soon as I find a decent surgeon I'm going to have them cut off my studs. Going to get me purged. There's nothing to fear if you get purged.'

They chew this over for a while, the occasional fly twanging into the heater, sizzling, popping.

'Sounds like you heard a lot of stuff,' says the second speaker. 'But did you hear about her lover?'

There are some muttered assents and several admissions of ignorance. Sensing the gossip, all lean closer. 'Heard he's hideous ugly. I heard that what people think is a goat is actually him!'

There is some laughter at that. The Vagrant smiles to himself.

Another voice whispers into the night, young sounding, anxious. 'I thought the First was her lover and they have half-breed babies. Lots and lots of them.'

The Vagrant stops smiling and there is a round of derision and a thwack of a palm against the side of a head.

Something like thunder rumbles in the distance, something like lightning flashing on the northern horizon. Conversation fades away as faces turn towards it. Sporadic but regular it comes and goes. People hunker down, pulling blankets tighter round their shoulders.

'What is that?' asks one.

'That's why we're on the road,' says another. 'Looks like they're going to do to us what they did to the colonies.'

Nobody needs to ask any more details. They do not need to see the flames to understand that there is fire, do not need to hear the screams to know that those left behind are dead.

Nobody sleeps well that night, kept awake by consciences, fears and the buzzing of hungry flies.

In the morning, the group set off early, making the most of the pre-dawn light. Worried glances are cast back over shoulders but there are no lights in the sky, no sign of fires or fighting.

The group parts company with the road, following a recently made path through fields less sodden than the ones before.

Delta's sword shifts in the Vagrant's grasp, agitated. He frowns, looking around for trouble. He sees nothing at first, then hears it, a quiet hissing in the background all around him.

Unaware of any strangeness the group continue on.

The Vagrant readies the sword, regularly checks his surroundings. Picking up on his unease, Mazar begins checking her rifle.

As the first rays of the red sun begin to ink in the fields around them, they see buds breaking the earth. An hour ago there was nothing but now the fields are unmistakably full of tiny shoots.

Oversized birds flop down from the sky, seed hunting, worm catching. They do not yet have the courage to attack the travellers, content with the other bounties offered close by.

Another hour and the shoots have reached ankle height, the hissing finally understandable as the sound of thousands of stalks sliding against the skin of the earth.

Delta is appalled.

Reela is delighted. She runs about, Jem and the Vagrant chasing after, touching every plant she can. Plucking a leaf, she sniffs it, goes to taste it.

'No!' exclaims Jem. 'It's dangerous.'

Reela pouts and gives a sly look at a nearby plant. Before she can reach for it, she is lifted into the air, feet kicking in surprise before landing on the Vagrant's shoulders.

Soon the group are having to weave around the young stalks that grow fast and thick all around them. The second sun is well into the sky now, baking shoulders and tops of heads.

By midday the foliage is swollen, greenish skin stretched full of fluid, leaves sprouting like sails, a patchwork canopy. Birds sit heavy on the branches or waddle about on the ground, too full to fly, walking oranges with feather crowns, not long for the world.

By late afternoon the group leaves the forest behind. When the suns begin to set the first of the new plants bursts open, spreading seeds and mulch in all directions. Another follows, then another, as if some unseen signal has been given. Smaller pops, equally messy, come from a series of avian explosions.

Fluids drain quickly into the fields, absorbed for the next day's cycle.

The group neither see nor care, their attention firmly ahead. The worst of the tainted fields have been crossed and beyond the field they now walk is a valley, topped with man-made walls and squatting bunkers. A multitude of flags fly from poles, dizzying in number, and there are tents and makeshift houses everywhere, a city of scraps and offcuts.

Crucible.

Genner makes his way along the line of new arrivals. The most useful have already been identified for him: glass cutters, meat runners and one or two traders with rare machine parts. Normally his people would handle this for him but there are some things that must be seen firsthand.

He moves quickly along the line, taking little interest in the thin, desperate faces.

As he nears the back he sees them and his face falls. Being of the Lenses, Genner quickly collects it again, coming to a stop in front of the Vagrant and giving a smart salute.

'It's been a long time,' he says.

The Vagrant's eyes narrow a fraction as he nods.

Genner's chip has already identified Mazar. One of the military elite, with near perfect performance scores, it does not surprise him that they wanted to make a squire of her, is curious as to why they didn't. He notes she is believed to have been killed in action.

It also identifies Jem. Though he already knows the information, Genner reviews it on instinct: a survivor of New Horizon, he was held by an infernal known as the Demagogue for more than a decade before joining Vesper and becoming her lover. Low levels of taint suspected. Purging required.

'And you must be Reela,' he says, crouching down to come level with her scowling face. At the same time he prepares to update her entry. 'I'm Genner. I'm helping your mother here. Would you like to see her?'

Her scowl breaks and she nods several times.

'Good, I'll take you to her,' he says while adding: *Taint manifesting through skin discolouration and patterning. Condition worsening rather than improving. Suspect mutation is already underway.*

He is about to add more when he spots the silver shins on the other side of her shoulder. For a moment his eyes track up, peering into the dark of a hood, then words fly from his mind and he goes to one knee, lowering his head.

Fear thuds through every heartbeat, rapid, as he tries to understand. Why is Delta here? What does it mean and what will she think of his actions? Will he be judged and if so, will he be elevated or cast down?

But Delta does not deign to look, much less to see. It is as if she is not truly there, a ghost in her form, drifting in the background.

He feels a tap on his shoulder, masks his irritation and looks up.

'Can we go now?' Jem says. 'We're getting a lot of attention out here.'

'At once,' Genner replies. He leads them past the other

hopefuls queuing for entry, all too aware of Delta at their backs. His attention returns to the Vagrant and the sword he carries. Her sword. Questions form in his mind that he has no answers to. Unlike many in the Empire of the Winged Eye, the Lenses are trained to question and investigate, to consider facts from multiple angles. He wonders if Delta is here against her will or whether she supports Vesper's work, or if she is simply curious. He keeps such thoughts to himself, observing quietly, collecting data.

They are waved through the outer walls, coming into Crucible's chaotic innards. Temporary structures are all around, some colourful, some faded, all with purpose. Desperate people flit from stall to stall, looking for ways to make their savings stretch. All around them, deals are done, labour exchanged for trinkets. He knows that less savoury markets have already sprung up, a sudden revival in Necrotech. He has not moved against the traders yet, wanting to learn why anyone would want the redundant interfaces now that the art of animating dead tissue is lost.

He is aware of various factions moving like sharks through the crowds. The scavengers of Slake working for Gorad and Gut-pumper. The First's nomads, pretending to be independent traders. There are even a couple of the Man-shape's puppets to be found.

Genner shakes his head. There are too many agendas in the mix, too many ways things can go wrong.

By the time they arrive at the dome, Vesper has come down to meet them. Genner salutes and stands aside, becoming an unobtrusive figure on the sidelines.

'You're alive!' Vesper shouts, breaking into a run.

The Vagrant smiles, Reela doing the same a beat after.

251

Just before she gets to them, Jem steps in front and the two embrace.

Some of the lustre fades in the Vagrant's face.

'Jem!' she practically shrieks his name. 'Oh Jem, I feared the worst.' She pulls back, looking at him. 'Are you hurt?'

'Just a few knocks, nothing serious. I'd kill for a good meal though.'

'Yes, although we're rationing so don't get too excited.' She steps back, looking around him. 'Is that my Reela?'

Reela nods but as Vesper kneels down the girl backs away.

'She's been through a lot,' Jem mumbles.

Vesper straightens, looking away. 'I'm sure she has. When you've had a chance to rest, I want to hear all about it.' She steps towards her father, then stops, sudden.

Two swords hum, making the air quiver. An eye at Vesper's shoulder stares, probing, while the one in Delta's sword seems to shrink briefly within the hilt before rallying. 'Is that?'

The Vagrant nods.

'I don't understand.'

'It's a long story,' Jem mutters.

The Vagrant nods again.

Vesper looks at the group, taking in each face before turning back to her father. 'Where's Uncle Harm?'

The Vagrant steps closer to her, takes her hands in his. He shakes his head, slow, sad.

'No!' she shouts. Then: 'What happened? How did he? No, no . . .'

While the Vagrant pulls her into his arms Genner updates his files. Even while he does this, he watches them all. How Jem stares at the floor, how the sword that Vesper carries seems to radiate anger, casting its gaze from Delta's sword, to Delta, to Jem and back again, calculating.

Briefly, Delta looks across at the two blades, then flinches as if struck, turning from the group. Genner does not know how The Seven should act but he is sure it is not like this. Why is Delta not bearing Her own sword? Why does She trail round after these people? If he had not known better, he would have mistaken the immortal for Reela's minder.

There are patterns here he does not yet understand but he knows that time will reveal them. All he has to do is remain quiet and wait.

CHAPTER FIFTEEN

Vesper reclines on a mutigel cube, getting her head together while Jem chats in the background. It occurs to her that she ought to have settled into the room by now. It is a functional space without personality. Vesper wishes she were somewhere else. She wishes she were home. But there is no home to go to anymore. The Seven have destroyed it.

'We need to talk about Reela,' Jem says, chewing on a flavoured vegetable stick. 'I know this has been hard on her but she's getting into bad habits. You know she hasn't uttered a word since we left the Shining City?'

'No.'

'Not a single word. And you know it's your father's fault? Reela's started copying him and he's encouraging it.'

She realizes that she should probably be getting ready and slowly starts to pull on her boots. Jem continues to talk. He sounds angry. She should probably do something about that.

'Reela nearly died following him into the ocean.'

Vesper nearly drops her coat. 'What was that?'

'I said she nearly died. Suns knows what would have happened if I hadn't gone after her and pulled her out. But he doesn't care. I'm starting to wonder if he's actually looking for a way to get himself killed, and us with him.'

'He loves Reela. He always has.'

'When you love someone you look after them, you don't abandon them.' He waves the vegetable stick for emphasis. 'I'm telling you, you need to do something about him. He'll listen if it comes from you.'

Vesper shrugs into her coat and moves the shoulder plates into position. She hates it when her family argue. The thought comes to her that Uncle Harm will sort it out, followed by the sure knowledge that he won't. That his soft voice will never take the heat out of their arguments again. She covers her mouth, clamping the sob inside before it can escape.

Jem doesn't notice. 'Sorry to go on but it's been unbearable, cooped up with him all this time. He hates me. Never says it of course but I see it in his eyes.'

She moves to the door, nods. 'I've got to go. I'll see you later.'

'Already? Is everything alright?'

She doesn't turn to face him, picking up the sword and slinging it over her shoulder. 'Yes, everything's fine.'

'But you are going to speak to him?'

'Yes. I've just got something to take care of first.'

Full of people, the audience chamber has an energy to it. Vesper drinks it in, accepting aid from any quarter. The leaders of the fragmented world are mostly present, together in the same space for the first time in living history. Representatives from Slake, New Horizon, Red Rails, West

Rift, Verdigris and the Thousand Nails all sit in their designated areas, staring down at her.

She is mindful of the empty spaces waiting to be filled by the First and Neer, and of the many people who have journeyed to her still waiting to be given a voice.

But there is no more time. She has to act now.

Vesper spreads her arms wide. 'Welcome. I can't tell you what it means to me that you're all here. I know we didn't exactly plan it this way but before I get to what's coming, I wanted us to take a moment to appreciate where we are right now.

'For my whole life, it's been about survival. There was a war on, and people were either fighting the enemy to hold onto their homes or fighting their neighbours to get enough to eat that night.

'They say that the Usurper won the Battle of the Red Wave but that it lost the war against the Empire. That's only half true. The Usurper did lose the war but the Empire also lost. And everyone in the middle lost too. There were no winners in that conflict.

'Since then we've all been fighting over what's left. Well, I say, no more. I say there's another possibility: one where we meet, as we're meeting right now, and make a different kind of future together. A safer future where we build something better.

'We're at the very start of what I hope is a new age, and what we decide here,' she spreads her hands to encompass them all, 'will shape the world.' She pauses, lets it sink in. 'So with that in mind, there are a few simple rules that you've already been apprised of but I want to reiterate here. One, everyone has the right to speak their mind. Two, everyone has the right to be heard. Three, everyone has the right to speak without interruption. Four, everyone has a right to hear the truth and only the truth. Five, this is no place for angry words or insults. Six, any of you who have a matter to lay before us are welcome to come down to the floor and do so.'

She smiles, sheepish. 'That's all for now but rules will probably develop as we find need of them.'

For a while the various delegations talk amongst themselves, leaving her to stand alone, exposed, unsure of what is to come.

The Man-shape is the first to speak. It has been ensconced on a high, hooded throne, modelled after the one in New Horizon. The back of the chair curls over, casting the Man-shape's head in shadow, hiding it from view. Because of this, the assembled are spared the sight of its mouth contorting to make the right shapes. 'This is a statement of intention. I am here to make peace with you. I have served those making war on your world. It did not work. Your world changed us. It forced us into new forms. We did not ask to be this way just as you did not ask for us to come. Your world changed us and we changed your world. It is our world now. We must find a way to coexist or we will surely destroy each other.'

Vesper inclines her head in the Man-shape's direction, grateful. There are gentle noises of support from the direction of Verdigris' delegation and from the prince of Red Rails.

'Thank you, Man-shape. Who wishes to speak next?'

The rulers of Slake sit on elaborate seats constructed of sparkling chrome. Gorad leans forward, the old woman's

257

smile patient, painted. 'My colleague, Gut-pumper, has a thought.'

Gut-pumper leans over as well. 'More of a question, really.'

'Yes,' agrees Gorad, 'more of a question. All of this talk of peace is well and good.'

'Lovely,' adds Gut-pumper.

'But the thing is, the Empire of the Winged Eye isn't interested in peace. They've been blowing up everything between here and the Shining City and it doesn't look as if they're going to stop anytime soon.'

'So my question is—' begins Gut-pumper.

'—His question is, when are we going to start talking about the Empire and how we're going to fight them?'

'We also wish this question to be answered.' This new voice comes from amidst the West Rift delegation, distorted by a breathing mask, anonymous. The group has not identified a single leader, deliberately obscuring their command structure.

Vesper feels the attention of the room focus on her and the sudden bloom of heat on her cheeks. 'I've heard what the Empire are doing and of course we have to be prepared to fight if it comes to it.'

She hears her words barked back from a few places, turned into exclamations. 'If it comes to it? If it comes to it!'

'Yes!' she says, raising her voice. 'They haven't listened to anyone else but they might listen to me. Before we fight I'm going to try and reason with them.'

Gorad taps her cane three times to get the room's attention. 'If I remember correctly, rule number four says we have to have truth and only truth here. So, I hope you'll forgive my . . .'

258

'Being blunt?' suggests Gut-pumper.

'My plain speaking, but when you set all this up, you spoke for the Empire. Now it looks to me like you don't speak for them no more. Looks like they want to burn you as much as the rest of us.'

'Maybe more,' adds Gut-pumper.

'So, if I'm honest, I'm wondering why we should listen to you at all.'

Vesper's throat dries up. She has to fight to keep from drawing the sword. It is furious and she is furious and, pent up, that fury swats away any words of peace before they can get out of her mouth.

From the area reserved for Verdigris, Tough Call clears her throat. 'Way I see it, none of us would even be here if it weren't for Vesper. We'd be behind our walls waiting for the Empire to pick us off one by one. If it weren't for Vesper we'd all have been eaten by the Yearning years ago. I know most of you by reputation but I know Vesper by deed. She saved my city from a plague. Didn't have to but she did.

'I reckon she's earned the right to have my ear. I don't reckon any of the rest of you can say that. With or without the Empire, I say that Vesper is the only one that we all actually trust. Unless you want me to run this show?' Tough Call looks around, meeting the eyes of the other delegations. 'Thought not. So until someone better comes along, how about we stop acting like gutter scavs and start listening.'

The Thousand Nails roar their approval and Vesper's next breath comes easier. 'You have to decide for yourselves if you want to listen to me but I have Gamma's sword, and that makes me the only one that The Seven might listen to. And if they don't, I'll stand with you and I'll make sure we win. I have my own knights and my own soldiers that will fight with us.' Somehow, the sword is in her hand and her voice acquires a new resonance. 'And I have bled for all of you. Is that not enough?' She sweeps the tip of the sword from one end of the room to the other. 'It's up to you. Listen or don't listen but I stand here. And I will speak. And nobody, not you,' she points at Gorad, 'or you,' she points at Gut-pumper, then extends the sword straight out to her right, 'and certainly not The Seven are going to stop me.'

There is a long silence, filled by the vibrations of the sword. As the room stills again, Gorad and Gut-pumper exchange a look.

'In that case,' says Gorad.

'Yes, in that case,' agrees Gut-pumper.

'In that case,' repeats Gorad, 'we're all ears.'

Vesper strides out of the dome, needing air, needing to be alone. She manages to sheathe the sword though she still feels its power tingling through her.

Normally she would go to her room and shut out the demands of others but the space is no longer empty and, guiltily, she realizes that the thought of speaking to Jem is not a comforting one.

She makes her way up the side of the valley, having to scramble up in places. It isn't dignified but she doesn't care. It feels good to concentrate on something simple.

As her body attends to the demands of the climb, the events of the meeting play out in her mind. Words are dragged over, analysed. Several times she winces at the memory of her tone, or how she struggled to answer a question, or the way some of the other leaders stared at her. Even worse, she finds gaps in her recollections, where the memory is emotional only, disconnected.

She reaches the top, flopping down, savouring the quiet. On the opposite side of the valley there is a great deal of industry. Fortifications continue to be built, and new arrivals appear in regular spurts, hurried, looking warily over shoulders.

But on her side it is quiet, there is no reason for anyone to be there.

The buck does not need a reason. He goes where he pleases and, for the moment, that is close to Vesper. Nearby tufts of grass are picked at, restlessly, his dark eyes often on the lookout.

Vesper reaches up to stroke his flank. If she closed her eyes, she could almost be home, a child, innocent again, dreaming of adventures in the Shining City.

Then a voice slaps her back to the here and now. 'A nice view, yes?'

She groans. 'Ezze?'

'Yes, and it is good that I have caught you here.'

'Not now, Ezze. I need a bit of time alone.'

'Ah, but this is the best time for us to be speaking, uninterrupted by others, where the only tongues wagging will be ours.'

She looks up, sees her father slowly working his way up the side of the valley and sighs. 'Go on then.'

'As you know, great lady, these are hard times. Ezze has been working hard to give the people what they need. Much of this is like the children playing, and after a quick talk, they leave, fresh meat on one shoulder, leather balls on the other for the recreation and all is well.' He chuckles for a moment before letting his face fall. 'But!' He holds up a finger, dramatic. 'There is one thing even Ezze cannot sell.'

He waits and Vesper sighs again. 'And what's that?'

'Much as it brings great sadness, Ezze admits that he cannot sell hope, not without you, great lady.'

'What are you talking about?'

'Always, you inspire. When the people see you striding about, your hair ready for war and your eyes flashing like the lamps. But this is only in the day and it is in the night that the fear creeps in. Imagine how it could be if the people could be touching you at night!'

Vesper grits her teeth. 'Seriously, what are you talking about?'

'Little Vespers!' exclaims Ezze, brandishing a small doll. Padded insides covered with flexible plastic give the texture of human skin, with face and clothes painted on.

'It doesn't even look like me!'

'The people will not care so long as they are thinking it is you.'

The Vagrant is not far away now. She gives him a wave. He doesn't wave back, his attention on Ezze.

'And who is this?' asks Ezze. 'He looks like a man from the Winged Empire. This is good! Their needs are always interesting!'

'I doubt he'll want to buy anything.'

'Then watch as Ezze brushes away those doubts with the best offers around. See how the man gets quicker with anticipation!'

Vesper frowns, and an eye opens at her shoulder, curious. The Vagrant is moving faster, his hands clenched tight at his sides.

'Ah,' says Ezze, opening his arms. 'I see you are a man of purpose. You have come to the right place. Whatever help you need to fulfil this purpose, Ezze can provide. Just unfold your desires and we will soon find a suitable product to match them.'

The Vagrant comes to a stop in front of Ezze, his chest rising and falling, air whistling angrily through his nose.

'This is not our first meeting, no? There is something familiar about the unhappiness in your eyeballs. Do not be sad, friend, if something has not been to your liking, perhaps we can trade?'

The Vagrant's hands slowly rise, opening.

Vesper's frown deepens and she starts to get up. 'Father, what is it?'

Ezze's eyes widen. 'Did you say fa—?'

The Vagrant's hands encircle Ezze's throat and squeeze.

'What are you doing?' Vesper says. She goes to intercept but one of the sword's wings grips her shoulder, telling her to wait.

Sweat patches appear on Ezze like magic, at armpits, across the chest, beads popping up all over his face. He begins pulling objects from his pockets, holding them up so the Vagrant can see: a rat-fur moustache, a diamond choker made with real plastic, an unidentified tablet.

The Vagrant continues to squeeze and more things appear: a sausage with dubious filling, a highly polished molar, an actual diamond.

None of them catch the Vagrant's attention.

Veins now rise under Ezze's skin, the sweat pouring freely.

'Don't kill him!' shouts Vesper. Again she is about to intervene, again the sword squeezes her shoulder. Surprised, she looks at the sword for confirmation. An eye is staring at the scene, drinking it in, gleeful.

Something in Ezze seems to break and the man sags. In defeat, he holds up a single platinum coin.

The Vagrant seizes it and Ezze drops to the floor, gasping. While the merchant wheezes at his feet, the Vagrant examines the coin, then tucks it away. He looks down at Ezze and his fist lifts. He looks from Ezze, to his fist and back again, his expression dark. Then he glances at Vesper.

'Father?' she asks.

The Vagrant sighs, his fist becoming a wave.

As the pressure at her shoulder eases, Vesper moves to join him. 'Was that really necessary?'

He nods, confident, and she feels the sword thrum in agreement.

'Oh . . . okay then.' She looks down at Ezze. 'Are you alright?'

Unable to flap his mouth, Ezze flaps his hands instead.

'I think you were right when you said you can't sell hope. The dolls aren't going to work out. People are going to have to make do with me.' She turns to the Vagrant. 'Come on.'

She leads him away, the buck trotting after them, leaving Ezze to gasp in the dirt.

When it is clear the threat has passed, he slowly sits up, rubbing at his neck as he watches them leave. He notices that an eye remains open at Vesper's back, looking at him, its silver wing raising in a gesture that, if it came from any lesser creature, he would swear was obscene.

Vesper and the Vagrant walk for a while, enjoying each other's company. 'It's strange seeing you in that armour,' she says. 'When I was little I used to imagine you dressed that way, like the knights in the stories Uncle Harm used to tell.'

At the mention of his name, tears spark in their eyes but Vesper manages to keep talking. 'I know that really you were in that dirty old coat but in my mind, you'd always throw it off before fighting your enemies, and underneath it you were in sparkling mail from head to toe. It's funny what we think as children.'

The Vagrant nods.

'I used to think the sword was enormous but over time it's got smaller.'

The Vagrant points at her, then holds out his hand at chest height, lifting it up.

She laughs. 'I got bigger, I know. That's not what I mean though. When I didn't know the sword, it was this scary thing I'd always been told to keep away from. At first I was so scared of it I didn't think of it as a person, like us. Then one day I realized it had feelings too, that it wasn't this force of nature. It was just angry, and sometimes it could be scared too.'

The Vagrant tilts his head, noncommittal.

'I believe the same is true for The Seven. Everyone else sees Them as something better than us that's beyond question, but we've met Them. We know They're not perfect.'

This time, the Vagrant agrees without hesitation.

'If I can find a way to get Them to listen, I'm sure we could find a non-violent way to do this. There's already been too much bloodshed.'

The Vagrant puts a hand on her shoulder, gives it a gentle squeeze.

'Do you think I can get through to Them?'

He tries to smile but amber eyes only manage melancholy. Whatever else she is about to say is swallowed down as Genner arrives. 'What is it?' she asks.

'The Empire's forces are almost on us. I've communicated your desire to talk to them.'

'Have they responded?'

'Not yet.'

'We should be ready for when they do. Tell Samael to gather my knights and meet me in front of the wall. Send word to Doctor Grains that he is welcome to join us. In fact, make it clear to all the delegations that they can send representatives with me if they want to.'

Genner starts to turn, then stops, uneasy. 'Are you sure that's wise? Your knights are using some kind of derived Necrotech, and Samael is clearly infernal. If you take them with you, it will damage your chances of getting The Seven to listen.'

'But if I hide them, then I'm saying I'm ashamed, and I'm not! I'm proud to call Samael a friend, and I'm proud of my knights.' She sees Genner's look of concern and resists the urge to shake him. 'Don't you understand? If this is going to work, The Seven need to see us as we are. They need to adapt to us.'

'I understand. For what it's worth, I hope I'm wrong.'

Vesper dismisses him, and she and the Vagrant go back to Reela's room. Mazar reports there has been no trouble as she unlocks the door, allowing them both to go inside.

Delta appears to sleep in one corner, a battered coat draped over her like a blanket. Reela lies next to her, pretending to sleep also.

Vesper looks at them, the sword does the same. Her face becomes stern. 'Wake up,' she commands.

In the opposite corner of the room, Delta's sword stirs while Reela screws her eyes shut tighter.

'Wake up, I said!'

Silver eyelids flicker but don't open.

The Vagrant edges forward, scooping Reela off the floor and into his arms. Vesper draws the sword as he steps to the side, well out of her way.

For a third time she demands Delta's attention, the words seeming to thrum on the sword's edge, echoing, and Delta's eyes stretch open as if in shock.

Vesper allows her own to close, the sword seeing for the both of them. 'You've slept long enough. If you want to stay here, the least you can do is take an interest in what's happening.'

Slowly, Delta raises her head, making eye contact.

'I know that you don't agree with Alpha. Join your voice to mine, together we have a chance to end this before things escalate.'

Delta's words come softly from silver lips, like teardrops falling. 'He will not listen.'

'We don't know that!'

A little certainty returns to the immortal's expression. 'We do.'

'Even if that's true, the others might. It could be enough.'

Delta turns away and her sword rattles on the floor.

Vesper's voice lowers, becoming older. 'Must I always be the one to go out there? Must I always be the one to suffer?'

'But I have suffered.'

Vesper shakes her head and opens her eyes. 'Come on,' she says to the Vagrant. 'We have work to do.'

But as she moves towards the door, a sound stops her.

Delta's sword is trembling on the floor. Alone, it lacks the strength to sing, but it manages to make itself heard, tapping on the ground, forcing out notes with effort, dull, muted.

The Vagrant goes and picks it up, offers it to Delta, hilt first.

The immortal remains where she is, curled upon the floor, curled within her wings. Vesper gives her one last look before walking out.

Slowly, the hilt of Delta's sword lowers. The Vagrant sighs. Reela sighs.

Delta's sword hums again, louder now, motivating, and Delta looks at it, a pained expression on her face.

With a stamp of her foot, Reela goes over to Delta and grabs her little finger. Hold established, she starts to walk after her mother.

The Vagrant raises an eyebrow.

Delta does not resist, flowing to her feet, a giant silver balloon gliding behind a stony faced girl.

They pass through the doorway, leaving the Vagrant and Delta's sword to stare, then follow.

While the journey south has been swift for the Knight Commander, it has not been pleasant. They have met little resistance, driving back the enemy by their mere presence, and yet he has felt a lowering of morale. For as they have travelled the sheer scale of the problem begins to show itself.

Gloomily, he watches the alien scenery go by his window. It is one thing to fight a demon or to cleanse a tainted body but what do you do when the environment itself needs purging?

He considers putting the fields they cross to the torch but

will they have to stop to bring flame to every blade of grass? And what of the deeper soil and the stone underneath that? What of the mountains around them? What of the very air itself?

It is too big a thing to contemplate, and in the end the Knight Commander takes solace in his position. His job is to fight military battles, and he is happy to let The Seven worry for the world.

One of his officers looks up from a screen. 'Knight Commander, our scouts report movement from the enemy base. A small force is coming out, heading our way.'

'What do we have on them?'

'They're on foot, armed but weapons stowed. The Bearer is there . . . as is our former Champion.'

The Knight Commander hears the surprise in the man's voice and is glad that he already knows of the Champion's survival. 'Anything else?'

'Sorry, sir, I'm just confirming the report . . . Yes, they say Delta Herself walks with them, sir. How can that be?'

How indeed? 'I asked for information not questions, captain.'

'Sorry, sir. The Order of the Broken Blades is present, as are a number of others, including a Dogspawn!'

He paces the length of the command centre twice, considering what is to be done. 'I take it there's been no word from Obeisance?'

'None, sir.'

'Resend my request. Notify me the moment you hear anything. I want a unit of our best brought forward, no more or less than the Bearer's party, match them man for man.'

'Yes, sir.'

'Have our generals prep their troops for action but mark me, they are to hold position until I give the order. And keep the sky-ships back, I doubt their cloaks will hold up to the Bearer's scrutiny.'

'You're not actually going to talk to them, are you, sir?'

'Don't look so worried,' he says, as much to himself as to the captain. 'Are our scouts in place?'

'Yes, sir.'

'Good, remind them that they are to close the door and hold it closed, nothing more. I don't want any heroics.'

'Understood.'

'Be sure that *they* do, captain.' He marches towards the exit hatch. 'Only disturb me if Obeisance calls or the sky falls down.'

He knows he walks a delicate line. To attack without sanction would mean his doom one way or another. To not answer the Bearer's call would look like weakness. He has to act, and hope that Obeisance responds while the enemy are still in his grasp.

CHAPTER SIXTEEN

Most of the delegations decide not to accompany Vesper. Flat Head of the Thousand Nails is one of the exceptions. Though her advisors would prefer the Usurperkin stay behind, Vesper is adamant she be included. However, she does consent to putting Flat Head towards the back of the group.

She and Samael walk at the head of it, the Vagrant and Delta of The Seven behind them. Instead of her sword, an old coat trails from the immortal's fingers. The Order of the Broken Blades march alongside, with Doctor Grains and his followers coming after, flags to the Winged Eye fluttering, bright against the dull sky.

Though the field has been punched full of holes and traps for the unwary, a single pathway remains through the centre, untouched. An easy path for enemy soldiers to take, a lure to funnel them towards death.

For now, it serves a different function, allowing Vesper and her retinue to traverse the space with dignity.

She gestures ahead, glances at Samael. 'What do you think?'

271

He looks at the force opposite, a strange mirror. For each of their knights, the Empire of the Winged Eye has fielded one of their own. For each civilian, a soldier. Where their group is a mix of styles, the Empire's makes clean blocks of colour.

Behind them rises a wall of human and machine, a backdrop of menace, a promise of things to come. Above them, the sky is strangely empty. Of Alpha's palace, there is no sign.

Scout whines by his feet and Samael murmurs, 'I do not think they are here to talk.'

'Then why haven't they attacked?'

He has no answer for that.

The Knight Commander waits for them, standing proud of his officers. He cuts an impressive figure. A tall man made taller by his armour.

As Vesper goes forward to meet him, Samael touches her arm. 'Don't trust him. He's hiding something.'

She gives him a bleak smile. 'I know, don't worry about me.'

The two face off in the space between their groups.

'Bearer.'

'Knight Commander.'

'I assume you have something to say to me?'

Vesper nods. 'I do. Quite a lot, actually.' She pauses, frowning at her reflection and the way it distorts in the hard edges of his visor. 'Starting is always the hardest part . . . I'm glad that you're here, you've always been kind to me.'

'That was before you betrayed the Empire.'

She glances skyward, then back to him. 'Let's get to it then. Actually, before we do, can you take off your helmet?'

'What?'

'It feels strange not being able to see your face.'

He makes a sound, part surprise, part disapproval. She waits him out, and after another grunt, unintelligible, he takes it off. The face underneath is lean, covered in lines of stress. She sees a man out of his depth, doing his best to mask the panic.

'That's better. Actually, that's really the point I want to make. It's much easier to talk when we can really see each other, just like it's much harder to kill when you know who you're fighting.'

'I do not shirk from hard choices. The taint must be cut away, or it will consume us all. If you truly cared for the people behind you, you would purge them yourself, not indulge them like this!'

'Why?'

'This is ridiculous!'

'Is it? Then answer. Save me from my own ignorance!'

'Because the taint corrupts and kills, just as surely as the infernals do.'

Vesper tries not to laugh. 'Then explain Samael. He is a knight, an infernal and a friend. Explain why my daughter is tainted and yet able to hold hands with one of The Seven. Explain why it was infernals, not knights who had to step in to save the people we abandoned. Explain why I should submit to your judgement and not the other way around.

'You are asking me to kill innocents or to cut away pieces of their very soul and hope that something remains at the end of it, and for who? For beings that do not care if we live or die. Beings that did nothing while the world suffered. Don't you think it's convenient that The Seven act now, after the Usurper and the Yearning have gone? They were too afraid to act when we needed Them so why listen to Them now? Tell me!'

The Knight Commander takes a step back, involuntary.

'You can't, can you?' She pauses, her face softening. 'Do you realize I've known you for years and I've never even been told your name? I can't believe you were born as the Knight Commander, and yet that's what the Empire tries to turn us into, titles and roles. It's like they squeeze the person out of us. Everyone knows me as the Bearer. Not a person in my own right . . . just a means to transport the sword. But I'm more than a handle with legs, and you're more than a military office. It's time for us to acknowledge that. To stand as ourselves. Complex and conflicted and . . . and wonderful.'

She waits for an answer, watching as he struggles to make one. 'You have to surrender,' he says at last. 'It's your only chance.'

'Maybe. But I'm still waiting for you to tell me why it's the right choice.'

He shakes his head, unable to look her in the eye. 'I . . .'

From his helmet, the voice of Obeisance issues. 'It is alright Knight Commander, I will take it from here. Vesper, in the name of The Seven, surrender Gamma's sacred blade and Delta over to us, stand down your forces, open your doors and prepare yourself for Their mercy.'

'The Seven!' retorts Vesper. 'Are you even listening to yourself? There aren't seven of them. One is half dead and the other is here, with me. The Seven don't exist anymore. They are divided. That means that you don't have authority here, that's why we need to talk.'

Impassioned words make little impact on Obeisance's calm.

The Seven

'You forget yourself, Bearer. Your place is to serve Gamma's blade. You are part of an order, just as much as I am. Even within The Seven there is a hierarchy. First and foremost of them all is Alpha and I speak for Him. In His name, I tell you to surrender or be destroyed.'

'It doesn't have to be like this. You know Them, Obeisance. Reason with Them, please.'

'This is your last chance.'

Vesper does not hesitate. 'I will not surrender.'

'So be it.'

The helmet goes quiet and the Knight Commander puts it back on.

An eye narrows, staring up at the clouds. A moment later, the sword begins to hum. 'What's going on?' asks Vesper.

'Our deaths,' replies the Knight Commander.

Above their heads, a mile away but racing closer, is a warhead, attuned to the chip in the Knight Commander's brain. It streaks towards them, an angel of death, screaming.

Vesper reaches for the sword but the Knight Commander rushes forward, grabbing her wrist, forcing it down, her fingers only able to brush the hilt before slipping away.

The sword shakes helpless in its sheath.

The warhead breaks through the clouds.

In vain, Vesper continues to wrestle with the Knight Commander.

'I'm sorry,' he says.

The Vagrant has time to blink.

Commotion has broken out behind him. In front, the enemy are registering the end of negotiations. Guns point forward, swords slide from sheaths, singing.

No shots are fired but none need to be, the warhead bringing enough death for everyone.

Samael is running towards Vesper, and the Vagrant joins him, even though it is pointless. The Vagrant raises Delta's sword, trying to get it above Vesper's head, even though he is not fast enough to get there, even though it is pointless.

The scream of the warhead becomes deafening, its shadow casting over them all.

The Vagrant takes breath to sing but another beats him to it.

It is felt in the bones before it is heard, reaching the heart before the ear has time to register it. A songlike shout, a call of defiance.

A force from behind pushes the Vagrant, making him stumble, a great downdraft that nearly has him on his knees.

Screaming, the warhead stops directly above their heads.

The warhead stops screaming.

The warhead stops, caught, a pair of silver hands either side of it. Without power of its own, only Delta's wings hold it aloft.

Hesitantly, together, the Vagrant and Delta's sword look up.

They see Delta's song surrounding the warhead, suppressing, not quite containing, but forcing the explosion into slow motion. Metal buckles beneath Delta's fingers, going molten, the shell of the warhead disintegrating as fire bulges, threatening to wash out in all directions.

Delta's wings sweep around the flames, head lowering, cocooning them with her body.

There is a boom, muffled, far away, and then Delta is

falling. She does not have far to go. There is a thud and then the only movement comes from the smoke curling upwards from wings and limbs and chest and head.

The Vagrant has time to blink before Samael reaches Vesper and the Knight Commander. The half-breed grabs the man's right wrist as Scout's jaws close around his left. Gauntlet and jaws squeeze together, and bones break, synchronous, canine and infernal strength more than enough to snap flimsy wrists.

The Empire's knights move to assist their leader, and the Vagrant moves to intercept them. Though outnumbered the Vagrant has some advantages. He carries Delta's sword and he is known to them, a legend of sorts, a mystery.

Such things give the knights pause, their opening attacks more salutation than slash. The Vagrant swings, singing, and his opponent makes a pretence of a parry, blasted backwards into the people behind him.

Another comes at his left, swinging for his neck, and he meets the attack, stopping it in its tracks. Eyes lock over crossed swords. Though the Vagrant is the more skilled of the two, the other knight is younger, stronger, and reinforcements are right behind her.

The Vagrant narrows his eyes, aims a kick at the other knight's knee. There is a satisfying crack and the Vagrant feels all resistance fade, pushing his opponent into the dust.

A natural pause occurs in the battle, brief, where Samael is forced to release the Knight Commander, drawing his own Necro-blade in order to meet the coming storm. The Order of the Broken Blades are at his side now. They form a barrier in front of Vesper just as the Knight Commander is swallowed up by a wall of Seraph Knights.

277

Empire soldiers spill out to either side of the living wall, moving to flanking positions.

The Vagrant sees their situation but is already engaged. The enemy are finding their courage and he has become the nearest opportunity for glory. Attacks come thick and fast, growing bolder. He finds Delta's sword distracted in his hand, dragging left to where its immortal counterpart has fallen. Gritting his teeth, he pulls against it, forced to give ground to keep his head.

He is not the only one. While the blades that Neer and Samael have created are impressive, they cannot hold against the legendary swords of the Seraph Knights.

Moving as one, striking and singing in harmony, the Empire advances. With each step, they bring their swords down, each cut accompanied by song that sets the air shimmering. Sound made physical, pushing, burning.

It is too much for Scout, who turns and runs while Samael flinches away, the infernal parts of his soul trying to curl in on themselves.

Bravely, the Order of the Broken Blades resist. Veterans all, they have received the highest training of the Empire and fine tuned it with years of fighting at Vesper's side. They use every technique at their disposal trying to temper the Seraph's song with their own, but it is not enough.

A Necro-blade shatters and moments later, its wielder falls, blood running from his ears. Two more barrages and another of Vesper's knights goes down.

'Retreat!' shouts Vesper. And suddenly she is at the Vagrant's side, then past him, virtually face to face with the enemy.

Essence boils around her, unseen but felt, and the Seraph

Knights instinctively lean back. She draws the sword, sweeping it wide, roaring. Air explodes outward, an arc of blue extending well beyond the metal.

The Seraph Knights are blasted backwards, their swords tumbling from their grasp.

She sweeps the sword back again and even though the Vagrant is behind her, he winces, uncomfortable.

Armoured figures fly from their feet, away from her, to land in heavy heaps. 'Retreat!' yells Vesper a second time.

Oaths taken to defend clash against oaths to obey but the Order of the Broken Blades do as they are told, running for the safety of the walls.

The Vagrant turns, finds that Doctor Grains is not running, the small group from Verdigris down on their knees, murmuring the rite of mercy over and over.

He grabs Grains' shoulder, shakes it, but the man refuses to budge.

'You are the ones who need to fear, not us.'

The Vagrant lets go and continues to retreat, pulling Delta's reluctant sword after him.

Having taken up positions either side of Vesper, the Empire's soldiers begin firing, twin hails of bullets, horizontal, scissoring into the fleeing force.

The Vagrant inverts Delta's sword, twirling as he moves, song and steel deflecting shot after shot. But Delta's sword is sluggish, and many get through, the majority confounded by his armour, making dents, bruises. Three brush his more exposed side, slicing through plating and clothing to nick the skin. Three more scars for his collection.

As he spins he catches glimpses of Vesper's knights, some getting lucky, some managing to fend off the worst of the attack, others faltering, their strides losing rhythm, their bodies falling into the dirt.

He sees several shots find Samael, tearing through his battered armour. The half-breed lumbers on however, showing no sign of injury.

Instinctively, his attention returns to Vesper. He squints to make her out through hazy air, blue tinted, rippling as if viewed through water. She walks backwards, eyes closed, singing, the sword making slow circles in front of her. Bullets collect at her feet, thousands of petitioners paying respects. Not a single one has found her.

Delta's sword has been fixed on Delta's prone body, getting more agitated the further behind it is left. Now it looks up just as two mirages resolve into sky-ships.

All at once the Empire's forces focus their fire. Soldiers with their rifles, Seraph Knights with blade-touched song, the cannons of the sky-ships and the metal snakes, firing from range. All focused on Vesper.

He catches a glimpse of her jumping backwards, the sword moving so fast it appears like a series of giant fans, trails of light building a second skin in front of her, and then she is buried in smoke and fire.

A second volley is fired before the bombardment pauses, the Empire's forces seeming to lean forward as one, straining to see what lies beneath the unfurling smoke.

The Vagrant is running, not towards safety as Vesper desires, nor towards Delta as her sword desires. He does not register the counterattack from his own side. Does not see the First's sky-ships chasing off the Empire's or the footprints of the projectiles, range finding, walking their way towards the enemy soldiers.

The Vagrant reaches the smoke as it thins to wispy fingers and gasps.

Vesper still stands. Her head lolls to one side, her left shoulder drooping, a puppet missing several strings. The plates on her jacket are scorched, the white fabric burnt black, seared in places to her skin. But Vesper still stands, the sword held upright in a trembling arm.

The Vagrant dashes in front of her, hauling her over his shoulder. Around him, chaos reigns, shots firing in all directions, explosions and shouts merging, the echoes of one becoming the other.

He runs, this time for Crucible. Vesper's body is limp against him, save for her right arm that sticks out, arrow straight, allowing the sword to glare behind them. Delta's sword stops resisting, silver wings covering an eye that no longer wishes to see.

The Vagrant keeps going.

Shockwaves and near misses send him stumbling, ears give up trying to process sound, resorting to a one-note ring, dull, persistent. The world becomes unreal.

The Vagrant keeps going.

Finally, Vesper's right arm drops, flopping against his back. Though her fingers loosen, the sword does not slip from her grasp. A lucky shot ricochets off his hip, turning him but not dropping him. Several times he trips on a body but doesn't fall.

The Vagrant keeps going, past the walls, into safety, past staring eyes and gawping faces, he keeps going.

The Knight Commander stands on deck once more, creating the illusion that things have returned to normal. They have not. Beneath replacement bracers, slender casts hold his wrists straight. Meds reduce the swelling and allow him to focus, though he still has no use of his hands, unable to dress or attend to matters of base biology without assistance.

He looks out onto the battlefield, trying to make sense of what has happened. A part of him hopes that Vesper is not dead, though there is little logic to the thought. Her end is coming one way or the other. *Is it not better that her suffering end now?*

Most of his thoughts concern Delta, however. As absurd as it sounds, he cannot escape the idea that one of The Seven has acted to save him. He had been ready to die, as all of them are, should the Empire require it. It would have been a glorious death, one that would surely have been added to the stories. The logical part of his mind tells him that Delta was simply saving Vesper but he does not believe it, turning the idea of his importance to Delta over and over in his mind, thrilling to it.

'Sir, Obeisance wishes to speak to you.'

He goes to wave a hand but fingers ignore the request, forcing him to lower his arm. 'Put her through.'

Her image resolves and he takes a moment to marvel at it. To him, she seems unshakeable, her tone, her greeting the same as ever. 'Knight Commander.'

'Obeisance.'

No mention is made of the fact that she presided over an order that would have seen him dead. No apology is given, none is asked for. 'Report.'

'Delta is inert on the battlefield, I do not know Her status.'

'She is alive. What of Her sword?'

'It remains with the enemy. Vesper, that is,' he corrects himself.

282

'The Bearer was critically injured and heavy losses were inflicted on her party. It appears that they have developed some kind of technology that apes our swords, however it is inferior.'

'It is profane. Is the Bearer in our custody?'

'No.'

Obeisance's hairless brows raise. 'No?'

'Gamma's blade protected her, as did her own forces. And they prepared the ground, making it hard for our land vehicles to pursue. The First fielded a sizeable fleet of sky-ships and while we could have defeated them, it would have been costly. I thought it better to—'

'We accept your judgement in these matters, Knight Commander, and trust that you will have made more significant progress when we arrive.' He inclines his head. 'Is there anything more?'

'I had several scouts in place ready to cut off the Bearer's escape, yet none of them acted. We've received no communication from them and all attempts to locate them so far have failed. It is as if they've vanished.'

'Troubling.'

'Yes. We are aware of no major detonations in their area or enemy troops. A mystery I am keen to solve. There is one last thing. A number of the civilians you mentioned did not flee. Most were killed in the crossfire but one or two survived. I wouldn't normally trouble you with it but they were flying our flag and all of them are pure. No taint. They claim to have information that may be valuable to us and wish to serve in any capacity they can.'

'See them cared for, their injuries treated and have them dressed in new clothes. Let us make an example of them, Knight Commander.'

'It shall be done.'

When she is gone he returns to the window. 'Captain,' he says, 'do we have eyes on Delta?'

'We do, sir.'

'What's Her status?'

'Her eyes are open, sir. She's . . .' he turns in his seat, fearful. 'She's looking in our direction.'

A sense of buoyancy fills the Knight Commander. *It is ridiculous but could it be that she looks for me? Could it be that she sees me?*

Several of his officers are looking at him now, the captain voicing a fear for all of them. 'What does it mean, sir?'

What indeed? Inwardly, he smiles, at last able to recycle one of the many lines fed to him by Obeisance over the years. 'It is not our place to interpret The Seven, captain.'

'No, sir. I'm sorry, sir.'

'Back to work, all of you. The Seven are watching so be sure there are no mistakes.'

The command centre is filled with the quiet sound of activity, people tucking uncertainty beneath their tasks. Satisfied, the Knight Commander stares at the distant gleam of perfection in the dirt, wondering what it means for all of them.

One Thousand and Twenty-Three Years Ago

Days become like fragments, a part of one jumping to a part of another, disjointed, incoherent. In her more lucid moments Massassi is able to appreciate how far she has fallen. Like a diver returning briefly for air before being lost to the depths.

Mini eternities are spent studying the ceiling and there are many blank spots, though whether these are due to inactivity or failing memory she cannot say.

A host of afternoons stretch, long and pleasant, being walked through gardens by her beloved creations and Peace-Fifteen. She enjoys the sun on her face, and the warmth on her heart, shone continually at her by Alpha, Beta and Delta. These afternoons feel to her like one, a single experience divided up and portioned out.

Occasionally, she is drawn to her workshop, the need to create remaining even after all else is gone. Though Massassi has given away much of her essence, some ghost still tugs at her, a tiny thread of dissatisfaction, a sense that her task is not finished.

Peace-Fifteen does her best to fill Massassi's days with good news and pleasant experiences, anything to keep her from another project. But arguments about health and self-care have never held much sway with Massassi and, seemingly out of spite, the more Peace-Fifteen makes things easy, the more difficult Massassi becomes.

Sunny days pass, morphing into weeks, months, years, a golden age of peace and prosperity for the Empire of the Winged Eye.

For Massassi they are like sands shifting around a fixed point. A tunnel of time with another project at the end of it. She is merely waiting for that time to catch her up.

And one day, sure enough, Gamma comes. She takes Massassi's arm and leads her to the workshop, putting tools into her hands and stepping back.

A change comes over Massassi then, a shifting of posture, a return to purpose.

And she works.

This time a man takes shape in the silver, similar in general to his brothers yet very different. Massassi does not craft as sharply as before, making features more abstract, like a mask, the face seeming ancient even when new.

Not long into the process, Alpha arrives. He takes up his customary position, as does Beta who follows. Delta joins them not long after, assuming a place at her brother's side, another silent witness in the ritual of creation.

A harness holds Massassi in place now, supporting her weight, monitoring her health, separating the dozens of tubes that lacerate her body. Food and medicine is taken in, waste removed, all without interruption.

She works, sleeps, works and sleeps, not having to leave

the spot. She prefers it this way, wishes they had designed the set up years ago.

A sword is made, simple and clean.

When the time comes to bring life, she raises her hand, the iris in her metal palm opening. For a moment nothing happens and then it comes, an exhalation of essence, easing from one body to another.

Epsilon's birth is gradual, gentle. Unlike his brothers and sisters, Epsilon's eyes are pale misty things, the pupils hard to discern.

No, Massassi thinks, *that is not it.*

In her mind, she goes straight on to making another, a sister called Theta. Then, without pause, a seventh, Eta.

In reality the three creations are ten years apart.

And yet they do seem of an era, a different generation to the ones that came before. Epsilon, Theta and Eta share common features and behaviours. They travel constantly together, speak little and seem preoccupied. The three follow Massassi everywhere, on walks, in her room, equally attentive whether she is muttering, bathing, complaining or sleeping.

Alpha makes use of the three when it pleases but mostly ignores them, going back to the business of running the Empire. Beta goes with him, but studies the trio when other duties allow. Gamma tolerates them mainly because she is elsewhere and Delta keeps her distance, finding their presence disturbing. Though in most ways they seem inferior, she feels that her three younger siblings are privy to a secret the creator has kept from the rest of them. Some hidden knowledge that haunts them, keeping them apart.

It is as if they are holding their breath, waiting.

CHAPTER SEVENTEEN

Jem shakes his head. 'Look, I've bandaged a few cuts before, but this? I can't. I don't even know where to start.'

The Vagrant has not been here long and already the room's smell is dominated by smoke and burnt skin, strong enough to taste. He points again, desperate.

Vesper's breathing is laboured, her body covered in injuries that cross each other, a giant homogenized wound.

Where possible, clothes are loosened or cut away. However there are many places where skin and fabric weave together, binding, a succession of hybrid scabs. Jem's hands hover over them, unwilling to take actions that may be regretted later. 'We need a doctor. I'll do what I can but we need someone else! I can't do this alone.'

Mazar is sent for and a call for any skilled physicians to present themselves is made. Most take one look and walk away, unwilling to be connected with any failed treatment.

In the end, Mazar and Jem decide that any action is better

than none. The Vagrant hovers over them all, amber eyes unable to watch, unable to look away.

'This is pointless, she's too badly burned,' states Mazar. 'She won't survive.'

Jem and the Vagrant look at her, shocked.

'Best to accept it now.'

But they do not accept it and soon Mazar is taking off her gloves and readying what few tools they have. As they begin to cut and clean the Vagrant starts to sway.

For Jem, it is too distracting. 'Keep over there, I'm trying to concentrate!'

'Wait,' says Mazar. 'He's bleeding.'

The Vagrant seems as surprised as they are. He looks down to find that blood is caked around a small hole in his hip. Contemplating it, he sits down.

They continue to work, like makeup artists treating a kidney failure, a feeling of gloom descending. Increasingly, Mazar shakes her head.

'Sir Samael!' blurts Jem. 'Where's Sir Samael?'

From his slumped position against the wall, the Vagrant shrugs, and Jem jumps to his feet. 'Fine, I'll find him. Mazar, do whatever you have to, just keep her alive.'

Mazar mutters something but keeps working.

The Vagrant moves to follow, but somewhere between intent and action there is a failing, and he remains where he is.

Time passes with cruel speed as Jem searches. Nobody seems to have seen the half-breed or his Dogspawn. Rumours of Vesper's fall are already spreading like wildfire and Jem is bombarded with questions he cannot answer. Where is she? Is she dead? Is she dying? What is going to happen now?

Eventually he finds Samael sitting on the edge of New Horizon's delegation. A tiny no-man's land, demarking the borders of human and infernal domains.

'There you are!' he gasps, catching his breath.

Samael does not respond.

Jem slows as he approaches, noticing the slant, odd, of Samael's back, and the way Scout is flopped on one side, flanks pumping raggedly.

'Are you okay?'

Only Samael's mouth moves, his voice far away, making Jem lean down to hear it. 'Their weapons are poison to us.'

'Were you hit?'

'Yes.' He points to two holes, one on his chest, the other by his ribs, and the matching ones on his back. Half-breed eyes read Jem's shocked face and the concern underneath. 'We will survive. Not that it matters.'

'What are you talking about? Of course it matters. Now come on, Vesper needs you.' He turns to go and manages two steps before realizing Samael hasn't moved. 'Weren't you listening?'

'I'm no use to her. Today has proven that.'

'Today isn't over, and she's dying. You have to help.'

It takes Samael a moment to heave himself off the ground but then he is able to move fairly quickly, Scout left behind to whine, self-pitying.

When they get back to Vesper's room, they find Reela has managed to sneak in. She sits next to the Vagrant, holding his hand. A small replica of his misery.

Jem nearly loses his temper. 'How did she? Why didn't you-' He shuts his mouth, resolving to deal with it later, and leads Samael to Vesper's side.

Mazar has been busy while he was away. Smearing the remains of their burn medication on the worst areas and applying Skyn to the others. 'I've taken out the shrapnel that's near the surface and tidied her up as best I can. She's still alive, somehow.'

'It's the Malice,' says Samael. 'It won't let her die.'

They all look at the sword, and the way her fingers remain curled around the hilt.

Somehow the time away makes the shock of her injuries fresher. Jem covers his mouth. 'Can you help her?'

'That depends on the Malice.'

'But you'll try?'

'Yes.' Though his knowledge comes from an alien source, few knew more about the inner working of the human body than the Uncivil. A master of manipulating essence and flesh, living and dead, she was the architect of Necrotech and all the cults that sprang up around it, and her knowledge floats within the soup of Samael's soul.

He pulls off a gauntlet, turning his hand until he finds the rent in his palm. Feeling nothing, he is forced to do this by sight. Then he presses it against one of Vesper's open wounds, letting his essence probe the edges of hers.

Though the sword remains inert, he feels it tense, knows it is watching him from inside her.

'What is it?' asks Jem.

'Nothing,' replies Samael.

'Is there anything we can do to help?'

'Yes. I'm going to need some raw materials.'

'What do you mean?'

'A body.'

Jem swallows. 'Alive?'

'Or dead. So long as it's fresh. And hurry, I do not think the Malice will tolerate my closeness for long.'

Alone at last, Jem scrubs at his hands with a worn fibrous pad. With water being rationed, only a few drops can be used, making it as much a case of scraping off the top layer of skin as it is of cleaning it.

No stranger to dirt, or to the sight of sick or dying people, today has taken him from his comfort zone and well beyond. The weight of the cadaver against his palms remains, though he has not carried it for over an hour now, and the smell of Vesper's injuries still plays in his nostrils.

He pulls a face, tries not to retch, and continues scrubbing.

Footsteps are heard behind him. 'Not now.'

'I'm sorry to bother you,' says Genner from the doorway. 'But I wanted to know how she's doing. The other delegations need an update.'

'How is she doing?' Jem's hands stop their work and his shoulders slump. 'I'm not sure where to begin answering that question.'

Genner waits and when it is clear Jem isn't about to elaborate, asks, 'Is she alive?'

'Yes.'

'Good,' he replies, though nothing in Jem's expression suggests that to be the case. 'Is she stable?'

'Yes, I think. I don't know. Better than she was.'

'Has she given any orders?'

'No. She's not ready for any of that yet.'

'Are you saying she's conscious?'

292

'Look, she's not up to visitors and I wouldn't say she's awake like we are now.'

'What would you say?'

Jem sucks in an angry breath. 'Can't this wait? Suns! She's half dead!'

'I have to make a report. There's an army sitting out there that could attack us at any moment and a lot of very nervous people waiting for news. This all hinges on Vesper. Without her, I don't know what they'll do. I've already got requests from all the leaders for an update, and several of them have made it clear that they won't rest until they get an audience with her.

'Jem, they want to know why you and Mazar dragged a dead body up there.'

'No they don't, believe me.'

'That's not a satisfactory answer.'

'It's the only one I've got.'

He hears Genner's sigh. 'I'll stall them as long as I can.'

'Whatever,' mutters Jem, starting to scrub once more.

Three figures use the last of the day's light to pick their way across a churned field. They wear crisp clothes, simply cut, austere fashion favoured by the Empire of the Winged Eye.

Recent injuries have vanished, an illusion of meds and makeup, and if any notice them stumbling, it is easily attributable to the uneven terrain.

All three are unarmed, unarmored, exposed. Easy targets. But no bullets, arrows, darts or explosives come their way and eventually they come to a stop in front of Crucible's walls.

The middle of the three figures speaks, his voice broadcast

through speakers on a score of Empire vehicles, the sound carrying for miles in all directions.

'My name is Garth Grains, I was a doctor and council member of the city of Verdigris. I've been sent here on behalf of the Empire of the Winged Eye to make you an offer.

'When Vesper came to make her arrogant demands, we chose to give ourselves over to the mercy of The Seven. We had nothing to fear from Them. Why should we? We had done nothing wrong.' He gestures to his companions. 'As you can see, our faith was rewarded and we have been recognized as loyal subjects. There was a lot of talk about the Empire destroying everything they came across in the south. These are lies spread by the infernals and their lovers. The Empire is here to protect us. If you are tainted you will be purged, but if you are strong, you will come through it pure and worthy.

'So I have this message: to the good people of the south, if you present yourselves here, where I stand, by midday tomorrow, you will be spared. Come without weapons or anger and you will be received in kind.

'To those tainted by the touch of demons I say this: do not despair! You have a chance for salvation. One chance. Kneel before the Empire, here, by midday tomorrow and find your humanity again.

'I also have a message for the infernals among you. To them the Empire says this: your time is coming. The Seven have come at last and They will end you.'

Grains kneels in the dirt. 'We are here to offer you an alternative. We are your friends. Know that the Empire will only destroy its enemies. Until midday tomorrow, we will wait here, ready to deliver you to mercy. After that, we will go and righteous judgement will fall upon any who remain.'

Genner watches the different groups assemble in the dome. Rumours have been flying around the camps; of the Empire's offer, of Vesper's health, of bodies being moved in the night.

Urgency has driven them all together, a shared need to find a way to navigate the storm. But nobody holds the centre space, leaving a Vesper-shaped absence that none of the other leaders dare to fill.

There is a lot of muttering, of people looking at each other across the floor, but Tough Call from Verdigris is the first to speak. 'Reckon somebody has to get this thing moving and it might as well be me. Way I see it, we're fucked any which way we look at things so we might as well do something. Sorry about Grains by the way. That's my bad.'

From his shadowed throne, the Man-shape speaks. 'I assume you all know that their offer of amnesty is woven of lies. There is no mercy to be found for any of us.'

'Speak for yourself,' says one of the group from West Rift. Genner cannot be sure which one.

Bickering begins, distrust spilling over into argument. Positions are taken, predictable. The Thousand Nails, New Horizon and Red Rails having no option but to fight, the others trying to decide if either path available will end in their survival.

'What we need,' says the Man-shape, speaking into a sullen pause in the vitriol, 'is the counsel of an expert. While Vesper is not here, we must turn to her advisors, let them advise us.'

With surprise, Genner realizes the infernal is pointing at him.

'Samael tells me you were of the Lenses. You know how the Empire thinks. Tell us, what will they do?'

Genner feels exposed, doubly so under the infernal's gaze. Training keeps him calm however. 'Honestly? I doubt most of you would survive the purging, you're too far gone. And even if you did, the Empire is unlikely to look kindly on the leaders of what they see as a rebellion.'

Slake's leaders confer in hasty whispers, then Gorad leans forward, painted lips pursed. 'Really? Seems to Gut-pumper and I, that this would be the best time for negotiation.'

'There's a chance, I suppose. If you acted now. But the Empire don't negotiate. You'd be throwing yourselves on The Seven's mercy. They might let you live as an example but it would be on Their terms.'

There is further debate, though it seems that all sides know they are merely postponing the inevitable.

'Kill this doctor!' yells Flat Head of the Thousand Nails. 'Kill him now, rip off his head. Show our enemy strength. Show our people, no running away.'

Genner sees many of the others nodding in agreement. 'That's true,' he says. 'But I'd advise you to wait until midday tomorrow before you make that statement. As soon as you do that, they'll attack, and Vesper needs time to recover.'

'How is Vesper?' asks the Man-shape.

'She'll be back with us soon,' Genner lies, 'but the longer you can give her, the better.'

The delegations grudgingly agree to stay and fight together. Each leader agrees to keep their people on the right side of the wall, even a single defection sure to start a tide. The Thousand Nails are posted along the perimeter as a deterrent for any having second thoughts about staying.

Genner urges patience, promising that by morning Vesper will return and they can plan for the day's battle.

The meeting breaks apart, delegations returning to their separate camps to brood. During the night messages flit between groups, private, sharing suspicions and smaller, secret plans.

Regular requests are made for an audience with Vesper, all are ignored. Instead, Genner gives updates on her progress, vague, optimistic, completely fabricated.

And then, an hour before dawn, as the night begins to relax its grip on the sky, the Empire of the Winged Eye attacks.

Light floods across the field, filling it. There is a wide range of sources: miniature torches fixed to rifles or built into visors, great lamps set into the eyes of the metal snakes, searchlights fastened to the underside of the Empire's sky-ships, all cast back the night with disdain.

Guns flash and shells arc overhead, indiscriminate, paving the way for their ground assault.

Stealth has been abandoned in favour of a swift, relentless advance.

Though the offer of amnesty has proven to be a trick, it could be said that in the end the Empire does show a kind of mercy to those who surrender. Doctor Grains and his companions are dead seconds after the attack begins, reduced to atoms long before any shock or pain has time to register.

To begin with, there is only a limited response from Crucible, the defenders offering little in reply to the sudden onslaught. Taking advantage of their air superiority, the Empire's sky-ships shoot overhead. They make several passes before the First's nomads have time to scramble a response, dropping bombs on the early runs, and troops on the later ones.

Both are guided to the places where they can cause the most chaos by light-tags that wink, cheery, amidst the unfolding horror.

A few of the tags have sat there in secret, for weeks, but Genner has had to place the majority by hand over the last few hours. He has only just finished when the bombs start exploding. If any were paying attention they would see his silhouette ghosting away but the people of Crucible are too busy looking up.

At last, the defenders begin to respond. Tough Call comes charging from a tent, a different one, Genner notes, than she had said she was staying in, her Usurperkin marshals behind her. They all carry guns and launchers, relic weapons meant to support the Empire's soldiers that never quite made it to their destination.

At her order, they open fire, making up in accuracy what they lack in discipline, and one of the Empire's sky-ships is falling, already a ruin, the others pulling clear.

West Rift mercenaries rush to support the Thousand Nails at the wall, several gunned down before they can make it, none realizing they are being killed from behind.

As one of the First's sky-ships begins to lift off the ground, it explodes, sudden, without warning, showering ground crews in molten shrapnel.

Genner has only had the opportunity to sabotage one of the sky-ships but he knows the First's nomads will be too afraid to fly until the others are checked, buying more precious time for the Empire.

He does not stop to observe the results of his handiwork however, moving swiftly past people as they tumble from their tents, making for the dome itself and the climax of his mission.

Two of the Order of the Broken Blades stand at the entrance.

'Hold!' he calls as he runs towards them. 'It's me!'

'What's going on, sir?'

'The Empire betrayed us. They're everywhere. Hold the door at all costs, do you understand? I'm going to help Vesper.'

They salute him, attention returning to the night.

He passes several more of the order, and various members of the other delegations that stay here. He gives them instructions appropriate to their station. Telling some to arm themselves, others to hide, giving them purpose and destination, away from his.

In the corridor outside her room, he finds himself alone, the sounds of battle outside muted through the curving walls. For a moment, he pauses, gripped by uncharacteristic nerves. Despite having already done so before setting out, he checks his pistol is fully charged, that the darts implanted under the skin of his wrist are functional and that the charge he carries is primed. They are ready, and he has no time to be otherwise.

Another of Vesper's knights stands at the door.

'Any word?' he asks her.

'None, sir.'

'See that we're not disturbed.'

She nods to him, opening the door.

Inside, the room is stuffy, the air choked by strong chemicals and the kind of scents normally locked inside the body. Fortunately most of Vesper is covered over and Samael's armoured back obscures his view of the rest. He clocks the other occupants, pleased to see the Dogspawn is absent. Vesper's father and her tainted child slumber in a corner, Delta's sword laid across his lap. Its eye is open but looks elsewhere, fixed on a random spot on the wall.

Genner moves across the room until he is next to the half-breed, within striking distance of his target. 'How is she?'

'I have done all I can.'

'And?'

'I've replaced the damaged bones and patched the holes in her body. Cosmetic repair will have to wait. The Malice has been sustaining her essence. Now that her body is stable, I expect it to wake her soon.'

Genner has the sudden feeling of being watched. He looks over his shoulder, to find things unchanged. He double checks Delta's sword but it continues to stare in another direction. 'You've done well, Samael, but if you're finished here, the Order of the Broken Blades need you to lead them. The Empire is attacking and it's going badly for us.'

'What about Vesper?'

'The best thing you can do for her is to give her time. Hold back the Empire until she wakes.'

For a moment Samael simply stares at him, then he begins to put on his helmet, threading his long hair through the top.

'Don't worry, I'll stay and watch over her.' Samael stops to look at him a second time and Genner adds, 'Go! Now! Before it's too late.'

'Yes,' replies the half-breed, marching out with sudden speed.

Genner waits until the door has closed again before turning back to Vesper. In a way Samael's ministrations have made his task easier. She is an abomination now, soiled by the attentions of a infernally marked man and his dark arts. It helps too, that her body is so badly marked, makes it easier for him to distance the thing in front of him from the woman he has known for so long. *This is not a murder,* he tells himself, *it is a mercy.*

He is thankful that Gamma's sword is focused inward, its eye closed. Even so, he moves quietly, sliding the pistol from its holster with aching slowness.

Again, there is a feeling of being watched. He spins round to find no one there. The Vagrant still sleeps, as does Reela. For a moment he thinks the eye of Delta's sword is on him but a second glance reveals that no, it has not changed position.

Before he can turn back, there is a knock at the door and then it is opening. The knight that he spoke to before is there, another person, hidden, behind her.

'I told you not to disturb us.'

'I'm sorry, sir, but Savmir of Red Rails is here. He says he can save us.'

Genner crosses the room, pistol stowed so fast it is as if it was never drawn. 'Quickly then.' He keeps the sneer from his face as the self-proclaimed Ratbred Prince presents himself.

Richly dressed, plump, Savmir's mutations are well developed. He is tall for one of his kind, the top of his head nearly reaching Genner's collarbone, and elongated front teeth brush against a narrow chin. Coarse hair dusts his body evenly. 'Not you!' he cries. 'I need to speak with her. Urgent! Urgent!'

'She isn't ready. You'll have to make do with me. Now tell me, what have you got?'

Small hands hook around the edges of sleeves, squeezing in frustration. 'Our weapon! It is time to use it. We can turn the fight.'

'I don't understand.'

Savmir's lips curl into a hunter's smile. 'A secret. Prepared under your nose, in case we needed it.'

'You have a weapon that can defeat the Empire?'

'Yes. We must work together to maximize its power.'

'Agreed.'

'Come! Come! I will show you.'

Genner looks back at Vesper, torn, before allowing himself to be led from the room.

Delta's sword watches Genner go. Its eye does not blink. A silver wing taps on the Vagrant's thigh, taps again, taps two more times, rapid.

Humming with impatience, it tries again more forcefully, drawing up so that the wingtip can stab at him, forceful.

The Vagrant's hand moves, grabbing the wing before it can descend. He looks at the sword, nods, one finger to his lips. He is already easing himself up, his eyes on the door.

The humming quietens but Delta's sword continues to thrum silently in his hand.

Stepping outside, the Vagrant nods to the knight there, looking both ways down the corridor. He sees a rat's tail snaking away out of sight and gives chase, Delta's sword needlessly pointing the way.

A nearby detonation rumbles through the dome, forcing the Vagrant to lean against the wall. As it settles he sets off again, following the curve of the building's perimeter until he reaches the area set aside for Red Rails.

Usually packed full of ratbred, the abandoned space seems larger than it should. Additional hangings lower the generous doorway, so that the Vagrant has to duck to enter.

He passes by a few empty rooms. They are full of junk, arranged without care. Only brief glances are given before he moves on. Signs of gentle disturbance are visible, glasses tipped over, bowls of indiscriminate sludge, still steaming, unfinished.

Not a single ratbred is to be seen. But he hears one.

The voice comes from a room he's already passed. He takes a step back, looks again.

The room is still empty.

With a flap, Delta's sword pulls his right arm into the room. The Vagrant follows, ears straining to identify the source of the sound. He looks from wall to wall, checking behind a cabinet when he hears it again, a soft voice with a slight lisp.

It comes from a rug at his feet.

Leaning down, he pulls back the rug to reveal a hole. He and Delta's sword exchange a look of satisfaction and he is about to jump down when he notices a small shadow in the doorway.

Reela is standing there.

A number of expressions cross the Vagrant's face and he raises a stern finger.

She steps more into the light, revealing a grimy face, full of worry.

The Vagrant sees, his expression melting into one of sadness. His finger hesitates, then changes direction, pointing at the cabinet.

Reela runs and climbs inside. He puts a finger to his lips and she does the same. He musters a smile for her, then shuts the door.

Delta's sword virtually drags him back to the hole.

Without hesitation, he jumps down.

CHAPTER EIGHTEEN

The group is growing. As Savmir leads Genner deeper underground, more of his ratbred people pop from the shadows,
moving easily in the dark.

He dips his head to manage the tunnels, rough rectangular
shapes burrowed out and skinned in a substance Genner is
not familiar with. It is tacky to the touch, moist, and smells
fragrant. He is careful to keep his head clear.

The smaller sounds of battle do not penetrate the earth
above, but the rumble of the metal snakes can be felt through
the walls along with the roar of explosives, muffled.

All at once Savmir stops, whirling round. 'Do you see?
Do you see?'

'I see,' he replies. 'How far does this go?'

What poor light there is glints on Savmir's front teeth.
'All the way.'

'You mean we could bring our troops up behind them?'

'Yes!' hisses Savmir. 'Behind them, underneath them, anywhere we want!'

'Or we could collapse the tunnels right underneath them.'

'You do see! But must be now.'

Genner cannot help but be impressed. 'How did you manage all this without being discovered?'

'Are you listening? We must act now! Bragging will come later.'

'I agree,' says Genner, his hand sliding over the grip of his pistol. 'Does anyone else know about this?'

'No. A secret. Wasn't sure who to trust. Wasn't sure Vesper would approve.'

Genner runs his empty hand through his hair, a gesture to keep their attention on his face. 'She wouldn't have.' There are at least three other ratbred in the tunnel, and two of them are armed. One with a short spear, the other with a shrapnel gun. He decides to take them first, then Savmir, then the fourth one.

'Hey, did you hear—' he begins, pointing towards the ratbred with the shrapnel gun, just over her shoulder. As she turns he raises his palm, releasing the dart housed within his wrist. It streaks out, silent, burying itself just under her jaw. '—something?'

She looks at him, puzzled. Then her small eyes widen a fraction, barely noticeable, a sad last act of life. Without a word, she falls.

In the moment that the others turn to her, Genner raises his pistol. Even as he shoots the ratbred holding the spear, his other hand moves towards the charge in his pocket, Lenses' training forcing the mind to think three moves ahead: *After the armed threats are eliminated, kill Savmir, kill the witness, then collapse the tunnel.*

Light shines from his pistol, poking a hole straight through the forehead of the ratbred holding the spear. The weapon, held out to thrust, drops from senseless fingers.

Kill Savmir, kill the witness, collapse the tunnel.

He swings the pistol round, squeezing the trigger as the barrel lines up with Savmir's chest.

Nothing happens. No light, no death.

Savmir screeches in horror, rearing away.

It takes Genner a moment to register that something is wrong. His ears are suddenly full of noise, a rumbling sea contained in his head. He looks down at his pistol to see what the problem is.

But the pistol isn't there. Neither is Genner's hand.

Blood spurts, energetic, from the stump of his right wrist, spattering on the floor, dappling the edges of Savmir's toes.

Despite the shock, Genner realizes that the remaining ratbred are not the problem. He turns to find three eyes watching him. Two are human, amber, the other set into the crosspiece of Delta's sword.

Instantly, he revises his plan. *Collapse the tunnel,* he thinks. This was not the way he had intended things to go but, whatever happens to him, his mission will have been a success. *Collapse the tunnel.* He grips the charge in his remaining hand, brandishing it in front of the Vagrant like a trophy. His grin is manic and he takes satisfaction from the way the other man's eyes widen in realization.

The roaring in his ears grows louder, the edges of his vision losing cohesion. Though he cannot hear himself, Genner shouts out a last salutation for the Empire's glory.

The Vagrant pulls back Delta's sword.

Already primed and poised, it is a small matter for Genner to activate the explosive charge. The countdown is set to allow him time to leave but it doesn't matter, once activated, there is nothing anyone can do to stop the countdown. He wishes it had not ended this way, that Vesper had not forced his hand. But in the end his life and hers are nothing compared to the greater good.

Ten lights activate on the side of the charge. Immediately, the first goes out.

Delta's sword swings towards him but it does not matter, he has done what he had to.

For the Empire.

Delta's sword passes through Genner's elbow without resistance, parting hand, wrist and forearm from the rest of his body.

Before it can fall, the Vagrant snatches the explosive out of the air, caging it with his fingers. Nine lights shine along its surface. He looks at them, then to Savmir, who is trying to press himself through the wall with little success.

Genner simply collapses, his features locked in a grin.

Savmir screams again.

The Vagrant frowns at him, then notices the ratbred prince is pointing at the charge in his hand. Another light has gone out.

Eyebrows raise and then all three are running. Savmir and his remaining companion back towards the surface, the Vagrant going the opposite way, deeper into the tunnel.

There is no light here, save for the seven green ones on the charge, and the Vagrant stumbles often, catching his head on the ceiling, tripping, lips moving in silent, frequent curses.

Another light goes out.

The Vagrant keeps going, making good progress until the

tunnel splits into two. Unable to see the choice in front of him, the Vagrant takes neither, slamming into the dividing wall.

Air rushes from lungs and sparkles dance before amber eyes. Though he manages to keep hold of Delta's sword, the charge slips from his fingers.

A few seconds pass, precious, before the Vagrant snaps back to attention, sucking in breath. He looks down, Delta's sword hums at him, urging him on, and soon the charge is spotted again, a five-eyed spider, legless, staring up.

He reaches for it as another light goes out.

The distant rumbling of a group of metal snakes can be heard getting closer. Cocking his head to one side, the Vagrant listens.

He lets his ears guide him, moving closer to the sound. It is not above him, not yet, but it is coming his way. He presses the charge to the ceiling, and it adheres to the coating immediately.

The Vagrant doesn't pause to count how many lights are left, breaking into a sprint, Delta's sword pulling his arm straight, guiding, dragging him away.

And behind him, faster than seems fair, the last light goes out.

Samael marches out of the dome and into chaos. He does not have the kind of voice to carry over the cacophony so does not bother giving orders or rallying troops. Instead he takes stock, half-breed eyes untroubled by the poor pre-dawn light.

Above him, a sky-ship battle rages, the First's nomads pitting their skills against the Empire's pilots. It is too early to see which way the tide will go.

Tough Call rallies the bulk of the defenders by the walls, leaving the main camp mostly undefended. Shock troops dropped in by the Empire are making the most of the situation, running through civilian areas, firing indiscriminately at anyone foolish enough to be on the move. Fires rage in several places, more being started all the time.

Distantly, he is aware that Scout is curled in a corner, miserable, still recovering from the Seraph Knight's chorus. Though distracting, there is a comfort in knowing that the Dogspawn is hidden and safe.

Samael reaches for his sword and remembers that he no longer has one. A feeling of sadness, of failure washes over him.

Then he marches towards the nearest Empire soldier, who is in the middle of taking up a sniper position on the roof of one of the flimsy stalls. She sees him coming, shoots as he lumbers forward.

The first shot misses him, the second takes him in the shoulder, the spinning bullet seeming to hum as it passes through. Vision mists as his essence spasms, then clears again. He feels no pain from the impact, only a slight hangover from the bullet's essence-disrupting properties.

He ducks under the roof, punching up through thin fabric to get a hold of her ankle. With inhuman strength, he pulls the soldier through thin planks, down to his level. There is a struggle, brief, that ends with a neck snapping under his gauntleted grip.

A few more are hunted down before he spots a group of Empire soldiers, trying to come in behind Tough Call and the defenders at the wall.

This time he does shout, collecting a burning piece of

wreckage to wave over his head while running full-tilt at the enemy.

There are ten Empire shock troopers, each armed with weapons designed to kill infernals, though they are equally effective on humans and half-breeds. Samael doubts he will be able to take them alone.

Tough Call and her people seem understandably distracted, and it does not surprise him that the shock troopers notice him long before his allies do.

Out in the open, there is little for him to do but put down his head and run.

Shots fire, wild, missing, missing, missing again.

As he gets closer he sees a soldier flailing at his own face, trying to clear a visor thick with flies. The shock troopers all have night vision in their visors but a new kind of darkness has descended, one made of bodies tiny and black.

And then Samael is on them. He does not fight as a knight should, with discipline and skill. He has failed in that role and so gives it up, letting another side of his heritage take over.

He grabs and gouges, twists limbs, breaks bones beneath his fists. The swarm hums, drowning out any cries for help.

When the flies clear, all ten are dead.

Samael makes his way to what remains of the wall. Repeated bombardment has blown it full of holes, leaving plenty of room to see the Empire's advancing forces. Tough Call's people squat either side of the gaps. Those with ranged weapons trying to thin out the enemy while keeping their own heads, those without keeping low, waiting for their time.

The one-armed leader of Verdigris clocks his approach,

shouting to be heard even at close quarters. 'You better be bringing good news, 'cos I'm only bringing the bad.'

'How bad?' asks Samael.

'Word is, the West Rift commanders got blown to hell in their beds along with half their best people. I got what's left here. The ground's been torn to shit in all the firing. It's slowing down their snakes but it also means we can't deploy our brawlers. We're having to fight at range and that's a problem because they've got more guns than us. Reckon they've got more ammo too, we're running low.'

'That is bad.'

'Tell me about it! We need some infernal backup from your friends in New Horizon.'

'They're already helping.'

'Oh yeah? Well I need to see it to believe it. Get them here.' Before he can answer, she adds, 'I don't suppose Vesper is coming?'

'Soon, I hope.'

'It'd better be or there'll be none of us around to greet her.'

A dull boom from the battlefield catches their attention. One of the metal snakes drops half from view, headlamps sinking into the mud, a pair of eyes squinting in confusion, before vanishing completely. Another explosion, louder, comes from the metal snake. They cannot see the extent of the damage but can guess. There is a belch of smoke, then flames surge up from the hole, waving and wild.

The other snakes seem to pause in sympathy, bringing a temporary halt to the Empire's advance.

'Anything to do with you?' asks Tough Call.

Samael shakes his head.

Using the brief respite, Tough Call moves up and down the line, directing aid to the injured, fighters to where the wall is breached, bolstering flagging courage.

He is about to follow, not sure what else to do when a squealing figure catches his eye. Though dishevelled, the glittering from of Savmir is easily distinguishable from the other ratbred in Crucible. 'You!' he shouts, pointing a tiny hand. 'You! Come, now!'

Samael goes to Savmir's side, struggling to make sense of the other half-breed's babbling explanations. He does not question Genner's reported betrayal, the fact slotting cleanly into his mind with the ease of a truth already known.

A sixth sense has drawn Tough Call back to his side. She waits until Savmir is finished before speaking. 'This is our chance. Samael, take your knights, Flat Head and the Thousand Nails, and any infernals you can get. Get to those tunnels, use them to get in close. And make it quick, if they get to the wall, we won't hold for long.'

An eye opens.

Silver wings stretch before resuming their normal position. The sword begins to hum and, unseen, essence flows from it to Vesper.

She wakes, sudden, surprised, jerking upright, and slowly takes in the room. It is empty. Strange, she expected someone to be here. Jem or her father, Samael or Reela. Even Scout. But they have gone.

Relaxing her neck, she lets the weight take her head downward, until chin touches chest, then rolls it up to her left shoulder, down again, then up to her right, down again, and up.

313

Discomfort comes with the movement but it is far away, like a man shouting at her on the other side of a wall. She is aware of something but unable to give meaning to it.

Sword in hand, Vesper gets up and goes to the door. A member of the Order of the Broken Blades waits on the other side. Vesper frowns, unable to recall her name. She is usually good with names. 'Where is everyone?'

The knight stares at her, open mouthed.

'Did you hear me?'

'. . . I . . . sorry, they're not here.' There is fear in the knight's voice.

'What's wrong?'

'You don't know? We're under attack!'

The sword hums in her hand. It hears truth but there is a lie buried in there too, their fear connected not to the fighting, but to Vesper herself.

She smiles, and there is another slight discomfort, oh so far away. Instead of calming the knight, her smile makes them wilt further. 'You don't need to be afraid.'

Hurriedly, she nods. 'What are your orders?'

'Come with me.'

The two of them make their way to the base of the dome and then out, into the valley itself.

Above them, the night is weakening, preparing to give way to dawn. Vesper knows it is the gold sun that will rise first today. Some would say it is a good omen but she knows it doesn't matter whether the horizon glows red or gold in the next few hours. If there is to be any good, they will have to make it themselves.

She doesn't need to wait for the sunrise to see. Fires blaze all over camp, fed by smashed tents, torn crates, and the wreckage of a sky-ship.

Bodies and blood are everywhere, most belonging to the people that came for her protection, some belonging to the Empire. Survivors make hard choices. Many flee with whatever they can carry. Others try to reclaim the camp, fighting back the flames as best they can. Still others arm themselves, preparing a second line of defence.

Vesper walks past them all, ignoring the shocked looks and worried mutters that trail in her wake.

Up ahead she hears gunfire and shouting, the sound taking her back to Sonorous and another battle, many years ago. So far removed in time and space and yet so similar. Vesper shakes her head. She has heard enough of war's dirge, is sick of its irregular yet predictable beats, its one-note of misery.

'Stay here,' she says to the knight. 'Help where you can.'

'I will. What are you going to do?'

'End this, if I'm able. Can you pass on a message for me?'

The knight lowers her head. 'Of course.'

'Tell them I'm sorry.'

She turns to go but the knight calls after her, 'Wait! Who do you want me to tell?'

Vesper gives a slight shrug. 'Jem, Samael . . . Everyone.'

Then, to the amazement of the knight and the other defenders, Vesper steps through one of the many gaps in the wall, leaving its protection behind.

The metal snakes are close now, bearing down on all sides. Soldiers march between them, using the vehicles as moving cover. It doesn't take long for them to notice Vesper, and then word quickly spreads through the troops.

They don't shoot, not at first, mesmerized by her lone

trudging advance. Then word gets to an officer, who replies with a barking order to fire.

Still, there is a reluctance, a sense that somehow to shoot would be wrong.

A single shot rings out, and Vesper waves it away, casual, as one might a fly on a hot day.

Quickly, the officer unifies his troops, calls for fire support from one of the snakes. He watches Vesper drawing closer, ever so slowly as he gets the confirmation from the gunnery teams.

'On my mark,' he commands and his troop aim their rifles. Above and to his right, a metal head swings into position, picking out Vesper with powerful lamps. The officer gasps at the sight, wonders how the woman can stand, let alone walk.

He realizes that his troops are waiting for him and takes breath to give the order when the ground opens up beneath his feet.

There is a muffled gasp and he is gone from sight.

The soldiers have time to turn, to train their guns on the hole that took him before new ones open, whisking them away, one by one. In seconds the hole is so large that the metal snake begins to lean, then slide, half-swallowed by the earth.

Untouched and untroubled, Vesper keeps walking.

'Sir, snake five reports weapon failure . . .'

'We're down another sky-ship, sir.'

'Snakes and troops on the far side are struggling to keep pace with the main attack . . .'

'Something wrong with our scouts in Wonderland, sir . . .'

The Seven

The reports are coming in too fast for the Knight Commander to keep up with. He cannot understand why such a simple attack has become so complicated. They have the element of surprise, their saboteur has done his job well, and they have superior discipline and military might.

But somehow it has all gone wrong.

'. . . They're asking for permission to withdraw and repair.'

'Insertion team is down, I repeat, insertion team is down.'

'. . . What do you advise, sir? Our line is breaking.'

'. . . They've been checking in but only giving minimal information . . .'

He feels his lack of experience in the field keenly. His predecessor would have known what to do. A bitter voice tells him that Obeisance would know if she were here. Even Vesper, with her strange ideas, has a strategy superior to his.

'Shall I give permission to snake five?'

'Sir?'

'. . . I've tried asking for a more detailed report but I've been ignored.'

'Captain Thrail is at the wall, sir. Repeat, she is at the wall. She's clear to attack but unsupported as yet. Should she hold or proceed?'

It all hinges on him and he is failing to take action. He looks down at his splinted wrists. Functional hands are not required here and yet he feels diminished. Perhaps the meds are wearing off. He demands another injection.

'Sir?'

'Sir?'

'Sir?'

'Sir?'

He doesn't mean to shout but his nerves come out that

way. 'Tell Thrail to attack. Tell all other captains to follow her example and press forward.'

'Sir.'

'I don't want to hear about Wonderland or anywhere that isn't Crucible until after the battle, is that clear?'

'Clear, sir.'

'Snake five does not have permission to pull back, they'll have to repair as they go. Have it ram through the wall if it can't fire. Our troops will do the rest. No one is pulling back. We will not show weakness to the enemy.'

'Yes, sir!'

The Knight Commander turns to the window once more. Delta is still out there. She has not moved but they have, slowly advancing behind their army, yet Her gaze still falls in their direction. Surely there can be no doubt now: She is watching him. It is comforting to know that one of The Seven has noticed him. She has saved him for something and that makes his heart glad. A small diamond of certainty that he clings to.

So far the Empire's army has moved around Delta, their soldiers studiously ignoring Her, a respectful denial. To look is to wonder about the schism in The Seven, to question it. Only the Knight Commander looks.

'Sir, snakes three and six have been immobilized. They're under heavy attack.'

'What? How?'

Another officer cuts in. 'Snake two has gone dark.'

Then another. 'Sir, Captain Thrail has engaged the enemy. She's requesting immediate backup.'

The Knight Commander starts to make a fist and pain lances through broken wrists. He sucks in a breath through his teeth. 'I asked a question, damn you! What has immobilized our snakes?'

'They're collapsing the ground under them, sir. We've got hostiles engaging our troops on all sides.' The officer touches a hand to his ear.

'What is it?' snaps the Knight Commander.

'Infernals!' comes the shocked reply. 'We have infernals. They're in our lines!'

'Keep calm, captain, and order our Seraph Knights to pull back and engage the infernals. This is what we were made for.'

They have a moment to take solace in the idea before the next report comes in.

'Sir, I have reports that the Bearer is on the battlefield.'

'You're sure?'

'Yes, sir. She is alone and clear of the wall.'

The Knight Commander frowns. 'Where is she now, exactly?'

'Unknown, sir. The solider reporting in is injured. He says his unit was sucked into the ground by giant green demons. He's the only one left.'

'She can't have vanished. Find her!'

A suspicion drags him back to the window. He frowns, sure that he is right but needing evidence.

'Sir, what about Captain Thrail?'

'Do we only have one decent officer in this army? The other captains should be in position by now!' He shakes his head. 'Send in a sky-ship on a glory run, tell the pilot that their name will be added to the songs.'

'Yes, sir.'

Then he sees her, a grey spectre emerging from the chaos. It is as he suspected. 'Call the Seraph Knights back!'

319

'But, sir! They're already engaging the infernals.'

'Call them back now! Tell them to move to Delta's location. And summon my guard, I'm going out there. And get me those damn meds!'

'Yes, sir!'

With no small amount of relief, the Knight Commander leaves the command centre. His officers know the mission and they have their orders. *Let them win their own glory now*, he thinks, *and let it be a shadow of my own.*

CHAPTER NINETEEN

Inside the dome, in a room, in a rounded corner, Jem hunches, legs pressed against his chest, arms wrapped around his legs. He feels the noises of war on his back. Each explosion makes him jump, each cry makes him flinch.

He is rarely still.

The door to his chamber bursts open without warning, and, despite his instincts demanding he stay small and silent, he cries out.

A soldier dressed in armour, imperial, walks in. Her rifle is slung over her shoulder, and though there are no lights on, she spots him immediately, leaning down to stare, puzzled. 'What are you doing down there?'

'Mazar?' he asks. She nods and he adds, 'I'm hiding of course. Trying to stay alive. Do you want to join me?'

'I don't know,' she replies but she squats down at his side, awkward.

The dome trembles from some nearby impact and Jem grabs Mazar's arm. 'Sorry. I'm not very good in situations like this.' She doesn't say anything and he doesn't let go of her. 'I . . . didn't expect to see you.'

Her helmet turns to look at him. 'What?'

'I mean, I thought you'd be out there, fighting.'

There is a pause, then she says, 'I need your help. I don't know what to do.'

It is Jem's turn to look puzzled. 'You're going to have to—' another cry pierces the air and he ducks '—tell me more.'

'You're right. I should be out there. It's what I'm trained to do. The problem is I don't know which side to fight for.'

'I thought you were on our side?'

'I am. I want to make up for what I've done and win Delta's forgiveness. I have to. But flying you here and killing infernals is one thing, fighting the Empire is another. I spent my life training with these people. I know them . . .' she trails off.

Jem tries to stop himself from shaking. 'Look, Vesper is the one that makes inspirational speeches, not me. She'd probably tell you that Delta is on our side and that means you are too. Or maybe she'd say something about this being bigger than your feelings and that you can make a difference. I don't know.

'As for me, I want to live. Besides, I'd be no good out there. I'm no soldier and I don't have the stomach for fighting. It's easy for The Seven or Obeisance to talk of bravery. They're not the ones who have to bleed for it. We are, and we're not immortals and we don't have living swords to protect us. No, I tried being a hero once and it didn't work out.' This time it is a memory that makes him shiver. 'So I'm going to stay here. You're welcome to stay too. I won't judge either way.'

Mazar nods slowly, then settles more comfortably next to him. She still doesn't acknowledge his hand on her arm, neither does she remove it.

Only the biggest craters make Vesper detour, her path doggedly straight. She ignores the fighting around her, fending off stray shots without turning her head. Her right arm seems to move of its own accord, agile and sure, the sword always where it needs to be.

Nobody opposes her directly. Most of the enemy are too busy fighting for their lives, or content to find other targets. Fear keeps them at bay, and an inevitability in her manner they cannot bring themselves to question.

Soon she finds herself passing through the bulk of the Empire's assault force and out the other side, a brief place of calm before she gets to the Knight Commander's rearguard.

But her path takes her away from them at a tangent, towards a lone form of silver, mostly buried.

With her free hand, Vesper brushes away the dirt, uncovering storm-cloud eyes and a mouth turned with sorrow.

'Delta,' she says. 'I know you can hear me.' Slowly, Delta's head turns, facing Vesper and the sword. 'It's time for you to get up.'

Delta goes to turn away again and the sword hums, angry. Vesper stills it with a look. 'No,' she says, 'that isn't how this is going to be done.' She looks down at Delta. 'You didn't have to get involved in this but You did. You made a choice and You stood with us against the rest of The Seven. You put Yourself between us and harm.' She nods to herself, then adds, 'and saved my life and that of my friends. Thank You.'

The sword thrums in her hand, drawing her attention to

the Seraph Knights approaching from behind, and the Knight Commander and his entourage coming from her right, running as best they can through the mud.

She spares them only the briefest of glances.

'We stood up to them and offered to talk, and in return they betrayed our trust and knocked us down.' She brings her hand to her chest, 'I got up again. Now it's Your turn.'

Vesper knows that in some ways the words are unnecessary, that Delta can look into her soul and read her intentions, just as the sword can read Delta's. Through its eye, she sees Delta's fear, and an ocean of regret, deep enough to drown a nation. She sees the desire to hide from it all and is reminded of the sword's desire for vengeance when she first used it. A different emotion, a different way to avoid the grief, but just as powerful.

The Seraph Knights are closing, the Knight Commander closer still, one jaw of the trap moving faster than the other.

Vesper holds out her hand. 'You're not alone.'

Delta sits up, her attention going to her own hands, empty, then to the area immediately around her.

'It's gone,' says Vesper. 'There's no blanket to hide under anymore, nothing to cling to. There's just me or them. It's Your choice.' She keeps her hand out.

Delta looks at her properly then, and liquid stone runs down her cheeks. 'You suffer.'

'Yes,' she admits, feeling the truth of the immortal's words. Her dream is broken, her body not what it was. 'As do You.'

Delta holds her gaze and takes her hand. Understanding passes between the two, solemn, resolute. The immortal stands and, immediately, the approaching forces slow, made wary by Delta's return to action.

The Seven

Vesper calls to the Knight Commander across scarred earth. 'I didn't want it to be this way.'

The man doesn't answer, just continues to advance. His entourage have weapons drawn, pointing at her, but not at Delta. She sees the Knight Commander give an order and those same weapons wink at her, discharging a volley of death.

She swings the sword, making an arc of blue, her song transformed into a light that steals power from the incoming projectiles, scattering them, harmless.

Delta speaks, the word resonant like a song. Just a word, but its echoes seem to endure, shimmering in the minds of those that hear her.

The Knight Commander's soldiers drop their weapons.

The Knight Commander drops to his knees.

Delta strides towards him and as she gets close, the others kneel too, unable to stand in the presence of her glory.

Silver fingers take the Knight Commander's jaw and tilt it up.

He looks into her eyes, his own shining with love.

Delta takes that love, and makes a chain of it, heavy, binding.

Vesper's whisper goes unnoticed against the spectacle. 'I didn't want it to be this way.'

The gold sun is the first to rise, shining brightly on the brutality below. Bodies languish in the mud, some frozen in the act of burying themselves, others on their backs, enjoying the dawn. A collection of tableaus, defying the lives that made them, enemy corpses unable to keep from getting close to each other. Here, a uniformed arm is thrown companionably over a green shoulder, there, a stilt-wearing fighter from Slake spoons a Seraph Knight, her arms wrapped tight around his neck.

The Empire of the Winged Eye has surrendered, the order coming, unexpected, only minutes ago. Samael sees little rebellion in the eyes of their soldiers. Most remain in shock, staring about like babes slapped for the first time.

He moves from group to group, making sure Crucible's forces adhere to Vesper's orders. 'No killing,' he rasps. 'Restrain them.'

There is reluctance, a mix of pragmatism and bloodlust, but they obey. Weapons are thrown into a pile, helmets with them, hands and ankles bound with a mix of chain, rope and wire.

He finds Flat Head checking bodies, seeing how many of the Thousand Nails have survived. He does not need to read her essence to know the news is bad. 'You've been shot,' he says.

She musters a grin, 'Yes! Many times!'

'How do you feel?'

'Strong!'

Samael sees the lie in her body as much as her words. 'You will get weaker. There is poison in your blood. Gather your survivors, bring them to me. I will help them.'

Flat Head slaps him on the arm. He does not feel it. 'We not need help. We strong.' She pauses. 'But we take help. Sign of friendship!' She slaps him on the arm again for emphasis.

Though the sights are grim, there is one thing that lifts Samael's spirits. Scout has returned with the dawn. Recovered and well rested, the Dogspawn bounds across the battlefield drawing attention to the wounded. There is a simple joy in his work. To Scout, this is not a disaster, it is a game, and his barks are playful, excited.

The Seven

The fighting has been intense, horribly efficient, with losses high on both sides. The salvaged armour used by most of Crucible's forces is no match for imperial artillery. *It should have been worse for us*, he thinks. Walking between groups of newly bound prisoners, he begins to understand.

For many of the Empire's soldiers, this is their first true battle. A far cry from the scared little settlements they've smashed along the way, or the odd lone half-breed, encountered and hunted down. No amount of reading about the infernal prepares one for actual contact. Meditation on death is no substitute for actually seeing it. *They were not ready.*

In the golden light of the morning, the Empire's failings are all too easy to see. Metal snakes show signs of damage caused long before the fight started, old wounds poorly treated. Equipment shows its age, veteran warriors, their rarity.

A tug on the thread of essence that links him to Scout pulls him from grim musings. The Dogspawn has found something.

Samael looks over to see a red tail, ragged, sticking up from the mud. Unsure how much of the curiosity is his own, he drifts closer to Scout, who is already digging.

Through their bond, he knows Scout is hunting for a familiar scent. Then, realization jolting through his mind, he joins in. Wet earth is clawed away in clumps, heavier bits of stone pulled out and thrown aside.

Gradually, they excavate a hand, then an arm, then a shoulder, all armoured, filthy.

As Scout continues to work the body free, Samael crouches down, establishing a grip under the armpit. The hand spasms for a moment, then feels the side of Samael's arm. After a moment's pause, it establishes a grip on his bracer. In a slow, smooth movement, the half-breed straightens, making the ground gurgle.

With a final muddy burp the Vagrant is brought back into the world. Delta's sword comes with him.

Scout barks. He knows this body!

Samael pats the Dogspawn, then stands the Vagrant up, examining him for damage.

Though the Vagrant lets Samael take his weight, there are no obvious wounds, and after a few moments, the half-breed steps back.

The Vagrant coughs, spits out something black, wipes his mouth. Only then does he seem to take in his surroundings. His lips draw into a line and the eye in Delta's sword seems about to close when something inside it rallies, opening again, looking, seeing.

When the Vagrant turns back to Samael, his eyebrow is raised in question.

'She is out there,' he replies, pointing away from Crucible. 'With Delta.'

The Vagrant nods to Samael. One hand rises as if to stroke Scout's head but, as the Dogspawn looks up, eager, the Vagrant's fingers seem to wilt inwards and the affection reduces to a second nod.

Then, he is walking away.

The red sun makes its way into the sky, giving a bloody wash to the proceedings, and a second, less-defined shadow.

Walking in the rut left by caterpillar tracks, the Vagrant makes his way towards the far end of the field, where a line of people kneel. Nearby, two figures stand, framed by a solar disc.

He keeps going, squinting, until squelching footsteps draw Vesper's attention.

She turns towards him. 'You came. I knew you'd come.' She looks at his face, sees the shock. 'I haven't had a chance to see myself yet. It's bad isn't it?'

Tears seem to bleed from his eyes as he nods. He closes the last of the space between them, reaching out carefully, as if she were made of glass. They embrace, the two swords watching each other, awkward, at their sides.

When they part, she sighs. 'How is everyone?'

The Vagrant shrugs.

'Is Reela okay?'

The Vagrant nods, musters a little smile.

'Good, and Jem?'

He shrugs again, making her frown. 'I have to go and see. Look, this isn't over yet, you know that don't you?'

The Vagrant nods.

She points to a shape on the horizon, a black smudge like a pupil in the eye of the red sun. 'The rest of The Seven are coming. We have to make sure all of the Empire's soldiers are secured before they get here. And I need to speak to whatever is left of the delegations one more time.' She pauses, her voice losing some of its command. 'And I need you to be with me, I mean for what's coming. I can't do this alone.'

He nods, immediate.

'You know what I'm asking?'

The nod is slower this time, definite.

'Thank you.'

They turn towards Crucible together, leaving Delta to stare, solemn, at the horizon.

One Thousand and Nine
Years Ago

Sleep seems to lose its grip on Massassi. She spends her days outside, watching the sun make its way across the sky. Epsilon, Theta and Eta stand further back, watching the watcher. All four of them seem to be waiting for something.

Peace-Fifteen has tried asking but might as well be a shadow for all the older woman acknowledges her. As for the three silver figures, they do not speak. Mostly they ignore Peace-Fifteen entirely, and for that she is grateful, for when they do look at her, she feels pity and the urge to run away.

But she does not, for she is a loyal creature. While Massassi sits in her harness, Peace-Fifteen administers her medications, sustenance and hygiene. She notes with concern that Massassi is requesting a further reduction in rations. It is as if there is less of her to feed.

When Peace-Fifteen tries to argue, she is ignored. When she questions, she is ignored. Massassi's gaze is only for the sky now. And if the rays damage her eyes, she does not complain.

The Seven

There is an intensity to her that frightens Peace-Fifteen. It reminds her of the way her mistress used to watch the Breach in the early days.

At night they carry Massassi back to the workshop where she murmurs to herself, working through dark hours on little pieces of platinum. No longer strong enough to create another like Alpha, she makes coins, each infused with a sliver of feeling, a moment of life. They take from her in insect sized bites. It is a slow diminishing, a whittling away of the soul.

Meanwhile, the Empire continues its job, patrolling the Breach, staying vigilant for signs of new fractures. The divide between citizen, soldier and knight grows deeper. Beta wisely keeps only the finest families in the Shining City, the ones that Alpha approves of. He moves the others away to less desirable locations.

A new generation is trained, furnished with skills and stories from the old.

Though happiness is as rare as ever, the Empire of the Winged Eye is stable, safe in the hands of its immortal leaders.

Massassi has succeeded in her task. She has prepared humanity for the day when the infernals will come, armed them, trained them, given her own blood and being, ensuring that things are ready, and will remain so after she is gone.

And yet she does not rest.

Every day she studies the sun and every day ends without satisfaction. The scar is still there. A thin line of darkness running right down the middle that only she can see. No matter what she makes, it remains.

It appeared the day she almost died, a three pointed fracture to mirror her wounds. And though she has healed, though the sun has healed, both of them remain marked.

Massassi does not know why this is, does not understand the link between her and the world. She knows only that it exists, and that the sun's fate is tied in some way to her own. In some way, she is the bastion of this reality, an anchor that must remain strong, even after death. And so at night, she works, until the coins fill every corner of her workshop, a treasure hoard of self, fragmented.

Even when the sense slips from her and her jaw begins to hang, slack and drooling, she keeps going.

Days of sun and nights of making platinum moons in miniature repeat, seeming endless.

But they are not.

A last coin is made. It falls clinking with the others, setting them off too, echoing, echoing as Massassi lets her hands fall on her lap, becoming still.

For such a dramatic life, it is a small and lonely end.

Peace-Fifteen finds Massassi shortly after. Anger rises through the grief. She cannot believe that the old woman would dare to die in the scant few hours she wasn't there.

From their scattered positions across the world, The Seven stop as one, all looking the same way, all looking up. All looking at the sun.

Minutes have ticked by and now they see the black line on its surface too. It grows quickly, a vertical band of darkness. For a fraction of a second, the sun dims, seeming to wink down on all below.

Then, without sound but with light so bright it sears the vision from any mortal eyes turned that way, it explodes.

CHAPTER TWENTY

Walking towards Crucible, Vesper has a view of the devastation. Large parts of the field have collapsed, exposing bare roots and building foundations, like a bottom lip pulled away from old teeth.

The makeshift wall has been obliterated, only a few bumps in the earth suggesting what was there the day before, and only two of the bunkers remain intact, the others broken or smoking or both.

Amidst the wreckage, wounded are found, dug out and helped to safety. Meanwhile the trade for scarce medical supplies has already begun, a new kind of war, with very different rules.

As she gets closer she sees the Empire's forces slumped together, bound and watched over, their guards angry, hurt, looking for an excuse to lash out, to make the prisoners pay.

'Listen,' says Vesper, making everyone turn to her. 'You came here to receive my protection, and you have it. Now, the people who have surrendered their arms are also under my protection.'

Assent is given, the potential for violence receding.

Vesper and the Vagrant continue, not stopping until they stand where the wall used to be.

The fighting has been heavy, brutal, explosives employed to devastating effect. New craters pepper the ground, the largest made by a fallen sky-ship, the impact so severe that only shreds of wreckage remain.

She sees a Usurperkin limping towards her, is aware of the way the Vagrant tenses at her side. The figure is familiar but she cannot place him. Strange, she thinks, she is usually good with names. The Usurperkin wears a tattered marshall's uniform, one of those favoured in Verdigris. There is dried blood in his ears that has run down, staining both sides of his neck.

'You're one of Tough Call's people, aren't you?'

'Yeah, I'm Max.'

'Are you hurt?'

He looks surprised at her question. 'Yeah but this ain't about me.' He clears his throat as if about to say something important, the effect spoiled slightly by his inability to meet her eye. 'We wanted you to know that the boss held the wall. Those Empire bastards didn't get through.'

'Then I owe you and Tough Call my thanks.'

'Not a one of them,' he continues. 'They piled it on thick and she stood right there with us. When she ran out of rockets she used a knife and when that broke she used her fist . . . and . . . and when that broke . . .' Max shakes his head. 'We wanted you to know what she did. We want you to tell the others.'

The Seven

Vesper rests a hand on his forearm. 'I will, Max. You have my word.' She squeezes, then asks, 'Where is she? I'd like to see her.'

Max leads her back to the dome. The Vagrant follows as far as the entrance but then splits off, hurrying towards another section while she and Max go to the rooms allocated for Verdigris. There are new cracks in Crucible's walls, a few shards of daylight getting in where they shouldn't. One falls across Tough Call's face.

There are others here. A Usurperkin called Maxi, covered in bandages, who wipes at her eyes, and Ezze, who for once appears humble.

Vesper nods to them and goes to Tough Call's side. Most of the woman's body is covered, giving the impression of someone merely sleeping.

Leaning down, Vesper whispers goodbye.

A few ratbred have returned to the dome already, setting their rooms to rights. They tense at the sound of the Vagrant's boots hurrying down the corridor. He gives them apologetic waves as he passes, moving on before any questions can start.

One door is passed by, then another. He goes through the third one, ducking late, the hangings pulling at his hair. A few strides take him to a cabinet. He crouches down, pulls open the door.

Inside are some folded clothes, rumpled by the indentation of a small bottom, and nothing else.

The Vagrant's hand goes to his mouth.

He stands up, checks the back of the cabinet.

Nothing.

A quick glance round the room reveals plenty of orna-
ments, all shiny or studded with glass. Many are on their
sides. Not one of them looks like Reela.

He runs over to the rug, still folded over, and looks down
the hole.

Nothing.

Hand still pressed to mouth, he stands there, his face
caught in an expression somewhere between intense thought
and panic.

Behind him, there is a soft giggle.

The Vagrant's eyebrows shoot up.

He nods to himself, the worry lines easing, then turns to
his left, until he faces in the opposite direction.

Nobody is in sight.

He scratches his head and gives an exaggerated sigh.

There is another giggle behind him, stifled, louder.

He turns again, faster this time, catching a glimpse of hair
trailing off to his left, and the bottom of a foot raised in flight.

Another sigh and he tilts left before turning right, catching
a naughty-faced Reela in the act.

He shakes his head at her but is usurped by his own smile.

She smiles back, cheeky, and he shakes his head again, at
himself, before sweeping her into an embrace.

They cluster in Vesper's room: the Vagrant, Jem, Samael and
Vesper. Reela has been put next door with Scout, and the
sounds of running feet and happy barks form an incongruous
underscore for the otherwise grim proceedings.

'I need to know the state of things before I speak to
everyone,' says Vesper. With difficulty, she adds, 'I've already
seen Tough Call.'

For once, Samael's whispery tones are appropriate. 'The Thousand Nails have taken heavy losses and over half the survivors are wounded or suffering essence poisoning. I will help those I can but they are not what they were.

'The West Rift delegation was hit worst. Their leaders are dead, their numbers decimated.'

'What about New Horizon? Red Rails? The Order of the Broken Blades? And where is Genner?'

The Vagrant looks up at the name. He catches Vesper's eye and shakes his head.

She seems to deflate a little. 'Oh . . . Sorry, he's been with me so long I thought . . . Do you know where his body is? I'd like to see him, if there's time.'

The Vagrant looks away.

'New Horizon is still with us,' says Samael. 'I don't know exactly how they fared but the Man-shape seems happy. Without their support the Empire would have killed us from the inside. The ratbred of Red Rails didn't get involved in the fighting but their tunnels allowed us to bring the fight to the Empire.'

'I see. What about the Order?'

'We remain but the Necro-blades are unworthy.' Samael lowers his head. 'I failed you and I failed them. I'm sorry.'

'No Samael, if anyone failed here, it's me. Please, look up. This isn't over, and with Genner gone I need you to be strong, now more than ever.'

He meets her eye. 'I am yours to command.'

'Good. Anything else?'

'There were civilian casualties. Although the Empire's main attack was held at the wall, a smaller force were dropped in at the start of the battle.'

The sword hums softly at Vesper's side. 'They came to me for protection . . .' There is a pause, awkward, then she adds, 'How have people taken it?'

'A few have fled. Most have stayed. A large number have asked to fight.'

'Then we need to give them weapons. Tell Gorad and Gut-pumper to see it done. We can worry about compensation for Slake when all of this is behind us. Is that it? Good. Samael, convene a meeting of the delegates. The rest of The Seven are only hours away and we need to be ready.'

As the group breaks up and Vesper starts for the door, Jem approaches, tentative. 'You're not actually going to fight them are you?'

An eye regards him, incredulous. 'Of course I am. There's no other choice now.'

'I know there has to be a battle. What I'm asking is do you have to be at the head of it? You've been asking about everyone else, but what about you? Those people out there, they don't care about you. They just care about themselves.' He makes a vague gesture in her direction, his hand not quite touching hers. 'Haven't you given enough already?'

'I'm not doing this because I want to, I'm doing it because I have to. There's no one else, Jem. Just me. I made this happen and I have to see it through to the end.'

'But what if there's nothing left of you at the end?'

Vesper closes her eyes. 'This isn't the time.' She knows this will anger him, keeps talking to smother the argument before it gets going. 'Look, I can't fight The Seven and you at the same time. Help me. Keep yourself and Reela safe. When this is over, we can talk.'

'This will never be over.' He looks at her, pained by what he sees. He steps aside.

'We'll talk after the battle, I promise.'

Jem bites back a reply. The taste of it lingers in his mouth, bitter, long after she has gone.

The buck wanders the grasses on the far side of Crucible, keeping well clear of the people and their grim business. Terrors of the previous night are already forgotten, the suns as warm as they ever were, pleasant on his back.

A questing bleat catches his attention.

It is the doe.

At the sight of her, four legs freeze in place and his jaw locks. Calling to her drives her away so he does not do that. Chasing her drives her away so he does not do that either. The buck has no idea what to do and so he stands, rigid, his eyes on hers.

Slowly, she approaches, pausing sometimes to behead a nearby flower, her eyes flicking to his as she does so.

The buck sways, eyelids flickering, vision suddenly blurry. Somehow, he manages not to faint.

She bleats again, a call for attention already received, and trots closer, until her head is inches from his.

The buck does not move, holding his breath, keeping his body still.

Those final inches fall away slowly, a bearded mouth brushing his cheek.

Blissfully, the buck closes his eyes. She nuzzles him a second time, more firmly and it is suddenly too much. He opens his mouth, bellowing joy.

The doe leaps, straight up.

Several birds fly away.

Not long after, the buck is alone again. He hangs his head, making a series of low bleats, miserable.

Vesper walks out to the central space. Above and around her, the delegations quieten, as much through shock as respect. By now they have all heard rumours about her injuries and recovery, but for many this is the first time they have actually seen her.

The infernals lean away from the silvery essence running though her like flaming mercury. The humans, seeing nothing but the physical, wonder how she still walks.

All present are attentive, waiting for her to speak. Since the battle, there has been a new kind of respect for her. No longer just a diplomat or sword carrier, or the one that allegedly closed a distant Breach. She has been transformed into something other, a figurehead, a legend, a thing they can no longer fully relate to. They are in awe of her.

A memory comes to Vesper of the Shining City and the sea of reverent faces at the steps of The Seven's sanctum, and with it a feeling of terrible loneliness.

She looks up at the various delegations. Savmir and his ratbred appear ruffled, nervous. Ezze sits uneasily in the space left by Tough Call, Max and Maxi just as uneasy at his side. West Rift's section is poorly populated, and the First's box remains empty. Flat Head seems propped up in her chair, chin resting heavy on her fist. Only Slake's painted delegates and the Man-shape seem unchanged.

'Last night,' she says, 'you did the impossible. You stood against the Empire of the Winged Eye and you won. They came at us with their war machines and their soldiers when we were least ready, and you did not fail.

'The cost was high.' She takes a moment to look at each group in turn. 'It was too high. Our worlds will never be the same again. But we won. A lot of us were strangers to each other but we fought side by side and we won.'

She lets the positive note fade away. 'I wish I could say the battle was over but it isn't. Alpha's sky palace is coming. It will be here before midday.'

They all know this but her words bring the reality home a second time. Heads shake and dark words are exchanged. Vesper holds up a hand and they fall quiet again. 'Listen to me. They say that no one has ever stood in battle against The Seven and survived. Maybe that's true.' There is another rumble of unhappiness that cuts off as she continues. 'But The Seven no longer exist. Gamma and Delta are with us. The bulk of their army has fallen. We can do this. Together.'

At some unseen signal, Gorad and Gut-pumper lean forward. 'Gut-pumper was wondering about that army . . .' says Gorad.

'Yes,' agrees Gut-pumper, 'that Empire army we're looking after.'

Gorad nods. 'Why haven't we killed them? Be safer to. Much cheaper to kill them than to feed them.'

'Hard to tame,' murmurs Gut-pumper.

The Man-shape raises a hand, indicating that it would like to speak. At Vesper's nod, it begins. 'I too have thought about this problem and I have a solution that will save resources and be of benefit to all sides. Give them over to us.'

'What would you do with them?' asks Vesper.

'Repurpose them, as we would our own after a defeat.'

Vesper looks hard at the Man-shape, then at each of the other delegates. 'Is this really what you want? I thought we were here to do things differently than before.' She draws herself straight. 'I didn't order those people restrained just so I could kill them later. I did it because there's more than one way to defeat an enemy, and there's more than one way for us to live our lives.'

Ezze clears his throat. 'Great lady, Ezze hears you and is struck by the vision of your splendid words, but many of us are unworthy of the greatness. We are more interested to be living and having enjoyment of the food.'

'Who will watch them?' asks Savmir. 'Cannot fight and watch. Cannot split our fighters. Too many enemy as it is!'

'This won't be like last time,' replies Vesper. 'Those too injured to fight but well enough to hold a weapon will watch the prisoners.

'Alpha's sky palace can't be fought like a regular army base that's on the ground. It doesn't matter that there're more of us, they'll just glide overhead and bomb us out of existence. To bring our numbers to bear, we need to bring them down to our level. In order to do that, we're going to need to get people up and into the palace.

'We have the First's remaining sky-ships in addition to the ones the Empire surrendered. We'll pack them with our finest and use them to board the palace in multiple locations. If we're fast, we can force them down, allowing the bulk of our army to attack.'

She gives them a moment to take it in. 'I'd prefer to take volunteers for the raid. The casualties will be high.'

'Where will you find pilots for the extra ships?' asks Gorad.

'And how will you stop the Empire ships locking down?' asks Gut-pumper.

'The Empire's sky-ships won't lock down because it will be the original crew piloting them.'

She hears a mutter, perhaps from the West Rift box, 'So much for volunteers.'

'They have already volunteered, it seems we are not the only ones to doubt The Seven's wisdom.'

'Can we trust enemy?' asks Savmir.

'They cannot lie to me,' replies Vesper. The irony of her own lie does not escape her. While it is true that the Empire's pilots are willing now, it was not so before their meeting with Delta. Vesper keeps this detail to herself, another smudge on the window of her dream.

'Are you going, Vesper?' asks the Man-shape.

Without hesitation, she raises her head. 'Of course. I wouldn't ask people to go if I weren't willing to myself.'

'I am confused. You know that The Seven will sense the Malice. They will come for you.'

'I'm counting on it. While They are trying to bring me down, it will free the rest of the raiding party to complete the mission.'

The Man-shape remains unconvinced. 'What if you get shot from the sky before you land? What hope will the mission have then?'

'There's going to be more than one lure. Delta is going up too, and I was hoping you would join us. Your presence will draw them just as fast as mine.'

Everyone turns to the Man-shape's shadowed head, waiting for it to answer. 'No,' it says at last. 'I am here seeking life, not death. However, I will send Guttershamble and the Faceless Prince in my place.'

343

Was that comment aimed at me? she wonders. *Am I seeking death?*

The sword begins to hum in her hand. It takes her a moment to realize it is not reacting to her. Frowning, she closes her eyes, giving herself over to it.

As she concentrates, she becomes aware of a slight vibration in the floor, like the purr of the earth. The sword pulls at her, drawn by something outside the dome.

She is not the only one disturbed. More and more of the delegates sense the tremors now. Some reaching for weapons out of habit, others moving for the exit.

The Man-shape and the other infernals are first to the doors, moving with the speed of those that know something the others do not.

In a matter of minutes, the dome empties.

Vesper is the last to leave, moving with a more measured pace than the others. She is weary rather than afraid, resigned as much as ready.

Beneath her feet, the ground trembles, regular, the heartbeat of a giant, louder, closer.

Squeezing the hilt of the sword, Vesper goes outside to meet it.

Delta of The Seven turns away from the rising sun and her approaching brothers and sisters in the sky, her gaze going towards the new arrival.

Above, Alpha's palace pauses, five silver figures moving to the same side of the battlements.

In Crucible, people rush to high ground. Those with scopes and vision enhancers employ them. Those without, squint.

The infernals sense it before they can see it: the coming

of one of their own. Not since the time of the Uncivil or the Usurper have they felt such power. It is fear-making, thrilling, and they are drawn to watch like flies to fire.

And there is plenty for the humans to see too. A shape is materializing, visible despite the distance. Familiar, bizarre, moving in a way that shocks the brain.

Someone shouts, voicing the thought they all have, lending credence to the impossible sight. 'It's Wonderland!'

Others agree, the word spreading from group to group. For it is Wonderland, but transformed. No longer simply a city, it has become a living creature, the towers like rows of spines on its back.

It moves on a skirt of rippling bone, hundreds of giant vertebrae flexing together to give the city a gliding, almost graceful approach.

Lights sparkle, on towers, on walls, thick studs of them making a belt of jewels between the bone-skirt and city gates. They are a riot of colours, joyous, each one lovingly restored.

Such is the majesty of it all that for a while, all anyone can do is watch.

Then, Delta returns to her vigil. Scopes and eyes across Crucible return to the sky, and Alpha's sky palace rotates towards the new threat, Wonderland.

Vesper finds her way to Samael's side. 'It's the First, isn't it?'

'Yes,' the half-breed replies. 'It is complete again. Wonderland is its shell now. That was the Uncivil's dream but she was destroyed before it was complete. Now Neer has seen it through.'

'With your help.'

'Yes, with my help, and the First's.'

She nods, realizing that Samael has known about this for some time. She quickly puts away any anger at being kept in the dark, focusing on the needs of the moment. 'This is it, Samael. This is our chance. Scramble the sky-ships.'

'Yes,' he says but does not move.

'If you have something to say, there's no time to be shy.'

'I wish to volunteer for the raid.'

Vesper shakes her head. 'I'm sorry, but I need you on the ground. If all goes well, we'll meet in the palace somewhere. And, Samael?' she adds. 'If something happens to me, I'm relying on you to hold this together. I'm sorry to lay another burden on you, but you're the only other one that can get the infernals and humans to listen.'

'I hope it doesn't come to that.'

'Me too! Now go, we need to make this count.'

While sky-ships are prepped and run through last-minute checks, Vesper jogs to the edge of Crucible, raising the sword and singing softly. There is an answering cry, and soon after she is rewarded by the sight of Delta flying back towards her.

It is almost time to go and there are too many goodbyes. In a way, she is glad.

The Vagrant strides through the throngs of rushing people to stand before her. They look at each other, condensing a lifetime of feelings, of things said and unsaid, into a nod.

A strange movement in her periphery draws her attention from him: Guttershamble and the Faceless Prince are making their way onto a waiting sky-ship, two mashed corpses shuffling towards a second end. The sight repulses her. She wonders if anything is left of Gutterface, the infernal they were made from, and if they are even still capable of independent thought. There are hints in the wrecked figures of something greater, but they are hard to find.

After a moment, her eyes travel to the sword. *Are they any different to me?*

The sword has little sympathy for such thoughts, glaring at her until they are burnt away, leaving her focused again.

She looks up as Delta lands. 'Ready?' she asks.

The reply is whispered, as much felt on the ears as heard. 'I do not want to face Alpha again. I am afraid.'

The mention of Alpha's name does not make Vesper feel afraid. If anything, she and the sword feel a frustration that slides into anger, tinged with disappointment. 'Dig deep. Don't let the fear win. And remember, You're not alone. I'll see You up there, okay?'

Delta assents and Vesper runs to another sky-ship, jumping in without hesitation.

From the open hatch, Mazar shouts that they are ready to fly. The Vagrant starts to climb in, beckoning Delta to follow.

But she does not.

She is thinking of the last time she met her brother, Alpha. Her essence remains bruised by his anger, throbbing at the recollection. She wishes there was something to cling to and looks at her hands. They are empty, only dark smudges on her palms where once she held a coat.

The other sky-ships are nearly loaded. It is important that they all leave together to have the biggest chance of success. Delta knows this but cannot bring herself to go in.

Vesper says that she is not alone but, in this moment, Delta feels more alone than ever before. She is estranged from her brothers and sisters, adrift, and her purpose is unclear. Even her sword feels wrong to her now.

Engines rise in pitch, ready, urging her to hurry.

And then it strikes her. There is something that would bring comfort.

She leaps up, soaring towards the dome. In seconds she has flown through one of the larger cracks and is gliding down an empty corridor. She stops at a room, ducking through the doorway.

A man called Jem stands up. He sees her hand, beckoning, and goes to say something that Delta does not want to hear. Her essence ripples out. *How dare he!* She wants such a little thing. *It is not his place to pass judgement.* A single look is all it takes for Jem to close his tainted mouth and step away, to keep stepping away, mindless, until his back hits the wall.

Once more, she looks to Reela and the girl comes, a small hand snaring one of her silver fingers.

At the contact, Delta feels the tension ease slightly. *Now, I am ready.*

CHAPTER TWENTY-ONE

A dozen sky-ships rise together, light spearing down from their engines. They stay low at first, skimming over the fields that surround Crucible, following the curve of gentle hills, speeding stealthily towards Alpha's sky palace.

From a distance, Wonderland and the floating fortress appear to move slowly towards each other, with dignity, more like participants in a ritual than combatants.

Even the first volley of missiles seems as much display as attack. They streak, screaming across the sky, crashing into Wonderland's towers and walls, and little clouds bloom, flowers of smoke with flickering eyes.

In seconds they are gone and Wonderland continues forward, untroubled.

The sky-ships continue as well, flying low until the shadows of the palace fall across them. Together they peel away from the ground, a volley of arrowheads shooting straight up.

As gun turrets along the battlements swing towards the

new targets the formation breaks abruptly, each sky-ship fighting its own battle to survive.

Inside one of them, the Vagrant sits. His hands press against his face, as if trying to hold something inside. From his lap, Delta's sword watches, nervous.

Each sudden movement makes the Vagrant jolt. His chest heaves and cheeks puff out before he swallows, settling just in time for the next one.

A small hand rubs his back in sympathy.

He looks up and gives Reela a watery smile before lowering his head again.

She carries on rubbing his back.

After a beat, the Vagrant lifts his head again, before turning slowly to look at Reela.

Amber eyes blink several times.

Reela is still there. She waves at him.

The Vagrant's mouth drops open.

Outside, a set of booms grow louder, gunfire tracking closer to their position. The sky-ship makes an abrupt turn in the air and Reela lurches right, feet leaving the floor. Her flight is arrested by the Vagrant, who catches her, plonking her into the seat next to his. The Vagrant gives little shakes of his head as he straps her into place. When he glances down at Delta's sword, it is looking at Delta, accusing.

The Vagrant sighs into his hands.

There are more explosions nearby, more flips and spins, each one matched by the stomachs of those in the hold, then a thud and a screech as the sky-ship skids to a stop.

Already the hatch is hissing open, Mazar readying her

rifle as she comes from the cockpit. She ignores the others, her eyes for Delta alone.

'We're here.'

Vesper's sky-ship dives in, risking a bad landing in order to be a harder target. Given the nature of the palace, landing spots are limited. There are a few designated pads, two courtyards or the possibility of squeezing onto one of the rare pieces of flat roof. Because of this, it is easy to predict where the sky-ships will approach, The Seven's elite forces already moving into ambush positions.

Vesper watches the ant-like figures scrambling below, feels yet another stab of remorse at the waste of talent. Bile is swallowed down before she gives the order.

Small pods spit from the sky-ship, firing the crew at one of the gun towers while Vesper leaps from the hatch. The sword is held high, silver wings spreading, navigating rich currents of essence.

Meanwhile the sky-ship accelerates, plunging itself like a dagger into the palace below. Too late, the ants try to scatter, their ambush inverted.

Vesper forces herself to watch the explosion before turning her attention to the tower.

The soldiers manning the turret are focusing their attention on the pods, waiting for each to land before blasting it off the battlements. She glides down above their heads, coming to land on the cannon's steaming barrel.

Reversing the sword, she plunges it into the control panel, causing the two operators to leap back in alarm. They reach for sidearms, neither able to take their eyes from the apparition in front of them. One of the soldiers misses his holster, his hand drawing air instead. The other raises a pistol, shaking.

Vesper swings the sword in a wide arc, letting out a single note, sharp. No steel touches the soldiers, but the force of the song blasts them both backwards. Heads rock, slamming into the wall, and sense falls from faces.

Meanwhile, the pods pop open, one after another. A motley crew made of the best that Crucible has to offer. 'Go,' she tells them.

They nod, scattering quickly as she raises the sword again, this time issuing a challenge. It blasts out, bright and loud, even above the sounds of battle.

And then, on the other side of the palace, just visible over rooftops, streets and courtyards, five figures spread their wings, taking to the sky.

Reela slips from her seat, running over to Delta. The Vagrant goes to follow but in his haste he fumbles the clasp, contemptuous straps arresting his movement and throwing him back into the chair.

He makes a grab for Reela but she has already gone beyond his reach, moving to stand by Delta.

The clasp confounds him a second time, then a third. Bemused, the eye in Delta's sword watches him.

Mazar drops out through the hatch, her rifle giving a warm welcome to those nearby. Delta follows, Reela compliant at her side.

Finally, the clasp parts and the Vagrant tumbles out, running headlong through the hatch and into a courtyard.

Already, skirmishes are taking place all around, in the streets, across battlements, the forces of the palace organizing themselves into hunting parties, dividing the prey between them.

A group of soldiers come running into view led by a pair of knights. Delta takes Reela in the opposite direction, a door opening at her approach. The Vagrant and Mazar block the doorway, preparing themselves for battle.

As the knights get closer the Vagrant's eyes flick to theirs, to little details in the way they hold their swords, one with the point dipping like a ramp, the other held aloft, flagpole straight. They are familiar styles to match the faces under the helms.

He moves to engage them, making the knights a wall between him and the soldiers' guns behind.

They come at him then, their blades taking turns, running him through a series of parries that he recognizes, that, years ago, he showed them. It is a form of respect, a recognition of their history before the proper fight begins.

It is also an ideal opportunity to strike.

The Vagrant does not take it, letting the swords ring out in sequence, one against the other, letting Reela and Delta get further away.

Though ritualistic, the Vagrant is still forced to give ground, the two knights pushing him back towards the wall, closing down options as the ritual comes to an end.

The last parry rings out and all three pause. One sword held high, the other low, Delta's sword at a level between them, waiting to see which needs to be met first.

The knights break rhythm, attacking together, one blade going for his neck, the other his knees.

Ducking low, the Vagrant feels a blade sing over his head, the song pushing down on him, as Delta's sword forces the other away.

He sees an opening, hesitates, a thrust that could slide up under a breastplate to bring death becomes one that swings down, cracking an ankle.

While one knight staggers, the other attacks, sword held in two hands.

The Vagrant meets it, his parry augmented by song, throwing back his opponent.

From his left, a shot rings out, sparking the stones by his feet. Before he can react, the knights are attacking again, battering the Vagrant's defences, looking for an opening.

Two blades slam into Delta's sword together, pressing down. The Vagrant's elbows begin to bend, one of the silver wings digging into his shoulder.

The Vagrant bares his teeth, takes breath to sing again when a grinding sound of metal on stone comes from behind him, from the floor, distinct.

He looks down, the knights, despite themselves, copying the movement, all three watching as a trio of grenades rolls between the Vagrant's legs, then through the knights' to come to a stop a few feet past them, where the soldiers are.

The Vagrant looks up in time to meet their young eyes and see the knowledge in them, before they are ripped apart, armour, skin and bone, gone. He pulls the sword flat to his chest, singing out, and the last of the grenade's fury disperses around him, flames licking the wall either side.

'Come on!' yells Mazar. 'The Seven are moving!'

She is right. Their shadows fall tenfold around him, a flight of immortal birds. Two of the shadows are blurring together, shrinking, deepening, as the immortal that casts them descends.

The Vagrant doesn't bother to check which one, following Mazar through the door at a run.

Not all of The Seven come for Vesper. Beta parts from the others, diving away into a nearby courtyard. Smoke belches up to meet him and his wings hack through it scythe-like, then he is gone, a slowly expanding hole left behind.

The others, Alpha, Epsilon, Theta and Eta, all remain airborne, heading straight for her.

Vesper has a moment of grim satisfaction. Her plan has worked, Alpha's hatred of her has proven more important than any tactical concerns. Reality comes soon after. Four immortals are coming for her, where one would surely do. There is no hope of survival and she has to swallow the knowledge that she is going to die in this palace. Again, no fear comes at the thought, just determination. If her life is to be the price of victory, she has to sell it high.

And so she runs.

Along the battlements she goes. Twice, she swings her sword, scattering soldiers who stand in her way. There isn't time to destroy the next turret she passes but she allows the tip of her blade to screech alongside the barrel, impairing it to an unknown degree.

Up above, Alpha draws his sword. A low thrum sounds as it comes free of its scabbard, a death knell. He raises his sword towards the heavens, then lowers it to point straight at Vesper.

She is still running, head down, trying to reach the relative safety of a turret. An eye watches for her, however, and her sword arm moves so that her fist is behind her head, the blade running down her back.

Alpha's mouth opens, and a single note barks out. Between his weapon and his target, the space explodes in fire, blue-white.

When it has passed, the turret is rubble, and the entrance that would have taken Vesper deeper into the palace, into cover, is no more.

Vesper herself is still moving, groggily, her right arm pulling her forward even as she struggles to clear her head. She scrambles across the rubble and keeps going.

Alpha points again but this time he doesn't sing. Epsilon, Theta and Eta draw their weapons together in near synchrony, a beat of wings carrying them up, ready to dive.

She is close to one corner of the battlements now, where another tower joins the two walkways. She is so close, so nearly there.

Eta swoops in behind, missing narrowly, close enough to buffet Vesper forwards, wingtips slicing fabric but not drawing blood.

An eye watches Eta pass, narrowing.

Whatever thought the sword has is put aside for Theta's attack. Vesper spins, letting momentum carry her through the air backwards, managing to parry the attack as it comes down, a diagonal slice of death.

Swords and song ring together, charging the air. Theta shoots past, starting a majestic turn, while Vesper is sent reeling, bouncing once on the floor before hurtling through the tower's door.

She rolls, graceless, backwards, before coming up on her feet. Somehow she manages to turn the right way, controlling the momentum, letting it carry her forward into a running beat.

Eta lands on one side of the tower, Epsilon on the other but she is heading towards neither of them, plunging down the stairwell.

A man in Empire uniform is coming the opposite way, fleeing something else. He screams when he sees Vesper, throwing himself against the wall. She ignores him but, as her mind clears, she notices the sounds of violence below.

The respite of the stairwell is brief, the tower spitting her out into a street where Empire forces do battle with Guttershamble and the Faceless Prince.

Their bullets sting, slowing the two infernals but not stopping them. She has a glimpse, stark, of Guttershamble grabbing one of the soldiers, crushing his skull in its rotten fingers. Another soldier flies through the air, her legs missing.

All their lives, the people of the Empire have lived in the shadow of the infernal threat and now it is in front of them, a nightmare made real.

Vesper turns away and runs. She has put two streets between her and the carnage before she hears Alpha's cry of outrage.

She keeps running.

For a while, Alpha's anger, and that of his brother and sisters, is directed elsewhere. She uses that time to put as much distance between them as possible. What she needs is a way deeper inside, where flight will be difficult. None presents itself, forcing her to keep moving.

But she is no stranger to the palace. Through the essence that links them, the sword whispers memories of another time and her vision shifts. The buildings around her begin to change, structurally the same but lit differently, by a single, stronger sun.

'Thank you,' she whispers, and the sword hums acceptance.

Behind her, she hears the sound of four immortals singing together, engaging the infernals. They will not stand long but it doesn't matter.

She knows exactly where she has to go.

It does not take long for Mazar and the Vagrant to catch Delta and Reela up. The two move at a stately pace, hand in hand.

The corridor is only wide enough for two, forcing them to match the immortal's strides. The Vagrant exchanges a look with Mazar, frustration passing between them as they check the urge to push, like a pair of dogs keen to be off the leash.

Just as they turn a corner, the Vagrant checks behind and sees Beta in pursuit. He does not run either, though he seems to gain on them in agonizing inches.

They meet few others in the palace, hallways strangely empty, deserted. And when another person is seen, they kneel immediately, deferent, allowing Delta to pass unhindered.

The walls are decorated, the Empire's history inlaid in silver, layer upon layer of images and words, grand, glorious, a foundation for unshakable pride.

Many of the images feature The Seven, working miracles, dispensing justice. There is a permanence to them, a sense that no matter what else transpires, be it demonic or human or otherwise, that afterwards, The Seven will remain.

Gamma's fall is nowhere to be found on the walls however, neither is Delta's betrayal.

They are nearly across the hall when Beta enters behind them. Without anger, he calls his sister's name. Nuances are loaded into the word. Joy in seeing her, sadness in the way things are, hope of reconciliation.

It is the kindness that knifes into Delta. She stops walking, her own essence a conflicting bubble of emotion.

Beta continues his approach, sword held down at his side, relaxed, its eye watching the Vagrant. Again he calls Delta's name and this time, she turns, her eyes drawn to the dark voids of his own.

'Beta,' she says.

The immortal smiles at the sound of his name, and the love she infuses it with, his pace more enthusiastic now, the gap between them closing.

Mazar drops her rifle, falling to her knees.

Reela and the Vagrant stare, uncertain.

Beta, still smiling, comes close, Delta able to do nothing but bask in his approval.

Gently, without taking his eyes from his sister, Beta reaches out, touching Reela's hand. His essence brushes the girl's, making the tainted marks on the back of her hand flare red, then white, burning. Her body locks, rigid, a scream trapped behind the bars of her teeth.

Surging forward, the Vagrant raises Delta's sword, trying to cut through the hold. But Beta's sword comes up of its own accord, guiding away the Vagrant's strike, a light touch to divert his momentum.

Delta's sword slides against Beta's until the two hilts catch together.

Without turning his head, smile still radiant, Beta flicks his wrist, launching the Vagrant across the room. He slides across the floor, turning slowly on his back, Delta's sword skidding away.

Beta and Delta commune, their essences coming together, sharing thoughts and emotions. Not the smashing of rage that she experienced with Alpha, but gentle brushing, arguments passed back and forth without judgement.

Reela continues to burn, a slow moving fire that follows the lines of her taint, creeping from hand, to wrist, to elbow, leaving a nerveless limb behind.

Her hand slips free and Delta blinks, breaking contact with her brother.

Reela falls, and storm-cloud eyes follow her down.

Delta blinks again and her expression darkens.

Beta's smile wavers. He raises a hand, palm out, a mute appeal. Surely she understands that he was only doing what is right? Surely she would not be angry with him for doing the creator's will?

Delta's essence flares and Beta takes a step backwards.

Meanwhile, the Vagrant rolls over his new bruises, collecting Delta's sword from the floor.

He sucks in a breath, pressing down with his free hand, and stands up.

One Thousand and Nine
Years Ago

When Massassi dies, something of reality dies with her. The pressure that has borne down for so long, from another reality, pushes harder. Old wounds on the sun's surface reopen, the cracks widening, tearing and splitting it apart.

But Massassi's death is not total, for much of her essence remains, housed in the hearts of her seven creations, in their swords and, in lesser quantities, in the weapons of the knights and the soldiers, in the essence-powered machines of her Empire, and in the thousands of little coins she has made.

A single human, scattered piecemeal, then wrapped in silver and platinum.

And, like a solar mirror, the sun's death is not total either. It is broken, diminished, the whole returned to the value of its parts, but not gone.

For days, fire fills the sky, a series of distant explosions that spell death for millions of those that watch, helpless, earthbound. The nights become strange, flickering things, with pale strobing flashes hinting at the astral violence viewed on the other side of the world. True darkness is swiftly forgotten.

While people run and hide and mostly die, The Seven watch, unmoving, grief-shocked.

Days and nights pass. The death toll, crop failures, mass blindness and scrabble for resources seeming discreet beneath the apocalyptic reverberations above.

Meanwhile, The Seven watch.

There is general agreement that the world is going to end but, despite a number of convincing arguments and passionate doomsayers, the sun does not fall from the heavens.

When the skies finally clear two suns are revealed where one was before. Lesser, weaker; one red, the other gold, orbiting each other in small lazy circles.

Though diminished from their former state, the suns endure, allowing life of a sort, and the Empire, to continue.

The Seven gather at the place where Massassi died. Peace-Fifteen is waiting for them. She asks a simple question. 'What do we do?'

For a while, The Seven do not answer. Massassi has created them to withstand the ravages of time, to be leaders, champions, symbols of power and permanence. She has tried to prepare them for every problem she could think of through a combination of intelligent design, of balancing one against the other, and teaching them, sharing her knowledge and skill.

The one thing that she did not consider, did not prepare them for, was her death. The Seven's love for their creator is paramount, a glowing wondrous thing that unites them and gives them strength.

Gone.

The Seven

In its place is grief. Massassi, their maker, their teacher, their beloved, is dead. Something of themselves is dead too, gone forever, and they know that things will never be the same.

This is problematic. They have been taught that their role is to guide humanity, to preserve the glory of the Empire and to prepare them for the coming threat. But such a task is impossible, pointless.

For their creator is gone, her perfection cruelly taken from them, the Empire of the Winged Eye has been reduced to a shadow of what it was. They cannot bring Massassi back any more than they can restore the sun.

Peace-Fifteen knows better than to rush The Seven, so she waits, the question hanging between them.

What should they do? What can they do? The Seven are not of one mind.

Alpha cannot bear how far the world has fallen, to even look upon it brings him pain. He cannot understand how his creator could abandon them to this existence, or why she did not warn him.

Beta tries to consider the long-term problems but each solution turns quickly to another issue in his mind, and another, and yet another, a succession of disappointments leading to failure and death.

Gamma's grief is tinged with anger, at Massassi, at her brothers and sisters. They all disappoint. She feels helpless, bitter. Though she does not love her creator as the others do, her tears fall just as freely.

No thoughts run through Delta's mind in the first years. She is carried in stronger currents of emotion than any of her siblings. They do not know what to do with her, torn between admiration of the depth of her love, envy of it and, in Gamma's case, frustration.

Epsilon, Theta and Eta weep too. The thing they have waited for has come to pass and yet life continues. They are broken by it, saddened by it and also dissatisfied. *Perhaps,* the three think to themselves, *this is only the beginning.* And yet it feels so much like the end, they cannot fully believe it.

But something has to be done. The wishes of the creator must be respected and her body must be honoured.

The Seven set to work on the construction of a suitable tomb. A giant cube of metal, balanced on one corner and raised seventy feet into the air. Inside, the walls are covered in tapestries, detailing the life and works of Massassi. Every achievement made glorious through the filter of The Seven's loving eyes, shining bright, eclipsing any ugliness.

It is the only thing The Seven create themselves.

So pleased are they with their work, that they decide to make a home there, a sanctum where they can be alone with their grief.

Massassi's remains are stored within the cube, and an order is created to maintain it. Acolytes that live and die within the walls, unsullied by the outside world.

Hidden away in their chamber, The Seven find a measure of sanctuary. They share memories of a better time, singing of their creator and their love for her, unpicking every detail of the years blessed by her living presence.

Usually these reminiscences result in tears of liquid stone that harden in the air, forming a shell of sorts over silver bodies. A set of living tombs within a tomb.

Only the brave or the foolish interrupt them.

Peace-Fifteen is not sure which she is when she presents herself. She knows that her very presence disturbs them and yet she comes anyway. The Empire of the Winged Eye is falling apart and something must be done. The Seven must take action.

In gentle, humble language, Peace-Fifteen makes this clear. Her life has been spent dealing with an extremely difficult and dangerous old woman, and it surprises her how transferable her skills are to the immortals.

And so they take action.

Peace-Fifteen is elevated by them, turned into a bridge between the grieving Seven and humanity. Hair is stripped from her, removed at cellular level. Nails too, are taken, leaving her smooth skinned, unblemished just as Massassi was. She is cloaked in feathers and renamed Obeisance.

The role is an odd one, nursemaid, messenger and icon rolled into one. Obeisance takes to it quickly, and soon, Seraph Knights set out, bringing order to the world once more.

And slowly, the Empire recovers. Its people are not what they were. The old pride has gone from the outer colonies, replaced with deep fear and superstition. The vast armies have been reduced to a fraction of their former size, and many of the satellites that orbit the world are now empty shells. Even the watch on the Breach itself is reduced, an outpost standing where legions were before.

A status quo of decay establishes itself, the Empire's decline incredibly slow, barely noticeable from one generation to the next, but there, worsening by fractions of degrees.

Obeisance is not allowed to die, the role taken over by one of the daughters of Peace-Fifteen, and then one of her granddaughters, and onwards. Each is trained by her predecessor, shaped to appear and act the same, a thread of continuity for The Seven to cling to.

While Alpha, Beta and Delta bury themselves in nostalgia, and Epsilon, Theta and Eta content themselves to wait, Gamma fumes, restless. Of all of them, she loves Massassi the least, is the most removed from her siblings.

And so, when Obeisance comes, it is often she who answers.

And when, a thousand years later, the Breach finally opens, it is she that rides out to meet the demons, alone.

And it is she alone that pays the price.

CHAPTER TWENTY-TWO

The Vagrant sees his chance. Delta is advancing on Beta, furious, her hands pointing at Reela then spreading to encompass everything before stabbing towards Beta again.

The other immortal backs away, his replies uncertain. Clearly Beta is touched by her argument, his nature making him listen and consider before refuting.

Mazar remains on her knees, doing her best to stay small.

Briefly, the Vagrant looks at the girl lying on the floor, cradling the arm that Beta touched. Her face is screwed tight with pain and his own creases in sympathy before turning back to Beta.

The immortal is on the defensive, distracted by Delta.

Circling round, trying to keep out of Beta's eye-line and the eye-line of his living sword, the Vagrant advances. He moves closer, getting within a few paces of his weapon's reach.

Carefully, he goes, carefully, then a sudden rush of movement, a step, two, pulling back Delta's sword, singing out, swinging hard for Beta's unguarded back.

Beta's sword notices too late, its eye swivelling in shock, transmitting the warning to Beta via their essence link. There is the beginning of the motion that would become a parry, if there were just a few more precious seconds.

But Delta's sword does not ring with the Vagrant's song, the blade stiff in his hands. It holds itself rigid, so that the sound smacks dully along it, sapping the energy. Silver wings strain against his swing, forcing the Vagrant to drag it down.

When the blow lands, it is without force, a tap on the back, impolite.

The Vagrant has time to look surprised, then angry, at Delta's sword before Beta has turned, his own blade rising with indignation.

Delta tries to intervene, reaching out to her brother, her hand cupping his face, guiding it back. Whatever she is about to say is cut off however, the palace shaking from multiple impacts.

There is a pause, long enough to register the vibrations in the floor and wonder what causes them, and then there is a groan from outside. A not-quite-human sound that comes from the walls and the agents that bond buildings together, stretched, tortured.

Slowly at first, the Vagrant begins to slide away from Beta. He frowns, looking down at innocent feet. As his momentum increases, the Vagrant leans forward, arms waving for balance.

Something is pulling at the sky palace, rotating it. The floor tilts dramatically, becoming a hill, steep. Beta and Delta automatically step up, their wings holding them stationary as everything revolves around them.

The Vagrant is not so lucky.

He flails, falls onto his front. There is nothing to grab onto but the toes of his boots squeak on the polished floor, finding purchase.

Mazar spreads herself flat, an armoured starfish sliding slowly away.

Reela rolls past him. He misses her but she manages to get hold of his ankle, causing them both to slip a few more feet.

Briefly, the floor tilts back again, not quite level but enough for the Vagrant to stand. He helps Reela up. Sweat runs cold on her face, one arm pressed close to her side, a few wisps still smoking up from the back of her hand.

Delta and Beta turn together, towards the wall, both appearing to see something shocking.

The Vagrant looks the same way, squinting, Reela copying.

They see nothing strange about the wall, it is as it has always been, a smooth canvas decorated in silver. Miniature figures remain as they were, innocent, frozen in their telling of ancient history.

Beta and Delta continue to stare, and so the Vagrant and Reela continue as well. He is about to turn away when there is a boom, loud and close, and the head of a bone lance erupts into the hallway. A sharp cone, like a giant arrowhead, five feet across. As they watch, four lines become visible along its length, allowing the cone to split apart, anchoring itself to the wall. A dark tunnel is revealed in its centre that appears the bastard child of a chute and a throat, lined in muscle and grey flesh.

Reela grips the Vagrant's hand a little harder.

The tunnel convulses, the end they can see braced firmly as the rest of it bucks. A gurgling, retching noise bubbles from the depths and then it spits out a body onto the floor.

It is one of the stilted warriors from Slake. As she hauls herself upright, another of their number is disgorged, then another, the hallway rapidly filling with slime-covered fighters, armed and ready.

Around Beta, the air begins to hum. He points his sword at the tunnel and, with a single beat of his wings, surges towards it.

Blue light crackles into being, forming a nimbus that covers Beta from the tip of his sword to the top of his shoulders, as wide as his wings at the base.

Partway through the charge, Delta's hand flashes out, hard fingers locking about a silver ankle. She pivots in the air, taking the power of Beta's movement, transferring it side-ways, so that he completes a rapid orbit of her, a sparking, singing satellite.

Delta lets go, launching her brother down the hallway. It is a brief flight, followed by an impressive crash. Instantly, Delta gives chase, leaving the Vagrant, Mazar, Reela and the warriors alone.

They share a look before heading off in the opposite direction.

Vesper pauses by a window, looking out on the battle taking place across the sky palace. Wonderland has come alongside now, multicoloured tower-tops peeking over the battlements of Alpha's palace. Though the living city is lower down, it is not out of reach. Many of the city's vertebrae-legs have curled upwards, snakelike, to reach up, puncturing the sides of the palace. As more and more attach themselves, they begin to flex together, pulling the palace down to Wonderland's level.

The great engines of the sky palace pull back, making everything shake, alarming, managing to lock it in the air at a strange angle.

Turning from the window, Vesper rushes on, stepping out into the open. With the palace off-balance, people roll like bits of litter, scattering downwards. A lucky few dangle from pillars or posts, or dive into nearby doorways.

Vesper dares the sloping streets, the sword held out to one side, wings catching the currents, holding her steady. Part gliding, part bounding, she races along, fixed on her destination.

Though she is fast, she cannot match Theta of The Seven for speed. The immortal swoops down from some higher place to fly alongside, keeping pace easily. Theta points her sword at Vesper, singing a note of outrage, simple, that launches light, blazing and blue, straight at her.

Vesper brings the sword round with a counter-note, splitting the fire, moving through the gap. However, the sword cannot parry and guide at the same time and Vesper's stride loses momentum.

Theta attacks again, forcing another parry, forcing Vesper to abandon herself to the mercy of gravity. She slides down the palace on her back, sword held up, diverting the angry song before it can touch her, while Theta follows, keeping on the pressure, waiting for the opening that will surely come.

Vesper slides further down, batting away another strike, barely, the power of Theta taxing her voice and muscles to their limits.

At first, neither notice one of the giant bone-legs of Wonderland rising to meet them. Tendrils twitch along the upper half, translucent worms tasting the air, and the cone-shaped head flickers in Vesper's direction, then splits open like a four-fingered hand, to snatch her mid-fall, pulling her away and into the air.

A second leg lashes out for Theta, a giant spider swatting at a silver fly. The immortal tucks in her wings, corkscrewing to safety. Meanwhile Vesper dangles from the first limb, like a prize in a fair.

Above her, the sky stretches in unbroken glory, the suns glaring down at her like a pair of mismatched, angry eyes. Below, she sees her feet dangling, and past them, the angled floor of the palace, and the judder of battlements, half a jaw of wide-spaced teeth, blunt, square. Through them, she catches a view of Wonderland and the ground, far, far beneath.

The sword stares at the limb, seeing the essence of the First, whole again, radiating an alien majesty. Vesper ignores its misgivings, too busy trying to catch her breath to worry about the future.

Abruptly, the view is snatched away as she is swung back towards the palace, deposited carefully on the side of a building that juts out like a ramp from the tilting streets.

'Thank you,' she says.

There is a sense of being regarded, and then the bone-limb retreats, joining the other one as it tries to smash Theta out of the sky.

Vesper doesn't wait to see the result. She lowers herself off the side of the building, climbing through an open doorway.

From there, the sword leads her on, finding ways deeper into the palace, where the grinding of machinery can be heard, and the heart of the floating fortress beats.

Down stairwells and along passageways she goes, all spotless, generously sized. Few venture this deep inside the palace, a series of doors standing between would-be explorers and the inner chambers. Each one is four inches thick, heavy slabs without handle or keyhole, and there are many of them.

As Vesper approaches, the sword acts as a key and they spiral open, vanishing into the walls without trace.

The last door swishes away to reveal a large chamber, spherical, nearly half a mile across. Most of it is filled by another globe, the light drive that works hard to keep gravity at bay. Walkways line the edges, allowing access to different parts of the great engine.

A handful of robed engineers scurry from place to place, their worried faces caught in the glow, ghostlike, scowling. The fact that the palace is leaning does not matter here, clever gyroscopes keeping the chamber level regardless. But despite this, and their best efforts, the engines are struggling.

Vesper's arrival soon gets their attention. Though their duties keep them isolated, the engineers know who Vesper is. They know the sword as well, and they have no idea what to do about either of them.

Like sheep, they scatter as she approaches, stopping at a safe distance to watch, nervous.

She works her way up until she is running across the top of the engine on a path that ends, abrupt, like a diving board above a soft-glowing star.

Once there, she and the sword start to sing. Not the battle

373

song of the Seraph that hardens sound into a weapon, but the gentle hum of a parent helping their child to sleep at night.

It is a simple four-note refrain that rises and falls, repeating, calming.

In response the engines cease their groaning, their radiance reducing, their efforts easing. Vesper continues her work, lulling the light drives to sleep.

Alpha's sky palace stops fighting the pull of Wonderland. As a result, it floats level once more, and begins a stately descent into the embrace of the living city.

Meanwhile, the armies of Crucible swarm forward, collected by the strange bone-limbs of Wonderland. Each one is part of a necrotic transport system, sucking up individuals into the inner workings of the city, transferring them from pipe to pipe, until they reach one of the bone-limbs already anchored to the palace above and are regurgitated. Many are inserted this way, bolstering the numbers that originally came by sky-ship and turning the tide of battle. Those less fond of travel by necro-pipe, and those augmented for climbing, make their way to the base of the palace, firing ropes or webbing, or in some cases, simply jumping the distance with superhuman prowess.

These brave invaders scale the outer walls, hoping to find a way in before the defenders notice them.

The Vagrant emerges onto one of the battlements, Mazar and Reela close behind. The fighters from Slake overtake them with ease, their curved stilts propelling them forward in bouncing strides. Each one carries a length of cable, coiled, that they unspool over the side, a lifeline for others to climb.

While they work, amber eyes take in the situation.

Fierce fighting goes on all over the palace, the Empire struggling to hold back the forces of Crucible. As more and more people pour into the palace, the odds move ever in Crucible's favour.

But there is another story unfolding above, as four of The Seven battle their way towards Wonderland's heart. The bone-limbs fight together, orchestrated by the First's will, an unrelenting assault of stabbing and slashing, with each lining up ready to take over as soon as the one before is done.

Theta, Eta and Epsilon match this display of coordination, flying together, each covering the other, alternately flying over and under limbs, lashing out with their swords and song. It is like watching a group hack its way through an angry forest. The going is slow but there will be only one result.

Alpha is more direct. A single swing of his sword takes the head from one of the limbs. Blue flames burn around the wound, tinting green as the infernal essence catches at the stump. Briefly, the limb flails, miserable, before the flames snuff out, something cutting off the flow of essence from the rest of Wonderland. This saves the First from further pain but leaves the limb to flop, dead and useless.

The other nearby limbs hesitate, standing upright, paralysed snakes that allow Alpha to proceed unhindered.

If Alpha can reach inside the shell of the city, he will be able kill the First, and without Wonderland, the forces of Crucible are lost.

The Vagrant frowns. He taps Mazar's rifle and then points at Alpha.

'No way,' she replies. 'You can't ask me to do that. Delta wouldn't want me to.'

There is a hint of questioning in her voice but there is no time for the Vagrant to argue. Alpha is diving lower. Soon he will be lost amid the sparkling towers.

The Vagrant looks at Delta's sword, nods towards Alpha. An eye meets his gaze, frightened but steady, and he takes one of the silver wings in his free hand.

Mazar begins shaking her head. 'Don't do it,' she urges.

The Vagrant releases the wing, kissing the tips of his fingers and touching them to Reela's forehead.

She wraps her uninjured arm around his leg, holding tight.

Gently, he unpeels it, pushing her away. Clearly, the girl intends to contest the issue but Mazar drags her back. 'Don't do it,' she says again.

The Vagrant leans out over the battlements and points Delta's sword at Alpha's back. Both man and sword seem to sag momentarily before straightening. His mouth opens and sharp song comes out, is caught by the blade and focused, making a line of blue fire, streaking.

Down it goes, an ethereal comet, straight, unerring, until it strikes Alpha square in the back. At this distance the song has lost much of its power, more a slap in the face or a flick of an ear than a real attack.

Somehow, this is worse.

A quick flicker of a wing whirls Alpha round, sky-blue eyes finding the Vagrant instantly. Another beat and he is flying up at them, at speed.

The Vagrant waves Mazar and Reela back, urging them away with a frantic wave of the hand. They go, though Reela resists, her feet kicking in all directions, heels drumming against Mazar's armour.

Satisfied, the Vagrant readies himself for Alpha's charge.

As he draws nearer, Alpha levels his blade with the Vagrant's chest, before giving his response to the challenge.

The Vagrant's face falls.

The eye in Delta's sword widens in fear.

And everything between them explodes.

Alpha's rebuke reverberates, passing through every corner of the sky palace, every part of Wonderland, even reaching Crucible, startling men and goats alike.

In the streets of the palace, on its battlements, and in various corridors, infernals, humans and half-breeds pause, taking a moment to appreciate that they are not the target of the immortal's rage.

Delta and Beta cease their argument, curiosity drawing them outside.

And in the bowels of the palace, an eye glances up, Vesper's following. A curse escapes her lips and she starts running, despite the knowledge that she is already too late.

The Vagrant blinks against the dust, rising from his crouch. There is space in front of him where moments before there were battlements. A circular gouge that encompasses a section of floor, allowing new views of the levels below and an uninterrupted view of Alpha's charge.

Alpha is only twenty feet away and closing fast, his sword remains focused on the Vagrant, a second blast of song coming hot on the heels of the first.

The Vagrant tries to parry but it is like blocking a hurricane. Though no flame touches his skin, the force pushes him back, until heels hang over the courtyard.

Before the Vagrant can recover, Alpha attacks a third time, thrusting forward, adding the power of his arms to that of his wings.

Delta's sword bravely puts itself between them, wings trembling, eye half closed.

If the Vagrant does try to augment the parry with song, it is overwhelmed, lost in the roar of fire and rage.

The point of Alpha's sword strikes the flat of Delta's pushing it into the Vagrant's chest, punching him into the sky.

Like a leaf, he tumbles, head over heels towards the waiting courtyard. He sticks out his arms, instinctive, useless, falling just as fast as before.

Delta's sword is slightly more effective, the silvered wings that make the crosspiece stretching wide, using currents of essence to slow their descent.

Even so, the landing is an ugly, lopsided, rolling thing. The Vagrant comes to a stop, his armour scuffed in every place, his face down, his eyes closed.

Above, Alpha circles, building up to something. Blue fire trails from his sword, growing steadily brighter.

There are other combatants in the courtyard, but both Crucible and Empire forces clear the area, united in their desire to avoid what's coming.

Only one person is going the opposite way. A small figure, cradling one arm, who has finally escaped her captor's grip; she rushes over to the Vagrant, kneeling at his side as Alpha completes his second circle.

Her arrival catches the attention of Delta who has been watching for some time. Sympathy crosses her face and she takes a step forward before Beta's hand finds her shoulder, stopping her.

A small silver wing and a small hand nudge the Vagrant, eliciting some kind of noise. It is not a word, not even a grunt but its meaning is clear: no.

Neither girl nor sword respects it, nudging harder.

The Vagrant looks up, irritation spurring him to consciousness, but fading as the situation presents itself.

Alpha makes a third circle, faster, as the Vagrant struggles to his feet.

The trail of fire grows longer, almost making a hoop as Alpha pulls up with a powerful wingbeat.

The Vagrant raises Delta's sword, stepping in front of Reela.

For a moment Alpha seems to hang in the air, and then he is turning, diving, his wings folding close to his back, his sword so bright that the air shimmers in fear.

Like a meteor heralding the end, he comes down.

As Alpha's song grows in strength, Vesper pushes herself to run faster. The sword urges her on, humming with worry. They make a strange sight as they storm along, and people on both sides of the conflict hurl themselves aside rather than get in their way.

She bursts out into the open in time to see Alpha's dive. The Vagrant is just a shadow underneath it, a stick man with a stick sword with an even smaller shadow behind.

Without pausing, Vesper leaps into the air, spinning, singing out. As she completes her turn the sword points at a space where Alpha will shortly arrive, blasting it with song.

Unwittingly, Alpha races to intercept it, his attention so fixed on the Vagrant that he doesn't see it coming.

She is not strong enough to knock him from the sky or

to take away the force of his attack, but she is strong enough to divert it, sending Alpha off at a tangent, to crash into a nearby building.

The immortal dives straight through the roof, straight through several floors, and a shockwave blasts out, shredding the walls and rippling the floor. What is left collapses, the roof folding in on itself, no longer supported.

Vesper skids to a stop at the Vagrant's side.

He nods to her, one eyebrow cocked.

'Are you ready for this?'

He nods again and she knows he is lying. She finds herself smiling anyway. 'Me too.' Her gaze moves to Reela. 'You need to go hide, now.'

The girl shakes her head.

'Reela!'

She shakes her head a second time, stepping behind the Vagrant.

Vesper sees the fear in her girl's face: of the battle, the violence, of her own mother. She tries to soften her expression and reach out to her daughter when the rubble that was once a building blasts into the air, and Alpha climbs out.

'It didn't have to be this way,' she murmurs, making the Vagrant turn his head, puzzled. 'We take him together, okay?'

The Vagrant nods.

Alpha is upright now, bits of debris falling from his shoulders as he strides towards them. The collision has not marked him, and exertions have taken no toll on his strength.

The closer he gets the more the difference in height is pronounced.

'You've lost,' says Vesper. 'Look around You. The army

You sent has surrendered, Your palace has been anchored and is being overwhelmed as we speak. But there's still a chance to save lives. Order the Empire to stop fighting and I can stop this right now.'

But there is no relief to be found in Alpha's eyes. It is like asking the mountains for mercy. He continues to advance.

Vesper's expression hardens. 'The Empire needed You for years. They prayed for You to come, and You ignored them. I know why.' She glances over to where Delta stands, Beta's hand still restraining her shoulder. 'You were scared.'

Alpha's sword begins a low, growling hum.

'You were scared of the Breach, so while generations suffered and Your own sister sacrificed herself, You hid in Your room. Then You were scared of the Yearning, and while good people—' her voice chokes for a moment '—sacrificed themselves, You hid in Your room. Only now, when the biggest threats have passed do You decide to come out. And what do You do? You kill the very people you're supposed to be protecting. And why?'

Alpha is nearly within sword reach now, and his blade is already rising to strike, the hum becoming a roar.

Vesper carries on, shouting above it. 'Because You are scared again! You're scared of what You let happen to the world, and rather than take responsibility for it, You—'

Alpha's sword comes down.

Two swords meet it and the collision is thunderous, driving Vesper and the Vagrant backwards. The two exchange a look and the briefest of nods before assuming positions of readiness.

'And rather than take responsibility for it,' Vesper continues, 'You'd just destroy everything. Because purging is easier than understanding. Because if You get rid of us . . .' She tails off, meeting another of Alpha's attacks, the Vagrant lending his strength to hers.

Again, one blade strikes two, again, they hold fast.

'If You get rid of us, You don't have to take responsibility for us, or for Yourself, or for all the ways You failed. I'm asking you again: Surrender.'

Alpha's answer is immediate, furious, his sword raining down in a series of strikes, each falling like a hammer, heavy and fast, forcing his enemies back.

The Vagrant fights well, but he is just a man, and his link with Delta's sword still fragile. Vesper fights well, moving as Gamma would, a match in skill and anger. But she too is mortal, with muscles that tire and a body that is already broken.

Moreover, to match Alpha's song, they push themselves. Throats quickly burn, straining, their own efforts ravaging them from within just as Alpha's whittles from without.

For a time, Vesper does not have the space to sing and speak, using everything she has just to survive. They are holding Alpha, but they will not be able to do so forever. Something has to change, and quickly, if they are to win.

Every time she thinks she sees an opening, Alpha has already closed it. He and his sword read her intentions even as she conceives them.

The sword gives her the same advantage, meaning neither side can surprise the other. Gloomily, she realizes that Alpha does not need to do anything but wait.

For all her talk, the taking of the palace will mean nothing if The Seven still stand. And if she falls, the alliance with the infernals falls too, and Crucible will fail.

The Seven

There has to be something I can do!

But Alpha's attacks send any possible plans fleeing from her mind, forcing her back, and back again, each time a little more weary than before.

The Vagrant is getting slower too, his parries only just joining hers in time.

She knows that somewhere behind her is her daughter, can only hope that the girl has found a safe place to hide. At the thought of Reela, there is an accompanying surge of guilt. *It shouldn't have been this way for her. This is my fault.*

Something pricks her finger and she looks over to see that the sword has stabbed her with a wingtip. It is telling her to focus. More than that, it is telling her to attack.

As Alpha's blade comes down, she steps aside instead of meeting it, letting the Vagrant face it alone. She hears the ring of sword on sword but, without her aid, he is overwhelmed, blasted backwards, tumbling out of her periphery.

She has got an opening but has abandoned her father to get it. *Another sacrifice*, she thinks. *Another betrayal.*

The sword does not give her the luxury of remorse, driving her forward.

Somehow, the idea that she would dare to attack surprises Alpha. He is already wrong-footed, preparing to strike again in the place where Vesper was.

He manages a clumsy parry, her sword sparking off his blade and then a second time against his shoulder. Before he can recover, she presses her advantage. Alternating high and low, striking quickly, feinting. An anger fuels her, giving her much-needed strength. Vesper is not sure how much of it is hers and how much the sword's but she doesn't care, happy to use it regardless.

383

Stumbling away, Alpha does all he can to keep the sword from biting him. His own weapon races to put itself between him and danger. On his back wings flick out, stabilizing, then sweep in turn, trying to buffet Vesper, break her flow.

And she is buffeted, but she does not fight it, allowing the sideways momentum to add to her slice, breaking Alpha's guard and drawing a dark line across his silver chest.

On the one hand, the injury is minor, more cosmetic than anything else. On the other, it is historic, massive, a spoiling of perfection. Alpha is no longer quite as the creator made him.

An eye blinks in surprise, staring at the mark it has made, and a feeling of wrongness locks Vesper into place.

Alpha swings out, bellowing with a wild rage even the sword is not ready for, blowing out the candle of Vesper's resistance.

The flat of his blade catches her in the ribs, making several crack, and she somersaults backward, a limp-limbed gymnast that fails to plant her landing.

CHAPTER TWENTY-THREE

Samael has come deep within the heart of Wonderland. He is drawn here. Since his last visit, the empty necrotic pipes have become active, pulsing with life, filling the veins of the city with the First's essence.

This was to be the Uncivil's dream. A shell capable of sustaining her growth, and allowing her to travel the world as she wished. Power and freedom, a complete package. Though the Uncivil has been destroyed, her dream lives on, in Samael and Neer and the bones of the city, the three of them coming together to restore it, making a shell fit for the greatest infernals.

Now there is no doubt that Wonderland lives again. The sense of the First, rejoined, whole, is intoxicating. With his half-breed eyes, Samael can read the flow of essence in the city. A swirl in one pipe tells him that Crucible's armies continue to be transported onto the palace, a bunching of cloud in another indicating pain and fear.

He moves quickly down dark corridors, finding Neer hard at work. 'Managed to pierce the shell,' she says without turning from the scorched wall. 'I cut off the flow of essence before their blasted fire could get here but we've lost another limb.'

'Can you repair it?'

'Of course I can,' she replies. 'Give me a few months and the raw materials and I'll have Wonderland good as new.'

'I see.'

'Those winged bastards are breaking through. You have to stop them.'

'I can't stand against The Seven.'

'Problem is, Wonderland can't either. Against one of Them maybe, but three?' She shakes her head. 'It's hopeless. But if you weighed in, distracted a couple of Them, maybe then we'd have a chance.'

He nods, not needing her to guide him to where Epsilon, Theta and Eta are. He can feel their song even from here. 'What defenders do we have?'

Neer tuts. 'We have apprentice Necroneers and stock, none of them are much use in a fight.'

'Give them to me.'

'Fine, but don't get them all killed!'

Samael ignores the comment and reaches up to pluck a fly from his shoulder plate. It does not resist, allowing itself to be placed on the white skin of his wrist, in the space between gauntlet and bracer.

He does not feel it bite but senses the sliver of essence being absorbed, along with his call for help. Samael sends the fly away, unsure if the Man-shape will come to their aid, unable to wait for the answer.

'Goodbye,' he says to Neer, and perhaps it is his imagination, but her answering grunt seems softer than usual.

The Vagrant gets up, retrieving Delta's sword as he does so. One hand is pressed flat on his chest, and a wheeze now accompanies each exhalation.

In front of him, Vesper is prone on the ground, the motionless, charred body bearing an uncomfortable resemblance to a corpse.

Behind him, Reela whimpers.

Compared to the multiple scrapes and scuffs on the Vagrant's armour, the single mark on Alpha's chest seems trivial. And yet, there is nothing trivial in Alpha's reaction. His voice turns the air into a sphere of liquid fire around him, and where he steps, prints are left behind in part-melted stone.

He is stepping towards Vesper and one does not need to read his essence to be able to guess his intent.

The Vagrant looks over to where Delta and Beta stand, hoping for support. Beta's dark eyes are unreadable and Delta does not meet his gaze.

Alone, the Vagrant moves to intercept Alpha. His limping shuffle isn't enough to put him in the immortal's path, so he swings out, the end of his sword clipping one of Alpha's wings.

There is a neat sound, a 'shing', and two feathers spin their way to the ground.

Alpha stops.

The Vagrant swallows, raises Delta's sword.

Alpha's head turns towards the Vagrant and the hatred that had been raining down on Vesper focuses on him like a force, physical.

The attack comes immediately after, a blurry set of strikes.

Each time the Vagrant parries, there are flames rather than sparks, that fly in all directions.

Mist begins to rise from his armour, and the gauntlet that holds Delta's sword shimmers, the skin of the metal becoming tacky.

The Vagrant's song is barely audible and grows rapidly weaker, the notes sounding tortured, the aura around Delta's sword flickering, fading away.

Somehow, he continues to hold his weapon up. Each of Alpha's strikes knocks his sword arm wide but it is always back in position before the next lands.

He is dying, but in a slow, dogged fashion.

And Delta's sword supports him, forcing his arm to move when his muscles give out, watching for him when tired eyes blink against the sweat and heat, taking his sad little notes and making the best of them.

Alpha's sword comes down, it comes down, the sheer force of it breaking the Vagrant from the inside, shuddering bones, wrenching the heart.

Smoke comes from his throat now, and the metal on his gauntlet and right forearm begins to melt. He stands, but Alpha's sword continues to come down.

Delta's sword fights almost alone now, puppeting the man as best it can. But it is not without limits. Another strike, the next in an endless blur, comes down, meeting little resistance, striking hard.

A crack appears along the blade, turning the note into a screech.

Neither Alpha nor the Vagrant notice, but when the next attack comes, Delta's sword spins from the Vagrant's broken hand, and he falls.

Delta's sword clatters next to him, its eye staring upwards, bulging, shocked.

The Vagrant does not get up. His arm twitches, useless, at his side. One knee rises only to flop down again. His head remains at an angle, smoke curling from his open mouth, a faulty exhaust.

Alpha turns from him, knowing, wanting him to see what will happen next as he walks over to Vesper.

But amber eyes strain elsewhere, seeking out Delta, who remains removed, an observer.

His tongue moves over dry lips and air passes through a red-raw throat to whisper a word, given shape by a cracked, bloody mouth.

'Please . . .'

In Wonderland, they throw themselves in the path of Epsilon, Theta and Eta. None of them can hope to win the fight and so they do all they can to slow them down, making barricades and obstacles, and when they fail, their bodies are used to block the way.

Half-breeds and broken-bladed knights fight shoulder to shoulder, soldiers from a dozen locations united under Crucible's banner.

It feels strange to Samael to be hanging back. If it were up to him alone, he would be joining the defenders' lines, most likely at the front.

Perhaps they will consider him a coward. The thought troubles him, for the truth is that duty makes him wait. Vesper's orders were clear: if she does not survive, he needs to endure, so that the alliance between human and infernal endures. He can see the wisdom in this. He is a living bridge between the two, and he has the Man-shape's trust and the First's gratitude, as well as a position of sorts within the Empire.

It still rankles to not commit.

He cannot help but notice that while some of Crucible's forces have diverted here to aid Wonderland, the Man-shape has not come. It has sent some of its minions, even a few lesser infernals but none of the great ones are here, aside from the First itself.

Fear has kept them away. Few things can threaten the Man-shape or the Backwards Child now, but The Seven are among them. Perhaps, if they had come, allied with him and the First, they would have been able to mount a credible defence.

But they have not and when the three immortals break into Wonderland's heart, they will destroy the First from the inside.

For this reason, the people that still live in the city have joined the fight, a mix of children and young adults, raised by Neer. None of them have a chance against The Seven but they go anyway, because it is better than doing nothing.

Samael respects that. Soon he will be doing the same.

'Please!' says Reela, her face, tear-streaked, turned to Delta's. 'Please! Please! Please!'

The immortal regards the girl, well aware that her brother, Alpha, is moving over to Vesper, intent on revenge.

Beta's hand has been on her shoulder for some time now, a calming restraint.

She shrugs it off, feeling his dismay as she does so. The hand does not come back however, nor does he stop her as she leaps forward, gliding across the space between them. She passes Alpha, who ignores her, arrogant as ever, banking past Reela to retrieve her sword.

It feels different in her hand. *It has changed,* she thinks. *And I have changed too.*

She knows Alpha so well that she feels his movements as much as sees them. The ground whips underneath her as she comes back towards her brother, passing him on the other side as he lifts his sword.

Turning sharply, the momentum whirls her round, bringing them face to face. Alpha glares at her, dares her not to approach and she remembers their last meeting.

And she is afraid.

Her sword sends a wave of courage up her arm and into her heart. It is natural to be afraid because she is standing up. At last, she is standing up.

Alpha does not notice, turning his attention to Vesper and her death.

Her wings beat, driving her ever faster towards him.

When Alpha's sword arcs towards Vesper's chest, it finds Delta's in the way.

He pulls his strike wide, then points for her to stand aside. She shakes her head.

He orders it, and she shakes her head.

He threatens her, and she does not deign to respond.

Alpha raises his sword, the threat made physical, and a third time she shakes her head.

From the sidelines, Beta calls out, a voice of reason, ignored.

With a roar, Alpha's sword comes down, striking Delta's.

Song meets song and steel meets steel with explosive force.

Cracks recently made yawn wide, and Delta's sword breaks apart in a shower of slivers and essence, silvered.

Delta groans, falling to her knees, staring shocked at the ruined edge jutting, too short, from the hilt.

Then, she looks up.

And Beta looks up.

Even Alpha's rage is doused, his eyes going the same way as his siblings'.

Minutes pass in silence.

Then, in the sky, the red sun falters, its light fading as if suddenly covered with a veil. Details are easier to see on the muted orb, a new set of dark lines in one corner, spreading fast.

Another minute passes before the cracks meet each other. There is a second flicker, a deeper diminishing, and then the sky lights up and blood washes over the heavens. Under the strain, the red sun breaks, spitting out a chunk of itself to birth a third body, another smaller sun.

Samael stands ready with empty hands. A number of tools that the Necroneers use are easily translated into weapons, but he has left them on their hooks. It feels strange not to have a sword.

Some of the brightest of Neer's students are with him, guarding the door to the chamber that contains Wonderland's nexus, the one place where every necrotic pipe connects, where the greatest concentration of the First's essence is to be found.

It has been a long wait, the minutes stretched by nerves, listening to the sounds of battle getting steadily closer.

But for a while now, silence.

Samael waits it out, unwilling to be drawn into a trap. Their mission is to delay Epsilon, Theta and Eta of The Seven, not engage them. Besides, none of the young women and men here are in a hurry to die.

As the time stretches on, he cannot shake the idea that something is wrong.

'Stay here,' he rasps at the others and walks towards the last place he heard fighting. It is not far to go. In the dimly lit corridor, he sees bodies, some burned inside and out, others in pieces, a thick carpet, uneven.

But none of The Seven are to be seen.

Samael continues, following the carnage in reverse order. He is forced to climb in places where the fighting was heaviest. Many of the faces are known to him, if only in passing. Half-breed eyes find none among the living.

A bleak part of his mind considers that Neer will be pleased. There is a lot of raw material to work with, speeding her efforts to repair Wonderland.

Three figures come into view, walking slowly towards Wonderland's surface. Their wings are curled close at their backs, and all three heads tilt up.

There is nothing on the ceiling of note and it soon becomes apparent that they are looking through it, not at it. The Seven are hard for him to read, their essence too bright, too harsh on the eye to see details but he thinks they are worried.

Despite the many dead around them, none of the silver figures bear a single injury.

Eventually they reach a hole, blasted recently in the roof. One by one, they spread their wings and take to the air, leaving Samael to stare after, finally able to see the thing that has drawn them away.

For now, Wonderland is safe from The Seven but, when he looks up at the sky, he feels no relief.

Through Reela's tears everything looks blurry. Her mother is lying on the floor, too still. Her grandfather's eyes are closing. The sky is red and angry, and clouds unlike any she has seen are appearing on the horizon, thick and dark and fast, driven by unearthly winds.

Delta is on her knees in front of Alpha. Both look up, open mouthed, at the sky. Beta, nearby, does the same.

Meanwhile, three more winged figures come in to land. They too have been looking at the sky but now their eyes, and those in their swords move as one, to the sword in her mother's hand, to Delta cradling her shattered blade, and finally, to Alpha.

The immortal seems to jolt under their stare, jolting a second and third time as Delta and Beta turn their attention to him.

Alpha spreads his arms in something approaching a shrug, his look is beseeching and although she hates him, Reela briefly forgets, wanting to go to the immortal and give comfort.

Before she can, however, the others speak, their sentences blending one into the other, circling around the space where Alpha stands.

'First and greatest of us you were . . .'

'Were, but now fallen, the saddest of shadows . . .'

'Shadows have been made, a third where there were two . . .'

'Two of our sisters cautioned you . . .'

'You did not listen . . .'

Gradually, Delta rises to her feet. The others form a circle with her, their wings spreading, enclosing Alpha within.

'Our purpose was to protect and preserve . . .'

'Preserve that which the creator held dear . . .'

'Dear to us was Gamma and we abandoned her when we were needed . . .'

'Needed to do our duty . . .'

'Duty that we have forgotten . . .'

Under the weight of their judgement, of his guilt, Alpha sinks to his knees, the others leaning forward, making a dome.

'Blindly, we followed . . .'

'Followed you to ruin . . .'

'Ruin for our sisters . . .'

'Sister's sword . . .'

'Sword that is broken like the sun . . .'

Reela can feel their song building, just as the storm builds on the horizon, a roiling darkness that stretches from floor to sky. The sound makes her skin itch. She wants to run away but does not know where to go. Instead, she squats by the Vagrant, the game of copying him forgotten. 'Please wake,' she begs, 'please!'

The Vagrant does not move, and the voices of the immortals grow ever louder.

'You will lead us no longer . . .'

'No longer will we be muted . . .'

'Muted voices will rise together . . .'

'Together, we will take your voice . . .'

'Your voice is ended, for the good of all.'

Reela holds on to the Vagrant's arm, burying her face in his chest, pleading for him to wake as the winds howl and crimson clouds break over Wonderland and the sky palace, smothering everything, blotting out the sky.

CHAPTER TWENTY-FOUR

While winds rock buildings and scream through streets, and lightning flashes amid boiling cloudscapes, infernals and humans huddle in their homes.

Within Wonderland, Neer stands over her work-slab, tutting to herself. The subject of her disapproval is a man's body, riddled with scars and burns. 'Seems like a lot of work if you ask me. Better to replace most of the parts. Better yet, just transfer what's left into a new shell.'

Samael shakes his head. 'He won't like that.'

'Well, it doesn't really matter what he likes. Look at him! He's not in any state to complain.'

'True.'

'Besides, he looks like the kind of person that will only break whatever we give him. Waste of effort if you ask me.'

Samael nods, good natured. He knows that she will do as he asks eventually.

'At least let me scrap the arm.'

'Why? The bones are mostly intact. If you rewire the

nerves in his fingers and repair the tendons he should regain function in the hand.'

Neer huffs, 'Partial function.'

'Yes, it won't be perfect but he will prefer it.'

'At least it won't be hard to find a good skin match.'

'About that, I don't think he'd want another's skin.'

'Don't push your luck. I'm fonder of you than most people but there are limits.'

'Don't worry about the match, use a synthetic sleeve for his right arm and hand.'

'Alright, but it'll be ugly as hell.'

'Do you wish me to stay and assist?'

She gives him a hard look. 'No, I've had quite enough of your help already.' Two of her extra limbs lock into place to stabilize her, while another two start lining up tools. Meanwhile, her fleshy fingers click together, summoning aid. 'I'm going to use this as a teaching case, might as well get some good out of the time.'

'Thank you.'

He leaves her to work, going to another room, where Scout comforts Reela, allowing her to absently stroke his patchy fur. All around them is the presence of the First, it presses down on Samael, a pressure headache that is hard to ignore.

As he steps into the room, she looks up at him, small and afraid. 'Will he?'

'He will live.' The girl crumples with relief as Samael sits down next to her. 'Now tell me how it was I found you at the sky palace.'

'Delta.'

'She took you there?' Reela rubs her eyes and nods. 'Did you see Vesper?'

'Yes.'

'Alive?'

Reela gives a miserable shrug.

'She was hurt badly?'

A sniff, then a nod. Samael can see the worry radiating from the girl. 'What happened to her?'

'Took her.'

'Who did?'

She frowns, searching for the words, then shrugs, helpless.

'Can you show me, in your mind?'

Reela looks unsure but Scout barks encouragement and she tries, her face folding in concentration. Samael pulls off a gauntlet and puts a finger just inside her bottom lip, pressing it to her gum.

He feels her memory taking shape on the edge of her essence, opens himself to it, and closes his eyes.

Instantly he is rewarded with a sight of Beta standing over Vesper's body. He is trying to take the Malice but it does not want to go, stubbornly refusing to be removed from Vesper's curled fingers.

He hears crying, Reela's, in the background but Beta ignores it. He puts his hand on the Malice, and though Samael cannot see it in her memory, he is certain that the immortal and the sword are communing.

After a pause, he bends down and picks up Vesper and the Malice, carrying them both away.

Samael withdraws from the memory. 'Don't worry,' he says. 'Your mother is still in the sky palace. I'm going to go and get her out.'

*　　*　　*

The battle has long been over but the storm continues with no sign of calming. Combatants forget their feuds with each other and hunker down. The few remaining Empire soldiers hide in Alpha's sky palace, praying for guidance, finding none, while Crucible's fighters retreat to Wonderland, sharing rations behind glittering walls and making idle predictions about what will come.

In Crucible itself they flock to the dome, the tent city unable to withstand the heavens' elemental punishment. People pack in tight, arms rubbing against each other, sweat mingling in the stale air. Every inch of space is used, even the remains of the ratbred's tunnels are turned into extra sleeping spaces.

Infernals from New Horizon are forced to squeeze in with the other factions, uncomfortably close. The greater ones fold themselves into cramped spaces, staying there, motionless. The lesser ones barely contain their delight, chirruping and salivating at the sight of so many people, all within reach of their jaws.

None bite though. A mutual respect keeps everyone honest, and where that isn't enough, proximity and lack of opportunity step in.

And so Crucible's alliance endures despite the storm. In the dome and in Wonderland, little moments of decency light up the dark. One woman offers another a little of her food. A half-breed with no thumbs slowly feeds the bound Empire prisoners, and a merchant from Verdigris tells a story so dirty that one of the listeners snorts drink from her nose.

There is little dignity to be had; the storm has gone on long enough to force people to attend to the body's daily needs. Bottles, still warm, are passed along lines, as are helmets, repurposed, held upside down and at arm's length. But despite this, despite it all, a warmth grows between the survivors, a weak flame kindled in the dark, fed with shared experience and growing understanding, mutual.

A sphincter opens in the wall, allowing Samael access to the tunnel. It is the inside of one of Wonderland's bone-limbs, and it will enable him to climb straight up to Alpha's sky palace, sheltered from the storm, by far the safest and quickest method of travel. Samael wishes there was a second option.

He clambers inside, having to slide his armoured shoulders in. There is a slick squishing sound as the tunnel accommodates his bulk and then he is lying flat, horizontal.

'I am ready,' he says, and feels the shift in essence around him. Clearly, the First has heard.

The sphincter closes at his heels, sealing him inside, and then muscles begin to work, bunching, rippling, driving Samael up the tunnel at a forty-five degree angle. A thick wall of tissue and a layer of bone protect him from the elements outside but he still feels them, muffled, as they buffet the limbs, making them sway from side to side.

Like a pip stuck in the throat, Samael is vomited upwards in convulsive jerks, until he spurts out onto a hard polished floor.

He has left Scout behind with Reela, as much to stop the girl from trying to follow as to look after her. Now he regrets the decision, missing the Dogspawn's keen tracking senses.

Standing up, he flicks mucus from his visor and takes stock. The hallway has taken some superficial damage but remains striking. The ceiling is high, built for things greater than him and decorated in silver, each shape painstakingly made, crafted by loving hands.

He feels uglier just looking at it.

Down empty corridors he wanders, searching for signs of life. The fighting has been heavy in the palace and nobody has yet cleared up the mess.

Occasionally the floor rocks under his feet, and he realizes that Wonderland has become an anchor, steadying the palace against the worst of the winds.

A woman dressed in the armour of an Empire soldier stands up from behind some rubble. She has a rifle in her hand but it points away from him. She is familiar, one of the ones brought to their side by Delta.

To his eyes, her essence is fascinating, corralled into an unnatural shape by broad lines, footprints left by Delta's touch. Within them, she has freedom to think and act but she cannot ignore them, cannot cross them.

'I'm on your side,' she calls out. 'My name is Mazar.'

'Yes,' he replies. 'Why are you still here?'

She swings herself over the rubble and approaches him, slinging her rifle over a shoulder. 'I didn't want to stay, believe me . . . but I'd rather die than climb into one of those giant arsehole tubes.'

Samael pauses for a moment. 'I hadn't thought of them like that.'

Mazar just looks at him.

'I'm here to find Vesper, do you know where she is?'

'Yes. I can take you if you want but I should warn you, The Seven have her.'

'I know.'

'And you still want to go?'

'I want to help Vesper.'

She doesn't say anything else, guiding him through the palace. It is clear she does not know the route by heart but has made signs to guide them, little arrows made from bits of rubble or weapon fragments.

'Is no one else here?' asks Samael.

'There are others taking shelter but they're clustered over there,' she gestures over her shoulder, 'and I doubt they're going to come out.'

'Because of the storm?'

'Because they failed.'

They continue walking through corridors that would normally be guarded. Empty, they seem too large, hollow.

Samael works his jaw a couple of times before deciding to speak. 'This may sound hard to believe, but I know something of how you feel.'

Mazar glances at him but doesn't reply.

'I once tried to help someone from the Empire who was dying and she turned me down. Her soul was torn, I could see it bleeding away. By the time we met her condition was severe.' He pauses. If he still needed to, he would sigh. 'She said she would rather die than let me come near.'

'What happened to her?'

'She died.'

'And what has this got to do with me? Are you saying I'm dying too?'

'No. No, I didn't . . . Forgive me, I'm not the best at this. I remembered the story because it was the last time I tried to reach out to someone from the Empire. I'm hoping it will go better this time.

'But you're not like her. You're not sick and you're not

dying. The situation is different. I just want you to know that I understand.'

They reach a crossroads. An abandoned gauntlet lies on its back like a dying crab, the digits curling towards the palm. One finger has been straightened. Mazar attends to it, then follows it, turning left.

'Do you understand?' she asks. 'Prove it.'

'Many years ago, I was just a fisherman who worked at Six Circles. But when the commander of the Knights of Jade and Ash found me, he gave me some of his essence, turning me into this. He had need of my skills and to gain them, he imposed his will over mine. I was still myself. My thoughts were my own, but now I had some of his thoughts too. They were stronger than mine. I don't know how to put it into words . . . but when I look at you and see what Delta has done, I cannot help but feel sympathy.'

Mazar's answer comes through gritted teeth. 'Are you trying to say that we're the same? That what some demon does is the same as being touched by Delta of The Seven?'

'No. It is not the same. What the infernals do is different, more complex. My desires were blurred with my creator's, whereas Delta has pressed Her orders onto you in a way that leaves them distinct.' He holds up his hands, apologetic. 'I've made you angry, and that wasn't my intent. We may not be the same but I think there is something common between us. We are both victims.'

'What's your point?'

'Just that I think I understand what it's like for you, better than most. But I'll say no more. I probably shouldn't have spoken at all.'

They walk a little further, then Mazar stops and shakes

her head, swearing under her breath. She shakes her head a second time and looks away from Samael. 'It's like She's in my head, watching me. I have to get Her forgiveness, do you understand? It's there all the time. I need it! It doesn't matter what I do, She's there, waiting for me to do better. Even when I sleep! You said I'm not dying but it feels that way.'

Samael stops by her side, 'I understand.'

'Yeah, maybe you do. It doesn't change what's happening though.'

'No.'

She curses again, quiet. 'But I . . . I'm still glad I could say it out loud.'

'Yes.'

'So maybe, if I ever see you again after this, maybe it would be okay to do this again.'

Samael holds her gaze for a long moment, his half-breed eyes searching the depths behind her words. 'Yes, I would like that.'

The worst of the winds do not touch the bottom of the valley, and fighting has dug new hollows in the earthy walls, making shelter for those small enough to take advantage.

The buck is small enough, backing inside so as to become invisible. Though protected, he remains wild eyed, terrified, screaming. Like a lighthouse in the dark, his bleats lure another through the churning, smoky air.

When the doe arrives, his mouth closes. She is a bedraggled figure, windswept, and nearly falls into the hole with him.

Panic draws them together, magnetic, until bodies press, necks touching, chins resting on each other's shoulders.

Frantic heartbeats calm, finding a common rhythm. As trust builds and warmth spreads, they shut their eyes, letting the full weight of their heads be taken.

Somehow it seems as if the noise of the storm is less frightening than before. Thunder remains shockingly loud, the flashes of lightning turned a dark orange through closed lids, but they jump less, and do not cry out.

Despite the rage of the elements outside, the buck and the doe relax, safe in their pocket of peace.

Mazar comes to a stop in front of a large circular door. They are deep within the palace now, in the central keep that is dedicated to The Seven and their acolytes.

'She's in there.'

Samael looks for a handle or means of progress. 'Can you open it?'

'No.'

He lifts his hand to knock.

'Wait!' says Mazar. 'You might make Them angry.'

Samael tries to laugh but it comes out as a wheeze. 'My existence makes Them angry.' His fist connects with the door three times. 'You don't have to wait with me,' he adds.

Though her feet take a step backwards, she does not leave.

Samael waits while the echoes of his knocking settle, then knocks again, a second round of three, a pause, another.

Mazar moves a little further back.

The door spirals open, smooth and sudden, revealing a corridor, and in front of it, Obeisance. As ever, she is dressed in her cloak of feathers, unruffled. As she looks at them both, Mazar goes to her knees.

Samael does not. 'Where is Vesper?'

'She is within. The Seven are deciding her fate.'

'Take me to her.'

Obeisance bristles. 'Do not presume to order me, abomination.'

He considers this. The reaction does not surprise so much as depress. A part of him wishes to rip her bald head from her hairless body. Another, to corrupt her essence and drag her before The Seven. Let her experience life as a half-breed and then see if she retains her arrogance.

Instead he says, 'You have surrendered. Unless you produce Vesper, it will be this abomination that decides your fate, and The Seven's.'

It is Obeisance's turn to consider. She does not need long. 'This way,' she says.

Samael and Mazar follow her, the latter at some distance.

They come into a larger chamber, filled with display cases, all artfully edged with intricate letters, ugly history made beautiful through calligraphy, grand, looping. Several of these cases are open, their contents removed. Tools that once belonged to the creator, taken out and dusted off, put to work once more.

The sounds of industry have stopped now, and Samael sees five winged backs in a curved line, examining something he cannot see.

Alpha of The Seven stands to one side, his hands chained in front of him, his sword chained to his side, a muzzle of black iron clamped over his jaw.

Samael senses little emotion from him, the immortal still deep in shock. Obeisance lowers her head, respectful, as the other five turn.

He feels their eyes on him, then their revulsion hitting him like a wave. Four swords glare at him, itching to be drawn, while a fifth sits, inert, in Delta's arms.

Beta notices Mazar then, and beckons her closer. He, like his brother Epsilon and his sisters appears excited about something, and nervous. He begins to speak, the others soon joining in.

'Come, come and bear witness . . .'
'Witness what we have wrought . . .'
'Wrought iron to hold anger . . .'
'Anger that caused such pain . . .'
'Pain we have inflicted, and now regret . . .'
They point at Alpha, who flinches away.
'Now he will listen . . .'
'Listen while we promise . . .'
'Promise to change . . .'
'Change for the better . . .'
'Better now that we are in balance.'
They part, allowing Samael to see a figure standing behind them. A naked statue, brushed from head to toe in silver, strange, yet familiar: Vesper. Her new skin does not erase her scars but it mutes them, grooves in the metal that snag the light. In her hand, she carries the Malice.

Though smaller and wingless, there is a likeness between her and the rest of The Seven that Samael cannot help but see.

'Long have we waited . . .'
'Waited and watched . . .'
'Watched when we should have acted . . .'
'Acted when we should have helped . . .'
'Helped our people, our world . . .'
This time, five fingers point at Vesper.

'For the first time, we have created . . .'

'Created and healed . . .'

'Healed Delta's sword and Vesper's body . . .'

'Body and blade restored . . .'

'Restored in form and number.'

Five hands open, and five faces beam with joy.

'Two fragments join . . .'

'Join to make one . . .'

'One that joins six . . .'

'Six that become Seven . . .'

'Seven, as we were made to be.'

An eye opens and Vesper's follow. Samael feels her smile, weary, before it reaches her face. She lifts her free hand, waves. 'Hello.'

CHAPTER TWENTY-FIVE

Eventually, the storm passes. Winds clear and clouds disperse, leaving a bruised sky, and three suns where there were two, a gold and two red, a lesser and a greater.

A sky-ship takes Vesper back to Crucible. The journey is short. Vesper wishes it were longer.

'How are you?' asks Samael.

'I'm going to miss my hair,' she replies, making him wheeze, amused. 'Honestly? I don't know.' She holds a silver hand up to the light. 'This doesn't look like mine anymore. But then, well, I haven't really looked . . . right? Is that the word? Anyway, I haven't felt myself since I was burned.' She stops and looks at him. 'I think it's going to take a while.'

'It gets easier,' he says. 'And if it helps, you can have some of my hair.'

She puts her arms around him, ignoring the clink as they connect with his armour. 'I love you, Samael.'

The sky-ship touches down and she moves to the hatch. Though she does not need them, she is wearing boots, just as she is wearing clothes. Affectations to help her and her people adjust.

They have gathered outside to greet her, a strange mix. Even a glance tells her a lot. Very few West Rift faces can be seen, and the Thousand Nails no longer match their name. Grief and loss and injury mark many of the survivors, but the sword shows her other things too, a scattering of hope, and a rippling of awe at her arrival.

She catches a glimpse of Jem in the crowd and resolves to speak with him as soon as she can.

As she climbs out onto the wing of the sky-ship, they fall silent. 'We did it. There are a lot of dead to mourn and a lot of injuries to heal but we did it. The fighting is over. Now we have to do the hard part.' She pauses. 'Now we have to find a way to live. Together. Better than before.

'So I want you to think about what needs to be done, talk with your friends and family, and your leaders. I can't do this on my own. Today we reflect, recover and take stock. Tomorrow, we plan and get to work.'

They cheer for her, a couple discharging weapons in her honour, but she can see divisions in the crowd already, new groups and agendas taking shape.

Tomorrow, she tells herself. *I'll worry about that tomorrow.*

Cracks run the length of her room in the dome and it is colder than it should be. Vesper doesn't notice for herself but deduces it from the goosebumps on Jem's arms.

They stand an awkward distance apart. Too close to be formal, too distant for comfort.

'Don't be afraid,' she says, and taps her chest. 'It's still me under here.'

410

He reaches partway across the gap. 'Can I?'

'Sure,' she replies, trying to sound normal.

Fingers brush against her shoulder. 'You're warm!'

'Yes.'

'That's a relief, I was worried you'd be . . .' He glances down. 'Look I have to ask, can you feel it when I touch you?'

'Sort of. It's not like before but I know that you're touching me.'

'So how is this going to work?'

'What do you mean?'

Jem covers his mouth, awkward. 'I mean, can you still . . . you know, get close?'

'You're asking if we can kiss?'

'Yes. And other things.'

She sighs. 'I don't know. We'll just have to find out.' A little twinkle finds its way into her eyes. 'Would you like to find out?'

'Sure, yes.'

Vesper puckers her lips, waits. She frowns when Jem doesn't come any closer. 'What is it?'

'Do you think maybe you could put the sword down first? I don't like the way it's looking at me.'

'Oh, sorry.' She doesn't try to explain that, more than ever, the sword is a part of her. *One thing at a time.*

The sword is put down, and the two kiss.

Though she no longer touches the hilt, the essence link between them remains, stronger now. It reminds her of the thread that connects Samael and Scout.

An eye rolls at the comparison, indignant, and Vesper giggles.

Jem immediately pulls back. 'What is it?'

411

'Oh, nothing.'

He smiles at her. 'No, it's okay. It does feel funny, like I'm kissing you for the first time again.'

She puts aside the thought that she didn't really register the kiss at all and focuses on the memory instead. 'The first was good, wasn't it?'

'Yes, and the second. I think I bumped your teeth with the third.'

They both laugh.

'Good times,' murmurs Vesper. 'It feels so long ago.'

'A lifetime,' adds Jem.

For a few moments, they stand, lost in memories.

Jem looks up at her. 'What's going to happen now?'

'That's a good question. I'm going to meet with the other delegates and try and thrash out a way forward. Crucible will finally be doing what it's supposed to.

'I want to make sure that the people not connected directly to any of the larger groups are looked after, and I want to make sure that we keep channels of communication open between all sides. If I can, I want to establish some basic rules in the way infernals and humans interact with each other. We managed to remove slavery from New Horizon, perhaps we can do the same in Slake.' Her face twists as she considers the factory city's leaders. 'Maybe.'

Jem takes a step back from her. 'Are you serious about all this?'

'Of course I am.'

'Then you have to apply those same rules to The Seven.'

An eye narrows, Vesper frowns. 'That makes sense.'

'And you have to help the people who have been brain-slaved.'

'What do you mean?'

'I mean Mazar, and people like her. They can't think for themselves anymore because Delta did something to their minds. It's sick and it's wrong, and you have to stop it! And if—'

She holds up her hands. 'It's alright, Jem. It's alright. I agree with you. I'll do what I can to help them.'

The sword shows her Jem's anger, and the way it flickers over his essence. It points out the little hints of taint too, disapproving. She gives it a warning look and an eye looks back before showing her more, that Jem blames her as much as The Seven for their predicament, that there is revulsion too—

'Enough!' she says, her voice taking on a resonance.

Jem steps back, alarmed.

Silver wings shrug and an eye closes.

'Don't worry, Jem.' She adds, 'I wasn't talking to you. It was the sword.'

Concern lingers on his face. 'For a moment, when you spoke, you didn't sound like you.'

'No?'

'You sounded like one of Them.'

'I suppose I did.'

He looks at her as if studying a relic. 'It's more than just silver skin, isn't it? They've changed you.'

'Yes.'

'What does it mean?'

'Jem, I'm still getting my head round it as well. And The Seven are having to adapt just like we are.' She points at the wall. 'Out there, I have to look like I have all the answers. But in here, I just want to be me . . . I want to have some time to scratch my head and to feel like it's okay that I don't

413

know what I'm doing. Maybe even to ask some questions myself.'

He doesn't quite meet her eye. 'Yeah, of course. I'm sorry.' There is time enough to notice the lack of conversation before he adds, 'How are you?'

'Physically? Well, I'm tired but I'm not in pain. I feel as strong as I ever have, stronger maybe. Otherwise . . . a bit of a mess. I'm trying not to worry too much until after this is done.'

'When will that be?'

She shrugs. 'When the delegations have finished their discussions. A few days, a week, maybe two? We'll have some time for ourselves then.' The thought of it brings a fresh wave of fatigue. 'Actually, I think I need to rest now. It's going to be a long day tomorrow.'

'Sure,' replies Jem. 'I'd better go and check on Reela anyway.'

She nods, moving to the sword as he goes to the door. An eye watches him go, pleased. It is a relief to feel the sword in her hand again, some small tension easing at the familiar weight.

To her surprise, she finds she is no longer tired.

A knock at the door breaks Vesper from her reverie. She has not been sleeping exactly, but drifting through memories, hazy, of another time.

'Come in.'

The door opens and a purple-skinned woman enters. She is short, with chubby hands. Four extra bone-limbs have been grafted to her hips, giving her a scuttling, spider-like gait.

There is something familiar about the woman's face. Vesper tries to place it. It was many years ago that they met, when both of them were girls. She was in Wonderland and the other girl was called . . . 'Runty? Is that you?'

The half-breed cackles, an ancient sound from a young throat. The sword draws her attention to other things. The soft glowing eyes, transplanted, green, like the ones her Uncle Harm used to have, and, more importantly, that a certain surgeon general of the Uncivil did. Through the sword's eye, she sees the way the essence has not quite settled within the shape of the body.

'Neer!' she says.

'Yes! It's me. What do you think of my new body? A little tainted maybe but I think there's a good few years in her yet.'

'But I thought only the infernals could transfer from one body to another.'

'That's only because we'd never done it before. It had always been an idea the Uncivil intended to try but she could never quite figure it out. The First though, that's another matter. It's a wily bugger, been playing with moving essence between human hosts for years.'

'Wait,' says Vesper, a hint of horror coming into her voice, 'what's happened to Runty?'

'The First has her. Was part of our deal.'

'I don't know if I like the sound of that.'

'Ha! Listen to you. I didn't come here to get your approval, girl. I'm not one of your little followers. I came here to see what all the fuss was about.' She looks Vesper up and down. 'Very interesting! I don't suppose you'd let me take a closer look?'

'No.'

'Don't let your ignorance hold us back. We could learn so much from a quick study of your insides. I'll put everything back the way I found it, you have my word.'

'No!'

Neer's face sours. 'Fine. The other reason I came was to drop something off.' She clicks her fingers and two robed figures enter, strange bulges around their middles. Between them, they carry a stretcher with a man on it, mostly bandaged. Puffy bruises decorate the only visible patches of skin.

It is strange to see the Vagrant looking so frail. Vesper feels tears itching her eyes.

'Now before you thank me, you should know it's not my best work. Samael wouldn't let me do a proper job so I've just restored the bones as best I can and put a sheath over the places where the skin won't grow back. Mainly on his hand.

'You can clearly see that this isn't the first or even the second time he's been worked on. If it were up to me, I'd just overhaul him from the skeleton up. But it wasn't, so this is what you've got.' She tuts at the Vagrant's sleeping form and then looks at Vesper. 'Ha! You even cry like them!'

In surprise, Vesper wipes a tear from her cheek and holds it up for inspection. It is grey and gritty, not quite what The Seven weep but not just salt and water either.

'Well,' Neer continues, a sly note in her voice, 'this has been fascinating but I'll be going. Give the two of you some time alone.'

Neer and the two robed figures leave, and Vesper looks at her father. She knows the delegates will be gathering soon but she cannot bear to leave.

'Can you hear me?' she asks.

The Vagrant does not respond.

'I know you've been through a lot and this isn't fair, but I could really do with talking to you.'

The Vagrant does not respond.

'Please,' she adds, the need in her voice making the word reverberate.

The Vagrant's eyes spring open. He blinks, alarmed, pupils gradually finding focus, then settling on Vesper.

'Hello,' she says quietly.

He favours her with a smile, sleepy.

Relief comes in a loud exhalation. 'I'm so glad you're here!' Gently, she takes his left hand. His thumb moves across her finger, probing smooth metal. He begins to frown. 'The Seven saved me. I was going to die, I think, from all the injuries. But they gave me a new skin and . . . well it doesn't matter now. The important thing is that I'm alive and so are you and we did it. The Seven have surrendered but tensions between the Empire and the south are worse than ever and I feel like I need time to deal with everything that's happened to us but there isn't any. It's all happening so fast and I know that if I don't take control of it then others will and I don't think Samael can handle this, I don't think anyone else can.'

Amber eyes struggle to stay open as she talks, a stream of consciousness made of worries, hopes and suspicions. When she finishes, the Vagrant gives her hand a weak squeeze, before being whisked away from consciousness.

She holds his for a while longer, waiting until his breathing has evened out before carefully slipping free. 'Okay,' she says, as much to herself as to the sword. 'I think I can do this.'

*   *   *

Vesper hurries towards the central area of the dome, her mind fizzing with what she is going to say. Absently, she notices teams of people trying to repair the damage done to Crucible. Superficial damage is left untended, decorative, all efforts going towards reinforcing critical sections of the roof. Metal bars are glued into place across the worst of the cracks, like plasters that are too small, injuries peeking out above and below them.

Crucible's interior looks like an old face, aged before its time. It does not get Vesper down. Somehow it feels appropriate to her. Like them, the building has suffered and, like them, it endures.

She sees uncertainty in those she passes. They are no longer sure of the best way to react. There is no etiquette to cover her unique status. Some kneel, others salute, a few wave hello, and one or two simply bury themselves in their work, pretending not to notice her.

Apart from the repair crews the dome seems quiet. With a start she realizes that the meeting has already begun. Running now, Vesper goes into the main audience chamber, to find it full.

This heartens her. After all the fighting, she had feared the delegates would have given up on her dreams of peace. But a quick look confirms that the south is well represented: Red Rails, Verdigris, West Rift, the Thousand Nails, New Horizon and Slake have filled their boxes.

At her request, a space has been made for the dispossessed, their hastily chosen leaders standing awkward, slightly bewildered.

Excitement growing, she strides down towards the central stage, only to find someone already there, holding court.

Neer.

'What's going on?' asks Vesper.

Neer's smile is cold. 'I'd have thought that was obvious. This is the place where we come to address the delegates, is it not?'

Vesper nods.

'And that's exactly what I'm doing. Wonderland is back in business, bigger and better than ever. As everyone has seen, our city is mobile now. We can take trade direct to those that want it. Do you understand? No more caravans and worrying about raiders and weather conditions. It's going to be a new age of trade, development and evolution.

'I'm proposing a consortium, on behalf of the First. Our doors are open to any that wish to negotiate. We also need keen minds and extra hands to join us. There's no shortage of work or opportunities on Wonderland.' Savmir, Gorad, Gut-pumper and Ezze all appear interested, their faces calculating.

'Wait,' says Vesper. 'We're getting ahead of ourselves. We need to talk about the release of our prisoners and how to help those worst hit in the fighting.'

'No we don't,' snaps Neer. 'We don't need to do any of that. You do. As for what I need, I've made my offer. After you're done here, you can find me in Wonderland, if you want to be part of the future.'

Vesper stares, stunned, as Neer leaves the stage.

Before she can collect her thoughts, Gorad and Gut-pumper lean forward.

'Gut-pumper has a question,' says Gorad.

'A quick one,' adds Gut-pumper.

'He was wondering how we are going to punish The Seven? Not you, of course,' says Gorad.

'Of course,' agrees Gut-pumper.

They look at her. They all look at her.

'Well, Alpha is being punished. He's in chains. They've made Him a prisoner for what He's done.'

Gorad's indignation is cartoonish, her painted lips opened in a wide 'O' shape. 'So old Alpha slaughters His own people, then comes for us, razing colonies to the ground along the way. Thousands in the north are dead, not to mention all of us good people what got the chop, and He gets to prance about in chains!'

'Generous,' mutters Gut-pumper.

'Maybe we're in the wrong business, Gut-pumper? Seems to me we should go around being murderers if Vesper here is going to give us a nice set of chains as a thank you! There's a lot of people here can't even afford a link, let alone a whole set.' Her voice becomes harder as she adds: 'Why isn't He dead for what He's done?'

There is a rumble, approving, from the rest of the dome.

'But don't you see?' asks Vesper. 'We can't kill Alpha without killing ourselves. The Seven's essence is part of our world. It helps keep the damage that the Breach did from getting worse. It,' she struggles for the words, 'keeps the balance from tipping too fast.

'When Delta's sword was broken in the fighting, the red sun broke too. There's a link there we have to respect. If Alpha was actually killed, it would destroy us all.'

'Convenient,' mutters Gorad.

'Most convenient,' mutters Gut-pumper.

'Can you prove it?' Gorad asks.

An eye narrows at Vesper's side. 'You'll have to take my word for it.'

There is an awkward silence.

Ezze clears his throat. 'Nobody is doubting your word, greatest and shiniest of ladies. But we are full of the worries and the questions. The Seven say you are one of Them now. Can you be of Them and still be one of us? How do we know that Alpha will not do this again when the chains are coming off? What is to stop the Empire coming back when they have recovered in a few years' time and burning poor Ezze?'

'What this comes down to, Ezze, is trust. Whatever I show you or tell you can be questioned. If you don't believe me, then I've already failed in what we set out to achieve here.

'But I think we've made a strong foundation. You trusted each other when our lives were at stake and proved worthy of that trust. You trusted me enough to come here in the first place. Now I'm asking you to trust me again.'

She waits a moment, pleased that nobody jumps into the space with a question. 'To answer you though,' she continues, 'I'm still me. That will become obvious as time goes on. Alpha will stay in chains until we're happy for them to come off.' She spreads her arms. 'All of us. Only an agreement from everyone here will be enough, and if that never happens, that's fine by me. As for the Empire, it needs to reintegrate itself. When it pulled back, you adapted to the changes, and now the Empire has to catch up. I can make that happen now.

'Gathered here we have the finest traders, warriors, engineers, Necroneers,' she smiles, 'survivors all! Together, there is so much we can achieve. But only together. So I have a question for all of you: are you with me?'

*   *   *

As the days pass, groups fall into alliance, like convicts chained by the ankles and wrists. One pulls the other along, until the whole is moving, knocking into one another, shuffling, awkward, but moving, and in the same direction.

While each of the delegates visits Vesper with their ideas for the future, so too do they visit Wonderland, to discuss more pragmatic things.

Two visions grow together, twining like trees, tangled, each lending strength to the other. Rights are discussed, for land, for the inhabitants of the world, old and new, and simple laws are set down to govern disputes on unclaimed territory. How these laws will be enforced is unclear but the principles are agreed.

Meanwhile, stories of the battle are shared. The best stick in the minds of the listeners, growing wings and flying outward, polished by a hundred tongues until names acquire a sheen, heroic.

Necrotrade returns as if it had never gone. Such is the need of the wounded, the greedy, and Wonderland's reconstruction, that the battlefield is picked clean of the dead.

By the end of the first week, no bodies remain, and by the second, not a single piece of blasted flesh is left unclaimed. Rain comes and goes, allowing people to get used to the three suns in short bursts. And then, as the delegations begin to pack, preparing for the overdue journey home, buds appear, new life, its shape as yet unknown.

CHAPTER TWENTY-SIX

It is dark when Vesper gets back to her room. Despite her transformation, she finds she still needs sleep. It has been slipping down her list for too long now, always making way for some new task or discussion. They are all so urgent, especially now that the first gathering at Crucible is coming to an end.

The door squeaks as it closes, the frame no longer in perfect alignment, and her feet chime softly on the hard floor as she walks. Jem's shallow breathing only becomes audible when she reaches the bed and lowers herself in.

'Good day?' he whispers.

'Long day,' she replies. 'Why are you whispering?'

'I have no idea.'

They both smile in the dark. 'It was a good day though. I've finally got them to agree that a body is the property of the family or the city of residence rather than the killer. And I think we're on the cusp of a preliminary route for Wonderland to travel. The First was trying to push its right to go where it pleases as a free individual, but even Neer had to admit that wasn't going to happen.'

'Are they all still going tomorrow?'

'Officially, yes. I think a few will hang back for private audiences, but yes, and I can't wait!'

'Me neither.' The sword tells her that there is more but she doesn't say anything, waiting for Jem to get there in his own time.

Sleep is just taking her when he speaks. 'Vesper?'

'Mmmnm?'

'I don't want to go back to the Shining City. I've been thinking about it for a long time. It isn't for me.'

'But our home is there.'

'No it isn't.' His hand feels about for hers. 'They burned it down. Purged,' he adds bitterly. 'I think they destroyed parts of the city too.'

'That's why we need to go back, to rebuild, to make it better.'

'No, listen. The Shining City isn't for me. Even if you rebuild it, that won't change the people.'

'But it will!'

'You're not listening. Let me finish, okay?'

His hand no longer holds hers. Her other hand squeezes the hilt of the sword. 'Okay.'

'It's going to take years for someone like me or Samael to be accepted there and I'm tired of waiting. I want to live now, while I can. There are opportunities in Wonderland. They've offered me a place there and I want to take it.'

'What will you do there?'

'They want me to be a diplomat for Wonderland. Surgeon General Ferrencia says she needs someone well travelled, and good with people.' His voice gets louder as excitement takes over. 'And she wants me! I could really be someone there, Vesper.'

'What about us?'

'Come with me. We can make a new start, as a family.'

'You know I can't do that.'

'Can't you? Why not? You promised we'd have time after Crucible.'

'I know but things have changed, I've changed. The Empire needs me now more than ever.'

Jem lets out a breath through his teeth. 'Actually, I don't think you've changed at all. But I have to do this, and I think Reela should come with me. You can still visit us in Wonderland, whenever you want. It's not like she ever saw you at the Shining City anyway.'

'No but—'

'She has to come with me. The truth is—' he hesitates '—the truth is, she's scared of you.'

There is no denying it. Vesper turns her head away. 'What about my father?'

'He can visit as well if he wants but Reela is my daughter and I won't have her purged or judged.'

'. . . Okay.'

'That's it? Okay? You're not going to fight me on this?'

'No, I agree. You're right. You're right and I'm sorry.'

'You know, you have a choice as well. You've bled for them, you've saved them all several times. It's okay if you want to walk away now, you don't owe them anything.'

She sighs. 'I wish that were true but I really am the only one. I'm the person holding this together, the one all sides trust. And I'm part of The Seven now. I am literally the only person in the world that can make this work. I wish I could just up and leave but I can't. I've sacrificed too much to stop now. I have to make the blood on my hands count for something. I have to make something good out of all this. It's the only choice I can live with making.'

'Okay,' he says.

'Okay,' she echoes.

Neither sleep. Something bugs Vesper, a piece of grit she can't quite bring into focus until: 'You mentioned Samael not fitting in. Does he want to leave too?'

'He does but he won't. It's the oath he swore to you, he feels bound by it.'

'I'll free him. He can make his own choice, like we have.'

They fall to silence again, but later that night, his hand finds hers, and this time it stays.

One by one the delegations leave. Each goes well, offering positive words and warm thanks to Vesper. All invite her to visit and say how much they are looking forward to the next gathering. Most of them mean it.

Savmir, the ratbred prince, gives her one of his rings, a band of tin, worn thin as a well-sucked lozenge. It is the spoils of his first trade, made as a youth. 'You share my bright future!' he exclaims.

West Rails leave her one of their knives, a very practical badge of brotherhood.

From Verdigris, she is met by Ezze and the Usurperkin twins, Max and Maxi. They make a gift of the city's flag, bearing the defiant arm of Tough Call. 'You will be seeing Ezze again soon, yes?'

'I'm sure I will,' she replies.

'This is good! We will meet as friends and eat as heroes!' The merchant slaps his belly, then adds in a more conspiratorial tone, 'And Ezze trusts there are none of the hard feelings with your father?'

Vesper simply smiles at him. 'I'm glad that you've been so supportive in the discussions. To be honest I'd expected you to side with Wonderland more often.'

'Opportunity is always good but monopoly always bad, unless it belongs to Ezze! And you are the favourite of our once-great lady. Tough Call may be gone but Verdigris remembers her. And Verdigris has lots of angry green-faced marshals so Ezze is forced to remember too!' With a last wink, the new leader of Verdigris goes on his way.

The remnants of the Thousand Nails come to pay their respects as well. Each shows her a new scar or injury as they pass. Flat Head comes last and points to a puckered circle of skin on her leg. 'Named her Vesper,' she says proudly, 'after you!'

Vesper thinks for a moment before pointing to a dark line in the silver of her chest. 'I think I'll call this one "Flat Head".'

Flat Head winces as she stands straight, straining scar tissue. 'Yes!' she roars, and squeezes Vesper's arm.

Even a Usurperkin's strength is not enough to cause Vesper discomfort any more. She takes Flat Head's arm and squeezes back, arranging her fingers around the bruises.

Soon, she is alone again, waiting for the infernals of New Horizon. Samael comes to join her, the two standing in easy silence together.

Flies begin to gather, forming a curtain around Vesper and Samael. The Man-shape steps through them, turning his back in order to speak.

'If you want,' says Vesper, 'you can turn round. We're hardly going to judge you on your appearance.'

The Man-shape's jaw distends into position with a click. 'Are you curious about my face?'

'No. Well, yes, a little. But what I mean is that I accept you as you are, as a friend.'

'That is meant as a kind gesture. I will not take you up on it. You see, I am proud of my vanity. It brings me closer to your kind.'

'Oh. I hadn't thought of it like that.'

'It pleases me to think that I was able to teach you something about humanity, but perhaps it is not such a surprise. After all, it is your uniqueness that we value, rather than your ability to fit in.'

'These days you fit in a lot more easily than I do, Man-shape.'

His reply is not without smugness. 'Yes. Yes that is true.'

'Thank you for coming here. This would have been an empty project without you.'

'I am glad to hear that you are well disposed towards me, and that, perhaps, you hint at feeling somehow indebted.'

Vesper braces herself. 'Why is that?'

'Because I desire something: When you go north, I wish to go with you.'

At her side, an eye narrows. 'You want to come to the Shining City?'

'Yes. This is the furthest I have travelled since my arrival in your world. It has ignited a curiosity in me. I do not know how far your sky will allow me to go, but I wish to test my boundaries.

'As we are friends, I will do you the courtesy of being

honest. The south is not safe for me any longer. Now that the First is restored, it is without doubt the strongest. If I stay, it will dominate me and force me to serve again. Sadly, I have gained a taste for command and cannot go back easily.'

'And Wonderland can't cross the sea.'

'Yes.'

'What about the other infernals? Will they go back to New Horizon?'

'No. They are mine. If I leave them here they will become the First's.'

'Wait, you're talking about a mass infernal exodus?'

'Yes. I fear the Malice does not approve.'

A narrowed eye has become a slit. Vesper glares at it. 'The Malice should know better by now.' She thinks for a moment, then nods. 'I'll give one of the island colonies over to you. A gift. Your infernals can live there safely while you travel further north. I doubt they'll be able to come as far as you anyway.'

'This is agreeable. I am going to stop talking now so that we may face each other and touch to show mutual appreciation.'

Vesper laughs. 'Yes.'

They do and it is strange. The Man-shape can feel its destruction close at hand, and yet it is safe. Vesper knows this, treasuring the courage and trust it takes to bring them in such close proximity. 'Go well, my friend,' she says. 'I'll see you soon.'

But the Man-shape does not leave straight away, going to Samael. The two touch heads, intimate, and Vesper turns away to give them privacy.

After the Man-shape and the flies have gone, she turns to Samael.

'I hear you no longer wish to be a Seraph Knight.' The sword shows her the half-breed's consternation, a swirl of shame, anger, and sadness overwhelming. Immediately, she regrets her words.

'No,' he rasps. 'I do wish to be a knight. I will always wish it, but I must face reality. I am not of the Seraph nor will I ever be. I have tried to honour that part of my heritage but, when it was tested, when I faced true knights, my swords were found wanting, as was I.'

Vesper watches the buck chasing the doe across the top of the valley. 'I think in the end, we have to go where our hearts tell us. We have to be true to ourselves. If you want to go to Wonderland, I'll let you. I'll make it clear that I have released you from your oath to me.'

'I . . . Thank you.'

'Don't thank me yet, I haven't finished. Do you remember when we first met?' Samael nods. 'You were with Jem and he said you were a knight, and when Duet scoffed at the idea, he said you were more of a knight than any other he'd met. You see, being a Seraph Knight is about more than having a singing sword or the right armour. It is about serving the Empire and protecting its people above all else.' She sighs. 'I'm going to set you free in public but in private I am holding you to the oath you swore. I don't trust the First or Neer, and I want eyes close to them. You will be those eyes, Samael. You will be my knight that nobody can see. You will watch them, and you will watch Jem and Reela for me, be there for them where I can't. Do you understand?'

'Yes.'

'Good. You can't stop being a knight any more than I can stop trying to change things. It's what we are.'

'Yes,' Samael trails off as the delegation from Slake approaches. It it markedly smaller than when it arrived, though those that remain are laden with new wealth. Gorad and Gut-pumper come to a stop in front of Vesper, planting their canes in the ground between them.

'Gut-pumper and I have come to say farewell.'

'Gorad would never say this—' begins Gut-pumper.

'Don't!' interrupts Gorad.

'—But she's actually quite fond of you.'

'I said, "don't"!'

Gut-pumper holds up a hand, curving it around his mouth as he adds, 'Says you're spunky.'

Gorad grips the top of her cane tightly. 'Whereas Gut-pumper doesn't like you at all.'

'Can't stand her,' he agrees.

'Too pious, he says.'

Gut-pumper nods. 'Full of shit.'

'Yes, he thinks you're doomed to fail but I don't agree.'

Gut-pumper gives an apologetic bow. 'Like the new look though.'

'Indeed,' agrees Gorad, 'suits you.'

'Well,' remarks Vesper after they have gone. 'I'm glad that's over.'

The once great army of the Empire sit in rows, their hands and feet bound, stripped of weapons and purpose. Hopeless, they wait, accepting food when given, talking little. A few have bruises, too fresh to have come from the fighting. A few more shiver, gripped by illness, struggling to stay in formation. But even in defeat, when all is lost to them, they remain mostly tidy.

The Knight Commander stares at the floor, the suns barely felt on the back of his head. Two shadows are made, and a third, much weaker, to the side. He cannot take his eyes off it.

Slowly, the shadows move, so slowly. His thoughts move slower still, unable to comprehend how it has come to this.

A boot interrupts them, appearing on the edge of his vision, quickly joined by another. The Knight Commander looks up to see the three suns reflected, dazzling, on a silver face. On instinct, he and the other soldiers lower their heads, deferent.

'No,' says Vesper, the word lashing out like a hand at their throats, holding them mid-motion. 'The time for burying your heads is over. Look up. Look at me.'

And they do.

'You, all of you, came here to fight in the Empire's name. You were willing to die for the Winged Eye. Such a death would be given glory by the Empire, and songs would be sung that would echo down the generations.' She looks at them all, and the Knight Commander feels suddenly smaller. 'You are all victims. Not because you lost but because you fought at all. This battle did not need to happen. Every drop of blood spilled was unnecessary, every life lost, a tragedy.

'I am told that many of the colonies have been utterly destroyed, that the death toll is massive. You were the tools used to make that atrocity happen. They lied to you, tricked you, turned you into murderers.

'Alpha has done more damage to the Empire than the Usurper ever did! Look up at the sky, does it look glorious to you?' She shakes her head. 'Does a single one of you think that you did right by coming here?'

There is silence.

'Liars! I see through you. You are thinking that you did the work of The Seven and that you did your duty. But Alpha was wrong. He was wrong! And The Seven were wrong too. They have brought nothing but misery and death because They were too afraid to face up to what They had allowed to happen.

'They are facing up to it now.'

The Knight Commander's throat is dry. He does not want to look at Vesper any more. He does not want to think. But he, like the others, is snared, a fish on a barbed hook.

'The Empire promised to give your deaths meaning. I do not. I intend to give your lives meaning. You will never wash the guilt from your souls or the blood from your hands. The Empire will never be free of shame in your lifetimes. But you will spend every remaining second you have trying to cleanse its name anyway, to prove that you are better than the roles the Empire forced on you.'

She points up at the sky until they all look, puzzled. 'Do you know what this means? I'll tell you. It means storms and shifts in the balance. It means buildings will fall, fields will flood and roads become unusable. It means areas will be cut off from the mainland. It means whole harvests will be wiped out and people will starve.'

Her finger descends to point at them. 'You are going to help those people in any way you can. You will take them supplies and food, you will rebuild what you have broken.

They will hate you all the same, but you will take their hate as fair due and get on with your tasks. And when you are called home, you will be able to hold your heads high, and come home to the Shining City to teach others what you have learned, and train a new generation to take over the work.

'You will not die heroes. You will live with your eyes open and you will take responsibility for who you are and what you have done.' She gives an order, and others come among them, setting them free.

'Now eat, you're going to need your strength.'

To the Knight Commander's surprise, Vesper does not leave, she sits down, opposite him.

He hears the clink of cuffs being removed, and bindings being loosened, he hears the thudding of his own heart, louder.

'I understand your wrists haven't healed yet.'

It takes him a moment to stammer a reply. 'No.'

'Then let me help you. You've lost weight, and you didn't have much excess in the first place.'

Like a baby in shock, his mouth falls open, and she spoons in a doughy compound, purple, that tastes mainly of sugar. Dutifully, he chews and swallows.

When she is finished she sits back and regards him. 'You've still never told me your name, Knight Commander.'

It takes a while for him to understand what she is saying, and another few moments before he can answer. 'Torran,' he manages finally. 'My name is Torran.'

Sunslight shines through plasglass, highlighting a sleepy form, bandaged and bedridden.

The Vagrant yawns and brings his left hand to his face. The swelling has gone down, bruises fading to watercolour marks. He lifts his right hand and flexes the fingers slowly. They respond without pain or discomfort. A coating of shiny black covers them, a replacement skin, synthetic. It extends from fingertips to forearm, following the lines of his injuries, faithful, the longest streak running almost to his elbow.

He has seen this substance before. It was used on the commander of the Knights of Jade and Ash over two decades ago, restoring the infernal so that he could continue his hunt for the Malice.

A flurry of memories present themselves, unwanted.

The Vagrant lowers his hand and lets out a long sigh.

Amber eyes soon droop again, his head turning slightly from the light.

He wakes to the sound of footsteps in the corridor, and hushed voices.

'Are you ready?' Vesper's voice.

'Yes.' Jem's voice. 'Now, don't make a scene, Reela. You don't want to upset your grandfather.'

The Vagrant frowns.

'Nooooo! Don't wanna go!'

There is a succession of hissed voices and then the door opens.

Vesper, Jem and Reela step inside, pausing as they see the Vagrant. 'He's asleep,' whispers Jem.

Vesper looks over her father. 'Apparently,' she mutters.

'Maybe we should come back another time.'

'No, the transports are prepping to go. It has to be now.'

Jem looks dubious and begins to pull Reela back out of

the room. 'He looks terrible. We don't want to put him under any more strain. You can tell him when he recovers.'

'I wake him!' declares Reela, slipping free. 'I'm best at wakings!'

Vesper and Jem's voices merge behind her as she skips across the room. 'Wait!'

'Be gentle at least,' adds Vesper as Reela takes the Vagrant's arm in both of her hands and shakes it back and forth.

The Vagrant opens his eyes, looks at Reela, then quickly squeezes them shut again.

Reela gasps and shakes his arm like a cat shaking a mouse. 'Wake up!' she shouts, thrilled. 'Wake up!'

Jem looks at Vesper and folds his arms.

After a while the Vagrant makes a show of yawning and stretching, then adopts an expression of happy surprise.

'Hello!' says Reela.

He gives her a tired wave and she leans back from him, eyes wide. 'Creepy hand!' she exclaims.

The Vagrant turns to look at it, then makes it into a claw and moves it towards her, darting in to tickle.

Reela squeals until he stops, then immediately demands more.

Jem has to clear his throat three times before the Vagrant takes notice. 'Vesper, you need to tell him.'

Amber eyes turn to her, challenging.

'I'm leaving for the Shining City. Jem isn't. He and Samael are going to live on Wonderland.' She pauses. 'And we've decided that it's best if Reela goes with them. I know this is a lot to throw on you but I need to ask where you want to go.'

Jem fails to hide his surprise. 'I thought you needed him to go with you?'

'Lots of people need him but we all have to make our own choices, for ourselves. You showed me that.' She turns back to the Vagrant. 'So, where's it to be?'

There is a long pause. Reela clasps her hands together and adopts a pleading expression. Jem keeps his face carefully neutral, while Vesper looks profoundly sad.

The Vagrant looks at Reela, then Vesper, then at his hand, as if searching for an answer hidden in the black ocean of his palm.

He looks up, lips pressed together, and points at Vesper.

Jem nods to himself, relieved.

'Thank you,' mouths Vesper.

Reela's face falls.

The Vagrant's finger moves to point at her, then up to Jem. Then he repeats the gesture, faster, pointing: Vesper, Reela, Jem, before resting his hand on his chest.

'Together!' says Reela.

The Vagrant nods.

'I'm sorry,' says Vesper, 'but we can't. I wish we could but I have to go back north and attend to the Empire. Jem has his own life to lead, and we need to think of Reela's future too. Please don't make this any harder than it already is.'

The Vagrant turns his head away from her, looking at Reela. He reaches for her hand but Jem is faster, pulling her back. 'I knew this was a mistake.' He glares at the Vagrant, then walks out, dragging Reela behind him.

'No!' shouts the girl.

Arms and legs flail, doing little to stop her backwards exit. Noises of protest continue down the corridor, fading in volume but maintaining intensity.

Vesper waits until they have gone and then sighs. 'I think it'd be best if you came with me.'

The Vagrant doesn't answer and Vesper sighs again, leaving him to his thoughts.

CHAPTER TWENTY-SEVEN

Vesper walks away from Crucible. A light rain patters unnoticed across her head and shoulders. Her people make last
checks before their departure, coaxing ailing snakes of metal
back to life.

She walks away from them as well.

Up the side of the valley she goes, scrambling in places
where mud slides beneath feet. She relishes the climb, finding
it easier than expected.

At the top, two goats look up from their grazing, startled.
'There you are!' she says, taking a step forward and opening
her arms.

The doe scampers away while the buck watches her,
puzzled.

'It's me, Vesper. Do you remember?'

At her voice he looks around, then back at her. His dark
eyes show no sign of recognition. 'It's alright, I won't hurt
you.'

She steps forward again and he retreats quickly. From a

safe distance, the doe bleats and he trots a few steps towards her before looking back over his shoulder.

'Oh,' says Vesper, lowering her arms. 'I suppose you're leaving me too.'

The buck screams, making her smile and the doe runs still further. 'Goodbye then. And good luck.'

For a while the buck just stares at her, and then another bleat from the doe sends him scurrying after.

Vesper waits until they are out of sight, wipes at her face and makes her way towards Wonderland.

The living city has settled somewhat, its skirt of bone-limbs bunching thick to make a base, a circular white cliff for Wonderland to perch on.

Several of these limbs have been pressed forward of their fellows, kinked, to form steps up to the main gates.

Vesper ascends them, again enjoying the feeling of exertion. Her legs feel as if they could go on forever even if her heart does not.

Teams of people crawl about the turrets like spiders, repairing, restoring, loving. Up close, it is easy to see the extent of the damage done, and to appreciate the speed at which Wonderland recovers.

She leaves the multicoloured splendour of the streets and makes her way into a grand building, with high ceilings and large windows. Waiting for her there, at a table, is a figure in smooth black armour.

She goes and sits opposite, placing the sword on the table but keeping her hand on the hilt.

The figure lifts the helmet, revealing Duet's face, and behind it, the essence of the First.

Vesper finds it still bothers her. The sword shows her a

concealed necrotic pipe that runs from the wall, through the back of the chair, through the back of the body. There is only an illusion of separateness, the thing that meets her merely the bud of a great tree. 'We're going soon. You wanted to talk?'

The First nods. 'Yes. It is important to me that we remain in alliance. Only I have the power to directly . . . threaten yours, and only you and The Seven remain to threaten me.'

'I'm not planning to threaten anyone, surely you know that by now. It would go against everything Crucible was made for. You're the one holding all the secret meetings, not me.'

'And yet you have entered into negotiations with the Man-shape, binding it more closely to you.'

'Is that what this is about?' She takes its silence as assent. 'Honestly, it's not about threatening, it's about the opposite. When you came to me, you asked me to stand between you and The Seven, right?'

'This is true.'

'And I did. I'm still doing it today.'

'I do not see the relevance of this statement.'

'I'm not helping the Man-shape so we can ally against you, I'm helping to keep it safe from you. I'm standing between you and the Man-shape. See the relevance now?'

'Yes. But which side will you take when the Man-shape comes after me?'

Vesper doesn't hesitate. 'That won't happen.'

'It is the way of my kind. It is inevitable. The Man-shape has had ample opportunity to find . . . accord with me. Instead, it flees north to gather its strength.'

'No, it isn't like that!'

441

'Then promise me, if the Man-shape returns to Wonderland, seeking conquest, that you will step aside.'

'How about this: I promise not to help the Man-shape dominate you. But I won't allow there to be war again, regardless of who starts it.'

'That is an interesting position to take. I look forward to seeing if such freedom is possible, without violence to enforce it.'

'It is possible,' she leans forward. 'With your help.' The chair scrapes as she pushes it back. 'Congratulations by the way. It must be good to be whole again.'

'Thank you. We are both greater than we were and this is . . . pleasing to me.'

'Well,' she says, turning to leave. 'I'm sure we'll see each other again.'

'Do you wish to say goodbye to your family before you go?'

She stops and shakes her head. 'They don't know I'm here. I've already said goodbye to them once, and believe me, that was enough.'

The last bone-limb anchoring Alpha's sky palace to Wonderland is removed, and the vast soft-singing engine comes to life again. It cannot be heard from the outside but something of the sound escapes, a resonance that tingles teeth and tickles the body's finer hairs.

Samael watches it go from atop one of Wonderland's towers.

There is a stateliness to the palace's ascent. While it has received only superficial damage, the metal snakes that follow it on the ground crawl with injury.

442

The Seven

The Seven stand on the battlements, two appearing smaller than the rest. One because his head is bowed with chain, the other because she is. Vesper draws the Malice, offering a last salute, and Samael reaches for a sword that isn't there.

His empty hand hovers, before he holds it out. Not a wave, not a salute, but something.

Out of respect he stays in position as the Empire of the Winged Eye begins its long journey home.

Scout comes to join him, settling against his leg. The Dogspawn has enjoyed the run up the stairs, Samael can feel satisfaction in the pumping of flanks and the way Scout's mouth stays open, panting.

It takes a while for the Dogspawn to calm, longer than it used to, he muses. Scout is getting old. While Samael suspects his own body will take a long time to fully crumble, he knows that his companion is well inside his last decade.

Scout whines, sensing Samael's sadness, and he leans his head against his master, looking up.

Samael reaches down and strokes Scout, an act of reassurance, though he is not sure if it is for himself or the Dogspawn or if such things even matter.

They stay like that while Scout's panting comes to an end and the sky palace becomes a darker dot amid the clouds.

Gradually, voices approach, chattering and breathless from the climb. One belongs to his friend, Jem, the other to Mazar.

'When you asked me if I was happy with his offer, I thought he was going to sweat to death!' says Jem.

Mazar's laugh is a little high. 'He was terrified . . . of me.'

'Yes, isn't it great! I'm going to have to take you to all my negotiations from now on. I'm sure the Surgeon General will approve of you being assigned to me.'

Her reply is too low to hear and then the two of them are coming onto the roof to join him.

'Sir Samael,' calls Jem. 'They said you'd be up here.'

The two embrace. Mazar just gives him a nod whilst trying not to stare at Scout.

'I'm not a knight any more.'

Jem smiles his sharp-toothed smile. 'Maybe not to them, but you are to me.'

Abruptly, Samael desires to change the subject. 'How are you finding Wonderland?'

'I love it! There's so much going on, and so much opportunity. When I was at New Horizon, even as a child, it was all about survival. When I lived outside the Shining City, I was safe but kept out of the way. I was an embarrassment there, but here, I'm valued. I feel . . .' he smiles again, 'alive.'

'Good. And you, Mazar?'

She startles at the sudden inclusion. 'It's new to me. Strange.'

'That bad?' asks Jem.

'I don't regret it.'

'Give it time and you'll love it like I do,' he replies. 'There's so much to learn and we haven't even started moving yet.'

Mazar glances around. 'But doesn't that bother you? That we're living on a giant . . . thing?'

'No,' says Jem.

'Yes,' says Samael.

It is Jem's turn to look around. 'Have you seen Reela anywhere? I thought she was with you.'

'I have. She was.'

He looks around again. 'Where is she? Hiding I'll bet. Bad enough when she just had a small house and a field. Now she could be anywhere.'

Samael turns and looks out to the north, towards cloudy skies. 'I stashed her aboard the sky palace.'

'You what!' says Jem, his voice rising. 'How could you do that to us?'

Samael turns back to him. 'Are you sure you want to discuss this in front of Mazar?'

'I want my daughter back, I don't care who hears that! You need to speak to the nomads and requisition a sky-ship. We could still get her back if we're quick.'

'Very well. I did it because it was the right thing to do.'

'Stealing her was the right thing to do?'

'Asking her. I asked her where she wanted to live. You didn't. Nor did Vesper. I'd have expected you to know better.' Scout growls, cutting off Jem's attempt to interrupt. 'You don't want her here, not really. There is no room in your new life for her, no real desire in your heart to be with her. I'd know if there was.'

'I . . .' begins Jem.

'You would be too busy and there is no one else here to look after her. Scout and I would make poor parents.'

'Vesper will be even worse!'

'I agree. But I didn't send her back for Vesper.'

A range of emotions cross Jem's face then. 'I need to go. I have another meeting coming up. You coming, Mazar?'

Jem doesn't wait for an answer, hurrying away down the stairs.

'Go with him,' Samael urges. 'He'll come round, and I'll be there when he does.'

Mazar nods, but stops at the top of the stairs. 'See you tonight?'

'Yes.'

She nods again, going quickly after Jem.

It is much later when Neer comes to join him. 'What are you moping up here for. There's work to be done.'

'I was just reflecting.'

'On what?'

'On life.'

Neer sighs. 'You're not still upset about those bloody Necro-blades are you?' Her green eyes flash as she regards him. 'Suns and shit-storms, you are! All of that knowledge from the Uncivil rattling around in there, all of those gifts, and you're sad because you can't be a knight. Pathetic! Knights and idiots are always going cheap, but you, you're unique.'

'You don't understand.'

Neer waggles a purple finger at him. 'Don't I? You're upset because you worked on something and it failed. So you made a sword and you found out it wasn't good enough. So what? You think that's the end of the story?'

Reluctantly, he meets her eye.

'It's the start, you great shambling fool! You think I'm happy with this body, do you?' She cackles. 'Of course not. It's a prototype. A work in progress. It certainly won't be the last one I inhabit, and let me tell you, the next one will be much more palatable than this.

'If your ambitions are limited to pointy sticks, then by all means, make another one, make a better one. I have no doubt we can sell them. But swords aren't the future. We are. So stop whining like some child who just dropped their dinner in the dirt and put those special talents of yours to some use.'

'You're right,' he says.

'Of course I am,' she replies.

Perhaps, he thinks, as the two of them make their way into Wonderland's depths, *I do not need to make a sword after all*. His hand goes to Scout's head, and a new idea takes shape, to prolong life rather than snuff it out. The Dogspawn trots alongside him, barking, excited.

Delta of The Seven walks unchallenged through the sky palace. She carries her broken sword under the crook of an arm, murmuring to it, trying to soothe an eye that stares out, unblinking. Reela walks alongside her, holding her other hand.

It was not so long ago that the palace seemed massive to Delta. How quickly she forgot the outside world! Now, the palace is small, its familiarity stifling and dull. She used to feel safe here, as she did in their sanctum, but both places seem boring now.

Silver feet find their way easily, carried by memory, until they reach the right door.

Reela peeks inside, then holds a finger to her lips.

Delta stops talking to her sword and the two step into a room, half-lit.

The Vagrant is resting inside, eyes closed, chest moving up and down with easy regularity.

Reela taps Delta's arm.

Delta looks down to see the girl putting her finger to her lips again, then pointing at the Vagrant.

The two of them cross the room on tiptoes, Reela releasing Delta's hand as they reach the Vagrant's slab.

Very carefully, Reela tries to settle in next to him. However, the slab is narrow and she is forced to balance on the edge.

Delta watches, bemused, as Reela slides off.

447

Immediately, the girl is on her feet again. She mimes pushing the Vagrant over, and enlists Delta's help.

Two small hands join Delta's silver one to slide the Vagrant a few inches to the left. At some point in the exercise, stealth and care are abandoned, but despite the noise, the Vagrant doesn't stir, and Reela is too busy pushing to notice his suppressed smile.

Delta looks at the man. Reela has managed to push his legs further than his body so that they jut away at a forty-five-degree angle.

With a shake of her head, Delta rearranges the man so that he looks neater. Meanwhile, Reela climbs onto the slab and nestles into the Vagrant's armpit, pushing his arm out until it flops over the side of the slab.

Delta lifts his arm and places it over Reela's shoulder. Satisfied, she walks back towards the door. She only makes it halfway before Reela's voice stops her. 'Stay, please?'

A warmth fills the immortal and she walks back across the room, sitting at the other side of the Vagrant's slab. She sees that Reela is pretending to sleep too, her smile a match for the Vagrant's.

Delta is surprised how long the two pretend, Reela only stopping when the Vagrant falls into true sleep. Then he is shaken awake without mercy.

There are gasps of outrage, mocked, followed by tickles and laughter.

For the first time since the battle, Delta's sword blinks.

The break in the weather is only temporary, giving a false sense that the worst is over. It is as if they have passed through the eye of a storm rather than the end of it.

Wind and rain, dust and cloud, strange-coloured lightning, all batter the travellers returning north.

Safe within the bellies of metal snakes or behind the walls of the sky palace, they endure, though progress is slowed to a crawl.

There is plenty of time to think, to worry. Vesper takes advice on what the fallout might be and tries to plan accordingly, though such things seem pointless, even foolish next to the scale of the problem.

But Vesper is used to taking on impossible tasks, is fuelled by them.

Despite the storm, plans are made.

They reach the coast, transferring snakes onto ships and risking an angry sea. The journey is long, arduous, giant waves slapping the fleet, sometimes even reaching for the sky palace.

It is a testament to the design of the vessels that they can withstand such battering.

When the storm pauses again, infernals come out onto the battlements, packing all of the available spaces. They are strangely quiet, even the shriekers and growlers stilled to awe.

None of them have been at sea before.

None have ever been so far north.

The suns survive but in a weakened state, the reality of the world dealt yet another injury. Taint spreads further, in the air, in the sea, and demons find the suns burn less than before.

One of the vanquished colonies is given to the Man-shape and its followers. They name it *Vesper's Gift*.

The infernals disembark, eager to explore their new home,

quickly vanishing into buildings, broken, and caves that peek from the water's edge.

Only the Man-shape continues to travel north, leaving flies and orders behind.

Onwards they go, faster now, spurred by the proximity of home and the weakening of the winds, until cloudy waters clear, and green-capped cliffs come into view.

Onboard ships there is celebration. For Vesper there is relief. Finally, she can get to work.

The Vagrant walks towards familiar hills, his jaw set. The suns have settled into their new formation, the smaller red sun dancing around the outside of the larger two, and the sky is as blue as it ever was.

Goats have returned, some grazing, some dozing in the afternoon sunlight. It is as if nothing has changed.

The Vagrant keeps going, unmoved by bleats and stares, until he reaches a hill that was once a home. Where two buildings stood, there is now one, a small shelter. Of the other, there is only rubble, a black scar on the landscape.

The Vagrant moves towards it, guided by memories, uncompromising, to the spot where the front door was. One glance down and he stops, turning his head to the suns, letting the glare fill his vision until it blurs and water streaks down either side of his face. He takes a breath, shuddering and deep, lets it out and looks down again.

Harm's skeleton is still largely intact, an unwelcome memory to cap off years of happy ones; stories, laughter, kindness. Gone.

It takes a while for the Vagrant to dig a hole big enough. Though his wounds have healed, muscles have not yet found their old strength. Sweat mixes with tears and the sounds of labour as the day wears on.

When it is done, the Vagrant kisses the tips of his fingers and presses them into the earth.

After another round of tears he staggers towards the remaining building. From the deepening shadows he hears a snort, a greeting of sorts, and shakes his head, disbelieving.

If the goat is pleased to see him, she gives no sign.

The Vagrant sits heavily beside her and, after a while, begins to stroke her side.

The suns have almost set now, and the Vagrant's eyes follow them down. His head begins to go the same way but just as slumber seems certain, there is a crunch and the Vagrant snatches back his hand. Even in the poor light, bony gum marks are easy to see, making a crescent of red across the skin.

Amber eyes glare at the goat.

The goat snorts again, triumphant, before settling down to sleep.

Alpha of The Seven stands in a corner, unobtrusive, his chained head lowered. Theta, Eta and Epsilon box him in, minders, jailers, watchers.

In the middle of the room is a projector, rendering a version of the world in blues and greens.

Beta, Delta, Obeisance and the Knight Commander all look from it to Vesper.

Obeisance is the first to speak. 'We are here. We are yours to command. What is it you want of us?'

'Knight Commander Torran, you will prepare what's left of our forces to go and help those in need. We must relearn the state of the Empire and get food and supplies distributed.'

'At once,' he says.

'Obeisance, do we have still have Lenses in the field?'

'We do.'

'Good. I want to know all you can tell me about how the rest of the world is coping. Who is surviving, who is stable, and who needs our help.'

Obeisance inclines her head.

'I have a lot of changes I want to make here in the Shining City too, but don't worry,' she looks at the older woman. 'I'm not going to do them all at once.'

'Do as you see fit. We are yours to command.'

Vesper's answer rings out, bouncing from the walls. 'No! That time is over. No more blind obedience. We will do this together. If you have objections or questions, you can raise them here. I'm not going to get angry. Remember that with what I'm about to say.' She looks at them each in turn, feeling a jolt of encouragement from Delta as their eyes meet. 'Firstly, purging will no longer be compulsory. It has to be a choice, with the risks clearly explained, okay?'

She senses Beta's concern, knows his question without it needing to be asked. 'I'm not saying that the tainted can live in the Shining City. Not yet, anyway, but they should have the opportunity to live elsewhere rather than be purged or killed. In many cases there's no difference between the two.' She checks for further objections but none are given. 'Oh and we need a new name for the taint. Something less . . . loaded. I was thinking about calling it "the change" instead. It's something we need to understand and face up to rather than fear.

'Second, we have to stop teaching that all infernals are evil.'

'We have already done this,' replies Obeisance.

'Only in a weak way. Nobody really took it to heart, and The Seven's actions undermined all of that. This time, the word will come direct from us, and we need to back it up. I've been thinking about how to do that and I think it has to be through experience.'

The Knight Commander looks shocked. 'You want our people to experience the infernal?'

'Exactly!'

'Forgive me, Vesper, but this is madness. Even if the demons could be trusted, we would be wilfully spreading the taint.'

'The change,' corrects Vesper. 'Try it out.'

'Change or taint, the threat of exposure is just as serious.'

'I've thought about this too. There is an infernal that I trust, and that has enough control over its essence to not change others: The Man-shape. I've talked to it and it's willing.' She smirks at a memory. 'Actually, it's quite excited by the idea of meeting so many people. I want a house built for it outside the shields and a timetable developed for visitors. The first ones should be picked for their open-mindedness, we want good word spreading, not bad. I'll accompany them myself, to make sure everything's safe. You'll both be coming too, of course.'

Obeisance hides her discomfort ably, the Knight Commander does not.

'And Beta and Delta will be in the second round.'

Neither immortal objects, both having come to terms with the idea some time ago.

'Good! Third and last, for the moment, is the choirs.'

'What about them?' asks Obeisance.

'They have to go. From now on, parents should be told which baby is theirs and they should be allowed to watch them grow in the tubes. When the babies are ready to come out, the parents should raise and educate them.'

'But without the choirs, how will they know what to do?'

'Don't worry,' replies Vesper. 'I've thought about that too.'

Years pass and storms come and go, settling into a calmer rhythm, more frequent than before.

In the north, just past the Shining City, a new house sits on a hill. It is an unlikely structure, haphazard, with a lean to the roof, and a number of extensions sprawling outward that look as if they belong to other buildings.

It is the subject of many jokes.

It is also a home and a farm and a school. On days when the weather is bad, it is filled with noisy children and parents slowly recovering from shock.

On brighter days, everyone is outside, running, playing, talking and singing. Goats are named, adopted, milked and fed. The braver children take treats into what has become known as the lair.

Often, Delta of The Seven can be found nearby, cradling her sword and showing it what transpires. Sometimes they join in the singing.

A man with a black hand and amber eyes can be found here. The lines on his face made by smiling gradually catching up ones made from a lifetime of frowns.

In the evenings children gather round in a circle and he sits down. In front of him he places figures carved from wood: a tall knight, a taller woman, a giant with a girl's face, a child with a sword, a woman with a gun, and a man with a kindly demeanour, more carefully carved than the rest.

And, in a soft voice, he tells their story.

Acknowledgements

As we come to the end of the Vagrant's story, I can't help but feel reflective. It's been a strange and wonderful few years, and I've been lucky to meet with, and work with, a load of great people. Some of whom, I'm happy to say, have become friends. I'd like to shower general appreciation on all the book ninja at HarperVoyager who work from the shadows, and give a shout-out to the awesome Team Mushens, and to all the booksellers who have done so much.

Also, in no particular order, I'd like to thank:

Juliet Mushens . . . For being fabulous. For having fabulous cats and sending me pictures of them. For all the support, advice, and for making me smile. Over the last three years every single email and call from her has left me feeling better. Best. Agent. Ever.

Jen Williams . . . For her friendship, and for teaching me the true power of the dark side of the (email)force.

Natasha Bardon . . . For being the first person to cry over one of my books. For always making my stories better and longer (value for money!). Also for providing steak, pasties and cocktails at critical points in the publishing process.

Jaime Jones . . . For those covers! I can't imagine the series without them.

Joy Chamberlain . . . For saving the general public from my writing eccentricities! And for always being so positive about my work.

Emma Newman . . . For, well, pretty much everything really.

And you . . . For reading. Thank you. I hope you've enjoyed this journey as much as I have.